The Northern

The Northern

JACOB McARTHUR MOONEY

Published by ECW Press
665 Gerrard Street East
Toronto, Ontario, Canada M4M 1Y2
416-694-3348 / info@ecwpress.com

Editor for the Press: Michael Holmes / a misFit Book
Copy editor: Crissy Boylan

Cover Illustration and design: Ian Sullivan Cant

This is a work of fiction. Names, characters, places, and incidents either are the product of the author's imagination or are used fictitiously, and any resemblance to actual persons, living or dead, business establishments, events, or locales is entirely coincidental.

LIBRARY AND ARCHIVES CANADA CATALOGUING IN PUBLICATION

Title: The Northern : a novel / Jacob McArthur Mooney.

Names: Mooney, Jacob McArthur, author

Identifiers: Canadiana (print) 20250140578 | Canadiana (ebook) 20250140586

ISBN 978-1-77041-782-3 (softcover)
ISBN 978-1-77852-394-6 (ePub)
ISBN 978-1-77852-395-3 (PDF)

Subjects: LCGFT: Novels.

Classification: LCC PS8626.O5928 N67 2025 | DDC C813/.6—dc23

This book is funded in part by the Government of Canada. *Ce livre est financé en partie par le gouvernement du Canada.* We acknowledge the support of the Canada Council for the Arts. *Nous remercions le Conseil des arts du Canada de son soutien.* We would like to acknowledge the funding support of the Ontario Arts Council (OAC) and the Government of Ontario for their support. We also acknowledge the support of the Government of Ontario through the Ontario Book Publishing Tax Credit, and through Ontario Creates.

PRINTED AND BOUND IN CANADA   PRINTING: MARQUIS   5   4   3   2   1

Purchase the print edition and receive the ebook free.
For details, go to ecwpress.com/ebook.

For Oli.

Table of Contents

A Bridge to Canada   9

Windsor, Tuesday, July 8th, 1952   20

Windsor, Wednesday, July 9th, 1952   40

Windsor, Thursday, July 10th, 1952   76

Windsor, Friday, July 11th, 1952   109

Hamilton, Saturday, July 12th, 1952   139

Hamilton, Sunday, July 13th, 1952   169

London, Monday, July 14th, 1952   207

Niagara Falls, Tuesday, July 15th, 1952 248

Buffalo, Wednesday, July 16th, 1952   268

A Bridge to Canada   298

Historical Notes   305

Credits   307

A Bridge to Canada

THE NOON SUN HAD ME HALFWAY TO SLEEP WHEN WE SAW the bridge appear ahead like the hollow husk of a skyscraper.

The bridge broke through the city so high above us, it looked like we'd need a crane or an elevator to get there. Like it stretched not from riverbank to riverbank but from the look-off atop one great building to the next. Especially for Mikey, who had napped through most of Detroit with its other tall buildings and so had gone this far without sighting anything that size made by man, the effect was awed confusion.

"Is that going to Canada?" he asked, in Coach's direction but not loud enough for him to hear it.

"That is," I answered him.

The front of Coach's Hornet tilted up and I thought, This is it, we must be driving into the mouth of some great lifting machine that will place us on the span of the bridge, the end of America, and we'll all of us take its Canadian equivalent back down for our first touch of foreign ground.

"How'll we get up there, Coach?" I shouted to the front of the car.

Coach was driving the same way he always drove, as if he was napping in the back of a rowboat. He had his big sweaty head

9

leaned flush against the headrest, which at his height meant a few inches of combed black hair stood out, and his free hand dipped from the window like the needle of a record player. Coach had given up smoking after the war but said he often craved a cigarette when he drove. One would've looked at home loose between his fingers.

"Coach?" I repeated.

"Say 'excuse me,'" he sent back, glancing up to show me his eyes in the mirror.

It didn't seem like Coach had been up to anything a person could interrupt besides his train of thought, but we had been drilling manners since Minnesota, and the need to excuse yourself first before speaking to an adult was a core lesson.

"Excuse me, Coach," I said. "How do we get to the top of the bridge?"

Coach brought his hand in to rub at his upper lip, then hunched his shoulders and let his eyes drift further up until they were looking out the topmost sliver of the Hornet's front window. "Up there?" he asked, nodding at the towering grey suspension arcs that now squatted directly above us like comic book mountains.

I looked around. Somehow we had gotten up to the midpoint of the first tower. I leaned to my right and saw the river, and further down Detroit itself, growing around us several layers of road below. While we were talking, Coach must have navigated those roads, and now we were the ones looking down on the city from inside, but not on top of, the great iron mountain.

Coach had returned his attention to the road but kept checking back to see if I had a follow-up. He must have been confused because I had asked what would have sounded more like a Mikey question than a me question. The question of a seven-year-old, not a twelve-year-old. Of course you can't drive on the very top of the bridge; you drive on the part where the cars go.

"Never mind," I told him. "I got confused about how the bridge worked."

Coach rolled his shoulders. "The Ambassador Bridge is older than the both of you put together," he told us. "And nearly as old as I am. Millions of cars drive this beast every year, and there hasn't been an incident yet. Look around you, what do you see?"

Mikey jumped in. "Water, Coach."

"Where?"

"Both sides."

"Exactly. Equally on both sides. That means no corners, no turns, no opportunity to drift into the wrong lane or get cut off. This is the safest bit of road in America."

"Are we in America?" Mikey asked. "Like, officially?"

In the next lane, a blue truck with a red-cheeked driver nosed ahead of us and then fell slowly back until I could shift in my seat to see its licence plate, which said Michigan. Coach squinted, and we slowed down to join a line of cars waiting for admission into Canada. He brought his hand inside as a red coupe pulled up next to us on his side, not close enough to touch but close enough to feel you were in someone else's space. The woman in the driver's seat painted her lips in the mirror.

"It's not clear," Coach said, which was how he told us when he didn't know something. He looked around for a hint. "Maybe it's in between."

"Everywhere has to be a country," said Mikey. "Unless the river is its own country in between the others."

Coach shook his head. "I don't suspect that's the case. Best guess is you're in one country until someone tells you you're in another."

"Well, who tells you?"

Coach pointed ahead to where a little cabin made of concrete and timber stood, improbably, in the middle of the street. Like someone had built a homestead years before the roads came only to have the border set down all around it. A man in a grey and blue uniform appeared in front of us, waving us forward like he wanted Coach to park right there in his front yard.

"This gentleman here tells us," he said. "You two stay where you are and be your best selves while I speak with him. Remember, Mikey, to listen to your brother."

Coach parked the Hornet in the same spot where someone had just sped away up the hill into the town we understood from the maps would be Windsor. A few yards to our left, there was another little cabin and another man in grey and blue, now speaking to the red-faced driver of the Michigan truck through his window. The truck had lettering on its side, something in cursive I couldn't understand and then "New for 1952" in crisp stencilled letters. There was a whole column of us, cars and men in grey pants speaking into them outside little wooden cabins flanked by concrete barriers, and a line behind each of still more cars waiting to arrive.

The gentleman seemed surprised when Coach stepped out of the car, but this was because Coach was a salesman and needed to look someone in the eye, to join them at their level, when speaking with them. You asked to take a seat when speaking to a seated person; you stood when someone walked over to you in greeting. Coach's rules.

"Good afternoon, officer," Coach said, pulling his suit jacket closed at the belly. "My name's Miller. And yourself?"

The border man took two steps towards us and shook Coach's hand, never really pausing long enough for my liking as he scanned around the vehicle, taking in everything he needed in a single long pass of his eyes. I imagined he noted the car model (a 1949 Hudson Hornet, built to race as a stock car but suitable to slower jobs as well), the person greeting him (a tall man of about thirty dressed smartly but inexpensively), and of course us (two juveniles in the back seat, one older than the other, clearly brothers, looking like two photographs of the same kid at different ages on a living-room mantle).

"Good afternoon, Mr. Miller," he said without giving his own name, though he was close enough now I could read a tag that said Parcells. "Citizenship?"

"American," said Coach, producing a card, which I expected to be a passport or a licence but was just his business card, which to my memory showed his name and phone number but not what country he belonged to.

Officer Parcells read it over, putting his hand on his hip in such a way that it lifted his jacket. He didn't seem to own a gun. I made a note that if we needed, I could jump into the front seat, ignite the engine, gear us up like I had seen Coach do a thousand times, and be over the hill before they could chase us.

"Are you here on business?" Parcells asked.

"I am, sir."

"What about these two gentlemen, are they yours?" he asked, leaning over and pointing at Mikey and me.

"Yes."

"Sons?"

"Yessir."

This finally got Mikey interested in the conversation, and he quit whatever daydream he was having to attune to the lie. He looked up and seemed to take in the scene for the first time, which was enough for Parcells to show a reciprocal interest.

"Hi there, sport," said the officer. "What's your name?"

"Michael, sir," he said, drawing out the *Mike* in Michael like he was fending off a yawn. "And this is my brother, Christopher."

Parcells looked at me for the length of my name. "I see. Where are you from, Michael?"

"Minneapolis. Just nearby it."

"Is this gentleman here your daddy?"

He nodded yes. It was so quick and assured, even overacted, that I guessed they had spoken about it first; maybe Coach thought he needed to be rehearsed before we got to Canada, or maybe—and this tightened my stomach just a little—he trusted Mikey to go along with a fib but not me. He wasn't our father. Our father had died in a car wreck right after the war. Coach ran little league and owned a sporting goods store, and Mamma let him spend evenings with us and keep his shirts in our closet.

Parcells turned to me again, and without him asking the question, I found myself nodding as well. Somewhere in the car was a letter Mamma had scrawled out identifying Coach and confirming that she had given him permission to take us into Canada, but nobody moved to find it.

"Good. Nice to bring the boys out on an adventure." He handed Coach back his card. "What's your business?"

Coach seemed to relax a little, both because the man accepted we were his sons and also because this had now become an opportunity to preach about his work.

"I'm in the cardboard business. Collectible cards."

"Like baseball cards?"

"Exactly baseball cards." Coach signalled the man to follow him to the trunk of the Hornet, which he unlocked and swung open. We couldn't see them anymore but I knew the pitch well enough because Coach had practised on us before we left home and three or four more times on the trip. "I represent a concern in Utah called the Four Corners Baseball Card Company. We're a new operation so I suspect you haven't heard of us, that's alright. I'm employed to represent the company as an agent, and I have here several contracts to sign with young men playing baseball in this area. Are you familiar with the local teams?"

"Well sure," said Officer Parcells. "But there's no big-leaguers in Canada. All we have is the PONY League and the Northern."

"Exactly, friend. So what we at Four Corners do is we go and meet those exact boys, the ones just starting out their baseball careers, boys in the early rungs of the ladder like the Northern League, and offer to sign them up to use their names and faces on our cards when they get older and make it to the American or the National League."

We heard someone moving boxes around back, which had to be Officer Parcells, because Coach had set everything up exactly as he wanted and promised to club either Mikey or me if we disturbed it. Contracts pre-signed by Salt Lake in the top-right corner, example cards in the top-left. Clothes and toiletries folded along the bottom, and under them, under the Hornet's upholstery cut into the underside of the trunk, a thick envelope containing seventy-five new five dollar bills. American, all of them. Coach said the players could have them exchanged if needed.

Somewhere, too, maybe in the back or maybe the glovebox, was Mamma's letter that didn't claim Coach as our father but said he was a friend of our family and a good community man. He was taking us to see Canada and learn about the licensing business. Once before he had taken us fishing on Mille Lacs, but Mille Lacs being in Minnesota, there was no border to cross and no need of a letter or a lie.

The officer stopped sorting the trunk and came far enough around my side that I could see he was holding an example card; I couldn't make out the print but it looked like Ken Hubbs, who was the same religion as Coach's bosses, Mormon, and had made the majors last year with the Cubs. There weren't all that many Mormons in the big leagues, but those there were were Four Corners men. The couple that ran the company saw to this by writing to their local churches.

"How do you get them to sign? You pay them?"

"Yessir, five dollars," said Coach. "Though don't worry. I don't bring the currency for that with me on the trip. Players receive a certified cheque from our bank in Salt Lake within three weeks of signing up, that's our promise."

"Not many players from the Northern ever make the major leagues," Officer Parcells said. "Curious what happens to those contracts."

"It's true," agreed Coach, manoeuvring into an answer we had gone over on the trip in. "Most of the boys playing up here won't get to Tiger Stadium without a paid ticket, and won't get within a day's drive of Ebbets Field. We sign them all the same; it's cheap enough to do so, and then we wait to see who grows into a major-leaguer."

"Honourable enough," said Officer Parcells, handing back Ken Hubbs. "But what's with all the money in the back, Mr. Miller?"

I must have flinched or gasped when he said this because he looked down at me and gave a strange sort of smile. He had to have seen the envelope; maybe Coach hadn't put it all the way under the hole in the trunk or maybe the hole had been the problem—maybe it had called attention to itself.

Coach was great at reciting practised speeches but sometimes got himself tongue-tied under pressure. "What?" was all he could squeeze out in the moment.

"It's too much to bring into the country unaccounted for. Also it's all in fives even though you said you'd pay the ballplayers by cheque. Now, I can see my way to small exceptions, but I'm afraid you're more than double your limit. Have to understand, small bills like this commonly point to drug running. You three don't seem like the type, but who does, right?"

They were silent for a minute. I got the impression that part of this was a speech Officer Parcells had practised himself. They both wandered away and spoke some more out of earshot. I looked at Mikey, but he hadn't seemed to have picked up on the problem of currency limits. All at once, Coach surprised us by popping open my door.

"Boys, come help us move some things please," he said, fast and uninflected. Tight-lipped, he loaded a set of 1951 Four Corners All-Stars, an eighty-card collection of current and recent big-leaguers, not an actual All-Star among them, into my arms and marched us ahead of him towards where Officer Parcells was sitting. It was late in the day now and the air was a little colder, the sky above a bit darker, than the last time we had stretched our legs.

"Alright," said Coach, holding Mikey by the shoulders, "this is the full set. Do we have a deal?"

Officer Parcells nodded me forward and dipped his hands into the wooden box that held the cards. He flipped through a few like they were a stack of 45s. "You guys have a Mantle?"

"No sir, no Mickey Mantle," said Coach.

"Not even a Phil Rizzuto?"

"No sir. Most Yankees are Topps exclusives."

"Huh," said the officer, pulling a disappointed hand away and placing it in his lap. "Alright then, if you have a signed copy I'll take that. My boy is a pinstripes kid but I'm sure he'll figure out a use for these anyway."

Coach was angry though he managed to hide it. He stood up real straight: he was a tall man in a good mood but grew into a flagpole when you made him mad. "I'm afraid I don't keep signed cards in the sample set," he said.

The officer looked around a minute before reaching into his little hut and tossing us a ballpoint pen. "Easy fix. You at least know how Mantle spells his name I hope?"

Coach caught the pen and flipped it around in his fingers a few times. I knew he was thinking, but I couldn't tell if he was thinking about whether or not to do it, or about where on the box he should sign.

"Hold still," he eventually told me, and I kept the case as steady as I could while he pressed down hard to etch out two quick squiggles that both started with what could passably be read as *M*s.

Coach extracted the case from my arms and held it out to the officer, who took an oddly long time to recognize he had done so. Like he was pretending to have forgotten we were there and then pretending to have forgotten why.

"Aw thanks, friend," he eventually said. "You can stick that on the table inside and then go get your car and drive on."

The mistake I made on the way back to the Hornet was opening my big stupid mouth. Coach was approaching the driver's side door when I observed, really as much to myself as to him, that there was no point in signing the box, as it was just going to rub off in a day or two anyway. Coach reached out like maybe he was going to hit me, or maybe he was going to grab me, but instead of doing either he just kind of pushed me forward and I smacked my lip on the side of the car, my knee hitting the door as I stepped ahead to try and catch myself. It didn't hurt, but I did feel foolish. Worse when we realized we'd left Mikey behind with the border man.

He was talking Officer Parcells through the list of cards. Mikey had been handed card duty when Mom first told us we could go with Coach to Canada this year, and he memorized every player in last year's set. It hadn't come easy to him: Mikey was fast and athletic and some days even funny, but he was ass backwards in school and didn't take well to memorizing.

When I told him to get moving, he looked at me for a moment and I could tell my lip was bleeding but I refused to touch it. Coach was in the Hornet; I could hear its engine.

"Sorry mister, I got to go," Mikey told the officer, who again only begrudgingly recognized we were there, as if the second he had extracted something valuable from us we had started to flicker in and out of his vision. But Mikey was told it was impolite to not say a proper goodbye, so he moved right up in front of him and reached out to shake his hand, which Parcells did once it seemed unrealistic to ignore him.

"One last thing," Mikey asked as the man began to stand up to await the next arriving car. "Can you do me a favour and tell me I'm in Canada now?"

The officer did as much and then told us to go away.

Windsor, Tuesday, July 8th, 1952

	W	L
Buffalo Bisons	37	23
Akron Zaps	33	26
London Maple Leafs	32	27
Erie Sailors	29	31
Windsor Clippers	27	33
Hamilton Red Wings	21	39

Last Night's Games
Clippers 6, Zaps 7; Wings 5, Sailors 3; Leafs 2, Bisons 9

I DIDN'T FEEL ANY BETTER UNTIL I GOT TO LECTURE MIKEY about how all the Great Lakes were threaded together by rivers and waterfalls, and Coach didn't seem to feel any better until we got to the motel and the pretty clerk told us we could park for free because it was a Tuesday. We pulled in around five thirty, too late to think about making a run to the stadium to see if we could catch the Clippers or the Zaps warming up, though if Coach really wanted to we probably could've made the game.

Detroit was the biggest city I had ever been in, and I had expected it to be all right angles, all rectangles and squares, like when Mikey and I built cities out of woodblocks back home, but that didn't turn out. Its buildings had rounded roofs and stepbacks and all kinds of arcs and cones and other sacrifices to empty air. I expected a big city to fill out its space to the maximum, buildings right flush against the street. I swear that's what I saw in movies showing couples out walking in New York or London, but Detroit wasn't like that.

I was surprised then to get to Windsor and see it express itself in right angles. Square houses, rectangular office buildings. Not flush with the streets but square at least. No stepbacks. The streets were a perfect grid. Even the buses were giant awkward shoeboxes on wheels, no rounded edges or stuck-out noses on them. Our motel was three-quarters of a square opened out onto an empty swimming pool and parking lot. One far wall of it advertising waffles. Mikey had to pee so bad he couldn't wait until the clerk found our key, so I grabbed him and we ducked into the restaurant under a cloud of cigarettes and adult conversation. The dining room had that thin plastic sheet on all the tables meant to look like marble. You could see where smokers had burned holes through it to expose the wood. The men nearest me were drinking beer from short stubby bottles and talking about hockey. I guessed this was because they were Canadians, even though it was summer and one of them wore a Detroit Tigers cap. Nobody seemed to have a plate of food in front of them. No sign of the advertised waffles. The way the men leaned towards each other made me think they were gossips.

"The thing about gossips," Coach had told us somewhere after the Michigan state line that morning, "is they find each other. If you suspect you're in the presence of a gossip, the best advice is to make up a lie. But don't make up the same lie twice."

"What do you mean, Coach?" Mikey asked. This was before he ate lunch and fell asleep.

"Well, say they ask you where you're from, Michael. Tell the first one Fargo and the second Kalamazoo. Then, when they find each other, they'll have conflicting information. So anyone watching will assume they're just both making it up."

Coach had a way of telling you what he thought that made it sound like he had heard it from someone else and memorized it. This was one of those times.

Mikey went sitting down on the toilet while I used the urinal, and after I reminded him he had to wash his hands. We each spent a good few seconds in front of the mirrors readying our faces, pawing down loose hair, and making sure the collars on our shirts didn't stick out. Normally I'd only pay close attention to how I looked on a special occasion, and Mikey almost never did. I'm not sure what made him care now, maybe he was just copying, but for me I found myself considering how everyone who would see me now and for the next several days, except Coach and Mikey, would be seeing me for the first time. I was about to make a run of first impressions.

The first impression I imagined for myself was of a young man who might convince you he was an athlete if you didn't ask him to prove it. I was three inches taller since Christmas, and my face had lost the roundness I grew up with, settling now into a kind of peanut shape with a prominent forehead and chin. My hair was the colour of everyone else's in my class: blonde turning a half shade darker every birthday.

Mikey looked like me if I was seven, had never had the round face, and could prove myself an athlete whenever asked.

This wasn't my first time away from home, but it was my first time out of the country. There was the Mille Lacs trip, and before that, the fall Dad came home from the war, Mamma celebrated by finding us a lodge up north to spend a week but that was too long ago to remember. On Mille Lacs, I saw an airplane go due north from the horizon off the lake to the horizon over the forest, one long lazy arc that took maybe twenty minutes from start to finish and left a soft cloud trailing in its wake. That was the first time I watched one like that, and I always do it now when I see them. Dr. Hogan, Mamma's boss at the university, went away to a conference in Florida last spring and came back with the arrivals and departures schedule from the Wold-Chamberlain airport, so now I chart those slow climbers and fallers against that timetable. On Mondays and Wednesdays, for example, those are the big ones, the Northwest Orients from Tokyo via Alaska, due overhead the minute I get out of school. If the weather's right I can race one downriver—that's the Mississippi River, the last big curl of it—to Mikey's school and then home.

All the men and women in the restaurant were strange to me; the city was strange to me. Canada was strange. Even Coach, in his lies and surprises, became more strange with the distance covered. Everyone's a different person, maybe, when you take away their neighbours.

"The toilet here is taller than the toilets at home. Is that because people here are taller?" asked Mikey, and I told him that toilet size was standard everywhere, because that was the law. If they had a different law in Canada, I didn't know it.

When we got back to the front desk Coach made it seem like we had been gone a long time. The clerk was wearing a plain grey blouse with the motel company logo on it, but she had left it open so that you could see a little bit of her cleavage at the top. This was something I noticed but didn't dawdle on. Coach seemed to notice too, because he called the clerk pretty, which would have been the case no matter how she wore her buttons. But Coach more than likely would've kept it to himself.

There were no elevators or stairs, just a walk through dusty halls to our room. Somewhere along the way Coach commented that we were probably meant to get in our car and drive there. I made a note to remember to have Coach park at the other end of the motel next time. Coach had put me in charge of navigation, which he didn't really need me for so far, outside of some uncertain exits where we had changed interstates. But I was determined to take the assignment to its fullest and get us from all points A to all points B. I had sent away for city maps from the three Canadian cities we were planning to visit (though only Windsor and Hamilton showed up in the mail; I'd have to find one in London) and studied the path from motel to ballpark, plus locations of gas bars and diners.

The room was at the furthest point from the check-in desk. All the way around the motel, under the waffles sign but opposite the waffles. Coach had his bags and Mikey's, plus he carried his good shirt on a hanger ahead of him. My bag was light enough, but still it was a struggle to keep stride and I was breathing hard when we got there.

Coach fed the key in the lock and turned the lights on. I knew what to expect because I found a pamphlet for this motel in among his receipts from last year's trip. Two beds turned up with plaid comforters. A radio, a writing desk, a washroom with a soaker tub. No TV, though the pamphlet said they had a big RCA buried somewhere in a common room for guests to use.

"Paradise," Coach whispered in a funny tone of voice and threw the bags on the nearest bed. "This one's mine."

We unpacked and walked across the lot to the restaurant for dinner. They tried to serve Coach a mouldy piece of bread with his soup but he caught them, and they gave us the rest of the meal for free even though there was no mould in his soup or my chicken sandwich or Mikey's oatmeal, which wasn't even on the menu but they said they had some in back from the staff's breakfast and would heat it up for him because he asked. Mikey liked oatmeal.

Coach took the mould so well Mikey asked afterwards if it was some sort of Canadian custom, like mouldy bread might have been a national dish here or something. Coach said he was just being polite and looking to make a sale, was hoping he could charm them into the free meal, and this had worked. The smile-sale he called it: an expression he picked up from a vendor at the sporting goods store he ran off Main Street back home when he wasn't coaching or representing the Four Corners Baseball Card Company. All it meant was we were expected to come back for breakfast the next morning. The waiter said they'd have fresh oatmeal, and fresh bread if we wanted it, ready early.

There was not a lot to do in the motel room. I could tell Mikey had been hoping for a television, and he and I agreed on that. A boy one year ahead of me at school had gone skiing last break and broken his toe, so he spent most of the week curled up on the floor of the hotel room watching the television and drinking hot cocoa, which sounded a lot better than skiing the way he told it.

I had seen television a few times. Plus what is a movie house really but a bigger television you shared with more people. What I really wanted to do was change channels: the way he described it you could just scoot forward and adjust a little knob like you're fastening a button, and a whole different world would pop into view if you didn't like the first one. The televisions I had seen were basically movie houses: you shared them with the other people at the department store or the legion hall or once, briefly, only five other kids in the sitting room at Dr. Hogan's house when he hosted the secretarial staff and their families for a Christmas party. I had wanted to ask the apologetic waiter if there was a television on the property, but there was no time to do so politely and Coach would have been mad if I had interjected amid his sale.

Because the motel room had no television, we were left to speak to Coach all evening, which meant we were there to help him practise.

"First off," Coach said, sitting on his bed cross-legged in his undershirt and drawers, "who are you?"

"My name is Michael Johnson," said Mikey. "I'm a business associate of Coach's."

The way he chewed the possessive *s* in "Coach's" was adorable, and I knew Coach was aiming for precociousness, which took practice as Mikey was anything but precocious on a normal day, more likely to run up and down the aisles than sit still and participate as a prop man in the pitch. I wondered how he wanted me to be, at five-foot-five and in full control of my *S*s. Was I precocious too? I didn't think of myself as adorable.

"Nice to meet you, Mike. Who is this gentleman beside you?"

"This is my older brother Christopher. He is the logistics manager for this here operation. He is going into seventh grade next year and I am going into second."

I don't know when they'd drilled this bit; it was the first I had heard of any of it.

"Are we going to miss the sample set?" I asked, and if Coach was annoyed by this break in practice he hid it by looking at his notes.

"No," he said. "I brought a second to have redundancy."

Coach loved redundancy. Practice, for Coach, meant two things: fundamentals and situational awareness. When he took us through baseball, the fundamentals were running, hitting, and catch. Done to redundancy in long spring evenings that had the town's mothers complaining about their kids being kept out past twilight on school nights. Situational awareness meant rehearsal games and scrimmages, punctuated by lots of all-in meetings whenever someone made a wrong decision, throwing to second when the play was at third, as an example.

On the road representing Four Corners, fundamentals meant practising his pitch, which was more or less a single reusable speech he gave to audiences of young ballplayers in locker rooms or on fields, sometimes hotel lobbies and even buses. He had props that Mikey handed him or held up, and while the two of us had never been out on the road with him before this trip, we felt pretty confident about our fundamentals.

As it always was with Coach, the real challenge was in the situational awareness, which on the road meant answering specific questions or dealing with complaints or refusals. Once we raised an objection and Coach had an answer for it he liked, he wrote it down in his notebook and we practised it along with the pitch. Coach turned it into another fundamental, and that way he conquered his potential noes one at a time.

"Who are you?" I asked Coach.

He straightened his posture and smoothed an invisible tie down his undershirt. "Thanks for asking, friend. My name is Lawrence Miller. I'm an agent with the Four Corners Baseball Card Company of Salt Lake City, Utah. Have you heard of us?"

"No," I said. This no was just fundamentals disguised as an obstacle: we had already memorized all our lines. He had an answer for no. I wasn't sure if he had one for yes.

"That's fine. It's a big world, and even the smaller world of baseball cards is growing. You've heard of Topps, I imagine?"

"Yes," said Mikey, before I could.

"Bowman?"

"Yes," I said.

"Well, those are what you might call the old regime of baseball cards. I collected Topps when I was the same age as my associates here. Both are good brands, and they do fine work. What they don't do quite as well is represent the best interests of young athletes like yourself. And that's actually my job: to represent your interests to my bosses, and theirs to you."

Coach stood up and crossed the room to the writing desk. He talked into his address book, his bare hairy knees sticking to the back of the chair. "My company has a great deal of faith in young men like yourselves, that your baseball talent is going to bring you big things in this world. Not all of you, I should add, as nobody knows the future and you understand as well as I do that for every man in the major leagues, there are fifty in rooms much like this from Montreal to Miami. And there isn't room enough for everyone. Some of you will find other futures, and we bless your efforts in them. But others will move up. From the Northern League maybe into affiliated baseball with the PONY League, and then down to Florida or off to the PCL, and from there we all know it's just one hot step to Yankee Stadium or Shibe Park.

"We are a spiritual company. Founded by good religious men and run like a family. As a spiritual company, we are guided by faith, and that includes faith in you boys. And we'd like to represent that faith with an investment."

Here Coach reached into his back pocket and pulled a stack of receipts from his wallet. In the rooms, it would be a stack from Four Corners' envelope of fives, fresh from the printing press, with no wrinkles or creases, so that the stack seemed half the size it should be, a full team's complement of fifteen bills no thicker in Coach's hand than a diner menu.

"We're prepared to give you each, every one of you, from the greenest rookies on up, five American dollars today if you'll sign what's known as a licensing agreement. A licensing agreement is a contract that says if your future does in fact bring you to a major league field someday, then Four Corners has the right to print a baseball card with your likeness on it, and your exploits and accomplishments on its back. Just like these my associates are showing around now."

Mikey handed me Jim Waugh's mint condition rookie card from last year's set, showing him close-up looking off and to the right of the camera, somewhere on his way to going 1–6 with an ERA of 6.30 for the last-place Pittsburgh Pirates. I examined it with an impressed air and handed it back.

"I've no training in the law, but even I can make sense of this contract. You'll note it's written in plain English, and we've Spanish-language copies available if you prefer. It's only ninety words long and pre-signed by Elder Jamieson Forbush, our founder and president. Now I know Mr. Forbush personally and his wife, Anna, and their five children, and these are good honest people, I can promise you that. I'll leave a copy for your records and take mine with me back to Utah after watching you men play this evening."

Coach had left the writing desk to rehearse out the window to the motel's highway sign, but paused now like he was waiting for it to ask a question. He turned to Mikey.

"Michael?"

"Sorry Coach," Mikey scrambled. "What if when we get to Florida, Topps comes by asking for the same sort of contract?"

"It's no problem for us," Coach answered. "If you take a look, it says our contracts are non-exclusive. This means that if you want to have your face and name on cards produced by other providers, that's no quarrel with Four Corners."

"But Topps's contracts are all exclusive," I said.

Coach paused for a minute to look at me, smiling. There had been some debate about whether this should be drilled since Coach let slip that while he was working the Frontier League last spring, a shortstop for Billings had made the same objection, backed by a rumour sent upstream by a college teammate in the majors that Topps would make players rip up competitors' contracts. "Well, that's a good point, my smart friend. To be honest, I suspect and hope that by the time you get to the major leagues, exclusivity in these contracts will be a thing of the past. There shouldn't be Topps men and Bowman men, but rather baseball players paid fairly for their likenesses by whoever wants to use them. However, until then we've an escape clause for that very purpose. Meaning, if at any point between today and your debut in Major or Open-class baseball, you'd like to get out of this agreement, you can do so by mailing your copy of the agreement and our five-dollar investment back to Mr. and Mrs. Forbush at the address provided on the paper. Sound fair?"

We agreed it was fair and then spent another thirty minutes going over the contract together so I could help explain it to anyone who asked. There wasn't much to explain, but Coach told me that baseball players could sometimes be cautious around contracts and in need of a friendly walk through the clauses. Plus you always had one or two who couldn't read, or who came up from Cuba and didn't have English. He ended by telling us in a serious tone that Utah was expecting two-thirds uptake from the Windsor team; that meant double-digit players signing contracts.

At nine o'clock, Coach looked at his watch and sent us off to the payphone with a handful of nickels and a promise not to go too long. Mikey stayed close to me and watched the guests filter in for their evenings. The wall of keys behind the clerk suggested the motel was about half-full. From the desk by the phone you could see the Hornet alone in the lot. This place must cater to folks who rode the bus.

It was eight at home so we were risking Mamma being off to bed already but she said she would wait up and sure enough she picked up on the second ring.

"You two best talk quickly or you'll put Mr. Miller out of house and home the way they charge for long distance," she said.

"Hi Mamma," I answered. "We made it to Canada alright. Everyone is safe and accounted for. Coach booked us all into a hotel room that's real nice and saw to it we were fed."

"Where's your brother?"

"He's here."

"How would you grade his manners?"

"Acceptable in a good light."

"Good, good." She let out a long slow breath, and I could hear her drag over a stool. "So tell me about it."

I gave her a description of the highway system of the Great Lake states and some colour about how Canada was a different country but not a different-different country like Germany or Rhodesia might be. Everyone spoke English and treated each other about the same as they did at home. The money was different; it had the dead king on it because they hadn't had time yet to print bills with the face of the pretty new queen. Mamma asked if there were many coloured people in Canada—not because she was prejudiced, she sent a cheque every year to the NAACP—more I felt because she was trying to picture the place. She also asked if there were lumberjacks. I told her no lumberjacks and more coloured people than home, but fewer than Detroit.

"How was your day, Mamma?"

"Good enough. Campus is so empty this time of year I had Trudy from the regents' office over for lunch. Her boys are both at Scout camp up north. I tried to explain to her what you two were doing but believe I made a mess of it."

"Roger will be jealous when she says I'm spending time with Coach."

"Well," Mamma said, and from her voice I knew she was playing with the phone cord. She had a tendency to get lost in her sentences while she wound and unwound it around her ring finger. "I just told her that you were with a friend of your father's from the war and left it at that."

"You say it was Coach?"

"No. I don't think Trudy knows Coach is close to us like that."

Mamma filled me in on the campus gossip and the changing price of poultry. The phone had eaten three nickels by then so I handed it off to Mikey. He made me stand several feet away for privacy even though I told him he didn't have any secrets and therefore no need for privacy. I walked off towards the middle of the motel in search of a TV while he said hello and told Mamma about his oatmeal.

I found more closets than you'd expect a motel of that size to have but no TV. I wasn't away more than a minute or two, but when I came back Mikey was gone and the hallway was empty. I cursed a little under my breath and jogged down the hall to our room. The door was open and I heard Coach and Mikey speaking. I presented myself in the doorway.

"Don't leave your brother alone in a strange country," Coach said without looking up or taking a breath after whatever he and Mikey were discussing. "You're the eldest and you must be thinking of his protection. Always. He was scared."

"Mamma was there," I said, and Coach stood up like he was going to argue but instead walked off to the bathroom and closed the door.

Mikey told me he wasn't that scared and I whispered to him to shut up. He had two nickels left so I had him stack them on the writing desk while Coach flushed the toilet and sat back down on his bed.

"Coach," Mikey said, "Mamma said to make sure you hang your trousers up so the press sticks to them, otherwise you'll look like you work out of your car."

Coach reached over, whistling a song, and pulled the curtains back to show his pants hanging off the curtain rod. "Tell your mamma thanks from me tomorrow when you call her."

"She also wants you to come talk next time. She says she worries about you too."

Coach smiled. "You tell that woman that I'm not for worrying over. I've done this before and will do it again unassisted next month in the Dakotas."

We went over the schedule. Coach had us an appointment with the general manager of the Windsor Clippers tomorrow at three p.m. Just after player calls and before batting practice and bullpen. He knew the general manager, Mr. Simmonette, from last year and before that when he used to work for the Toledo team in the American Association. He said Mr. Simmonette was a good man, though his drinking kept him down in life. The Northern was small time compared to the job in Toledo.

Like the rest of the league, the Clippers had fifteen men on their roster and none had signed contracts before. Korea had held back a lot of military-aged players so this season's Northern League rosters were filled with rookies. There was no listed team captain but maybe they'd have one by this point in the season. Coach liked to make friends with the captains where he could.

The Clippers were a bad team, but the visiting Akron Zaps were in second place. We'd do Akron Thursday morning; their general manager was off on business tomorrow and wanted to be there to supervise the contracts. The field manager of the Zaps was a fellow named Sheridan who'd had the nickname Spitter when he pitched. He didn't sound familiar to Mikey so either he was older than sand or he was a minor league lifer. I had this all down in the notebook at the bottom of my bag. After Akron we were off to London and the historic Labatt Park first thing Friday to catch the baby Maple Leafs and the Buffalo Bisons on a two-game stint. Sunday would be a day of rest on religious orders, but we had asked Coach about maybe seeing Niagara Falls. London to Hamilton was a short trip and we'd have an extra day to do it because the Red Wings were off on Monday. We'd do them and the Erie Sailors before their first game, hopefully making the turn homeward towards America by Wednesday morning. Coach described the plan as leisurely and said he was surprised the bosses approved it. He had once worked two Northern League games—four clubs—in the same day: an afternoon game in Buffalo and then down the shore to Erie that night.

We could have stayed up late and slept in but Coach said we were tired and I knew Mikey couldn't help but get up before eight any day. No baseball tonight but lots tomorrow. We all showered, Coach going in last and hooting complaints about the lack of hot water left.

"You boys say your prayers please," he told us after, slipping his wet rear end into a pair of underwear.

I thought for a minute about what I wanted to pray for. At home, Mamma made us pray every day but because we were Catholic that usually meant we didn't have to make anything up, just say an Our Father and a Hail Mary and tuck in for the night. Coach was something else I couldn't remember. Not a Mormon like Utah thought he was but something long and chewy with vowel sounds. His prayers were like regular conversation, like God was sitting there next to you and you were pitching him your salvation. Mamma said Coach liked to say his prayers out loud before sleep and that we should get in the same habit so he didn't feel like an eccentric.

Mikey went first, swinging his legs over the edge of the bed and kneeling beside it, the motel bed so much bigger than his own at home that he couldn't lean over the mattress but instead rested his head against it, hands peeking over the side like he was a swimmer holding onto the edge of a dock.

"Dear God," he started, "I love you and you love me. Thank you for this trip. Please keep us safe. This is Michael."

Coach seemed to approve of that. He got down on his knees next to his own bed and bowed his head. "Merciful Jesus, I come to you every day a sinner. Please guide my hands so I may do your work on Earth. I'd be grateful if you'd protect and uplift these boys, the people here we meet tomorrow, and our friends and family everywhere. Please enter the heart of their mamma and ease her worry until we are home and her children are in her arms again. In your name, Amen."

He stood back up the way he always did, first to one knee and then pushing off from there to get back to both feet. I didn't know if that was from a war injury or playing sports, but it didn't seem to bother him any other time, just when praying.

I did the sign of the cross first, which neither Mikey nor Coach had done, and prayed quietly, just enough so Coach would know I was speaking out loud, but not loud enough that he or Mikey or anybody else could hear what I was saying.

Mikey had a bad habit of kicking you when he shared a bed. Maybe he dreamed about running or fighting, or maybe it was just his little brain flickering on, but he would get you under your knees or your butt or, if you were unwise enough to sleep facing him, he'd dig a heel right into your private parts. This was why I was awake already when at some point I heard him sit up in the dark of the room and sob.

"What is it Mike?" I mumbled.

He sat there a minute. I couldn't tell if he was looking at me or Coach or the door.

"Mikey, what is it?"

He put his hand out until it found my face and then said that he had a bad dream. I told him to go get some water so he did. I might have fallen back asleep because the next thing I remembered was him standing over me and saying he couldn't get back in the bed because it was wet.

"Wet how?"

He shrugged. I threw off the blankets and sighed. "You're such a goddamned incompetent, Mikey!" I was sure to whisper it but still woke up Coach, who rolled to his feet asking what had happened. I apologized and then told him Mikey peed the bed, which inspired a great wrathful awakening in my brother and he screamed at me that he hadn't.

Coach turned the lamp on and we all blinked for a moment over the dark oval on Mikey's side of the mattress, smeared a bit where he had slid off to the floor.

"Mikey—" I started to say before he interrupted to try and tell us it was just water from when he had gone to get a drink.

"That's no water, Mikey." I leaned over and caught the urine smell. "You wet the bed."

Coach was pressing his thumb and forefinger into the corners of his eyes. "Let's all calm down. None of this is a major problem. It's okay, Michael."

"Coach, I didn't pee—"

"I know, I know. It's probably just water."

I made a clucking sound and smirked at this and Coach looked seriously at me until I stopped.

"Michael," he said, "why don't you get changed and put a towel down and we'll worry more about it in the morning."

"It's not pee!"

"Well then, no need to even get changed."

Mikey stood his ground for a minute, looking up at Coach and then, darkly, at me, before giving up and running for the bathroom.

Coach fished out his watch and cleared his throat. "Christopher, maybe you should sleep on the towel."

"What?"

"It's not good practice to embarrass a person further when he's already embarrassed. You don't get results that way."

I closed my lips tight together and stared straight ahead.

"Alright," Coach sighed, "go get your brother and tell him he can sleep with me."

I didn't know whether that made me feel more or less angry. It lifted the insult of being asked to sleep on pee but replaced it with something new. A sense that I was being left out for my selfishness. Like having to deal with Mikey's aerobics all night was some grand joy and I was being told now I couldn't have it.

I knocked on the door and Mikey said I could come in. "I'm just getting more water," he said without looking at me, busily tending to the bathroom routine, throwing out a used napkin and washing his hands.

I watched for a moment and then told him Coach said he could share his bed if he didn't want to lie on the towel. This slowed him down, and he looked up at me with something, not a smile but a kind of looseness on his face like this was a solution he hadn't dared consider, but he knew well enough not to gloat.

"That's generous of him." He shrugged, opening the bathroom door.

When we turned the lights back off I still couldn't sleep. I heard Mikey flailing around and hoped for Coach's sake that he slept with his back turned. There were cars coming and going and, every now and then, a voice. A man and a woman came back laughing and giggling and eventually I could hear them kissing in the hallway while one worked a key into the old lock.

When I had prayed, I had prayed for happiness, which felt embarrassingly needful because people were supposed to pray for more basic things first: food and shelter and safety from diseases and war. Mamma said that, when you prayed, you should think of the soldiers who were in Korea or the ones who never came home from the last war, because that would make you grateful. Our daddy had made it home but not for long. He died a few months later in the way that certain other fathers or friends of fathers were rumoured to have died, that quiet shameful way where cars drifted off highways by themselves or men took fifty pain pills instead of the usual five. Unaccounted for deaths, grey ones. Daddy drove a car, a Ford Woody he had borrowed from a friend to go buy a sofa, through the wall of a warehouse outside St. Paul. He had injuries from the Pacific and got confused sometimes, disconsolate others. He outlived the war but didn't survive it.

One of the few things Mamma ever said about him after he died, and she had said it in such a casual way I wondered if it had slipped out by accident, was at baseball practice after I had been caught staring off into space and let a pop fly drop in front of me. On the way home she excused me by saying I did the same thing Daddy used to do; it wasn't that I was distant or daydreaming but rather that I was always in the moment *and also* watching myself from somewhere outside the moment. She said this was something that great and thoughtful men did but that it was also a curse, because this second-sightedness, this constant observing, this narration, it slowed you down. Made you come out of concentration more gradually and left you too deliberate for the kind of immediate-brained decisions needed for elite sports or combat. Single-sighters were good athletes. Fast drivers. Second-sighters wrote books or practised law or taught. Almost everyone at the college was second-sighted, Mamma told me, as encouragement. The college was our temple.

Mikey was a single-sighter and, despite being a good teacher and wanting to be a man who made his money with his mind, so was Coach. They were both strong athletes, Mikey probably a better ballplayer than me already and Coach apparently a great success in high school before the war.

Every president except maybe George Washington was second-sighted. Good generals are second-sighters, but Washington was a foot soldier too. Fighter aces were single-sighters. People who could think with their body had the directness of mind to only address the parts of the world that contained whatever they needed. No matter how big the canvas was in front of them, they could focus on a thing and experience it. Second-sighters couldn't. They built theories (like this, this whole idea was a theory) but were always too slow to react.

My daddy was slow to react sometimes, which maybe explained why his car hit the warehouse. He watched himself drive off the road. I don't know.

Coach's tell that he was a single-sighter came from a few different places, but the biggest was in how he had us practise for this trip. Rehearsing was about memorizing, not thinking through your problems. Piling everything you could onto the plate of single sight. Fundamentals. It was something that I thought would serve him well until it didn't. Mamma was a second-sighter, I guessed. It took second-sight to think of all this. She said I reminded her of my father, that when seeing me she also saw him. I wondered if this was also a curse.

Windsor,
Wednesday, July 9th, 1952

	W	L
Buffalo Bisons	38	23
Akron Zaps	34	26
London Maple Leafs	33	27
Erie Sailors	29	32
Windsor Clippers	27	34
Hamilton Red Wings	21	40

Last Night's Games
Clippers 6, Zaps 7; Leafs 5, Sailors 3; Wings 2, Bisons 9

THE NEXT DAY STARTED AT TEN IN THE MORNING. WE REP-resentatives of the Four Corners Baseball Card Company had slept in after all; once Mikey stopped kicking, Coach had managed to knock off but it took me another hour after that to do the same. The noise of the motel and its surroundings came in unexpected crashes all night. A woman threw a man out of their room over some insult. Tires screeched. A dog barked loud and close enough I sat up to scan the room for it.

Mikey's pot of oatmeal was warm and waiting for him when we got to the restaurant. Yesterday's waiter was gone. The woman who served us was the clerk from when we checked in. She was still pretty, and the better light of the dining room made that clear in new ways. Her blonde hair was in ringlets and piled on top of her head like Gloria Grahame, whose movies I was not allowed to see but I knew her face from posters. The woman's waitress outfit was just her clerk outfit with a waist apron. Coach waved us all hello and went off to the washroom as we sat down.

"Morning, boys," she said, leaning over with the bowls of steaming oatmeal in hand. "Cook said you'd come around looking for these."

I didn't go out of my way for oatmeal but was too distracted to say so. She bent over such that I could see straight down the cleavage of her shirt all the way, I swear, to the belly button below her soap-white breasts. It felt like I was looking through her, fully and scandalously, all the way into her. I pressed my spoon to my lips.

Gloria took notice and covered her chest with her hand the way people sometimes do to show surprise. Her face was red, but she was still smiling. I looked deep into my oatmeal, which sat there like wet cement.

"Anything else you boys need?" she asked. I shook my head but Mikey piped up for apple juice so I asked if we could also have two coffees, one for me and one for Coach. Gloria seemed unsure but didn't press except to ask how I took my coffee, to which I answered, "Medium."

Coach came back to the table as Gloria was putting down two mugs and a tray of milk and sugar. He looked pale and dopey; I was glad I got him the coffee. I watched her long thin fingers work on the table in front of me and paid her a confident grin.

"Thank you, miss. You're good at this."

She gave a quick laugh and thanked me for the compliment before leaving us to eat. I watched her tend to the next customer with just as much skill as she had done us.

"I need to use the washroom too," said Mikey. Coach told me to go with him, and I froze. I did not feel able to stand up in front of everyone and God and walk through the dining room at that moment.

"Mikey," I said, "you just went to the room before we left."

Mikey made a face because I was lying; he hadn't. Coach fixed his coffee with milk and looked at him and then at me for about as long, maybe a little longer. "Mikey, can you just go by yourself?" he eventually asked.

My brother sighed and slid off the chair. I put both my palms down on the tabletop and tried to focus my attention on the consistency of the oatmeal. Gloria was off somewhere in my peripheral vision talking about the weather.

"I didn't know you drank coffee," said Coach. I told him he could have it if he wanted. He drank his and then mine and didn't eat any food and by the end of breakfast his hands had started to shake.

We spent some more time in the room, with Coach leaving a couple of times to call Utah for a check-in and the clubhouse in Hamilton about plans to meet the Red Wings when our paths crossed. He seemed busy and fidgety, and I didn't immediately understand because of the coffees that this was him being nervous. I had never seen him nervous before. Wary often, angry now and then, and sometimes despondent, but never nervous.

We left for the stadium midday after one or two returns to the room to locate misplaced merchandise and Mikey's Minneapolis little league cap. I thought we were on our way, the engine running and the Hornet facing the road, when Coach excused himself one more time.

Mikey sat quietly for as long as he was able before bothering me. "You want to marry the waitress here," he said.

"I do not," I told him.

"It's obvious."

I crossed my arms in front of me. "I actually think it's you who wants to marry her."

"I don't want to marry anybody. I want to be a bachelor and live on the beach."

I escaped Mikey and went to find Coach. He had left the room door open but the bathroom door closed behind him. I worried a burglar could make off with the place, though I could hardly launch a complaint having just left Mikey behind in the Hornet.

I waited a few seconds without announcing myself and eventually I heard him retch and spit. The water was running in the bathroom but I could still hear him vomit, three times in all, before flushing the toilet and stepping out into the room. He was touching his face but stopped short when he saw me.

"What are you doing?" he asked. Not mad, but something else. Shy?

"Are you alright, Coach?"

He looked around for his suit jacket. "Sure. Must have been some bad oatmeal."

"You didn't eat any oatmeal."

He had a cup of water and was swishing it around in his mouth.

"Were you hungover?"

He spat. "What? No. I was with you two kids all night."

"Are you nervous about the Windsor team?"

"Hey. I do rooms like this a dozen times a year. They're nothing."

He was reviewing himself in the mirror and not looking at me. "And you know what? I called Forbush, and he says this room doesn't even really matter. The whole trip. We'll get the kids who make it to PONY League next year. This is just insurance. Mostly a charity trip. Outreach to impoverished ballplayers."

His tie looked fine, but he loosened it and started the knot again. "We're about—I'm about—to walk into that locker room and tell those children that they can either make five bucks today sweating their asses off playing baseball in front of nobody for no reason, or they can make ten doing that and also giving me their signatures. Now they're ballplayers, so I suspect they're all pretty gosh darned stupid, but I bet that's a deal even they can make sense of."

I could tell from the cussing that he was getting himself ready to pitch, and I knew it was my job to play along. I couldn't be sure if Forbush had really said this room doesn't matter, as I'd never spoken to the man and didn't know how he thought. But it seemed strange that he'd pay to send us out of country to a room that didn't matter. I served Coach up a question from our book of fundamentals. "Do you think those boys ever picture themselves on a baseball card, Coach?"

"Damn right they do, Chris. Every day since they were Mikey's age. And what we're walking in and offering them is an opportunity." He paused here for a second like he liked what he was going to say. "An opportunity, to dream that dream a little clearer."

He reached into his coat pocket and pulled out the pitch notebook to scrawl that last bit down. Then he stood up straight, swallowed hard, and told me we were ready to go.

You would need to get very close to Windsor's stadium to know it was home to a professional baseball team. There were no signs on the lampposts, no reference in the city papers. The Clippers languished somewhere in the bottommost third of Windsor's sports attention. There was a junior hockey team and a whole university's catalogue of athletic options. The assembly plant for Chrysler was churning out Dodge Kingsways, which were big dramatic coupes that looked like upper-class gentlemen with moustaches. The men who worked the plant came from farms all over the area and as far away as Nova Scotia. They brought their own interests: hockey and football mostly. The Clippers had been in the Northern League for a decade and never won more games in a season than they lost. The Tigers and the Red Wings beckoned from the American side of the bridge.

The street grid near us had a patchwork quality, giving way from city rigour and right angles to sudden lapses into rural character: a new two-storey retail building fronted on an empty meadow, a gas bar overlooked an orchard. The drive to the stadium was like flipping back and forth through time.

Like everything else about the Clippers club, the rented stadium was a poor fit for baseball. Windsor Stadium was mostly a football park, and the field had a Canadian football layout with the big *C* in the middle, which Mikey said stood for Canada but actually stood for centre. Hash marks were visible crawling up the third baseline, ending in an end zone that peeked out from under the temporary fencing the staff erected every time the Clippers' turn to use the field came up.

There was no native dirt anywhere. The best they had done was drag a few wheelbarrows' worth of ground in from elsewhere to assemble rough sliding pits that, because the football team didn't want trenches in their field, rose up from the rest of the infield like miniature pitching mounds. At our local park back home, before the field went in there had been a copse of spruce trees. Local men had dug out the stumps but left small hills behind in doing so, and this led to some unexpected bounces when ground balls found certain slopes. I had gotten used to it but didn't expect it to be a reusable skill for actual professional baseball. Which Coach assured me Windsor was.

All the seats in the park faced the *C*. When set up for baseball, the *C* was in shallow centre field. This meant that twisting to watch the batter's box all day demanded a sacrifice from your neck muscles that the team's performance did not make consistently worthwhile.

There was a grandstand along third base, another wrapped around home plate from dugout to dugout, and that was it. The first base side was open grass until you hit the forest some fifty yards away. The league had asked the Clippers to draw a chalk line indicating where foul territory ended, lest some ambitious outfielder be lost chasing a pop foul that carried all the way into the woods. It was a cold place to start a baseball career, and the fifteen Clippers were eager to see the back of it, either by playing their way to an affiliated contract or turning heel for college or Korea.

Even this hasty approximation of a ballpark required a winter's worth of compromise. The Clippers were set to be folded until two weeks before the season, despite a full roster and a modest clutch of season's tickets, because the stadium owners had put their foot down over kicked-up sod and other damages from converting the facility all summer. The Northern League's strange schedule for 1952 was caused by shuffling them back in at the last minute. This made Coach's job harder, as instead of sticking in one place for the usual week at a time, the teams moved on after two or three games, meaning we had fewer chances to meet with the players unless we wanted to chase them around Lake Erie.

The three of us were getting a tour of the situation from Eugene Simmonette, a small balding man who I would have guessed was fifty if Coach hadn't spent the drive from Minnesota using him as a dire warning against hard living, so perhaps he was really only forty. He was wearing a light grey suit and a straw boater hat, which was the exact uniform made famous among baseball men by Connie Mack, but the suit's colour had bleached with wear such that Mr. Simmonette instead gave off the impression of a grown man wearing a child's sailor suit. He pressed his knuckles into the flesh above his hips, his elbows pointing out wide and slightly forward, as he accounted for his team.

With us was Mrs. Simmonette, whose first name was Dora and who was either around fifty, like Gene, or aged by his hard living just as much as he was. She sat while we stood, her hands folded in her lap and her legs crossed regally. She had a blue blouse that said Clippers in cursive over the breast.

We were sitting up high in the long bleachers above third base cooling off from exercise. Coach had invited Mikey for a quick fielding drill before any of the players were around. He didn't invite me but in fairness I didn't ask, and I wanted to be careful not to rip my good shirt, which Mamma had bought last summer and which was tight through the chest and arms.

"We did well scouting the colleges down south this year, found our middle infield. It's appealing to have university men on the team—they lend some maturity—but after them it's all high schoolers I'm afraid. If you were good enough to make a local paper's sports page but not lucky enough to sign with a D league, we probably called you. I've a stack of newspapers in my office tall enough to knock over a horse."

"Anyone stand out?" Coach asked Simmonette.

"Pitching's a bit of a mess, and we don't hit for power well. But there's a kid from Ohio named Law that's a good find. He'll end up playing PONY ball or down in Texas if not this season then early next. Jamestown's already in my ear about him. A good talker too. Some days a little too good if you understand. Our captain's a fine fellow and a decent ballplayer, but he can't read more than a little and he's not keen to talk to suits, so Law'll be the guy you'll go through for licensing."

Coach moved his mouth around like he was chewing on something. "Yeah? This Law, is he honest?"

Mr. Simmonette smiled. "Like a tidal wave is wet, he is."

We stood looking around a little longer, watching some Clippers shag fly balls and listening to the groundskeeper shout orders to the crew assembling the fence. Eventually, Coach made a move like he was going to get his coat. "The facilities are charming, Gene," he said.

"They'll do for now because they have to," said Simmonette. "City is supposed to pitch in for a proper baseball stadium, but until then I'm afraid we're like the circus, setting up before the show and striking down after. Till then we won't be the prettiest operation you'll see this summer."

When Coach first met Gene Simmonette, he was working as team secretary for a Toledo club that played in the American Association in front of ten thousand people a night. Coach said he once took him to a prayer meeting with a couple of players and the Toledo equipment manager after Gene had slept the night bare naked in the visitors' dugout. The meetings couldn't hold him, and things kept slipping up until he got caught by the wrong authority figure and fired.

"Dora is helping us out a lot this year," Gene said without prompting. "She's been a real champion in that ticket booth."

Dora didn't look back at us or acknowledge the compliment, just kept on watching the players warm up.

"It's a good operation, Gene," said Coach, setting his jaw firm and nodding while he gathered his hat. "Where are the locker rooms?"

Gene kept staring out at the field and didn't answer right away. When he did, it was just by pointing to two portable buildings on the other side of the fence; they looked like big sheds or small storehouses. "Afraid those are them for now," he mumbled.

We finished the tour and Gene had the kid popping corn for nickels fix a free bag for Mikey and me, then we walked down the third baseline to the locker room where we had seen a couple of young men in Clippers white and blue enter.

As we got closer to the home clubhouse, we noticed a faded sign atop the open doorway. It read "Essex County Farm Supplies."

"Is that because the Clippers are a farm team?" Mikey asked.

"No," I said, "I reckon they're just borrowing this place from a feed store."

The building was made of some kind of thin metal and was open on both sides like an airplane hangar. The echo inside was such that once you cleared the doorway, every conversation descended upon you all at once as a reverberating growl. There were curtains hung here and there to organize the space. Pieces of equipment were piled in each corner next to signs spelling out names and numbers. An old wooden barrel on which someone had written "clean shoes" stood empty at the back. Squares of daylight big like automobiles patched the ground, which was all grass except where it was mud and someone had thrown an unfolded cardboard box overtop. I looked up to see bits of the ceiling were missing, showing clear to the bright blue midsummer sky.

"Poor kids," mumbled Coach. "They'll be in some state for a chat, I bet."

It wasn't until Coach expressed sympathy for the ballplayers that I realized I felt the same. The faces around us were young and sullen and looked more than a little underfed. The Clippers' shifting eyes found our bags of popcorn like a flock of gulls waiting for food to be dropped. In every classroom in America there were boys holding the singular dream of being a professional ballplayer, that great unlikely jackpot of body and brain that would give you the ticket out of adulthood. Ballplayers were a universal subject of envy: every adult path was arduous or dangerous or sad. Other boys grew up to hold jobs they suffered through. Or they went to war and died. Or came back and died. Or they came back to run sporting goods stores and coach baseball, give the remnant knowledge of their dreams to the hungry attention of the next boys, boys who were still keen enough to nurture theirs.

But ballplayers were endless boys. They went off to New York City to play for thousands and meet the mayor. They slept with movie stars, and let the world use their faces as avatars of hope: on chewing-gum wrappers, pajama tops, and, of course, cards.

But here were these boys in the squalor of their dreams. They had been pulled out of their lives by the gift of immaculate single sight and left here, in an empty foreign football stadium. The Clippers slugged along in the summer heat, with not even a working showerhead among them. I found myself shocked to feel sad on their behalf, to want to rescue them and their talents and take them anywhere. New York or Cleveland, sure, but even Minneapolis or Jamestown. Or home to the suffering of jobs. Just anywhere. To adulthood even.

I didn't know whether Coach was thinking all this or not, but he was certainly deep in thought. The first young man who noticed us wasn't in uniform but seemed to work with the team. He had a fitful moustache, an accent that might have been French or Cajun, and a funny speaking voice like his breath was always short.

"Can I help you?" he wheezed.

"We're looking to speak with Law."

"Reg?"

"Is there more than one?"

"Nosir." The young man turned and called into the echo. "Anyone seen Watch Me?"

Someone pointed towards the centre field wall where two players in uniform were playing catch. The taller one had the darkest skin I had seen on a man to that point in my life, while the shorter one was lighter, but not quite light like the three of us visitors.

Coach stepped towards them and cleared his throat. "Excuse me, I'm looking for Mr. Law?"

The players completed one more throw and catch and then the shorter one brought his full mitt to rest against his hip, looked from Coach to Mikey and me, and deadpanned, "I promise you neither of those children are mine." This made the tall man howl with laughter, and eventually Coach let go of a small smile himself.

Law tossed the ball back to the taller Clipper who jogged off somewhere in search of another partner. He took five paces towards us and stopped, his glove again on his side. His whole body projected looseness, a sort of ease, that reminded me of professional dancers from the movies. Like at any moment he might start to float.

"So what can I do for you gentlemen?"

Coach took so long to speak that I had began to wonder what I might do to start the conversation myself.

"We are baseball card agents," he said eventually.

"All of you?"

"My name is Lawrence Miller. I'm an agent from the Four Corners Baseball Card Company of Salt Lake City, Utah. Have you heard of us?"

"Yes."

Coach stalled and cleared this throat. He took a moment to pick the script back up, and this time I broke eye contact with Law and looked over. Coach had a hand on top of his head, like either he was trying to hold his thoughts in, or he had started the action of taking off his hat but never finished it. I hadn't seen him appear unsure in front of anyone before except for maybe Mamma.

"You have? Well. That's good, most players haven't. It's a big world out there, and there are lots of baseball card companies out there—"

"You haven't asked me my name, Mr. Miller. I received yours but you haven't heard mine," Law said.

"Oh. Sorry." Coach managed to get his hat off his head and was holding it out now like he was hoping someone would fill it with soup. "You said you were Law."

"That's my surname. I've a Christian name as well."

"Oh. And what is it?" Coach asked, although he already knew.

"Reg."

"Like Reginald?"

"Nosir. Like Reg."

"Ah," said Coach. And we might have stayed like that forever, soaking in the efficiency and balance of Reg Law's name, if it wasn't for Mikey and his consistent inability to recognize tension in an adult conversation.

"Why'd that man call you Watch Me?" he asked Reg.

I caught my breath and believe Coach did the same. Slowly and somewhat dramatically, Reg Law tilted his head towards my brother and smiled a big white-toothed smile. It was a contagious smile, casting the sort of fulsome mischief that caught up a whole room. "Who told you that?"

"The little man with the wheezy voice in the farm shed."

Reg looked around a minute, holding the foot-wide smile. "These kids, man." He laughed, before bending over to answer Mikey's question face to face. "I'm the kind of person who likes to perform for an audience," he told him. "Are you that kind of person?"

"Not especially," said Mikey. "I like performing things I'm good at but don't care if there's an audience."

While all this side chatter happened, Coach had reassembled himself and prepared a second attempt. He cleared his throat and addressed Reg.

"Mr. Law, Gene Simmonette indicated that if I wanted to speak to the team about licensing with my company, I'd best speak to you first as you were best positioned to understand the matter."

"In what way?" Reg asked.

Coach was ready for this. "On account of your education and, Mr. Simmonette told me, your intelligence."

Reg closed his mouth but held the grin, and started nodding to himself, like he knew he was being buttered up for some extra work before the game but he still appreciated the compliments that came with it.

"Alright then, Mr. Miller. What are your terms?"

Mikey stepped forward and handed Reg a card; it was the same Jim Waugh from last night's practice session. Reg took it delicately and flipped it over in his ungloved hand.

Coach dove in. "Thank you. We offer non-exclusivity through-out the length of a player's time in affiliated and independent minor league ball. Players are able, encouraged in fact, to sign any complementary details they'd like with other parties in the card business. And the licensing is limited solely to cards. We don't do stickers or out-licences. We won't sell your face to a soap company."

This whole time Reg was reading about the career of Jim Waugh. "How much do you pay today?"

"Five dollars, Mr. Law."

Reg turned the card over one more time and handed it back to Mikey. "No thank you, sir," he said.

Coach spoke too fast in his first attempt at a rebuttal and had to repeat himself to Reg. "Can I ask why?" was what he meant to say.

"On the whole," Reg answered, "I feel your offer is too low to be serious. A fellow two years ahead of me at State is with the White Hawks out in Iowa. A gentleman from Topps came by on their team picture day and offered twenty."

"Oh but you're not going to get twenty at this level of baseball," said Coach. "Topps and Bowman don't even send their men here."

"Well, why would they?" said Reg, looking around at the stadium. "Most people on this team aren't ever making it to the White Hawks. Let alone the White Sox."

Coach saw an opportunity to appeal as a fan. Reg was undervaluing himself and Coach thought it was an act, that he could leverage Reg's unspoken self-belief into a sale. "On the contrary, Mr. Law. My company has faith in young men like yourself, that your talent is going to bring you good things in this world. Not all of you, like you said, as nobody knows the future and you understand as well as I do that for every man in the major leagues, there are fifty in rooms like this from Montreal to Miami, and there isn't room for everyone."

Reg Law was rolling his ankles in the mud while Coach spoke the pitch, looking around as if to wonder what Coach meant when he said "room" in this open field enclosed only by pine trees and the side of a temporary shed.

"Some of your teammates will find other futures, and we bless their efforts," Coach went on. "But some will move up. We are a spiritual company by nature. Founded by a good religious family man and run as a family. As a spiritual company, we are guided by faith, and that includes faith in boys like you. And we'd like to represent that with an investment."

"That's outstanding," said Reg in a manner so flat it would be impossible to ever hear the word spoken again without feeling underwhelmed by it. "I'll tell you what. If you can give us each twenty dollars today, we'll meet your faith head-on and sign fully exclusive agreements with your company. Scratch out the non-exclusive clause. We're all yours."

Coach stammered. He didn't have the currency or clearance to offer more money and didn't know what Utah would think of the deal. Reg read this silence as a no.

"Figured as much," he said, taking a loose leather glove string in his teeth and pulling it to tighten the fit. "Here's the thing. You're coming down telling us you're doing everyone a favour offering non-exclusive deals because it lets us speak to the bigger boys when we're all bigger boys. Great. Except, this puts no pressure on those bigger boys to come speak to us now. You think we'll get paid by more ball card companies this way? Sure, but we'll get five from you, five from the sticker people, and cash those in for twenty from Topps in two years. Do you know what Topps would offer us if you never came by in the first place? The exact same twenty dollars. Or they'd wait for the cream to rise to the majors and give them a few hundred. You're not competing with those guys by volunteering to roll over for them, you know. You want to make life better for ballplayers? Offer twenty and get exclusivity. That'll make Bowman and Topps come down here early and offer forty each and eventually we'll all—me, you, the rest of these bums, your bosses—get what we want, which is for the ball card monopoly to become so expensive that the monopolists have to break down and share the pie."

I had never imagined a ballplayer would speak like Reg Law, and I was quite sure Coach hadn't heard one do so either. Ballplayers spoke in slang and backcountry lingo. Reg Law sounded like a news presenter. He probably didn't even like to use contractions.

"They did a study, someone, a couple of years ago," he continued. "Do you know what the face of a star major league rookie is worth in the licensing market, across all lines of business?"

Coach shook his head. His hat now hung from his fingers at his side.

"They said a million dollars a year. Which is about ten times what Joe DiMaggio makes in salary, and Old Joe is the most overpaid schemer in America according to the St. Louis papers. Did you know that?"

We didn't know it.

"And Joe sold his ball card licence to Topps when he got as far as San Francisco for a steak dinner. So no, I don't appreciate your offer of non-exclusivity. It's not a kindness. I'd like to take my chances elsewhere."

I didn't breathe for fear of missing something. Coach asked him if he spoke for the rest of the team, and Reg Law said no, by nature he could only speak for himself, but that he spoke *before* the rest of the team and that we wouldn't be able to move on to the others until the terms of a deal were worked out through him. Coach dug out his notepad and after a quiet moment's fumble asked if Reg didn't see the agreement as an opportunity to dream his dream a little more clearly.

"Due respect, Mr. Miller, but you don't know what I dream about," he answered.

Though that didn't seem like the natural end of the conversation, Coach said thank you all the same, and we turned and walked away.

After we got the door shut on us by Reg Law we were stuck with nothing to do. Coach tried to get the Simmonettes to help us, but Dora couldn't be located and Gene was at the Chrysler plant trying to scavenge up some sponsorship money. The Clippers field manager was not someone who spoke to reporters, let alone baseball card agents. This meant Coach had to call Utah collect. When he did he closed the phone booth tight behind him but even so, I got the sense that whoever was on the other end was angry about what had happened. Which was reasonable so long as they thought the trip mattered.

Mikey didn't seem bothered, but for me the conversation with Reg was enough to fill my head all day. It confirmed something that I was a little worried about, and maybe quietly a little excited about, this whole time getting ready for the trip, which is that while Coach was a good worker and polite and dressed himself well, he might not actually be a natural at this job, which required all of the above and also a kind of ease with others, a kind of fluidity, that he maybe didn't have. Too much fundamentals, not enough situational awareness, and moreover maybe not quite enough something else, some magic third thing that let you move easily from one mode of conversation to another without making it seem fake or getting you run over by the likes of Reg Law. Charisma maybe. Empathy. Or smarts.

The Zaps did their batting practice and then the Clippers came out and got ready themselves. The fences were up, bare and blue and maybe leaning a little past a right angle in certain parts of the outfield. Sometime after five, the PA system turned on with a high electric squeal that had everyone—employees and players and hangers-on and us—covering their ears.

It wasn't exactly clear whether we were going to stay for the game so I was trying to avoid getting too invested in the practice. I was watching Reg Law, who was scheduled to start at second base, dance around the infield turning double plays. More broadly, I took in the sight of my first professional baseball team. It was incredible to think that somewhere in America (or Cuba or Canada), for each of the very ordinary young men running about before me, there was a ball field, and from the vantage of each of those ball fields, these boys were all gods. The best their fields ever knew. Here they were calling after each other with nicknames, dropping fly balls, and playing practical jokes in the outfield. All local gods, each klutzy one. The worst among them would still be the best player I had ever seen before today. Mamma said it would be like that, that talent blended in with talent. You go to a symphony and everyone in the orchestra is a genius, but you don't notice it. I had never been to a symphony. Mamma had, when she was a kid, but she had never been to a pro baseball game.

I first noticed the girl in the red cap after Mikey and I came back from getting hot dogs at the food stand. They had just lit the grill, still an hour before the game, when Mikey popped up and plunked down his cash. We were their first customers and had to get the vendor's help to open their brand new ketchup bottle.

The girl in the red cap was dressed in a loose white dress but wore running shoes that looked like a boy's. She had a black-and-silver camera on a leather strap around her neck that I thought must have been expensive. It looked heavy, the way it bounced against her chest when she ran up and down the stairs. The girl was taking pictures of the players but from funny locations and angles. She ran all the way up to the top corner of the grandstand and took a picture of the whole field as the Clippers chased grounders.

I had decided to take the day off from noticing girls after the embarrassment at breakfast with the waitress. I noticed the girl in the red cap but not the same way as the waitress. She was further away and younger, maybe my age, and this made her familiar and less gilded. She had red hair three shades darker than the cap and her socks were pulled up far, which made her seem like she had come running out of an old magazine ad from before the war, here to sell me shampoo or tooth powder. Friendly and disarming.

Mikey saw me staring and asked who she was. I told him to go find out, and because he was fearless about strange kids, or maybe just because he was bored, he got up and tramped away in her direction. Worried what he might say when he got there, I stood up and followed.

Her name was Clara. Mikey asked if she was Canadian and she said no, American, so he said so were we. He asked what she was doing and she said taking pictures and then, curiosity sated, he just turned and walked back without me to where we had been sitting.

"Sorry about my brother; he's direct to the point of carelessness," I said, feeling as I said it that I sounded too adult and stodgy. I tried to lean against the railing, but it was loose and I had to catch myself to keep from falling down the stairs.

Clara smiled and looked away. In a minute she was fiddling with knobs on her camera and then I saw her shift her weight like she was making to leave so I panicked and told her that her camera was a Canon, which of course she knew, it was written on the front, and then followed quickly by asking her what year it was from.

She said she didn't know that, but it was a present from her dad, who got it sometime after coming home from the war, and that it was new then, so probably it was from 1946 or so, but that cameras generally don't get named after the year they were made. That was cars. The camera was called the II B.

"Or not to be," I joked and regretted it. She smiled politely one more time and then did nothing, and I did nothing, until she did the strangest thing. She lifted the camera up, aimed it at my chin, and took a photograph. I blinked stars from my eyes.

"I'm afraid I won't be able to show you a print of that," she said, turning something on the front of the camera. "We'll be in Hamilton in a couple of days."

"We'll be in London," I told her. "Are you with the Zaps?"

She looked down at me and nodded. "We are. My dad's the manager."

"Spitter?"

She laughed. A bark of a laugh, not a giggle. "Yes. His Christian name's Thomas."

I introduced myself and told her about Coach and the baseball cards. She was interested, at least at first, though she quieted as I told her more about the pitches and the rooms and the licensing contracts. She was travelling with the team this summer to keep her dad company and make sure he took his pills. She was the youngest of six girls. We found a spot near Mikey but not next to him for her to take pictures and me to watch the game. As ticket holders started to arrive, she focused her lens on them, either in wide crowd shots, which in Windsor were mostly just shots of empty bleachers, or in portraits which, unlike mine, she asked to take first. I wondered how much a roll of film cost her.

"What do you do with the photos?"

"I don't develop all of them," she explained. "But those I do I keep, except for the player ones, which all go in the album." She described the album, or albums, as keepsakes that she filled with photographs of every player on every team she could visit. Sometimes she would get the photos or the album covers signed. Then she turned around and sold them to collectors' stores.

"People buy those?"

"They do."

"How much do you sell them for?"

"Both my Frontier League sets last year went for thirty."

Thirty dollars. That was two, maybe three days' work at the university for my mother. Five at least for Reg Law. Four Corners could license the images of six ballplayers for that, and Clara here was just snatching them up and selling them.

Clara was thirteen. Lived in New Jersey outside of the summer baseball season. She was good at geography and English but bad at mathematics. All of her sisters had names starting with *C*.

These are the things you learn about someone with nothing but a half-empty minor league baseball stadium to occupy you.

"Was your daddy a pitcher? Is that why he's called Spitter?"

"Yeah. He threw the spitball. Which is disgusting and not legal anymore, but it was at the time so it was considered just as honourable as anything."

"Did he make the major leagues?"

"No, he was playing in Wheeling when he made my ma pregnant so he quit and joined the Navy. He was teammates with Tommy Bridges. He stayed in the Navy through the war, and when he got out, he went looking for coaching jobs. He gets a new one every year or two."

"You always travel with him?"

"Just this summer and last. My sisters before."

"What'd he do in the war?"

"He captained transport ships, the boats that brought the soldiers."

"Are you named after Clara Bow, the actress?"

She bit her bottom lip but didn't answer. The stadium was nearly full and I didn't know where Coach was. Mikey had taken a quick nap sometime after his hot dog and now was full of energy with nowhere to put it. He kept running up and down the stadium steps, weaving in and out of annoyed Canadians.

I was putting all my own energy into asking Clara questions and answering hers. She wasn't interested in Coach's baseball card job but had questions about Detroit and Minnesota. What parts of the country I had seen (basically just those two) and what parts I wanted to see (New York or California).

"Why do you call your father Coach?"

"Excuse me?"

I told her Coach wasn't my papa. That he was actually my baseball coach and Mamma had let us come with him.

"He must be a good coach if your mother let you come with him."

"He's not only our coach. He's a friend of ours and Mamma's. He comes round our house, helps us fix things. We eat dinner together a lot."

She took some time to fashion her next question. "Is he courting your mom?"

"Courting?"

"Are they sleeping together?"

I didn't know how to answer.

"Do you know what that means? Sleeping together?"

"Yes," I shot back. "I don't know. Maybe. They're friendly with each other."

"Where's your father?"

"He died."

"In the war?"

My breath whistled loud through my nose and my ears went red. Did I hate the question but still want to please its asker? How to square the instincts not to answer and to answer charmingly. The PA system came back on and started a song I didn't recognize. It had the backing of military drums but the floating quality of a hymn. It started quietly before the brass came in. It wasn't until I saw our neighbours standing up around us that I understood it was the Canadian national anthem.

"Yes. My father died in the war," I told her, lying but not feeling that tug of shame I usually felt when I told someone a lie.

The game was good. Fast and well played with several standout moments in the field, many of which revolved around Reg Law. Clara wasn't interested in sitting through the whole thing and took off on quests into the stands and along the far fence for photographs. She said she liked baseball fine, but given her volume of games she had come to find the faces in the crowd or the players at rest on the bench more interesting. We wandered down level with the field and she caught her father's attention from his office on the first step of the visitors' dugout, which like everything else in Windsor's park didn't actually dig down into the grass and so was a sort of elevated terrace that players had to step up onto to find their share of bench.

He was a grey-haired man with muscular shoulders but a round belly. He barked orders but softened easily, not just to wave back to his daughter but whenever the team needed a lighter touch. When commiserating over a strikeout or an error, he would place a thick hand on a player's shoulder and whisper some unknown kindness in an attempt to lift their spirit. The Windsor coach was his opposite, a man of no clear lines, all easy jokes and a relaxed back, until something went wrong and he came screaming out at his young players, gobs of spit visible from half a park away, arms flailing like an angry chimp.

In the fifth inning, with the home team down two, the PA came on to announce that day's attendance of one thousand. A suspiciously round number and, if I had time to count them all row by row, I wondered what I would have come up with. Something short of seven hundred, I'd bet.

Coach showed up just when my relief that we would be sticking around for the game was giving way to a concern that we might be left behind. Clara and I were in the shadow of the flagpole. She was watching two old men argue over dinner plans. Coach spoke with Mikey for a minute, bent over so their heads were within a foot of each other. He put his arm on his shoulder as they spoke and at one point brought his hankie out to wipe something from my brother's face. I could imagine, at least for Mikey if not for me, why someone would imagine he was our father.

"Is that your coach?" Clara asked, emerging from her interest in the old men to follow my eyes down the grandstand. I nodded, and she lifted the camera to snap off a quick shot.

We met up with them while Coach was showing Mikey the way to the concession stand.

"Christopher!" he said, stretching his back. "Do you want an ice cream treat as well?"

He smelled like the legion hall back home: sour and dusty. I sought out the secondary smells of wood panelling and bleach but didn't find them.

"Where were you, Coach?"

"I was working out of the pub across the street and eventually flagged down Simmonette and got him talking. His meeting with the car people was a bust. He says Law's an uppity loser, can't stand the sight of the kid. He'll get us a proper audience tomorrow afternoon; there's an all-hands meeting once a week here and we'll slide right in."

"That's good," I said, watching him fidget. He kept looking for a place to put his hands and couldn't find one. "Are you okay?"

"I suppose I'm not used to drinking during the workday," he admitted, blowing his nose. "Pub made me order a glass to go through my notes. Then Simmonette had a three- or four-an-hour pace I did my best to keep up with. Christopher, are you aware there's a young lady standing next to you?"

I blushed. "This is Clara, Coach. We met waiting for you."

"Beautiful," he said, extending a hand. "That's beautiful. I thought at first you were Queen Elizabeth."

She shook it and reminded him Queen Elizabeth was a brunette. She let slip her surname as well, which wasn't enough to trigger Coach's interest, so I made things plainer.

"Clara is Spitter Sheridan's daughter, Coach."

His eyebrows lifted and he stopped fidgeting. "Sheridan's daughter?"

We nodded. Mikey came back holding a dipped ice cream bar the same shape and only slightly smaller than a surfboard. The corners of his mouth were chocolate-smeared from where he'd tried to work his jaw around it.

"Dear me, Michael, that looks expensive," Coach said. To which Mikey shrugged and then lifted a finger like he had a point to make so the three of us waited patiently for him to finish swallowing enough surfboard to speak.

"Reg Law is there getting a Popsicle," he told us.

Clara and I looked at one another and then walked over to the edge of the grandstand. A crowd had emptied the seats in our area and was gathering around the frozen treats stand. In the middle, we could make out a slightly taller head covered by a blue ball cap.

After we jumped the stairs and pushed through the crowd, Clara, hunched over as she led me by the hand, bumped right into his back, a blocky "5" written against a base colour that, at closer range, wasn't white but the faintest of blues. I looked to the scoreboard. It was the bottom of the eighth inning. The score was Zaps 6, Clippers 1. The home team was at bat.

Everywhere around us folks were shouting questions or hellos and Reg Law, waiting in line like the rest of us, took them one at a time. A lady in an unseasonable wool sweater asked him what he thought of Windsor.

"Ma'am," he said, reaching out and shaking her hand, "I was born in Cleveland, Ohio, and spent all my time there short of college and a summer with my aunts in Alabama, and let me say to anyone who cares to ask it: I prefer this place to them."

"Reg, are you moving up this year?" asked a man.

"Not my decision, friend. I'm enjoying my time and all the good people in town. But if they want me to move up, I'd say yes."

"Reg, why didn't you swing at the 3–1 in the sixth inning?"

"I was still a little winded from playing the infield and didn't think I could run out a line drive. That pop-up that came next was more my speed."

I felt myself leaping into the space of the next question. "Reg, what's your favourite flavour of Popsicle?" was the best I could come up with under the strangeness of the situation.

Reg Law turned around to look at me, and then looked a little harder. "I've seen you before, right? You were with Mr. Non-exclusive earlier?"

"Yes, sir."

"And what about you two then," he said, pointing to Clara, who was pressed up against my shoulder. "Are you two exclusive?"

Someone in the crowd laughed. We didn't answer and Reg told us his favourite flavour of Popsicle was red. Clara said that was also her favourite and, not having any inclination to argue, I said red was the case for me too.

The line shifted forward. Someone held out a baseball and a ballpoint pen to Reg and he signed it, shaking the pen several times to get it to write on the horsehide. I asked Reg if he did this every game and he said no, never, but that he had always wanted to.

"One year in college the milkman came by so I ran up the hill to try and get a bottle but I should have known. Milkman doesn't come with milk in the evenings, just empties for the plant."

The crowd had stopped shouting questions and took instead to watching Reg wait patiently for his turn. I looked back at the field to see who was batting.

"Who's number six, Reg?"

"Local boy. Hollett. Bats ninth."

"You bat second."

He whistled. "Not if this line holds me up, I don't."

I leaned in a little and said, half whispering, that I was sorry things didn't go so well today with my coach and that maybe they'll have a better idea tomorrow after he talks to his bosses.

"Nah. It's not your daddy's fault," he said, even though I had just called Coach Coach. "It's just the role he's been asked to play. The whole world wants to make a buck off of ballplayers. Do you know what I studied back in college?"

"Nosir."

"Economics. Do you know what that is?"

"It's like money and stuff?"

"Superficially, sure." The line was down to one kid and then Reg. The kid had spent his time staring up at Reg with his mouth open, incredulous that a real live ballplayer would be standing there next to him desiring treats. And it occurred to me by watching the kid, who had to be physically spun around by his father to order a cone, that I should just as well feel the same. And this was not any ballplayer, but the best one on the day. Standing next to Reg was like standing next to the burning sun.

Reg corrected me. "It's not just money. Economics is the study of choices. What people do when they can't do everything, when they are limited by what's available."

I didn't speak back to any of this. The protective coating of Reg's friendliness had started to burn off right when I noticed it and so I was caught up in my nerves. I was tongue-tied, stalled. Getting lost in the company of baseball. Clara knew more ballplayers than I knew college secretaries but even she was quiet, maybe more silenced by the strangeness of the setting than the fact of Reg himself. Or maybe she just didn't have anything to say about choices.

"I'm saying that good honest men make bad arguments all the time. We argue from the position life places us, by grace of class, occupation, whatever. I write letters once a week to the commissioner of the Northern, a Mr. Eccles, and he's a good honest man, but he writes me back the arguments wealth affords him. People look for explanations for themselves, their lives, and your man thinks in his real true heart that if we ballplayers signed with his company, it would improve our world a little, because life has brought him somewhere where he is paid to think that. He has to think it, to make sense of himself. He's been limited by what's available to think."

"What are you paid to think?" Clara asked him, and I turned to marvel at her burst of assertiveness.

He laughed. "Well, ballplayers aren't paid to think, Red. But I find myself noticing that if you go up the food chain a few links, you'll see everyone is getting rich but us. I've never got a face-to-face meeting with Eccles, but he writes to me back on fancy cardstock. Can't come cheap."

The kid ahead of us got his cone and edged away, opening our view to the concession worker who, I was concerned to see, was Dora Simmonette.

She brought a hand to her lips and looked at Reg like he was a child out of hand.

"Mr. Law. You're here early."

"Yes, ma'am, I'm on my snack break."

A round of applause struck up behind us. Hollett had hit a single, and the leadoff hitter was walking to the plate. Nobody was warming up behind him. The Windsor coach was up and shouting at the players, surely wondering where Law had wandered off to.

"I'll have a red Popsicle. And two for my hoodlum friends here."

"We're out of reds," she said. A strange smile threatened the edges of her mouth.

"No red?" Reg balked, throwing a wink at Dora Simmonette though he kept speaking to Clara and me. "See, hoodlum friends, here I'm limited by what's available again."

"You're gonna be in trouble, Law," said Dora.

He leaned forward and spoke in a low voice, "And who's going to bring that trouble, miss? You?"

She smirked. "What did you want?"

"I'd like to hear some options."

She looked him over for a moment like she was chewing on a piece of gristle. "I got lemon and orange, and you don't got any more talking time," she said, nodding at the field where the leadoff hitter had just flied out on the first pitch.

Reg winced. "Oop, make it a lemon then, and whatever my two friends want on my tab."

She handed him the lemon. "You ain't got no tab."

He leaned in and kissed her quickly on the cheek, then turned and cruised through the crowd at a jog, biting at the Popsicle like an apple. He had it gone at ten paces and was licking the sticks as he hopped over the fence, wiping his hands as he stepped onto the field. A pinch hitter was striding to the plate but Reg waved him off and the wheezing Frenchman showed up with his bat, which he traded for the licked-cleaned Popsicle garbage. I didn't watch, but, in the papers the next day, the box score said he hit a double.

Clara and I took our lemon Popsicles and walked them around the edge of the stadium towards the visitors' barn. I could make out Coach and Mikey at a distance. Coach might have fallen asleep, leaned back in his chair with his feet on the seat ahead of him. Mikey's head rested in his lap.

"So," Clara said, catching a drop of lemon sugar as it fell from her mouth. "That was a heckuva thing, Law and Mrs. Simmonette. I bet you aren't sure if those two are sleeping together either."

I widened my eyes. This was a lot of speculation about the personal lives of adults for a new friend. "It's not possible. She's married and, what, twenty years older than he is?"

We waited by the doorway. The Clippers had scored in the eighth but then the Zaps had done likewise in their half of the ninth. The game was nearly over.

"That Law character is the only ballplayer I've ever heard say *isn't* instead of *ain't*."

"Reg went to college."

She shook her head like she pitied me. "Lots of men go to college and they don't come out sounding that much like they want to impress you."

I thought about that. Watch Me. Watching Reg all evening was like waiting for a thunderstorm to start. On the field and off, you always felt like an uncontained moment was building, like you were about to see the surprise you didn't know you'd come for.

Coach and Mikey stayed in their seats after the last Clipper struck out to end the game and the people around them got up to leave. They were just stirring awake when the players started plodding upfield towards us, two tired armies walking parallel in loose formation.

Clara congratulated the first few Zaps by name, and when Spitter appeared, she jumped up into a hug. He spun her around like a toddler, feet not touching the ground. She introduced me as Chris from Minnesota. He shook my hand like it was stuck in my arm and he had been called on by the townspeople to yank it free.

"What's your business, Chris?" His voice had the croak of a smoker but his breath didn't smell of it.

I told him about Coach and the baseball cards, and that we had an appointment to visit the Zaps tomorrow, and he stopped me short when, kicked up in a chair with one arm around Clara and another holding a beer, he asked me if we could move it up to tonight, so the players who wanted could celebrate with a good dinner.

I said sure, of course, though I'd need to check with Coach. Spitter checked his watch and asked if we could do it in half an hour. I looked over at the stands to where Coach had fallen back asleep while Mikey begged the grounds crew for a ball.

"Sure," I said. "We can meet you all at ten o'clock, Mr. Sheridan."

By eleven, I was standing in front of the mirror in the bathroom in our hotel room, fixing my hair and wondering whether it was good strategy to rifle through Coach's trouser pockets for nickels to go call Mamma. Was she waiting up? Would she call the motel and have the clerk walk the long hallway to knock on our door?

I poked around the corner to assess the scene. Coach was face down in his underwear, socks, and good shirt, snoring rhythmically, a stain of drool on his pillow like a cartoon speech bubble. Mikey was sitting up in our bed with his knees against his chin, staring back at me with eyes strained wide in a bid to force the appearance of attention.

"Mikey, go brush your teeth and say your prayers. I'll call Mamma and tell her we're both safe. Don't lock the door after me."

He released all his muscles at once and sloughed off to do what he was told. I got three nickels from Coach's pooled trousers and went to the phone booth. Mamma picked up on the first ring.

"If you waited any longer this would count as tomorrow's phone call too."

"I'm sorry Mamma," I said into my shoes. "We had a pitch after the game."

"After the game? Those poor young men probably just wanted to go to bed. How did you do?"

"We did good," I told her. "Coach did his part really well, and we signed fourteen players."

"Wow, well done!" she said with genuine excitement. "He must be proud of himself."

I remembered, but left unmentioned, my sprint across the field from the clubhouse, slapping Coach awake and telling him about meeting Spitter. Him cursing at me for accepting the offer, then Mikey running around the corner for coffee. Panicked rehearsals in the men's washroom. A trip to the car for cash and supplies. Coach smoothing out his jacket wrinkles with old receipts, lips mumbling rehearsal lines in the dirty mirror.

"How was your day, Mamma?"

"Good enough. There was a group in from Duluth on a campus tour. Hadn't seen kids from up north before. It'll be you on those trips soon enough."

I thought about this. The Zaps had an appointed college kid just like the Clippers had Reg Law, though in their instance it was Sheridan who mostly spoke to Coach while the player, a hulking square-jawed outfielder who had half the credits of an engineer at Penn State, did a lot more listening than talking.

Then Coach got to go into the room, or the barn, and give our pitch. It was all fundamentals and lasted three minutes. There were no questions. Coach pulled out his wad of fives and the Zaps gazed upon those bills like gold nuggets drifting down the Klondike. Ten signed right away while the other five asked to read it first. Of those, only one, a pitcher by the name of Darwin, declined. He said he had spoken to Topps already, which surprised the lot of them not excluding Spitter. He claimed he called up their headquarters and introduced himself, and they'd mailed him ten dollars and a contract with a self-addressed stamped envelope. Just like that. If it was a true story, none of the other players believed it well enough to ask Coach to take their fivers back.

"Were you waiting up for us?"

"A little," she said. "But I'm basically down for the night now."

Our phone was in the kitchen, with just the one low stool for sitting. Two rooms and a flight of stairs separated it from Mamma's bed. "Mikey's asleep now," I told her. "So's Coach even. I'm sorry it's late; we didn't get back until just now."

"It's fine dear, I'm glad you had success. Did you meet anyone interesting?"

I thought about Reg Law, him kissing Mrs. Simmonette. And about Clara. And Spitter. "Yes, Mamma, almost everyone I've spoken to seems interesting." She laughed at that.

After the meeting, while I was alphabetizing the contracts, Spitter came up with a whispering Clara beside him and invited us over for a lunch date. Coach, coming down from the coffee and the thrill of the win, pawed his face a moment and tried to remember our schedule. I told him we weren't due with the Clippers until mid-afternoon.

"We met a man who captained transit boats in the Pacific during the war," I said. "There's a chance he drove Daddy there or back."

"Oh," she said, and nothing more.

"Do you know the name of the boats he took? I might ask him."

"No, dear," she told me in a quiet voice. "I don't know the names of the boats."

For a moment, a great bravery rose inside me. I wanted to use the rare freedom of distance from her disappointed face to ask more about Daddy and the war. She would feel her sadness, frown her disapproving frown, maybe weep an unknown tear, but I would keep going because I couldn't see it, couldn't be stopped short by fear or the shame of asking.

In the end, the image of her crying in my mind's eye proved just as bad. The bravery was gone. I told her I should be able to call earlier the next day, and she said she knew I'd do my best. She asked me to promise I'd kiss my brother goodnight, and I did.

Kissing Mikey was more difficult than I expected as he had migrated, apparently as a permanent arrangement now, out of our bed and into Coach's. He was curled into a tight ball with his butt poking out the side of the blanket and his forehead resting on Coach's shoulder, in the same tripwire sleep he always slept. I tiptoed over, assessed my options, and placed a soft peck on his arm. He didn't stir, but Coach did.

"Turn off the light," he mumbled. The lights were all off but the light from the highway made it still seem like dusk.

"I will, goodnight."

He exhaled. A housefly buzzed over his head and landed for a second on his knee, then flew away again.

"Thank the Lord for Akron," Coach said, though I didn't know if he was talking to me or some character in his dreams.

"It's good news, but I had a great day either way."

Coach snorted, and I understood now he was more or less awake. "For you. I'd get canned and shipped back to Minnesota if I didn't get at least ten of those boys' *X*s."

"You said Utah didn't care."

"Shit," he said into his armpit. "Companies, they don't have to care to punish you. Forbush said I was three-fourths to done. And I can't lose this job."

A ripple of headlight lit the far wall over Coach's bed.

"I didn't know that," I said, unsurprised that Utah's coolness was a lie but struck by how worried Coach was about it. "You'd be fine even then though. You have the sports shop."

This was a strategy I'd develop when talking about money with adults. Mamma mostly. Bring the worst-case scenario into the conversation and live together for a few moments inside it. Sure, you'll lose your job. You'll lose the house. Medical bills will sink us. The Depression will come back. Where would that leave us? Starved and frozen? Good. We could live there, you and I, if we had to. Smile as you describe it, give it all a nickname.

"You wouldn't be out on your rear end, Coach. You'd just be more of a homebody."

"Kid," Coach said quietly, shaking his head a little. In the light from the highway I knew his eyes were open though he was looking at the ceiling, not me. "I've expenses you don't understand. Every job I take I have to."

I didn't understand what extra expenses Coach, a bachelor with a successful business and nothing frustrating his pockets but parking tickets, could have. I was going to ask him when one more car came down the highway outside and spread its high beams through the room so that the light shifted more fully onto Coach's upturned face and I could see that he was crying. The red in his eyes gave it away more than any wetness on his cheeks. I made to apologize, stopped myself, and left to draw a bath.

Windsor,
Thursday, July 10th, 1952

	W	L
Buffalo Bisons	38	24
Akron Zaps	35	26
London Maple Leafs	34	27
Erie Sailors	29	33
Windsor Clippers	27	35
Hamilton Red Wings	22	40

Last Night's Games
Clippers 2, Zaps 7; Leafs 4, Sailors 3; Wings 5, Bisons 3

C OACH NEEDED A SHIRT. WE WALKED AROUND THE BLOCK twice and decided there was no proper place to outfit a businessman this close to the highway so we drove downtown. Coach's good white shirt was stained at the pits plus Mikey had gotten chocolate on it when he fell asleep at the game. After shirt shopping, our new schedule for the day was: Sheridans at their motel for lunch, then a second attempt at the Clippers at three, and eventually maybe the ballgame itself at seven.

We had all slept in again and the shirt problem hadn't been understood until well after breakfast. Coach cursed at me for wasting time wondering where the motel's television might hide and said to instead make sure Mikey was properly cleaned up and then to wait with him by the car.

Once we found it, Windsor's chief shopping avenue was lined by three-storey buildings that all shared a pattern: a store on their main level, storage or office space above that, and then people living out of open windows at the top. I wondered if each building was owned and occupied by one family. The butcher, his back room, his kin. The upholstery store: same thing. If we wanted we could walk to the stadium from the shopping district, but Sheridan's place was further away.

Coach was talking to the man who ran the shirt store and who maybe lived two floors above it.

"Friend, do you take American currency?" he asked, leaning on the desk.

The man said they did and told him the exchange rate. I flipped the price tags on two neckties. They were one dollar each, Canadian. Which seemed like a lot given how little fabric it took to make a necktie. Mikey was sitting on the bench by the door and swinging his feet like little kids do. There was no one in the store but us.

The mannequins were half women. One perched undressed in the front window; maybe we had interrupted the man setting her up. She was recognizable enough from the top half, her skin painted to look the colour of underwear, that faded yellowy beige. A self-possessed smile. But her bottom half fell apart; she had no legs, just a lattice of thin wood slits expanding out into a wide cone that sat her on the floor. Like a human robot from a science fiction serial. It upset me to look at her. She had upsetting hands, the colour but not the consistency of leather gloves.

I backed away into a rack of hats. Half hats. The ad above called them "Circle Hats," and that's what they looked like, like someone had pressed a red pancake down over their ears. No brims or clips or anything.

I was about to pass them by when I caught a better look at the girl in the ad. She had a face like Clara's. Not her complexion or shape or anything, but her look, her expression. She held her smile the same teasing way, with the same underlying brightness. Clara had been wearing a red hat but not like this; hers was a proper Akron Zaps ball cap with a brim for the sun and everything.

The man at the desk measured under Coach's armpits. They were debating something and I got the impression that Coach thought the measurement was unneeded. He probably had his numbers ready when we got there.

I checked for Mikey. He had his nose down now in some sort of catalogue. I looked back to the rack of Circle Hats, exhaled, and took one, pushing it down the front of my pants where my shirt was hanging untucked over it. I looked at myself in the mirror. If I was examining, I might notice a lump, but who would look there anyway?

The man came back with a collared white shirt. Coach didn't try it on and had cash out and ready in advance. We were safely gone and back in the Hornet inside of five minutes. I tried to walk like there was nothing stuck to me.

The Zaps' motel looked familiar and turned out to share an owner with ours. It was another C shape, with another restaurant at one end next to the clerk's desk. It may or may not have hidden a television somewhere. The swimming pool, empty like ours, may or may not have been filled in certain seasons, though realistically if not July, then when?

I had packed the circle hat in an old samples box I found in the trunk and stuck it in my school backpack, which I was glad I had convinced Coach we'd need in case we ever found ourselves moving on foot. Coach brought nothing but his wallet. Mikey brought a small drawing pad to fight the boredom, even though Mikey didn't get bored. Some kids you needed to build a whole schedule for, but my brother could stare at a blank white wall for hours. Nobody thought of him as a reader, but he was always scanning through written material: menus or pamphlets or the labels on cans. Still, Mamma thought that the car rides and business talk might test his limits so she sent him with paper and some of my old coloured pencils.

I knew I wanted to see Clara again and listen to Spitter's stories. But I didn't fully understand what Coach wanted from the meeting. We had the Zaps' signatures. I brought this up in the car and Coach told me that salesmanship was about making contacts. Sheridan was a journeyman. This year he was in Akron but next year who knew. He made a friend of an equipment manager in Martinville three years ago and now he was the vice president of the Carolina League. I thought about this. Clara and I would part ways tomorrow, us off to London and them to Hamilton, and then who could say. Maybe some letters or maybe not. Eventually she would just become a contact.

The motel chain's downtown managers had meant to distinguish their restaurant by upgrading its decor and menu. While ours offered diner food and plastic tabletops, they had stretched upmarket. There were tablecloths and darker wood, but the floor was still sticky and you still got a sense that you best review your bread for mould. The Sheridans were in the far corner at a four-person table with an extra seat pulled in from a neighbour. I rushed ahead to beat Mikey.

Spitter Sheridan had that morning's paper spread out and, when she saw us, Clara made him scramble it away. Everyone shook everyone else's hand.

"Mr. Sheridan," Coach said, "you're kind to invite us over."

"No, no. We always try to make time for fellow travellers, don't we, Clara?"

We settled in and looked at the menu, which was maybe three-quarters the same as we saw at our place, the changes mostly steak over pork chops, salads over starches, and beyond that just fancier writing in the entree names and higher numbers beside them. There were waffles for brunch though no special signage announced this. I didn't know if I could bring myself to order again, as we had just had breakfast three hours ago. Coach and Sheridan talked shop about travel and the cost of transportation and then Coach answered four or five straight questions about the Hornet. Yes, it was hard to find parts for. No, he never took it racing. After a long stretch of this I realized I still had the menu in front of my face and had been using it as a shield. I placed it down in front of me, smiled at Clara who smiled back, and this seemed to serve as a sign that we were ready to order as a waiter appeared tableside.

Spitter asked Clara what was appropriate for him to eat, which I thought was odd. He caught my expression and explained that he had doctor's orders against certain kinds of fats. I didn't know there were different kinds. Clara was fiddling with unmarked pill bottles and lining up tablets by his plate. Mikey didn't bother to ask about oatmeal, ordered a chicken sandwich and a side of Jell-O instead. Coach had coffee and toast with fried eggs. I asked Clara what was good and she said nothing. I had a beef sandwich and she had the same.

They invited us back to their room to wash up. We passed some of the Zaps on our way; they recognized us and said thank you for the money. I wondered what they had spent it on. What would I have spent it on? Books maybe, or bus fare somewhere. A friend from school and I had once found a quarter on the street and used it to take a round trip to the city limits and back,

Mamma flushed and spitting when I wandered home an hour late from baseball practice. I peeked into one of the rooms and saw two unmade beds and two more cots stuck flush against the wall. The tall blonde ballplayer getting dressed had to surf across the cots to find the washroom.

"One of the benefits of travelling with a young woman," said Spitter, "is Akron pays for our own room."

He opened the door and I saw it immediately. Where our writing desk sat there was instead a squat grey cabinet with six dials. On either side were speakers, and in the middle, where older eyes might expect to see a radio tuner, there was nothing but a blank black square. A television. A National, which was a company I knew of out of Massachusetts that was selling cheaper sets for homes and businesses. Not cheap enough for Mamma, it turned out, but cheap enough for me to ask.

I tried to make like I hadn't seen it, but Mikey crossed the room immediately, barked at by Coach for not taking off his shoes. He stood for a second before the invention and then reached out and put a palm on the screen, like he was testing it for heat or he expected an electric spark.

"You have a TV," he whispered.

Spitter laughed. "Those things are butterfly nets for the kids, I'll tell you what. Hotel said we're the only room that has one. Used to be in the lounge." He reached over and spun a dial with his thick fingers. After a moment to ready itself, the machine showed a line of people on benches, all taking turns telling jokes.

"Who is this?" I asked Clara, as if the speakers' presence in her room meant she must know their names. She shook her head to say she didn't.

Sheridan respected that the Four Corners Company was a religious outfit but he still wondered if Coach could allow a small brown drink after lunch. Coach looked a little queasy from yesterday but still accepted. They sat in the chairs by the door and gossiped about Gene Simmonette. They told stories about the border crossing. And then, like all men did once relaxed in one another's company, they began to speak of the war.

I knew Coach's story from other meetings with other new men. He had been living in New York State, where he was born, and was already in a training base when Pearl Harbor happened. In some versions he was twenty-three, in others twenty-five, but I suspect one's age in stories starts to cloud after a certain number of years. He had enlisted the previous winter after selling his parents on the plan. His dad worked at a shoe factory that would soon make uniforms. Most New York recruits got shipped to Europe that summer, but because he'd signed up early, he was sent through the West Coast and entered the Pacific without ever seeing France or Italy. Midway came just as he finished Marine training and from there it was a few minor islands and then Guadalcanal, where Coach met my Daddy and which he often, in casual conversation, used as a stand-in for the war as a whole. He'd tell my mom that he hadn't had soup as good as hers since before Guadalcanal. That he hadn't eaten shellfish since Guadalcanal.

Daddy was injured, but Coach pressed on with the rest of the First Marines into 1943. He did Cape Gloucester and New Britain, which weren't so bad, and Okinawa, which was. Daddy met up with him again after a spell of clerical duty sometime before the summer of 1945 and the end of fighting.

Of course, this wasn't how Coach explained it to Sheridan. They spoke in numbers and names, all of which were code words for a narrative that they could match to maps and battles, lists of foreign islands and campaigns. The First Corps. Third Expeditionary. General Geiger and Colonel Kilmartin.

Sheridan, for his part, had spent his war in the Pacific as well. He joined the Navy as Clara had said and was at sea for Pearl

Harbor. He won his command and spent the war ferrying communications equipment, supplies, and men closer and closer to Japan until the A-bombs. The men compared dates and, to their memory, thought there was a reasonable chance they had shared a boat before. It was understood that Sheridan had an easier time than Marines like Coach or Daddy, but he didn't say so except to note, with a kind of lurching sadness that made it sound like a confession, how well he had eaten on-board.

All this remembering went on as the three of us kids pressed up against the comedy show and tried to make sense of the jokes. Mikey was sitting so close I could see the grey reflection of the image play against the wide-open whites of his eyes. At two o'clock, Clara excused herself to the en suite and the men quieted down with their drinks for a moment. I heard what I thought was water running before realizing she was peeing in there and blushed so hard my ears got hot to the touch. As she washed her hands, I slipped the sample box out of my backpack and wedged it between her pillow and the baseboard, and then Coach said it was probably time we went looking for the Clippers.

The version of Windsor Stadium we came to on Thursday was a bank vault. The day before we had wandered through the open gates and been on the field itself inside of a minute. Thursday, the gates were closed, staff were garrisoned at either side of the grandstand, and the only way in was conversation.

Coach paced the building from across the street before deciding which attendant to try to convince to let us through. He chose a young-looking woman with curly red hair and glasses.

"Hello," Coach said in a voice a half octave deeper than normal, "I've an appointment to speak at the team meeting. May we enter?"

The girl took the card he offered her. "I'm afraid there's a team meeting," she said without reading it.

"Yes, exactly. That is our appointment."

She glanced at Mikey and me. "For all three of you?"

Coach told her to go confirm with Mr. Simmonette. She backed away and into an alcove office where she made a phone call. Five minutes later she came back out. Mikey had crawled up the stone plinth of the building such that he was level with Coach's shoulders.

"Mr. Simmonette isn't available," she said.

"He's in the team meeting," said Coach, his politeness wavering but not the stiffness of his bearing. "As I mentioned, he's expecting us to speak at the team meeting this afternoon."

"I'm afraid you'll need to wait until after it's over," she said, and Coach pulled us back around the corner to regroup, his lips stacked tight in the standard expression of his anger.

"This building is fake," Mikey whispered. He repeated himself before either of us paid him any attention.

"How do you mean?" I asked.

"It's like a fake building from a movie. It has a front but no back or sides."

He was right. The stone facade was impressive but didn't go all the way around the property. Still, there were employees at both ends of the block.

"We can't go in the front or the sides," said Mikey. "But not that many people work here. I bet we can go in the back, through the woods."

And that's how our second approach to Windsor Stadium began: we walked in from the edge of Jackson Park, around the cricket grounds and through the mixed forest, high-stepping over fallen trees and bog. We came out across from the visitors' clubhouse.

Coach grabbed Mikey by the head and pulled him in for a playful hug. "My little genius, well done!" He was animated and pleased for the first time all day. While they celebrated, I must have caught Coach's eye because he straightened and cleared his throat. I tried to look away before he spoke.

"Are you happy enough, Chris?" he asked, smiling in a way that felt like he was giving me a cue, like he was prompting me to join in with them. It was such an atypical question I thought at first I had misheard it. Was I happy enough? How much is enough?

"Happy?"

"Happy." He was still smiling but no longer looking quite at me, and it no longer felt like a prompt to join a celebration.

"Yes, Coach," I said. "I'm happy."

He took off his hat and checked it for twigs and leaves, then glanced over and nodded like he had forgotten at first to react to my answer.

"Good," he said. "I only ask because it's hard for me sometimes to tell."

I was left considering whether or not this was true and how I felt about it as we tramped out of the woods towards the voices coming from the home barn. Coach didn't say anything on the rest of the walk. I wondered what he meant by the question and what he meant by not explaining it. More and more I felt like it was my job to try and understand what adults meant when they went silent.

There was an employee at the entrance to the barn, but he wasn't on guard duty. It was the young man with the moustache and wheezy voice from yesterday. He took a deep breath and wished us a good afternoon.

We did the same and walked through the doorway. The Clippers were gathered out of uniform, mostly in shirts and trousers. They were leaning on posts or sitting on equipment bags. In the middle, their coach was illustrating his theory of infield play through a series of profane outbursts. He had drawn a diamond in the mud with his boot toe and was pointing to where he wanted the shortstop and second baseman to go when approaching a double play.

His second baseman was the only Clipper less than dressed. Reg Law sat cross-legged on the ground, shirtless and wearing a kind of underwear I hadn't seen before, tight like briefs but stretched down his thighs like short pants.

He and Simmonette recognized us at the same time.

"Coach Dunn," Gene interrupted, stepping forward from the back of the crowd. "Apologies, but the men from that card company are here."

The Clippers coach flared his nostrils and looked around trying to spot us in the crowd.

"Now?" he growled. When he saw us behind him, Coach tipped his hat.

Simmonette signalled Reg. "Law," he said, "go outside and talk to the gentlemen while we finish up here."

"He'll miss batting prep," complained the coach.

"That's no problem for me, sir," Reg Law told his manager as he stood up and strolled easily towards us. "New pitcher tonight. You'll want us to make him show some control. That's clever. Bats on shoulders until two strikes in the first inning. I understand you."

We backed up as Reg Law came towards us and didn't stop until we were clear of the door frame again and standing in the mowed field. We heard the Clippers manager go back to talking, his voice rising and falling unpredictably, stressing words you wouldn't normally expect to be stressed and seeming to get mad at random in the middle of all his sentences.

Coach shook Reg's hand and they looked at each other for a long moment. Coach was smiling in the tiniest way, just enough that Mikey or I would notice it but so little that a relative stranger like Reg might have missed it. The sales smile, on its lowest setting.

"Good to see you again, Law," said Coach. "I wonder if you don't have a few more minutes to speak."

Reg put his fist to his hip. It was the same posture he'd showed us during our standoff yesterday afternoon, but this time without the glove or flannels and barely any clothes at all. "I've always time for conversation, but I'm not sure you want to hear it, Miller."

Coach nodded his understanding. "That's okay, Reg. Why don't you borrow the Zaps' barn and talk it over with my associate, then?"

It took me a second before I realized he was speaking about me. I was the associate. Reg Law seemed similarly confused, but Coach pressed on.

"My superiors at the Four Corners Baseball Card Company have insisted that we try again to come up with an agreement that will let us pitch the opportunity to your colleagues. That's their desire, but to be entirely honest with you, I don't think it'll work. You made yourself clear yesterday, and men don't change their hearts all at once like that, so I figure: why don't you and my young friend go and speak it out for, let's say, five minutes by my watch, and then I can tell them we tried. I don't personally feel I need to join you, and I don't hold you any ill will for your beliefs."

I was watching Coach with a tilt to my head. It occurred to me that he had practised this. But with who? Alone? Mikey? I thought I could detect his salesman's voice, but it had been so long since I'd heard him use it without already knowing the words he would say, I couldn't be sure.

"I believe you two met yesterday at the game," Coach continued. "His name is Christopher, and he has my full proxy should you manage to strike a deal. But again, I don't expect you to. No pressure."

The "no pressure" must have been directed to me. Reg blinked. He looked at Coach and surprised us with a hacking laugh.

"Alright," he said, signalling me to follow as he wandered off half-naked to the other barn. "Let's go then, young man. Better listening to you than Coach Dunn anyway."

I looked over my shoulder at Coach but he didn't give me any signs. He just pointed, with two fingers, in the stylized way certain umpires do when calling someone out. No pressure.

The Zaps' barn was the same as the Clippers' except they hadn't moved back in for the day yet; everything was still stacked and put away. There was a box of washed uniforms on an old oak barrel, the name of a laundry service printed on the side.

Reg wandered over to about the same place he had been sitting in his home clubhouse and sat down cross-legged again.

"So what do you have for me, hoodlum?"

I cleared my throat. Coach hadn't given me a sample set or any sort of prop. They were still back in the other barn with Mikey. I looked up, the sun poked through different holes here, but the effect was the same. Patches of sunlight gave the floor the appearance of a chessboard.

"Why aren't you all dressed for the game?" I asked him. "We came here the same time yesterday and you were all in uniform."

"Team meeting day," he said. "Coach Dunn is a traditionalist; we're supposed to look smart for the meetings."

"Why aren't you dressed, then?"

"I don't believe I own any clothes that would make me look smart."

"So you go naked?"

"No." Reg reached down to massage his knee. "I just change at a leisurely pace while he talks."

It occurred to me that this would mean he had to get naked in front of all his friends and teammates and stay naked even after they were dressed. I wondered how he felt about that. I supposed Coach expected me to pull a pitch, a new one, out of my head and deliver it on the spot, but I couldn't see a first step, so I kept asking him questions until I found one.

"Did you always want to be a baseball player?"

A ripple of pain flushed Reg's face as he continued to work on his knee. "I'm not sure I want to even be one now, if I'm honest. I didn't start playing until high school. It wasn't like it usually is, 'born holding a bat' and all that. I stuck with it because I was good, and I got a free ride through college for it."

"You don't like to play baseball?"

"I like it fine." Reg looked down at his knee, and when he spoke again, the speed of his answers had slowed. Every other thing he'd said since we got to the barn the first time had felt like a challenge, like he was saying things because we didn't expect them or to see what we would do. But then he got bored, or he came to the end of his flippancy. I thought I heard the honesty rush into him once the show and patter emptied out.

"I don't know." He sighed. "I suspect what I want most is to be free. Get to hit the road, travel the country, all that. Ball sounded like freedom from a distance."

"It isn't?"

He shrugged. "Nothing is. Not in the way you'd expect. Everything with other people is a compromise."

"Where do you want to go instead?"

He stayed quiet a minute. I thought he was looking from one leg to the other, like he was checking that they were the same shape and size. "Niagara Falls? Maybe I'd like to see Niagara Falls. It's not far; hope I get to see it before they ship me up."

I told him I thought he was the best player on the team yesterday, and he looked at me with heavy eyes. I couldn't tell what that meant. Then he asked me if I had a pitch to make.

"You already heard the pitch," I told him.

"Alright. Then tell me the next thing."

"Coach says money in hand is worth more than money down the road. Because you could take that money and spend it on something, or invest it, or grow it like a tree. Or maybe that down-the-road money won't even happen. So you should take what is certain and invest it. It's worth more than what you might have later."

"Invest it?"

"Yes."

"What do you recommend?"

I thought a little. There was a word on my tongue but I couldn't quite remember it. "Bills."

"Bills?"

"Yes."

"Did you mean bonds?"

"Wait. Yes."

He leaned far forward until his chin hovered in its stretch just above the knee he had been measuring. "Who's that redhead I saw you with yesterday? She your sister?"

"No."

"Girlfriend?"

"We just met yesterday."

He laughed. "Okay, slick. Say I play your game and throw away everything from yesterday about competition and the size of the pie. For now. Let's assume you're right, basic time value of money stuff. How much would I make if I waited until, say, AA to sign a deal?"

I didn't know what time value of money meant except to guess it was another way of saying what Coach had said. Coach had a habit of coming up with on-the-spot folk knowledge that mirrored things other people had already written in books.

"Maybe thirty bucks?" I guessed.

"Okay. And when do I get there?"

"Four years?"

"So are you about to tell me I should take your fiver now and buy some treasury bonds with it, instead of waiting on thirty dollars in four years?"

"No," I told him, knowing my objection lay down a path ballplayers tended to avoid, but feeling like Reg wouldn't mind taking at least a look there. "You can't assume there's a hundred percent chance you'd make AA."

Reg looked thoughtful but not mad. "Fair." He exhaled through his mouth. "What chance do you think I got?"

"What chance do you think?"

At the same time, he said four to one and I said fifty-fifty.

"Alright." He grinned. "Let's call it three to one. So the question is: Do I want five dollars today or a one-in-three chance at thirty dollars in four years?"

"Yes," I said.

He stayed quiet for a minute. Eventually, I saw him drawing some figures out in the dirt with his finger.

"I'll take the shot at the thirty," he said, wiping away the dirt math like someone was going to come by and steal it.

I wondered how much of Coach's five minutes had gone by. Not quite all of it, but I still had one more good thought. "You're forgetting what Coach said. I know you didn't like it, but Four Corners' contracts aren't exclusive. You can sign both."

"Maybe." He shrugged. "But I heard a rumour Topps men won't sign you now if you show up at their visit with a Four Corners contract in your name. They just skip right by you when they're handing out cheques."

I stopped short. I didn't know if this was a joke or not, or a story he was telling to trip me up, or what it was. "How could they know?" I asked him.

He shrugged. "Same way anyone knows anything, I expect. They ask. Now I bet you're wondering how they'd know they were getting honest answers, and I wondered the same when I heard. Maybe they think ballplayers are too dumb not to lie to protect their own interests. Or maybe they have a mole on the inside."

"A mole?"

"A spy. Like a real Russian spy. Somewhere in the House of Four Corners."

"Why would they not accept a player who had a contract?"

This was the first time it felt like he was frustrated with me. He slapped the ground beside him with both hands. "Because they're in the monopoly game, son! They're not in the sharing game. Same as the boys who own the teams and the boys who own the companies making the damned hot dogs! It's in their best interest to see Four Corners out of business, even if it means having to take a chance and ignore some rookie with five dollars in his dresser drawer."

I sat down in the dirt across from him, rested my chin in the palm of my hand. Everything people in business did was an attempt to kill someone else. With all the thrill and daring Coach spoke about when describing the adventure of the sale, I had to expect he didn't know about this.

"Don't be sad over it," Reg offered, picking up a loose pebble and throwing it into my lap. "It's a compliment to be a threat."

"Wouldn't you be unhappy if they put Four Corners under?"

"How so?"

"You always talk about competition. If they put the companies trying to compete with them under, you won't get what you want."

"You want me to gamble my thirty bucks on fairness?"

"No." I sniffed. "I just want you to get what you said you wanted."

He put his hands in the square of sun behind him and leaned back. He didn't say anything right away and I wondered if he was done talking and we were just counting down the seconds until the end of Coach's five minutes.

"Fuck, kid. That's a pretty good point."

All at once we heard applause from the home barn and then a round of whoops and hollers. Some slow-moving part of my brain thought it was for me, for getting Reg Law to maybe come around. Reg got up, shaking dirt from his underwear in a way that brought the stalk of his penis into view long enough for me to look away, and stuck his head out the door. The mustachioed kid was there by himself.

"Hey French," called Reg. "What's going down?"

French told him that the boys were thanking the baseball card man.

"Wait—" was all I got out before Reg blew the air out his cheeks and took off running across the field towards French and the rest of the team with me chasing behind him. "Wait!" I called again and sprinted out in front of him. I had a hand on his chest when I looked up and saw that he was grinning.

"Kiddo," he said, removing my hand from his bare chest. "You're too small to fight and too young to fuck, so get off me."

When we arrived at the home barn, Simmonette and Coach were standing shoulder to shoulder as Mikey made the rounds picking up signed contracts. My job, as we had drawn it up in practice. Coach caught my eye and gave us a toothy grin.

"You bastard sneaks," said Reg, still smiling. I couldn't make sense of his expression. Was he mad at us? Is this how he showed he was mad? A Clipper came by and smacked him on the shoulders, pushing a one-page Four Corners licensing contract into his hands.

And what about me—was I mad? Coach had used me to tie up Reg, but I had done well. So well, in fact, that I might just about have won him over. And all this time it was a diversion; he and Mikey were the real show. I stood there in the excited noise of the Clippers' clubhouse and tried to take stock. In the end, maybe, I was happy if Reg Law was happy. I still didn't know if he was.

But something else edged in at the periphery. What did Coach think I was good for? Was my skill talking to people, convincing them of things, or was I only good for wasting their time? And behind those questions another, harder, one came on with a surprise: Did Coach like me? Was I someone he thought was worth attention?

I shook these questions from my head and focused on the only one that was askable. "Reg," I called, and after another try got his attention. "Are you mad or happy?"

He glanced at me and made a motion like I should turn around. When I did I felt him signing his contract against my back.

"Can't be mad, kid. It's business," he told me, handing me the paper to pass to my brother.

Coach took us out for ice cream to celebrate our victory. We had signatures from all fifteen Clippers, now twenty-nine of the first thirty Northern-Leaguers who'd come our way. The Clippers, who had missed a paycheque a month back and ever since had been scrounging for spending money and plotting their revolt against Simmonette, were suddenly a pack of terriers with the scent of the whole world. Plans to go out for drinks after the game were quickly made contingent, by Coach Dunn, on a win.

Even Reg Law was excited. The players' plans inspired him to promise that he'd take a woman home, and from there the talk grew bawdy and specific enough that Coach pulled Mikey and me from the room and left us to compare favourite major-leaguers with the kid Reg had called French. I understood French's full name, at least his full nickname, to be "French Wind" on account of his being French Canadian and having a lung problem that made his voice sound like a thin whirl of wind. I was learning that ballplayers did not come up with the best nicknames. French Wind was French and windy. Spitter Sheridan threw the spitter. Every pitcher who ever pitched left-handed had the same nickname.

From the benches by the laundry rack, French, Mikey, and I watched the Clippers in their banter and play. When they were down, losing and broke, they looked to older men to set their levels. Their snapping turtle of a coach and their milquetoast GM. But now that they were up they needed no one but themselves. In-jokes mixed with strategy, insults with encouragement. The Clippers were their own machine, rolling forward up a hill.

The only folks unhappy were the Zaps, who had to wait until the meeting finished and were just getting off their bus as we left, our stack of fivers exchanged for a full set of signed contracts. Clara was carrying her father's duffle bag while he argued with the same stadium girl we had met earlier. The Zaps looked strong but tired. The new pitcher they had brought in from Wooster, pride of the local high school, was rolling his shoulders and trying to hold his nerve.

Another pitcher, the starter from the day before, was leaning against the stadium stone talking to a young man in glasses with a notepad. Press, I'd guess. Clara called out to say she'd see me once the game started. I said sure thing and three Zaps whistled at us, which was enough to get a quick "Lay off of 'em" from Coach Sheridan.

After we found the ice cream parlour and had our fill, Coach raised the question of whether we did, in fact, want to see the game. We all did. He wanted to be around in case the underdog home team got their win, as he hoped to join them for those drinks. More contacts, I gathered. I wanted to watch Reg again and help Clara take pictures. Mikey just wanted more baseball.

"Coach," I said, wiping chocolate off my cheeks, "when I was talking to Reg Law, he said that the Topps men might stop signing players with Four Corners contracts."

Coach rolled his eyes and smiled. "I bet Reg Law is the arbiter of all knowledge. You know what? I'm sorry I sent you away with that creep. He didn't try anything on you, did he?"

"It was fine," I told him. "So you don't think it's anything?"

"I don't suspect that Topps or Bowman think any more about us than we think about the ants under our feet, Chris," he assured me.

The game started with an unremarkable first half inning from the visitors, and then the new Zaps pitcher got going on the job of walking the home team. He lost the first three hitters to load the bases, then earned a strikeout off a curveball that dropped like the dead. Then another walk to allow a run, a single, a double, another walk, and a homer. It was eight-nothing for the home team before the stragglers even made it to their seats to fill out an attendance that would later be described as 1,100, though in our section, which was one-fifth of the whole grandstand, I only counted eighty-five.

When he walked the lead-off hitter for the second time that inning, Spitter Sheridan started a long slow march out to the mound. They were far too distant to be overheard but I still leaned forward in my seat next to Coach. Sheridan put a hand on the kid's shoulder and then reset it further down, by his bicep, with a good hard squeeze. The kid might have been crying; he kept wiping at his face with his glove hand.

Reg Law was waiting to hit next, giving the conversation time to play out. When Sheridan walked back to his above-ground dugout, he gave Reg a wave of thanks for his patience and Reg nodded back. He stepped up, allowed two curveballs to miss the strike zone, and put the third against the centre field wall for a double. Sheridan pulled the kid for a reliever. There was one out in the first.

We didn't see Clara again until the fourth inning. She said she liked to stay closer to her dad when he was losing; sometimes he got too excited and she would warn him to take deep breaths. It sounded like a good service and I wish I had the same. I told her about our success with the Clippers pitch and she didn't try to act impressed. When she walked to the right field pole I ran behind and pointed out some interesting fans to snap, but she didn't take me up on the suggestions. She was just going there and back for the exercise.

The game was 12–1 after four innings and in past years the league's mercy rule would have kicked in but they had done away with it for 1952. The Zaps were grumpy; the reliever threw a ball behind the Clippers' centre fielder and then hit the next guy in the back. Clara said very little and put away her camera. She caught me staring at her as the visitors got ready to bat in the fifth.

"What are you doing?" she asked.

"Sorry." I turned to face the field. "Are you okay?"

"We're losing."

"I thought you didn't care that much about the games."

"I don't care when we're winning, or it's close," she mumbled, spitting out a sliver of a fingernail. "I don't want him to get embarrassed."

It was dinnertime, and the run of diner food and ice cream had me pining for something more reasonable. However I was in a baseball stadium in Canada; there wouldn't be any chicken noodle soup on site. I asked Clara if she was hungry and she ignored me. I looked around for Coach and Mikey to see if they had bought food, and saw them back at our initial seats behind home plate.

There weren't any other fans in their area, and I could tell immediately they were bunked in to a serious conversation. I looked for Coach to point towards the play, to give deference to some sort of baseball moment, but he didn't. Coach was looking intently at Mikey as he spoke, and eventually Mikey looked up and stared back. I felt my breathing slow. I had a sensation like I was spying on strangers when I shouldn't. Coach wasn't mad and Mikey wasn't saying sorry. And then, at the thick end of a long slow quiet, they hugged. Mikey went first and Coach followed. It wasn't the usual side hug or bulldog hug that Coach handed out as quick compliments when a kid, even me some days, did right on the field. It was chest to chest, cheek to chin, and it lasted three whole pitches from the Clippers' starter.

I don't know how long I had been staring, but when I looked back Clara was gone. I watched her walk down the bleachers towards home plate, and settle in even closer, right next to the visitors' dugout, where one of the hangdog Zaps flagged Sheridan and father and daughter had a short chat.

I watched the rest of the game by myself while Coach and Mikey took in the lazy last innings of the blowout from their nest at the top of the grandstands and Clara hovered over her father's shoulder. Near the end of the eighth, nobody but me noticed as the game's losing pitcher, the young god of Wooster, made the long lonely walk along the edge of the woods beyond left field and into the Akron barn.

The Clippers' preferred place to drink was an Italian restaurant two blocks from the stadium in the direction of downtown. The owner identified himself as a retired ballplayer who had been their shortstop before the war, but that seemed to be an in-joke. The Clippers hadn't existed before the war and the gentleman did not look like an athlete.

Because it was technically a restaurant, and maybe because this was Canada and things were different, nobody seemed to care that Mikey and I were there. We sat in a corner booth away from the players and Coach got us chicken parmesans, which might as well have been the only thing on the menu because every player ordered one. They came out as big discs of breaded meat with cheese and tomato sauce piled on. The sauce was sweet like ketchup but lumpy like spaghetti bolognese. This was our third restaurant meal of the day and we were getting pretty good at it. Mikey sat with his elbows off the table and I managed to get the waiter's attention over the songs and shouting to have him bring us pepper.

Clara wasn't there, obviously. She had shuttled her father off the field by the elbow, his face flush like someone had slapped him. I had planned to chase her down for her address but couldn't make myself do it. Coach said he'd write Sheridan at the team address when we got home, but I wasn't sure we should do that either. I had made myself too friendly, ran ahead too quickly to earn any real closeness, and it simply wasn't there. We had taken some pictures together and that was it. Now I was just a lonely boy eating the cheese off his chicken and listening to the men sing songs.

Coach made his rounds. The Four Corners crowd didn't want him to drink, and the necessary adventure with Simmonette the day before had left him hungover, so he kept a water glass at our table and got it refilled every hour or so. If he had alcohol, it was just for cheers.

At one point, two of the Clippers got to back-slapping, and in doing so one spilled his drink on the other. They embraced, laughed it off, and more drink spilled, and the slapping got stronger, and both imperceptibly and all at once the celebration became a shoving match before the coach and captain jumped in to separate them. The players had been strangers two months ago and would be strangers again soon. They were from cities and small towns, they were white and Black, from points south and north. Some came from Canada and at least one from Cuba. They were thrust into brotherhood by the demands of matching laundry. All of their fun and games harboured violence. Their competitiveness snuck up on them in unexpected ways.

Reg Law kept mostly to himself, until the doors swung open sometime after eleven and three women in mixed attire walked in. Two wore pants and one was in an evening gown. I don't know where they could have all been together; maybe they had been acting in a play somewhere and walked over in costume. The tallest among them towered over Reg, and he rested his head on her breasts. I saw some city faces stare into our window and realized the restaurant must have closed. We had become a private party.

The only unwelcome visitor arrived around eleven thirty. Eugene Simmonette brought Dora with him, tapping on the window glass until the owner gave in and opened up. He crossed right to Coach Dunn, who was sitting deep in an upholstered chair with his feet on the table, and they had themselves a hushed exchange as the background noise of the room dialed down and all faces turned to watch the boss and his wife.

Coach made his way towards us. "I don't expect the general manager is pleased by this curfew breach," he whispered into his water. The whole time Gene and the Clippers coach talked, Dora Simmonette was sorting the crowd with her eyes. When she found him, Reg Law nodded through the maze of arms and slumped bodies. The three women were still there; one was sitting on his knee. Dora nodded back.

At some point the whispered argument ended and the Simmonettes agreed to a drink, which they took to the corner opposite us, even further away from the crowd and next to a stack of chairs. I watched Dora and Reg watch each other. One of the young women went to kiss his neck and he pushed her face away with the heel of his hand.

Mikey was the one who remembered to call Mamma. We found Coach wedged in with the Clippers telling stories and asked him for nickels. The restaurant had a payphone by the bathrooms. I let Mikey go first; he may have woken her up but she didn't seem to mind. He told her about the game. I hadn't bothered to ask him about his hug with Coach because he never told me anything, but I thought maybe if I stayed close I'd hear him hint at it to Mamma.

Coach and Mikey were forever slowing time. We'd be walking three abreast down the sidewalk, and all of a sudden they would be crouched wordlessly over a butterfly or bug. Or they'd be buried in the paper's sports section. I didn't mind: all trios are just duos with an extra orbiter, and Mikey was always more eager to impress Coach and be his friend and protege than I was. Mamma often asked me how Coach and I got along. She told me I had his respect, which she said like it was something you could hold or look at. I told her he was fine, which she treated like a placeholder answer. Like I was still making up my mind, still weighing that respect in my hands.

Mikey told Mamma the score of the game and a play-by-play account of the new Akron starter's rough outing. He told her what he ate for breakfast, lunch, and dinner. He told her that business went well. She must've asked him about Coach because he told her he was doing a great job. Nothing about their private moment in the bleachers made the news.

When it was my turn, there wasn't much left to cover. Mikey made for the dinner table, and I asked about her day.

"Boring," she said. "That place can get so lonesome with the students gone for summer. They drive me batty when they're around and I miss them when they leave. Isn't that funny?"

"That is funny, Mamma."

"What about you? Did you make any friends this week?"

I thought about Clara. The circle hat in the sample box wedged under her pillow. "A little bit, maybe. It's hard to get to know people when everyone's busy."

"That's true. Who'd you meet?"

"A girl, she's the daughter of one of the coaches. She's from New Jersey."

"A girl, you say?" I could hear the smile in her voice. "Well, get her postal details. We can send her some of the sheep cheese; it just showed up in markets this week. A taste of Minnesota."

I pictured Clara opening a box of smelly sheep cheese and thinking of me. "Yeah maybe," I said. "Hey, what did Mikey say he got up to today? He watched the game with Coach. I didn't see him."

"You know your brother, he gets into everything," she said. "Apparently he got an eyeful of television. And he told me you were doing a great job of taking care of him."

Dora Simmonette got my attention by suddenly appearing, or at least the back of her suddenly appearing, in the window looking out on the alley. Her hair was pressed up against the glass and she was sliding around. It wasn't until I saw Reg Law that anything made sense. He had his hands tight around her middle and they were kissing. She was moving her body up and down against his, and when they turned a few degrees he opened his eyes and saw me. I froze, worried they'd think I was spying, and mumbled a few words of acknowledgement into the phone so they'd know I was otherwise engaged.

Reg smiled in my direction. It was a strange smile, lopsided and sly. All the Clippers were drunk. Gene Simmonette was somewhere in the restaurant. Reg couldn't have known who would have a view of the picture window when he threw Dora up against it. I was glad Mikey had left to stake out a second helping.

"Who won the game today?" Mamma asked.

"What?"

"The baseball game."

"Oh." I cleared my throat and turned towards the phone. "The home team. Like Mikey said. They don't win a bunch, but they got onto a rookie pitcher and put up ten runs."

"Impressive and rare, it sounds like."

"Yeah."

"Is Lawrence there?"

"Who?"

"Coach."

I put the phone against my chest and looked out into the dining room. Coach was singing a song, or trying to, with French Wind. The song was in French and it would have been hard to make out even in English the way French mangled it, but Coach seemed to know it, or at least know the tune.

"He's around but working on making some contacts."

"Just tell him I asked about him and to come to the phone sometime."

"He doesn't like social calling."

"I know." In my mind she was rolling her eyes, which for her meant she knew someone was misbehaving but wasn't terribly mad about it. At least that's what it meant with me. "Just ask him if he'll make an exception."

We said our goodnights and hung up. Alone, I stood facing the corner of the hallway, away from the alley window, and let the remnant air out my lungs. When I turned around there was nobody there but the shuttered store across the way. I don't know if I was relieved or disappointed. I was curious but I knew in my body, like a wave of heat before a fever, that the alley window was a problem that would suck me into it if I stared.

The parmesans were done but Mikey got a plate of sweet cannoli from the kitchen. They were passing them out like birthday cake. I wondered if someone paid, and moreover how the five-dollar jackpots handed to all the Clippers were holding out. Each beer was thirty cents, and I saw the right fielder buy six at once. The food was maybe fifty cents a head, and what's more Coach said many of the Clippers had IOUs out around town, trading on the name of the team, since the chaos at the start of the season saw them fall behind on pay.

I looked over the crowd and saw Gene Simmonette alone, with two empty drink glasses and a third half-done in his hand. He was looking at the floor beside his table and smiling a little. The restaurant had grown a whole jungle of untrustworthy smiles. His was thin and overwhelmed and maybe a distant cousin to a smirk. Dora was gone and so was Reg, and I wondered if that was the joke, that he knew everything, but he still wandered into the team's party to drink three whiskeys and laugh to himself while his wife ran off with the infielder.

Mikey asked for my cannoli and I said sure. He had been chewing on his fingernails, the thumb on his right hand was red where he had bit it too far down and it had irritated the nail bed. I thought of Clara spitting out her own nails and shook my head until the thought released me.

"What did you and Coach do at the game?" I asked him.

He swallowed a bit of cannoli and shrugged. "He had lots of pointers for me. What did you and your girlfriend do?"

"She's not my girlfriend."

"Did you make love?"

"I'll hold you down and make you eat soap if you keep talking."

"So you did?"

"What's making love mean, Mikey?"

He shrugged. He was old enough now that, while I didn't stop myself from bullying him whenever he went looking for it, I at least thought about the oncoming future when it would be me eating the soap and not him. He was the best ballplayer on our under-ten team, and I might not have beaten him for that title if I was young enough to play. He was the tallest kid in his class and the fastest. In the fall he'd transitioned from baseball to basketball like a gannet bird diving into the sea.

"I want to go back soon," he said. "The men here talk too loud and you can tell they think all day about fighting."

I looked at him. Every now and then he had these little perceptive breakthroughs. Maybe the Clippers did think all day about fighting, or at least about winning, embarrassing a local rookie or stealing someone's wife. Fighting in whatever form you found it.

"It's okay," I said. "Coach'll drive us home soon."

"Do you think Coach is the same as them?" he asked as we watched Coach, who had finally traded in his water for beer, raise glasses with a pod of five Clippers and shout out something we couldn't understand in the noise.

"Not quite the same," I said, and meant it. Coach's grand reusable power was falling in with other people. He got along with the teachers at my school and with the unemployed loggers who came into the store to barter hockey equipment. He'd picked Mamma up from the college one day and she said she'd found him making small talk with the graduate students. People generally knew that he'd moved to town after the war but still asked him which of our high schools he went to. Coach had a gift for making people think he had always been there.

"He's never played ball professionally," Mikey said, apparently as agreement.

We watched the crowd a little and then I asked him again what he and Coach talked about and once again he just said, "Baseball."

"No," I pushed and sat down at the table across from him. "When he was talking right at you and you hugged."

He licked his lips and stared into the greasy varnish of my dessert plate. I waited.

"Coach said he'll tell you soon. It's best that he does it. He'll tell you when we get home to Mamma."

"Just tell me now."

"No, Chris." He swallowed. "I don't wanna. And it's not my business to. It's Coach and Mamma's."

And that was when I knew, or thought I knew, the underlying test of the trip. Coach was going to marry Mamma, or move in with her. Or the four of us were going to move somewhere all together. Into the city maybe or off to New York State. I knew Coach was trying us on for fatherhood, even if I didn't know why he'd tell Mikey first and not me.

Maybe Mikey was practice and I was the pitch. Mikey would be easy, eager to fall right into family life like he had spent the last seven years scratching at its door. But I would be the hard one; best to work up to me. I tried to picture what I'd say when Coach told me but nothing in the restaurant's wallpaper kicked off my imagination.

"It's okay, Mikey," I said, and rubbed his shoulder with my hand. "Thanks. Thank you. I won't ask again until I hear it from Coach."

Mikey exhaled. He looked up at the wall over the kitchen door and I followed him. The clock was approaching midnight.

"Can we walk home? To the motel?"

"I don't think so," I said. "But I can walk the block with you if you need it."

The city outside was still and cold. There were lamposts, but no private lights beyond the restaurant. French Wind stood in the alleyway, near the window, smoking a hand-rolled cigarette.

"Do they not let you smoke in the room?" I called to him.

He sniffed. "The air out here," he said, "it is better for my lungs."

Mikey approached French and I followed.

"Are you two enjoying the road?" French asked us.

We nodded. His cigarette smelled sweeter than we were used to but also more acrid, like the spray of a distant skunk. It occurred to me that it might be a marijuana cigarette, not the regular tobacco kind, which smelled lightly like headaches but never stood out so sharp. This smelled like the ones Mamma's old desk mate in the secretarial pool smoked, before she got fired and moved to Florida.

He came up the alley so we didn't see him until he was right next to us, pulling on French's shirt sleeve. Reg. French flinched enough that his cigarette danced on his lips.

"Fellas, come on," Reg said, whispering excitedly, "I've a show set up for you."

"Not them too, Reg?" French asked, I guessed about Mikey and me.

"Sure," Reg whispered. "If they can hurry there's space for all."

French licked his fingers and pinched his cigarette tip. I looked at Mikey, then we followed the men down the alley and up the fire exit.

The floor above the restaurant was dark but I managed to make out enough to guess that it was set aside for storage. One more flight up might have housed the owner or his staff. The lights were dim and I couldn't pick out objects. Reg pushed us through a door and into a smaller room, then further still until the three of us—Mikey, French, and I—were packed into a closet. I asked where we were but no one answered. Reg slid the door closed and left the room. We could still see a little out the slats.

Mikey made a noise like a lost cat. French shushed him and said, "This is a game he likes to do. He thinks it's funny or something. Just be cool, be quiet."

I felt a nervous buzz in my ears and reached out to steady Mikey, who was shifting his weight from foot to foot.

There was a door slam elsewhere in the building, and then a click and the lights came on. The room had a mattress and not much else. An ironing board leaned against the wall in the far corner. Three books without dust jackets beside it. On the bare floor, an alarm clock told us that the day was almost over. It was one minute to midnight.

And in the middle of the room, unzipping her dress, was Dora Simmonette. She let it fall and stepped forward. Her rear end was hugged tight by underwear the colour of old teeth. When she took her bra off, you could see the angry red line where it had stretched across her back.

I heard Mikey whisper "What?" and put a hand back to silence him. Reg Law stepped into the room, threw a quick grin towards us in the closet, and got undressed himself. The minute passed; one day became the next.

Windsor,
Friday, July 11th, 1952

	W	L
Buffalo Bisons	39	24
Akron Zaps	35	27
London Maple Leafs	35	27
Erie Sailors	29	34
Windsor Clippers	28	35
Hamilton Red Wings	22	41

Last Night's Games

Clippers 13, Zaps 4; Leafs 7, Sailors 5; Wings 0, Bisons 4

"CHRIS, CHRIS, CHRIS," MIKEY WAS WHISPERING. AN INCANtation or a plea. I grabbed him and he shouted, like I had squeezed free all the air in his body. The noise from the mattress stopped; I pulled open the closet door, lidding my eyes against the bright light and the scenes it revealed. Dora Simmonette, her voice soft and slurred, asking what was happening, and Reg, naked between us, his long wet thing jumping in front of him like a downed wire.

The door to the room was closed. Locked? The ironing board slipped and crashed against the floor. I pulled Mikey by the arm and ran—the door came unstuck and gave way. On all sides of us the darkness and then, down the hall, moonlight from the alley. I pushed Mikey ahead to the window, threw it open and jumped into the fire escape. As I was pulling Mikey out I heard Dora Simmonette scream at French Wind to leave. We raced down the stairs and out into the city, across the street and all the way to the river, Mikey so fast, the fastest kid I knew, before we stopped to find our breath, hands on our knees and gasping.

On the road the next morning, the Hornet smelled like gas. At some point since we last saw a highway the engine had started to leak, or a cap or filter had misbehaved, and now once the vehicle got up over forty miles per hour, the smell of gasoline invaded the cabin. Coach first acknowledged it as we were leaving Windsor and heading up the shore of Lake Erie before our expected swing north to London. Mikey said it was worse on his side but I wasn't certain.

I was worried the smell would make Mikey throw up because he hadn't eaten and seemed sick all day. Once Coach collected us outside the Italian restaurant the night before, we headed back to the motel and fell asleep in our clothes, waking sometime after nine and packing as best we could. Mikey and I hadn't said anything, not even while trying to orient ourselves on the walk back to the restaurant. All morning my mouth had been dry and fuzzy.

At breakfast the pretty waitress was gone, replaced by a short and tidy man who called me mister. Mikey didn't order food. They didn't have his oatmeal anyway so Coach wasn't too surprised. I ate eggs and asked for extra toast, which I folded into a napkin to bring with me in case he got hungry later in the morning. He didn't.

It wasn't until cleaning up to leave the motel that I asked Mikey how he felt. He looked sharp at me for a second, like it was an assault to even pose the question, then coughed and slipped away to the car.

I didn't know how I felt. We had stood in silence, the three of us, amid the slatted light in the closet while Reg and Dora did their things. I might've called it making love if Reg hadn't filled the quiet moments with insults, telling poor Dora how bad she was, how old or ugly. The mattress inched across the floor as they rocked back and forth together. First bit by bit away from us and then, after Reg switched positions with a wink towards the closet, advancing closer and closer until Mikey revealed our location.

Mikey had his forehead pressed hard into the farthest corner of the closet by the time he started begging me to leave. French was looking on, interested in what seemed like an academic way, like Reg had placed him in the room to evaluate his form or style. And I, as I tended to be, was stuck in between, feeling both ways. Sick and hypnotized and scared and excited.

What I wanted was to interview everyone who was there in the upstairs room. Give them all a truth serum and a pencil to write down their recollections. What did Reg think had happened? Was this a thrill he had given us? Did he feel he needed to trick us into coming? What did French think of us being there? Whatever had happened, it lived in the intentions of the men who took us to the room.

Or it lived beyond them. Inside the two of us. Mikey's shoulders shook the whole walk back. He didn't answer Coach when he asked us where we went. I had to say we took a walk. If the lie upset my stomach it was already too far twisted by then to rate. When Coach pulled him in for a warming-up hug, Mikey got both his hands up under his ribs and pushed away like a cat fighting being put in a crate.

And of course it lived in Dora Simmonette, who should not have been there by order of her marriage vows. What happened after we left? Did she strike Reg? French? We made so much noise escaping, surely she had seen us. It didn't seem like she knew we were there before we busted out. Once she realized, did she run out into the night as well, shaking and retching like Mikey?

If she ran, was it after us or away from Reg Law?

Did Eugene know? Did he spend the whole episode smiling into his beer bottles, aware of the show overhead? Aware of the practice of performing for an audience?

All morning I found myself stopped short and staring into space. Through the window of the diner. At the back of Coach's head. Directly into the motel room's white wall from no more than two feet away. I used the bathroom before we left without touching myself. I peed all over the seat.

I wanted to wrap Mikey up in blankets and carry him home. I wanted to be home, and never be an adult, and not know about the time value of money.

Mikey in the closet, groaning and covering his ears. When I reached out to quiet him, he swatted my hand. Mikey in the street after, his fists balled up tight, eyes slammed shut so hard the skin around them had blanched and wrinkles ran down from his hairline.

When I shut my own eyes to try and chase away the bad memories with good, there were black spots everywhere. I pictured the Clippers but not Reg. Canada but not the Italian restaurant. And saddest of all, no Clara. Never in any of the new city's novel spaces: the grandstand, the concession pit, their motel room. No Clara. I could picture the circle hat but not the head I wished to wear it. The II B but not the hands that made it snap.

Coach called Utah just before checkout to tell them his good news. The call was brief and one-sided and I wondered if he was expected to make it. Were these check-ins for them or him? He noticed a stain on his pants, some red sauce from the restaurant, and ran back to change. When he stripped to his underwear, I focused on the faded grey carpet. Mikey left the room to sit outside. I didn't know where he had slept last night, in Coach's bed with Coach or somewhere else alone. I was asleep ten breaths after putting head to pillow.

The gas smell was the first thing we talked about, several minutes into the trip. Coach, as if he felt he needed to fill the car with some sort of human noise, spoke his theories about what could be causing it. None of them troubling, he promised.

"What was your favourite part of the trip so far, Mikey?" he asked somewhere between farming towns.

I turned to Mikey and willed him to reply. He was staring at the back of the passenger seat. I poked him in the shoulder and he looked at me wild-eyed.

"Coach asked you your favourite part," I prompted.

Mikey blinked. "Well," he composed himself enough to say, "what I remember best was the second game. I like that the home team won."

"Me too," said Coach. "That Windsor club is a bit of a hard case—it's not clear if they'll be around next year—so it's good they get some wins. You'll see when we get to London, it's a very different scene. Money and fans. The commissioner of the whole league owns the team. The field there is gorgeous; it's maybe the oldest in the world."

"The whole world?" I asked, seeking ways to prolong the conversation that didn't require Mikey.

"Yep. A controversial thing to say in certain parts, but the Canadians will tell you Labatt's is the oldest ongoing ball field on God's earth. There were older ones before it, obviously, but they're all paved or plowed over by now. London's a baseball town; they've seen everything there. International League, Canadian League, Ontario League, even Negro Leagues."

I asked him something I didn't care about, which was what the difference was between the Canadian League and the Ontario League. My head was starting to hurt from the smell. I rolled down my window and leaned against the door, feeling the bumps and divots in the road with my cheek. I told myself that every stinking mile was a mile away from Reg Law.

I thought about Reg, not the image of Reg but the idea of him. Second-sightedness, the gift and curse of watching yourself live your life. And then the image of Reg snuck in with the idea and he appeared: smirking, naked, throwing a gesture of fake surprise at the closet as Dora leaned over his lap. Reg might have been that rarest of things, the second-sighted athlete, after all. Though his sight was only of himself. For himself. He didn't see Mikey crying in the closet. Or me worrying. He didn't see what would happen when Dora Simmonette found us out. "Watch Me" French had called him when we first met by the barns.

Coach had asked if I wanted to call over to the Zaps' motel before we left and get Clara Sheridan's mailing address. I said no thanks. I didn't know what I'd mail. Letters? Lists of my daily accomplishments? Report cards? Cheese? She hadn't acted like she liked me by the end; she acted like I was in the way of her work as a daughter. I wanted to picture her face but not feel that buzzing fullness I felt around her, that warmth and its demands.

The lake was endless, long like a river and stretched over the horizon like the sea. Coach said that it wasn't very deep, that you could walk out a half mile before it reached your chest. Because of the lake and its stubbornness, my side of the window didn't have the best view, and Mikey didn't make good use of his. We stopped in a place called Leamington—where they made ketchup for a living—to pee, and Coach bought a fresh bottle to bring home. This was the first souvenir I remembered him buying.

Lunch was at a highway diner not in any way unique from the diners we had been to in previous towns. Except they had patched closed an old side door with a road sign so that when you went in, a rectangle on the wall told the distance from some cut-off spot on the road to Toronto. When we pulled up, Coach and I realized that Mikey had fallen asleep. He sent me in for menus while we waited for him to wake. The menus were covered in such thick plastic it felt like holding a pair of plaques.

"What do you think your brother will want?" Coach asked. I said I didn't know; he wasn't hungry at breakfast.

"He upset about something?"

"Mikey?"

"Yeah. He didn't eat and hasn't said five words all day."

I thought about whether to tell Coach the whole story and have him figure it out. Who was to blame, whether we did anything wrong, what I could have done differently, and in doing so lift the queasy fog of the thing from my head like taking off a hat.

"He's just tired," I said instead. "Long night."

Coach thumbed through the menu. "It was indeed a long one. You kids did well staying up with the men. Did you talk to the players?"

"A couple. Reg Law mostly."

Coach shook his head. "That Law is something else. What did he try to tell you?"

The menu was full of pies. And not just dessert pies, also mushroom pies, kidney pies, all sorts of dinnertime pies. I was not interested. "This and that. He knows a lot about how money works."

"Does he now?" asked Coach like I was supposed to disagree with myself and say that actually, no, he didn't.

"He went to college and studied that stuff."

Coach made a face. "The thing about Law," he said, looking back to make eye contact, "is he's a decent kid but he's a full-on communist. You know what a communist is right?"

I blinked. "A Russian?"

"Not just Russians. There are American communists too. Law wants the players to own baseball; he wants regular nobodies to run the world. He doesn't believe in loyalty or family."

I nodded. I tried to imagine what that meant.

"Coach," I said, deciding this pause was as good as any to bring up what Mikey had hinted at yesterday, in the minutes before the upstairs closet. Moving in or moving out together or maybe marrying Mamma. "Do you want to have a family someday?"

Coach turned in his seat until he was looking straight out the front of the Hornet again. He put his hands at ten and two like he was about to start the engine. I waited.

"Did Mikey tell you something?" came his voice, slow and weighty, a shade deeper than normal.

"No."

"Are you sure?"

I swallowed and studied the menu photographs a little more. They sold roast beef sandwiches with that thin gravy dip. The beef and dip could also be piled into a pie.

Coach put his elbow on the car door and rubbed his eyes. "I don't want to tell your mamma right away that I told him. Can you keep that quiet?"

"Yessir."

"Better than your brother could?"

"Yessir."

"Well, come outside at least. Best to talk about it face to face."

I got out and stood on the gravel, ready for the pitch. There were two other cars in the diner's parking lot. The afternoon sun dug in my eyes. A warm ache, lower in my gut than the one from Reg and Dora, blossomed inside me.

Coach had loosened his tie and his hat was cocked lower over one brow than the other. His second pants of the day were bunched at the shoes and his shirt was only half tucked in. It was the kind of mild all-over dishevelment he could fix in five quick movements on his way to shake your hand. It was him at rest.

"Alright," he said. "So, it's true."

"What's true?"

"I didn't want to tell you, but your ma was never going to spill, and he's getting so old. Eventually you just got to be honest."

I didn't understand why he kept referring to Mikey and not to me. "What is it, Coach?" I asked him.

The door to the diner opened and a businessman came out holding a briefcase in one hand and a slice of pie on a paper plate in the other. He nodded at us. I nodded back but Coach didn't.

"Okay, Christopher. If your brother said that I was his father, it's because I told him as much."

I opened my mouth and shut it. The man with the pie was searching for his keys.

"What?"

"Again"—Coach wiped at his chin with his palm—"I believe it's your mother's job to say this to you but she just wasn't doing it and I felt it had become past time to—"

"What?" I took a step back, my butt against the side of the car. I felt a pain in my hand and looked down to see I had clenched it into a fist so tight it had begun to hurt. The ache in my gut rose towards my chest.

"I felt it was time to tell him because I think it will, it should, change how—"

"How? When?"

"How what, Chris?"

I didn't say anything. He scratched his chin until he understood the scope of my question.

"Right. Well, you know I moved to town right after getting discharged. Your dad and I were friends and I wanted to help him settle once he was injured. Right after he died, your mother and me started to date a little—"

"No, Mamma was pregnant when he died."

"I know that's what they told you, but no," he said, taking off his hat. "She got pregnant just after. From me."

I looked down the highway to the lake and then back to Coach. I brought a hand to my neck. The sweat there was cold and dewy. Reaching back for the car door handle, I opened it and flopped myself inside. From somewhere in the sparking machine of my brain, the door out of Reg's room came back like a lost answer.

Coach opened his own door and took his seat behind the wheel, quiet so as to not wake Mikey. Neither of us said anything. I listened to Mikey's easy breathing and the sounds of cars passing by us on the road.

"It doesn't make any sense," I whispered. "You moved to town in '46."

"August of '44. They let me home early because of my leg," he said. "Your Mamma didn't want you to think this was possible so she made up the bit about being pregnant when your dad died and moved the date of my arrival until after that. I gave the eulogy at his funeral. I did a bit from *The Red Badge of Courage*."

Another image from early in the trip bubbled up to interrupt me. Coach and Mikey caucusing on a picnic bench, bent into each other, whispering and drawing out a plan in the flaking paint of the table, with me somewhere around the corner of a spruce tree. Off to the side, separate.

"I don't believe you."

"I know, Chris. But I can quote you the book now if you'll hear it."

I thought back to the game yesterday, and it seemed like Coach had whispered magic words and it unlocked a certainty in Mikey and that was that. A certainty I could see at a distance but not touch. Why would Mamma keep a secret like that?

"How did you make Mikey believe you?"

"Your brother seemed to know it already. Or at least, he really wanted it to be true, and that made it easier. He went from never having a father to always having one right then and there. It was a lot, but I made him very happy."

I breathed in deep and felt my throat tighten. I forced myself to not imagine what that would feel like.

"Let's not speak about it too much right now," Coach continued. "We want to ease him into it. He seems a little shell-shocked."

Shell-shocked. Whenever Coach used expressions from the Marines I felt like he was gifting us reminders of our father. When he spoke in military time, fourteen hundred hours instead of two o'clock, it felt like he was telling us without making a big fuss about it that he remembered him, and that because of that he recognized our loneliness. Honoured our loneliness. But it felt different this time. This time, for the first time, he was doing it just for me.

Mikey lifted his head and rubbed his eyes as I was biting my thumbnail and Coach was writing down in his notepad the phone number for the London motel. I handed him the menu as we got out of the car and walked towards the diner. Coach gripped my shoulder and reminded me not to tell Mamma.

We took a seat beside the road sign. Coach said he wished he had a camera to show it to folks when we got home. This idea set me briefly thinking about Clara, and that daydream resolved in the ghostly sensation of smelling her shampoo, which was hard and medicinal and not especially pleasant without her company. The steam from the kitchen billowed out the open window by the counter at the edge of the dining room. There was one other person there: an ancient man in a military uniform bent over a pile of eggs.

I watched Coach care for Mikey. He pulled out his chair and helped him unfold his paper napkin. When the woman came to give us menus, he held up the ones from the car and told her we brought our own, with an ironic little smile that she clearly saw as charming.

"Mikey, Chris said you had a long night last night," Coach said, once the coffee had arrived and he was stirring in his milk.

Mikey looked at me. I didn't move.

"I'm just not used to staying up late," he said after the silence got the better of him. Coach didn't press him on that.

I ordered the roast beef sandwich and Coach got their club. Mikey asked for oatmeal, which they didn't have, and then agreed to a grilled frankfurter, which I thought was ambitious and of which he only ever ate the bun. The pies went untested.

"The lake is a puddle," Coach told us while we waited. "Did you boys know that?"

Mikey didn't recognize the question so I jumped in and asked Coach what he meant.

"It's all glacial. All of Canada is like that. Thousands of years ago, this area of the Earth, down about as south as home, was covered by a sheet of ice maybe a mile high. Imagine that."

Mikey looked up, imagining himself flattened under a mile of ice.

"And eventually the ice pulled back, melting as it went. All the lakes here, countless lakes, are puddles of melted ice. The biggest ones are the Great Lakes, of which there are only four, I might add. Huron and Michigan are one lake with two names, one big lake the shape of lungs. But anyway, there are more lakes in the country north of us than anywhere else on the Earth."

"Was the ice very heavy?" I asked. I knew the ice was very heavy.

"Yes, of course, the ice was heavy. That's why the area is dotted with boulders everywhere. The ice picked up rocks, dragged them for miles, and dropped them behind like bread crumbs."

Our food was cold but the beef dip was salty and rich. Coach and I split Mikey's frankfurter. When Coach went to the washroom I didn't know which important secret to discuss with Mikey first.

"He told me," I said.

My brother didn't look up.

"He told me he's your daddy."

"He's not my daddy," Mikey mumbled.

"What?" I nearly shouted this, sausage spraying loose between my lips. "He already told me he was. He told me that he told you."

"Saying stuff doesn't make it true."

I sat back in my chair and wiped my mouth. Mikey had his hands in his lap, gripped around his unused fork. His voice was small and soft. "Why'd you think he'd wait this long to tell me if it was true, Chris? Why didn't Mamma tell me first? Makes no sense."

I was surprised because it was my job, not his, to disbelieve things. It was my nature, not his, to be cautious. I hadn't been cautious last night and I wasn't again now. Mikey's little voice reminded me.

"You're just in shock because of last night, Mike. You'll know it better when you talk to Mamma."

It was only then that he looked up, and I wished he hadn't. He wasn't crying, or letting slip any kind of confusion, or anger, in either his face or his voice. He looked right through me, to the road sign behind my head and on into the nation of puddles to our north.

"I don't wanna talk about last night, Chris," he said, still calm but louder now, cutting off the ends of all his words. "If you make me talk about it, I'll scream. I'll scream and run off into traffic, do you hear me?"

"Mikey, do you want to go home—"

"I want to go home," he acknowledged. "But I don't want to leave the trip. Can you understand? Let's do our best for Coach and get back."

"Okay—"

"And not tell Mamma."

"Okay."

"Either thing, Chris." He reached out and jabbed my hand with his fork. "We're not telling anyone either thing, you hear?"

I pawed around for the best way to apologize for not protecting him and couldn't think of it. Coach rescued me by reappearing. He walked slowly across the room, taking in every piece of art on the wall, and when he found the waitress he offered to pay her early. She rummaged about for change and when he placed his hand on her arm, I could see him tell her to keep it. She blushed and said thanks. He gestured for us to follow and when he turned towards the door, the backlit sun made him a shadow, slowly shrinking on its way towards the car.

The gas smell had gotten worse. We were all full, or in Mikey's case full enough, and had to roll the windows down to stave off the nausea that came from huffing gas fumes after a feed of diner meat. The stink was so bad it brought out Mikey's first words to Coach, beyond answers to direct questions, since Windsor.

"Are we going to make it to London?" he asked.

"We made it from Minnesota, didn't we?" said Coach. "We'll make London no problem."

"Is there someone who could look at it there?"

Coach sniffed. "This isn't your bog standard Chevy or Ford, you know. This is a Hudson Hornet—they don't make them anymore, and when they did it was to race them around a track, not limp into some backwoods garage. We'll see if there are any proper greasers in Canada who can tackle this thing." He patted the dash like it was the head of a show dog.

I pondered life without the Hornet for a minute. The car was the thing, outside of baseball and the sporting goods industry, that Coach had spent the most time lecturing us on. He had bought it from a customer at the store who used it for one season doing runs back and forth from Chicago, whose newsprint business then went belly up and Coach got it for two hundred dollars cash. The engine was fire-truck red under the hood. The manufacturer had shipped it with safety features to keep the car out of peak racing condition and more suitable for the civilian road, but Coach knew a guy in Minneapolis who'd removed them. I was in the car once when it hit 120.

A car magazine I once came across listed the retail price for the Hornet at around $1,700, so the idea of Coach locking onto a situation where he could have his for a sliver of that had always hung high in the trophy room I had fashioned for him in my mind, and it served as counter-argument if I found myself questioning his ability in business when engaged with vendors at the store or, more recently, ballplayers on the road.

But now was not the car's prime. Either from its back-alley operation in the city or from overuse or just because it was a lemon, the five-year-old Hornet couldn't get within sight of one hundred miles per hour and suffered on hills and turns.

I kept looking over at Mikey, but I never got what I wanted from him. He didn't snap out of it, make some whimsical observation, some little ceremony, and he never came clean and told Coach what had happened last night. And he never told Coach he didn't believe he was his father.

And he never told me that he *did* believe it. He never blamed me for taking him to Reg. He never jumped across the car and scratched my eyes out, pushing himself on top of me and holding me down with the proof of his superior strength.

Matters became more serious for the car just before we turned north to London. We were halfway along Lake Erie's north shore. Coach was talking about baseball cards he had growing up, before anyone thought to collect or trade such things. When they used to eat peanuts off them or use them to roll cigarettes. He said he used to buy the boxes of hard candy put out by Fleer Corp that had team portraits and sometimes paintings of individual players packed inside. The art was cheap but you could make out who was who. Coach preferred Lou Gehrig to Babe Ruth.

The Hornet didn't come to a sudden stop, or catch fire, but just sort of slowly lost power, and once our thrust wore off there was nothing to do but steer her onto the shoulder and hit the brakes. Coach sighed. He wasn't angry; he was resigned.

While Coach got out to dig around under the hood, Mikey bit his fingernails and spat them out the window onto the patch of short shrubs by the roadside. The fifth car that passed us stopped, and a couple got out. The man in coveralls and the woman dressed smartly in a dotted dress.

They got talking to Coach and I heard him tell them about the Hudson Motor Car Company and how hard it was to find parts. At some point they must have offered to drive us to the nearest town to call a tow, because when Coach opened the back seat that's what we were doing. We gathered everything we could: the players' fivers, the example sets, some clothes, and stuffed the rest under the seats and in the trunk, then locked the Hornet up tight and hopped in the back of the neighbourly couple's coupe.

Presented with these strangers, Mikey was suddenly friendly and conversational. He asked them their names and what they did for work. Patrick and Carol. He fixed farm equipment and she kept house. He asked what kind of car this was, and they said it was a Dodge. He asked if it was hard to find parts for Dodges, and Coach gave him a sidelong glare.

The town they drove us to was basically an intersection. We found a payphone and dialed through until the operator connected us to a garage in London that did import cars. Coach informed the man there that the Hornet was not an import, and the mechanic said yes, he understood that, but he was familiar with them anyway and had worked on them before. Coach seemed disbelieving but accepted his offer to help. London was still an hour away, and whatever the man quoted Coach for the tow was enough to make him think, briefly at least, about just leaving the car to rot on the side of the road, but he agreed after some heated haggling.

The drive to town only took five minutes so we didn't expect a long walk back, but highway driving can be untrustworthy that way and we ended up just barely beating the tow driver to the Hornet. The whole way Coach was grim, tense with defeat, mumbling about how he wasn't going to make any money on this trip and wondering whether people were likely to buy more hockey sticks that fall to make it up. Mikey paced us both, looking back every quarter mile to wait for us to catch him.

The tow driver hooked in the Hornet and propped it up on its back wheels. He was a man with a healthy gut and a long droopy moustache that combined to give him the impression of a walrus. He exchanged some papers with Coach and at some point Coach wrote a cheque. He was putting away his tools when I realized the cab of the truck was full of equipment; there was no passenger room. The walrus had no plans to drive us to London.

I told Coach and he conferred with the driver. Walrus said he wasn't liable for passengers and that if we had wanted a taxi cab we should have called for one in town. Coach's face flashed red and he told the man that a reasonable service would offer a ride. They had a brief standoff where Coach seemed ready to hit the driver and the driver seemed ready to unhitch and head home.

While they were arguing, I caught sight of a larger vehicle coming towards us in the eastbound lane; it was a small bus or a large van. As it got closer, I could make out an oblong grate and then a sign above the windshield that read "Essex Foods." It passed by us and as I turned to follow, it flashed its lights and slowed down, then backed up and, just before the driver told Coach where to stick his American Legion card, it stopped beside us. After a dramatic beat, the passenger-side door swung open, and the beaming bright head of Reg Law appeared, whistling to get our attention.

The first person to take a step towards the Clippers' bus was Coach. I was caught between relief and dread while Mikey, for his part, was unreadable. The tow truck driver didn't seem to care; he kept working on detaching the Hornet until Coach waved him off and wandered over to Reg.

"Law?" he called out. "What are you doing here?" It was a Ford Transit Bus, not like the big city buses we had seen in Detroit but bigger than a van would be. It could fit a whole underfed baseball team in a pinch.

Reg smiled wide. "Off to play ball in Buffalo. Why, where's your gang going?"

"Nowhere," Coach said, scanning through the rows of tired faces in the windows. "Car broke down on the way to London. We're looking to negotiate a cab ride."

"Well." Reg ducked his head back into the bus and spoke with someone. Coach clasped and unclasped his hands in front of him while we waited. "We can't get you to London, but we can bring you to Buffalo or we could drop you off in Hamilton."

Coach looked at me. Once upon a time, I was the planner for our operation. We were supposed to see Erie and London play and get both of those teams. If we followed the Clippers to Buffalo instead, we'd get the Bisons there but no use speaking to the Clippers twice. Same problem in Hamilton, where the Zaps were headed now; we'd only get one team, the Red Wings, for that trip instead of both.

I looked back. Mikey had crossed behind the tow truck driver and was standing on the other side of the Hornet, with two vehicles and three bodies between him and Reg.

"I think sticking with London makes the most sense, Coach," I said.

"But we don't exactly have a ride there, do we?" He asked this of me but directed it to the tow driver, who just grunted under his moustache.

"We can call a cab."

"Do you have cash on hand for that?" Coach asked with a lilt of mockery in his voice. "Does the budget cover it?"

Reg looked into the bus again and then back at us. He shuffled his feet as if to indicate that the offer was time-limited and they needed to get going.

"Where would we stay in Buffalo?" I asked. "Our motel is reserved in London."

"Not Buffalo, no," Coach said, stroking his chin, surely already decided on the matter. "I've no interest in seeing Buffalo. But

Hamilton's on the way. We do Hamilton, see the Red Wings, then we can get a rental to London. If we're lucky, we'll even catch the Bisons in town before they leave for home. Otherwise we'll need to get them on Tuesday like you planned."

I looked at Mikey. He had crouched down like a cat, only his eyes visible from over the hood of the Hornet.

"That way we'll miss London and Erie," I stammered, knowing it wasn't true.

"No, Chris. We can go see Hamilton tomorrow, grab a rental and go to London for the car. Are they not playing there Monday?"

I said yes twice because the first time was too quiet to be heard amid the traffic sounds.

"Good. Then London and Erie on Monday, and worst case we go back to Hamilton again for the Buffalo team. If we get lucky, maybe even the Bisons tomorrow morning."

I shook my head no, though I didn't have anywhere to hang my disagreement. The tow truck driver arched his eyebrows like he was suddenly interested in who we might be with all these plans. I walked back to talk to Mikey.

"I'm going to ride with the tow truck man, and see you two in London," he said.

"You're not," I told him. I knelt down and grabbed his head hard with both hands and looked right into his eyes until he pulled away. "We're all going to Hamilton, Mikey," I told him. "And I'm going to keep you safe." He rubbed his ears.

It took us two trips to grab all our bags. Coach collected the tow driver's details and said he'd call the garage tonight. The Transit Bus was dusty and smelled of sweat. The whole team wasn't there. I counted eleven Clippers, plus bags of equipment and linen. French Wind at the wheel. The sight of French and the smell of dust and sweat brought me back to the room above the Italian restaurant, its broad, immobile ceiling fan and its chipped white paint. I shook my head.

The seat next to Reg was empty, but I walked on to the next row and pushed Mikey in next to the tall Cuban, who seemed stoically annoyed by our arrival, and perched half an ass on the bench seat. Coach shook Reg's hand and took the seat beside him.

"How long until Hamilton?" Mikey whispered.

"I don't know," I said. "Maybe two hours?"

"I want to go home, Chris."

"I know," I said. "I know."

Hamilton was faster than I thought. We spent the trip making stilted conversation with my twenty words of Spanish and the Cuban player's, whose name was Garcia, fifty or so of English. He had been playing baseball "forever." Canada was "nice." The weather was "cold at first" but "okay now." He asked how old we were and I told him with my hands. Mikey didn't ask or answer any questions but smiled when Garcia smiled.

I could tell Reg and Coach weren't getting along. Reg had a habit of leaning into him whenever he pointed something out on the road, and punching his shoulder when telling a joke, that I knew even from behind Coach didn't appreciate. One time, when the bus was quiet and Reg was at his loudest, I heard him ask about a reporter, who apparently had been inquiring into Reg's Popsicle stunt on Wednesday. Coach shrugged, and I saw Reg flick his eyes back towards us, locking with mine for a quick second before I dropped my gaze to the floor.

The bus moved slow on the open road. But the distance was so slight, this part of Ontario so much more tightly packed, that we made it there just after dinner. There was some conversation among the team about whether they'd drive us into the city or just drop us off at the exit. They had a game in Buffalo the next day and still needed to cross the border. A car with the rest of the team and some supplies would be nearly in America already.

The solution came from French Wind, who indicated that if they stayed on the road they could bill dinner directly to the club instead of taking it out of per diems. This made Hamilton a more appealing stopover, and had I known the first thing about the city I might have been asked to recommend a restaurant.

Coach went up to chat with French at the wheel. City lights had started to appear on either side of the bus, animating the dusk with little yellow eyes. A steady buildup of industry marked our entry into Hamilton. Ships were perched in drydocks by the lake, which my knowledge of the road atlas told me was now Lake Ontario, not Erie. We had jumped lakes, skipping Niagara Falls, since we'd left the Hornet behind. Coach was directing the Transit Bus, looking up from his notebook and pointing French down side streets. He was glad to get the better of the tow truck driver, I could tell. Even if we ended up dropping one fortune for a rental car, then another for a last-ditch hotel, he'd be happy just to win have won the argument.

After a U-turn to fix a missed exit, French wheezed out the news that the stowaways were getting off, and then they'd all head out for food.

"Hey Miller, are you getting dropped off somewhere a man could piss?" called Reg Law. Four other Clippers said something to the same effect before Coach Dunn, asleep until this time in the backmost row between equipment bags, shouted out that they could wait until the bus got where it was going.

"Aw, Coach, I'm not waiting for French to find five-star digs. I need to let it loose now," yelled Reg.

The Clippers who had joined Reg's call before it met their coach's disapproval were quieter now, leaving Reg to do his complaining alone. Up by the driver, Coach said it'd be fine, as long as the team minded their manners while in the company of civilians.

"Miller," Law chirped, "I'm a college man. I can chat up anybody." A few of the other Clippers whispered to each other and I got the sense they were exchanging jokes.

Coach didn't say anything, but when French finally parked outside a big Victorian house on the edge of the mountain that made up the city's east end, he nodded to Mikey and me and then to Reg. Two other Clippers stood up as well, the other half of the peeing party having apparently changed their minds in the face of Coach Dunn's headwind.

I got our bags and left, mumbling my thanks as I scooted past the blank-faced ballplayers in the dying light of the bus.

"Coach," I asked, "where are we?"

"Place is run by friends of the Forbushes," he said. "Friends of friends, at least. They gave me the address last year and said we could come to them for help."

"Did you call ahead?"

He sucked his teeth. "When would I have done that, Chris?"

I kept my eye on Mikey, who was staying back behind Reg and the Clippers. Reg for his part was stretching and joking with his teammates, dancing from the ball of one foot to the other.

"You get laid last night, Reg?" one of them asked.

"I'm too shy to tell, Berger," Reg said, crouching to throw a quick combination of jabs, ending in a lunging right hook.

The one called Berger laughed. "Too shy, Watch Me says. Not my experience."

Watch Me. I thought about Reg's occasional nickname again in light of last night and the sense I got from French Wind that it had happened before. That it might have even happened before in the company of teammates like Berger. What would someone like Berger think had happened?

Coach had walked down the laneway, smoothing out his pants where the bus had left them wrinkled. He checked his watch. I checked mine: seven fifteen p.m. Somewhere in this city, the game between the first-place Bisons and last-place Red Wings was in its early innings.

The house was well-maintained and had a brass knocker. Coach used it and then rapped a few more times with his knuckles. We waited long enough to grow nervous. The three Clippers had formed a polite line behind Coach, hands at their sides. Mikey was still hiding by the bus. I went back, grabbed his hand, and stood with him to the side.

Eventually the door opened. There was a woman in a long sleeping dress with a top that had puffy sleeves right to the wrists. She was older, but to a degree that was hard to place. She might have been seventy, she might have been fifty. Her hair was light grey but the lines on her face were subtle.

"May I help you gentlemen?" she asked. Perhaps slightly concerned at having opened her door to this many unknown men.

Coach spoke for us. "Ma'am, would it be possible that you are Darlene Young and that this is the Latter-day Saints' mission home?"

She looked at him for a moment, still holding the door with both hands. "Yes?"

"Wonderful." Coach cleared his throat. "My name is Lawrence Miller. I'm a business associate of Jamieson and Anna Forbush. My associates and I are baseball card agents for Four Corners. I was told by Anna that, should I ever find myself hard up for a place to stay in Hamilton, I could call on you to see if there was space in the mission house. I'm afraid we're hard up."

Darlene Young examined Coach for a little longer and then turned her head to take in the rest of the adults. The nervous clench in her forehead had not yet released. "You're all of you baseball card agents?"

"No ma'am," Reg Law spoke up, gesturing at the other Clippers. "Myself and these gentlemen are professional baseballers. Mr. Miller and the two young men are agents."

She craned her neck around the wall of athletes until she saw, for the first time, Mikey and me. "You two children are baseball card agents?"

"Yes ma'am," I said, my voice stammering a bit until Mikey dug out a sample card and contract from the stash of materials we had lugged off the bus. "Here," I added, taking them from him.

I handed the card and papers to Coach who handed them to Darlene. She gave the pile a studious thumbing over before gesturing towards the Transit Bus on the curb. "And who all is in there?"

"Other baseball players, ma'am" Coach told her. "We got a ride with them from Windsor. These three were only hoping to use the washroom, but the boys and I require lodging."

"Well"—she handed the papers back—"lucky for you we've got a free apartment. The toilet's in the downstairs hall."

She opened wide the door and watched the ballplayers as they took off their shoes. "I'm not a baseball fan," she said. "Are you three anyone famous?"

"No ma'am," Reg answered.

"What team do you boys play for?"

They told her.

"Are you any good?"

"No ma'am," Reg answered again, smiling as he strutted down the hall.

Darlene Young went upstairs to make up beds and left us in what looked like a communal dining room. Piles of books, too small to be Bibles, sat on a far table. A bearded man, not Jesus, hung on the wall. I counted fourteen chairs.

"Does this woman think we're all Mormons?" I asked Coach.

He said no, but she likely thought that he was at least. Mikey went and looked through the books. I pulled the first of our luggage through the foyer and stacked it on one of the chairs.

"Are we going to lie and tell her you are?" I asked.

He must not have liked the way I framed the question because he looked away and studied the woodwork of the table for a moment before answering. "If someone asks us directly, then we'll answer them. But the three of us are men who talk for our livings, so let's try to avoid getting stuck in that corner. Okay?"

Reg Law was first out of the bathroom, first to be stuck waiting around for the others in the doorway of the mission house. This was manageable until Coach decided to bring in the rest of our bags, which left him alone with Mikey and me for the first time since the room.

He winked. "You boys were sure lucky I convinced French to turn back for you, huh?"

We didn't say anything. Mikey was behind me, pushing his forehead into the centre of my back. "Thanks Reg," I mumbled, before the silence ate us all.

If he was disappointed by this modest gratitude, he didn't show it. "That was some party last night. And you two got to see Miss Dora in her glory, that must've been a thrill, was it not?"

He held his grin with confidence. I could feel Mikey's hot head between my shoulder blades. Reg was tall enough to know Mikey was hiding behind me, and I knew that he knew. But he held the smile through the whole exchange, until the second Clipper came back from the toilet and pulled him along to the bus, with Coach right behind him asking them to give the team his best. I looked hard at the man on the wall with the beard.

Darlene Young came by holding a tray with four glasses of milk and put them on the table. She asked if we had eaten and Coach said no need to worry about us. She repeated the question and Coach agreed to some bread and jam.

"Are the brothers due back soon?" he asked her. She looked at the clock and said maybe in an hour. They had been doing door-to-door service on the other side of town and the bicycle ride home would see them out a little longer.

"Are you travelling all the way from Salt Lake?" she asked.

"No ma'am, my base of operations is in Minnesota, just outside the Twin Cities. But I've known Jamieson since the war."

"I see." She sipped her milk and looked down into it the way cowboys in westerns looked into whiskey glasses. "Did you serve together?"

"I met the corporal in Australia on leave. We were in the same gospel study."

She took a slice of bread and spread an olive-coloured jam on it that the jar said was rhubarb. She caught me looking, winked, and pushed the cutting board towards Mikey and me.

"Jamieson's a good man and Anna a loving woman. They are credits to the church and anyone arriving on their name is a blessing in this house."

"Thank you, ma'am. We will treat you and your property with respect."

She nodded at Coach and winked at us again.

"Are these your sons?"

I didn't look at him, but Mikey did a little. "These are my apprentices," he told her. "But despite their age they are keen minds and plenty capable at work like ours."

"Well"—she moved the jam closer to Mikey because he hadn't had any yet—"I don't pretend to understand the Forbushes' business. I'm not a sports person by nature. But I like the company of children."

"Of course, ma'am," said Coach. "Do you have children of your own?"

She put her milk down on the table. Next to, but not on top of, a coaster. "One surviving. Two lost in the war."

"I'm sorry to hear," Coach told her. "Korea?"

"No sir. Your war."

"I'm sorry."

She took a deep breath and looked over at the bearded man in the frame on the wall. A small smile rose on her lips. "It's beginning to feel like a memory. In any case, they're in a better place."

We went back to eating our bread and drinking our milk, and nobody said anything until it was all gone. As we began looking around for our bags and a path upstairs, Darlene Young spoke again like she had never stopped.

"Joseph was our eldest. He was an Army man from the jump and shipped off from Halifax in '39, that was years before you Americans got your guns out, and we lost him at Dieppe. Then his younger brother Terrance sometime after Normandy near the end of things. Long wars, the both of them. I imagine they got used to it. I don't know details on what sort of mistake got them shot, but there they were."

"Wasn't usually a matter of a mistake, ma'am," Coach offered. "There was no sense to who came home and who didn't."

She didn't look at him, or us, or anything in particular. Little bubbles were popping on the surface of her milk. "Did you fight at all in France, Mr. Miller?"

"No ma'am. Strictly Pacific."

"Well, no bother." As if she had made a decision to stop mourning at least for that moment, she stood up and gathered the knives and the glasses. "I've more young men in my house now than I know what to do with. We've three pairs of companions on mission with us just this month. Should have five by the fall. There's work."

She left to put the dishes away and Coach sat pensive in his chair. When she came back, she showed us upstairs.

The room was basic and clean. Two small beds and an unfolded cot in a corner. A wash basin. A small bookshelf full of books with white covers.

"There's a shower and toilet of your own through there. You can expect a small racket when the brothers get home, but usually they're quieted by ten."

We thanked her and she left. Coach let the silence settle for a moment, then raised his arms at us. "Well," he said, "we went looking for some kindness and we found it, boys. Say your prayers in triplicate tonight."

Coach tied up the phone line calling London where they told him no new parts were required but that the Hornet needed engine work and it would take two days. He argued out the price and hung up, swearing under his breath quietly enough that a passing Mormon wouldn't hear it. Mikey read magazines and thin paperbacks with Jesus on the cover and I dipped into the same for a bit before moving on to the backs of Four Corners baseball cards as Coach sorted a rental car from a local dealer.

I inquired about calling home collect. Coach sighed and said sure but to be quick about it and to remember what he said about keeping our secrets.

"Yes Coach," I said and then added, "I'm not to tell her that you are Mikey's father."

This boldness got both of their attentions. Mikey shot his head up, as if an alarm had sounded in the house, before recovering back to his book. Coach just stared at me and eventually said yes, all pointed like I had talked back or something, but to be honest I just felt like someone needed to say the thing out loud. That whole day had been secrets and half truths, and I wanted to speak clearly. I wanted to say what we weren't all saying, at least the parts that didn't feel like my fault.

Coach showed me how to call collect and the operator connected us. Mamma agreed to the charges but warned me to speak quickly. Coach and Mikey were in the room so I kept things simple. I said we were safe but not what city we were in, that the trip was good but not that we lost the car. More obviously, I kept talk of the Italian restaurant to myself and didn't mention the ceiling fan in the upstairs room, left unspinning so long it had grown a skin of dust, and I didn't tell her about French's sour breath or the smell on his clothes from his cigarette.

She asked what our plans were for tomorrow. I said we might get up early to catch a team before they left town.

Her day was lovely. She had met an old coworker for dinner off-campus, a woman who quit last year to have a baby. It was one of her first times out alone since the birth. There was a story in the new *Reader's Digest* she was saving for me. She was doing groceries tomorrow and would get some cereal for our return.

Then she asked if Coach was there. I looked up and handed him the phone, which he accepted after briefly holding up his hands to say no.

He said hello, then listened for a while, then made a joke about having to remortgage his house to pay our food bill. Then he laughed and I could hear her laughing. He put his feet up and listened to her talk about her day.

Hamilton,
Saturday, July 12th, 1952

	W	L
Buffalo Bisons	40	24
London Maple Leafs	36	27
Akron Zaps	35	27
Erie Sailors	29	35
Windsor Clippers	28	35
Hamilton Red Wings	22	42

Last Night's Games
Wings 3, Bisons 6; Leafs 11, Sailors 4

"I THINK THEY WON?"

"No, no, as I understand it they lost. At least that's the best I could gauge from conversations near the stadium."

"The paper should be in soon. We could check what the baseball section says."

"Elder, the paper doesn't have a baseball section."

"I believe it does?"

"It doesn't."

Coach closed his eyes and rubbed his forehead with the back of his hand. Darlene Young had brought him hot water with lemon, which wasn't coffee, and he had just about asked for some before remembering that his fellow Mormons, at least practising ones on missions, didn't drink or serve the stuff.

The dining room table had six young men in pressed white shirts and black jackets, plus myself, Mikey, Coach, and Darlene. It was six forty-five in the morning. At six forty, I had asked, more as an attempt to make conversation among strangers than anything, whether the Hamilton Red Wings had upset the Buffalo Bisons last night.

Four of the Elders were from Utah. One from Nevada and the last from Florida. They were all in college, all nineteen or twenty years old. They had been in Canada for between two and four months, and would each be moving on from Hamilton soon to the next stop on their mission tours.

They had settled their plans for the day after trudging in last night at the end of work. It had rained in the morning and business was slow and dispiriting. They had spent most of the day around the docks, approaching factory hands and longshoremen on cigarette and lunch breaks to speak to them about the gospel and Joseph Smith. It was hard going. Today, for a change of pace, they had decided to split up, with two pairs working a suburb called Riverdale and the third heading out to spend the day at the library picking up families coming in for a weekend visit. Then they would meet for dinner and prayer before the Sabbath came to offer rest.

They didn't know who we were but were friendly and polite by training and probably also by nature. Coach struggled to make chipper conversation after his night sharing the single bed with Mikey, the cot left unruffled, so I was made ambassador. When they asked us where we were from, I said our operation was based in Salt Lake. When they asked what we were doing, I said we worked for a company run by church leaders there. When they asked what the business was I said we invested in baseball players who might one day be on trading cards.

The eldest Elder, whose name was Charles, was the only baseball fan of the group. He played on a church team back home and followed the Bees, the Salt Lake franchise in the Pioneer League.

"There used to be a Pacific Coast League team in Salt Lake," Coach came awake enough to interject. "The PCL is the finest league in America."

Charles was charmed by this compliment. He had blonde hair and red cheeks and his face was full, his head large, in a way that made him seem like a very big toddler. The other members of the mission were hopeless about sports, and he hadn't had the chance to proselytize on his second favourite topic for months.

"My father was a fan of the PCL Bees, before they moved to California. The new Bees won the Pioneer title the year before I left for college. We saw them clinch."

Mikey pulled out the sample box and showed Charles the cards, spreading a sample of the samples on the table, pushing aside the toast and butter Darlene Young had set out. The other five missionaries got up to give us space.

Charles was impressed by the design of the cards, though we didn't have his favourite player, Stan Musial, and only had four from his favourite team, the Cardinals.

The missionaries were able to give directions to the car rental but as they were on bikes, they couldn't take us there. It wasn't open until nine a.m. anyway, so we headed back to our room to pack and call a motel. We thanked Mrs. Young for her hospitality but said we couldn't impose on her another night. She gave the impression that she could go on serving us bread and jam for all eternity and it wouldn't set her back any.

Mikey had read the first thirty pages of a child's anthology of Bible stories and Mrs. Young offered to let him keep it as a souvenir. Coach was in the process of denying the gift, explaining that we were packing light and we boys had diversions enough already, when he launched forward and embraced her, holding the hug long enough that she put down her plate of jelly cookies to hold his head.

After Coach called a cab to take us to the rental outlet, he gave our host one last thank you. She invited us to the meetinghouse for sacrament the next day and Coach promised he would take the offer, letting her run back to the study to find some notepaper and draw a crude map. Once the cab came and we piled our belongings into it and then the three of us into its back seat, it was over. I waited for the weight of playing a character to fall from Coach's face. I waited for it to fall from mine. However, that never really happened. He turned to me and beamed, commenting on how kind Mrs. Young was to take us in. Mikey read his stories until I pushed the book away for fear he would get car sick. We picked up the rental, a '49 Buick, and Coach filled out so much paperwork he joked he might be buying it. We loaded all our things and headed out to the Hamilton stadium on a hunch.

The stadium complex was in the middle of the city, directly beneath the block letter "I" in "HAMILTON" watermarked across my mail-order map. Its centrepiece was a football field with seating for maybe ten thousand, but unlike in Windsor the baseball team didn't quite need to live inside the football team's building. There was a squat ballpark abutting the larger stadium's southern end, squished so tight against the back of the end zone grandstand that the left and right field markers were almost as deep as straightaway centre. Still, it was a proper ballpark with permanent seating and it looked like it would last the season, unlike Windsor's. Coach went to the trouble of speaking to two team employees and bribing a third with an American dollar to figure out where the Bisons had slept last night. He hit paydirt with the young kid cleaning the scoreboard. The kid pocketed the dollar and nodded across the street to where a Ford Transit Bus, a slightly shinier, better-maintained version of the one the Clippers travelled on, was parked in a lot outside an inn that may have at one point been a row of townhouses. The Bisons slept close to their work.

Coach slicked his hair back and had us jaywalk behind him carrying the props, shouting all the way to remember our cues and to be ready with the paperwork. When we got to the bus there was a woman driver there with her head under the hood. She came out wiping her hands on a towel. She had wild blonde curls and was wearing a white shirt with grey pinstripes that looked tailored like a man's. Coach presented himself to her.

"Ma'am, sorry to bother you. Can I ask who's travelling with the team today?"

"Travelling?" she asked, tossing the towel into a tool box. "We're all travelling."

"I'm sorry. I meant is the general manager riding with you?"

"Yeah but he's not here."

"Do you know where he might be?"

"He's taking a shit."

Coach nodded. "I see. And is the field manager around?"

As he said the word *around*, a whistle sounded and a low masculine voice began to shout instructions somewhere to our left. We turned to see a proper military parade, young men marching two abreast out the front doors of the inn, each holding a simple matching day bag and each dressed, not exactly the same, but all in black shoes with black pants and white shirts. The man with the whistle blew it again and then called for inspection. It was all we could do not to fix the wrinkles in our own clothes and join the line.

Coach whispered to the curly-haired driver, "This him then?" She rolled her eyes, said yes, and climbed into the vehicle.

We watched the Buffalo manager walk through his squad, commenting here and there on postures and cleanliness. When done, he stood back and told them that they should have really swept the Red Wings, and that they'd need to take Erie more seriously to avoid embarrassment. Then he sweetened to say he was proud of how they played last night at least, solving the riddle as to who won the game, and to get some rest on the trip home.

When the team broke for the bus, Coach stepped ahead with his hand out.

"Coach, may I have a moment?" he asked the military man.

The Bisons manager, who had shrunk a little into his age once the spectacle of the march and his speechifying finished, looked up clear-eyed and raised his brows into neat points as Coach began the pitch.

"My name is Miller, my associates and I are agents of the Four Corners Baseball Card Company out of Salt Lake City, Utah. I wonder if you've heard of us?"

The old coach admitted he hadn't, but that was no surprise as he didn't keep up on baseball cards and there seemed to be a new outfit hawking them every time he looked. His name was Gibbs.

"Understood, Coach Gibbs. Well, have you heard of Topps or Bowman?"

"No, Mr. Miller," said Gibbs, gathering his own bags for the bus. "As I said, I'm not familiar with your industry. Now get to the meat of it—what are you selling me?"

Coach picked up one of the Bisons' equipment bags and helped the kid responsible lift it onto the back. "I'm actually not a seller, Mr. Gibbs. I'm a buyer."

He went on to tell Gibbs about the licensing agreements. I handed him an example, and the older man dug a pair of reading glasses out of his front pocket and asked the driver, whom he called Edith, to hold off on the engine while he read. He asked Coach how long he'd need with the team and Coach said no more than five minutes.

Old Coach Gibbs boarded the Transit Bus and his team snapped to attention.

"Men," he began, "I've got good news. There are three gentlemen here from a new novelty card concern in Utah. They've a licensing offer. We all know I'm no law man, but I've read their paperwork. They wish to pay you to sign a non-exclusive agreement so they may use your faces and names in baseball cards should you be fortunate enough to ever feature on one. Now, you know I don't extend my authority to business matters, but if I can offer my advice, it's to consider the offer and accept it if you trust Mr. Miller, the agent from the card company. I'll leave him to make his case and go see if I can help our Mr. Walschotts find his way out of the bathroom."

With that, Gibbs stepped down and ceded Coach his audience. There was no room on the bus between him and Edith, so we hovered next to the door waiting to be called. The moment their coach left, the Bisons relaxed, waiting for the pitch like a pack of alley cats, stretched out or leaning over seats.

Coach took them in a minute and then began.

"My name's Lawrence Miller, and the company I represent is called the Four Corners Baseball Card Company. Have any of you heard of us?"

"No" came a quick reply from the back row.

"That's fair enough," said Coach, using a ballpoint pen to point at the speaker. "Well, maybe you know about Topps or Bowman?"

Someone did, and the pitch went smooth from there. The only colour came once Coach started talking about licensing fees.

"How much we talking?" asked a voice.

"Well, that's what matters most I guess, isn't it?" Coach joked to the empty air. "We're able to pay you five dollars for, again, a non-exclusive licence to your likeness and name. Now again, that's non-exclusive, meaning—"

"Can we have more?" I couldn't tell from my spot who was asking the questions, but it seemed each interruption was a new voice.

"I'm afraid I can't improve the deal beyond the five dollars," said Coach. "But what do you think would be fair?"

"A blow job?" said the next voice. The Bisons erupted into screams of laughter. Coach gave a thin smile. I took a step back from the bus and came down on Mikey's foot. He didn't yell but instead pushed me away with the palm of his hand.

"Sorry," continued the player. "I don't mean from you personally, friend, but rumour is Topps brings in their own girls and, you know, services are rendered as I heard it. Have you heard about that?"

"I'm not sure what Topps does, to be honest," Coach blushed, scratching at his nose as the laughter ebbed and quieted. "But Four Corners is a deeply religious company, so I don't think we'd do anything similar. That said, I hear Buffalo's a fun town, and I can't tell you how to spend your money."

The same gossip about the big companies refusing to work with Four Corners signees had made it to Buffalo, though the class consciousness of Reg Law hadn't met it. Coach advised them that he hadn't been told any such thing and that these sorts of stories tended to spread in a vacuum. By the end, nine of the fifteen Bisons signed papers. Five asked to take one home to show a parent or an uncle, and mail it in if okayed by them, and just one—a Quaker with a maximalist sense of what constituted gambling—said an outright no. When I popped up with a stack of contracts the players in the front row grinned at the gimmick of the child assistant, even more so when Mikey appeared to show sample cards. I helped them with the reading and made sure they marked the right boxes, then we stepped off the bus and wished them a pleasant ride to America.

Coach had made mention to one of the players that he'd grown up near Buffalo, and word of that had disembarked the bus and met the two men waiting outside, Coach Gibbs and Marshall Walschotts, the team's GM, whom Coach had contacted over the phone before the trip. As we thanked them for their time Walschotts asked what town Coach was born in, and Coach said Genesee County, which I didn't know because I had never asked.

"Near Batavia?" asked Walschotts, who was a slim man with a trim moustache and a nice grey suit. I couldn't picture him pooping though of course I'm sure he did from time to time. We all did.

"Pretty near," Coach said to his shoes, shuffling the signed papers until they formed a perfect stack.

"Well, we might have run in similar circles, though I reckon I have a few years on you."

Coach didn't respond but shook both their hands, and indicated to Mikey and me to do the same.

After we wished the Buffalo bus happy travels, Coach stood around in the parking lot for a few minutes trying to work out whether he should be pleased or disappointed.

"Nine signatures, it's not great," he mumbled, pacing back and forth in front of us. "The take-homers won't convert, they never do. Sometimes the office gets them back but years later, once those bums have bounced clear out of organized ball and are hauling scrap iron for a living. They can keep their papers then."

"Still, nine's not bad," I encouraged. "We had twenty-nine coming in, plus these, it's thirty-eight. We're averaging more than a dozen a club."

"We're giving free cash away to starving artists." He shook his head. "Should be pitching perfect games out here."

Mikey sat down, and this seemed to convince Coach to do the same. They perched on the sidewalk next to the inn, whispering their little secrets too low for me to pick up. I watched them a minute, waiting for the familiar cloud to billow in, not jealousy exactly but one of its neighbours. The idea that the people closest to you thought about each other more than they thought about you. This iteration of the cloud came with new colours. I remembered Mikey's face as he rejected the notion of Coach being his father, and then the look of them relaxed in the Windsor stands the day before, and I tried to square the two. Was Mikey in the stands a performance? A slip into fantasy? Was he lying when he told me he didn't believe it?

I walked over to examine the inn, found the main door, and entered.

The inn was nicer than where we had stayed in Windsor. Behind the clerk was one of those tall cabinets you see in post offices, with little shelves for keeping keys or messages, one for every room. The clerk was not as nice as our clerk in Windsor. He eyed me as I wandered over to his podium.

"Yes?"

"Good morning, sir," I offered in my most grown-up voice. "Is this establishment host to all of the visiting Northern League teams, or just the Bisons?"

Even though he wasn't writing anything down when I came in, once I had started with my question he had some important note to jot and didn't look up at me while he answered. "Are you seeking autographs?"

"No sir. I've a friend who travels with the Akron team and wanted to know if I could expect them here."

"Well." He sniffed and scanned another sheet on a different part of the desk. "We generally don't provide guest information. But if you have a name, I can leave a message if they arrive."

"My name, sir?"

"No, your friend's name. The name the room will be under."

"Sheridan. Spitter Sheridan."

"Your friend's name is Spitter?"

"Yes."

"That's their Christian name?"

"I don't reckon, sir."

He finished writing Spitter Sheridan somewhere and then held the pen with two fingers like he had fished it out of the toilet. "And the message?"

"Chris wants to know if Clara will be at the game. Meet at right field foul pole if yes."

I went back out and Coach and Mikey were tossing a stone they had found back and forth, bare-handing it and then lobbing it to one another, miming the tag at second base when they caught it.

"I think this place is too expensive for us. The staff is snooty," I told them, pointing behind me at the inn.

Coach didn't break his motion or take his eyes off the stone "You're surely right. I've a lead on our sort of place just the other side of the stadium. We'll grab the rental and check it out."

I stood in front of them with my fist on my hip. I wouldn't admit it, but I was doing my Reg Law impression. Light on my toes, bent a bit at the waist, with my head cocked to the side and my butt stuck out like I wanted someone to trip over it. It was a habit I had picked up since I first saw him do it at the Windsor park and couldn't shake. Maybe they were doing their Reg Law impressions too, in the smooth way they came out of their crouches to throw the stone back as they pretended to field his position.

"How long did you stay in Genesee County?" I asked Coach, who didn't flinch but did a double-clutch before tossing back to Mikey.

"Left in '41," he answered.

"Why? The war?"

Coach nodded. "Thereabouts. We hadn't declared yet but folks felt it coming." Mikey's toss floated left and he stuck a foot out to block it with his toe then leaned down and flicked it back with his wrist like he meant to skip it across a lake.

"Why didn't you go back?"

"To Genesee County?

"Yeah."

"Have you been there?"

Mikey looked over at me, holding their rock. I couldn't tell if he was mad or happy that I was pressing Coach about this. It had become impossible to read him; unless he was laughing or screaming, all other reactions had grown flat and imperceptible since the Italian restaurant. If anything he seemed to exist in a state of constant impatience, or maybe boredom. I had done this, asked Coach about his hometown, to try to shake free a bigger reaction. I dropped it at his feet.

"If the motel is close enough, let's park there and walk to Lake Ontario. Mamma said to make sure we collect sight of as many Great Lakes as we can, and this'll make two."

They didn't answer but as I turned towards the stadium and the car, I heard them stop playing and then the sound of their steps behind me.

The motel Coach had picked out fit the mode of our style perfectly. Like the Windsor one, it was C-shaped. This version had no emptied swimming pool but instead a giant wooden statue of a tiger stalked the sidewalk. The paint had rubbed off its back where guests had braved to pat it. The motel had twenty rooms on one floor, though unlike the last accommodation, the rooms all opened to the outside, not a central corridor.

Coach parked the big loud Buick and we left our things behind. There was another tiger cat, smaller and made of some sort of cheap ceramic, inside by the desk. The clerk was not a tiger but rather a short man in a blue jacket, maybe ten years older than Coach. We introduced ourselves. Coach acknowledged that we were early but asked if we could at least park there for the day.

"You're correct. Check-in isn't for two hours," the man said, addressing Coach but giving quick eye contact to Mikey and me. "But it's good you came by; I've taken two messages for you already."

"Two messages?" Coach asked, surprised.

"Indeed, the first was from a Mr. Cassels. And I quote: 'Can only meet with team at nine a.m. Charity drive in afternoon. Otherwise: tomorrow.' The second is a Mr. Leahy, requesting call-back. London number as attached." He handed Coach two pieces of cardstock.

Coach read the notes. "Thank you for taking these," he said without looking up.

"Don't normally get many notes for future guests. Will you be expecting more?"

"No." Coach held his hands up as apology. "I don't plan to make you be my secretary all weekend. No one really even knows we're here."

"Imagine the messages if you had told anyone. You're okay to park all day. Room number twelve. Feel free to take a map of the city's attractions."

He handed me a folded map and circled for us the stadium. The map was larger and more colourful than the one we had brought from home. I made a mark on Clara's inn across the street. We thanked him and went to the payphones.

"Who are Cassels and Leahy?" I asked.

"Well," he said, fishing out some nickels, "Cassels is the GM for the Red Wings, and it sounds like we missed our shot. While we were floundering with the Bisons, his team was across the street in their locker room and now gone from our reach until at least after tonight."

I must have made a dismal look.

"Oh it's not so bad," he went on. "No good trying them after the game. On a Saturday night, they'll be at the tavern before the umpires file their scorecards. We can get them tomorrow before we head to London. Just because there's no games in Ontario on Sundays doesn't mean there's no practice we can't tag along to."

Mikey pulled a hard mint out of his pants pockets. Maybe he'd snagged it from the motel clerk. "And who's Leahy?" he asked.

"Well," Coach said, scratching his neck, "I know who he is, Mike, but not how he tracked us down. He's a businessman in London looking to get into the card business. Seeking some advice as I understand it."

"From you?"

"Yeah from me, wise guy." Coach reached out and rubbed Mikey's head. "Only I told him we'd be in London by now. Christ knows how he found us here. Suppose we can ask."

Coach called Cassels and got approved to visit the afternoon practice at the stadium tomorrow. Afternoon meant we'd need to leave Monday morning and try to get to London and pitch both the Leafs and Sailors in one day, but that trip wasn't long so it should still work. I gave Coach a thumbs-up when he raised his eyebrows to ask me.

Coach's London businessman friend turned out to have had the nerve to contact Four Corners in Utah pretending to be his cousin, wondering why he never showed up in town last night. They checked the mission house, was told we took other rooms, looked up the number of the motel Coach had used last year, and passed that on to Cousin Leahy. This man knew where we were going before I did. Coach listened to Leahy for several minutes, an impatient frown lining his mouth, while Mikey and I took turns walking the curb like it was a balance beam. He may have said ten words before hanging up the phone and half of them were "sure."

"Alright." Coach emerged from the phone booth, stretching his arms. "We have some time to ourselves. What are we to do with it?"

"Niagara Falls!" Mikey burst out shouting. He had opened up a little since the Buffalo pitch but this was the first time raising his voice all day. I looked to Coach.

"Mmm, I'm not sure we have that much time, fellas. What about something in Hamilton?"

I consulted my new map of attractions. Nothing seemed attractive, and I didn't think I could negotiate our way back to staking out Clara's hotel.

"I could see a movie," Coach offered, and Mikey agreed to the idea. Our local house had shut down after a fire last winter so we had all three of us been starved for pictures. I wondered if something so standard as a movie house could be any different from country to country.

We found a local cinema and got tickets to the new Robin Hood picture. Mikey fell asleep on Coach's shoulder so I ate his snacks, sneaking glances at Coach's face in the Technicolor glow. I wondered what he thought about in the quiet moments between action sequences, whether he thought Maid Marian made sense, whether he considered Little John to be Robin's friend or his assistant, whether he thought the Sheriff was too bad to be believable. I didn't ask him but I thought obsessively about his opinions. I watched him watch the world the cinema house presented, and the minutes sprinted by.

We came out surprised it was still daylight, spoiled with sugar and rubbing our eyes at the sun. When we got back to the motel the clerk gave us a look and said we had a third message. He handed it to Coach.

This one was in a different hand, as it was left for us in person. It said: "I'm in town for the foreseeable. Need a favour. —Reg L."

We stood there blinking at each other like toads. "You don't know another Reg L., do you Coach?" I asked.

Coach shook his head and walked us back to the room. "I don't even properly know this one."

"What's he doing here?"

Mikey and I both followed Coach into the room though we hadn't taken off our shoes yet, like the idea of making a run for it hadn't been fully put to rest.

"Not sure." Coach shrugged. "The Windsor team was on their way to Buffalo. Maybe he got cut?"

"Or promoted?"

"Maybe, though they usually put you on a train."

"What does he want?"

"It's unclear, Chris." Coach frowned, incurious to our run of questions. "If it's something I can help with, I will, but frankly if it's a big request, he may need to take it up with somebody who likes him more than I do."

Mikey, in a voice so low it sounded like he had buried himself under pillows, asked, "Did he say where he is?"

"He did not. Suspect he plans to find us instead of us finding him. Maybe he'll be at the game."

"I don't want to go to the game," Mikey said.

"You'll go to the damned game." Coach surprised us by standing up to make his point and Mikey dashed into the bathroom and closed the door. Coach, for his part, didn't force it open. He placed one hand on the door but didn't push, and instead rubbed at his temple with the other hand. "You two were meant to see some baseball on this bottomless money pit of a trip, and that part at least we're going to fucking execute, do you hear?"

I flinched a little when he said *fucking*, which I hadn't heard him say before, at least not in anger. Coach whispered forgiveness from God and sat down.

"He's been queer all trip," he told me. "Kid crosses an imaginary line between countries and suddenly he's a different person."

"He's just tired and not used to travel," I said, and studied the map of Hamilton until Mikey slinked out, red-faced, and sat on the bed to read his Bible stories, his shoes still on his feet, dangling over the edge.

Coach eventually bribed Mikey out of the tiger-themed motel and to the Civic Stadium with promises of ice cream and a ball cap. Mikey's little league cap had gone missing somewhere in Windsor. In my mind, it was hanging in the skunky closet above the Italian restaurant, but it had to have gone missing before that. A new cap never materialized; there was no sales stall on site and nobody seemed to be selling them in the shops around the complex. He could have had a hat advertising the local three-down football team, whose mascot was also a tiger, but demurred. The sun was working on him. He would come home with hair a half shade fairer than he left and Momma would say he looked younger.

Dinner was frankfurters again served on paper plates and topped with pickled cabbage we both just picked off and left on the bare ground beside us. Coach didn't eat. I kept my eyes on the crowd, trying to parse out a strategy should I see Clara before

Reg, and another for its opposite. Mikey kept himself between Coach and me while the stadium filled up comfortably, the boost of Saturday baseball making up for the drag of a last-place team.

The Zaps wore their grey and reds and the Red Wings red on white, and the haze in the air from the industrial city made it hard to tell who was who until they split into camps for the game. Spitter Sheridan was parked on the first step, a proper dugout this time behind him. When the Hamilton pitcher jogged out to the mound he got a partial standing ovation from the fans nearest the field. Someone later told me he was local, a kid who had played on this field in high school and then made the professional team on a tryout. Coach dug through his pockets and produced a folded-up scorer's sheet, a grid of diamonds with space for names in the left-most column. He began to take us through the mechanics of the sheet. You filled in batter names and tracked their progress on the diamond next to them, drawing lines from base to base and adding the position numbers of whoever fielded the balls. It wasn't normally Mikey's kind of distraction but I suspected he liked having a project and Coach left him to it, weighing in to help adjudicate decisions, base hit versus error and the like, and assist with the notation on unusual plays. There was a proper public address speaker, a man with a thick Canadian accent that added phantom *W*s to the middle of words like *player* and *order*, and he helped clarify the calls.

From our spot near third base, I could see into the visitors' dugout but also clear across the park to the right field foul pole. It wasn't as accessible as I had hoped, as it was slightly obscured by the corner fencing, but it seemed empty. I was hesitant to leave Mikey to check.

After three columns in the scoresheet, the score was still 0–0 and the pace had been brisk. It was only half past seven. The Akron shortstop caught a bad bounce on a grounder that found an unswept pebble and had to go off for medical assistance when the ball caught him in the eye. In the interruption, Mikey popped his head up from his paperwork and said he needed the bathroom. Coach and I traded looks and I volunteered to go with him to stave off his electing to make me. The concourse was lacking in signage so we had to walk most of the perimeter of the field. By the end, Mikey was hopping from foot to foot and grabbing himself in a way Mamma would have slapped his hands over. I was concerned he'd make a mess again like he had done to the bed in Windsor. Eventually, we located a portable toilet, waited a couple of agonizing minutes, and he dipped in.

As I waited, I caught sight of a tall man with a dark complexion nodding in my direction and while he didn't quite look like Reg, it was enough of a start to get me thinking about how to handle bumping into him out here alone. I'd take him to Coach to discuss his favour. Or no, I'd speak to him myself and send poor Mikey back to Coach solo and away from that creep's face. Or would sending Mikey back solo create a risk too? Ideally we'd come upon him as a trio and Mikey and I could wander off to leave the men to adult matters.

Mikey took longer than normal. The breeze coming in from the lake had cooled the air and some of the locals were wearing long sleeves. I moved towards the toilet door and was just about to knock when it flung open and Mikey came pouring out.

"You alright?"

He nodded, wiping his hands on his trousers.

We took three or four steps towards the stands when Mikey wrinkled his nose.

"What?" I asked.

"Piss."

"Did you have an accident?"

"No—" He bent down to examine his lap before looking at me, succumbing to a wide, wild grin and then covering his nose and mouth with his hand. "You though."

I looked down. It took a moment to make sense of what I saw. My brown trousers were darkened in the front, a shock of liquid the size of a dessert plate across my crotch and thighs. "What?" I asked to nobody, to myself I suppose.

Mikey pulled at his hair and laughed, then darted ahead of me. "Oh my gosh, Chrissy, you did it. You pissed yourself!"

The crowd around us was moving in every direction, and when I stopped short I became an obstacle as strangers flowed around me or swerved to get by. I stammered, sweat cooling on my forehead in the wind. "Mikey, come back" I croaked out, then I saw someone leave the portable toilet and jumped in behind them, locking the door before the next person in line could complain.

I looked at myself. For the first time, I could feel the wetness; cold on my legs and sticky over my underwear. There was toilet paper on a roll, so I wiped down the front until the paper started coming off in coiled flakes like dander. I unzipped the trousers, pulled off the wet underwear, and tossed them into the toilet with a plop, then went to town on the crotch of the trousers with more toilet paper, tears in my eyes, until in the dim light of the portable I could tell myself they looked normal.

I wiped myself dry, and then checked my eyes and cheeks to understand whether someone could tell I had been crying. I eased into the trousers and dusted away the flakes and then just sat there on the toilet in the low light until my heartbeat felt normal and I could imagine how I would look at Mikey.

Mikey. I wasn't supposed to leave him alone. I swept open the toilet door and caught the sound of an angry middle-aged woman calling me an inconsiderate brat. I didn't see him. Running around the concourse to our grandstand I didn't see him there either, and didn't get a glimpse of him until I was charging along the field-level seats, no longer hung up on how I might look, and then down the third baseline where he was sat next to Coach, alone in their row, with the scoresheet on his knee. I climbed the stairs and filed in next to them.

"Where were you?" said Coach.

"Bathroom," I answered, hugging my knees and leaning forward. Mikey said nothing, but he smiled a little and I felt in a preposterous way like that at least was a silver lining, that he had found it funny. Maybe I had made his day.

The underdog Red Wings scored in the fifth and again in the sixth. There was an unusual play in the top of the seventh when Spitter Sheridan's replacement shortstop got caught in a rundown as the first and second basemen played catch and he did wind sprints between them before eventually getting tagged. Mikey was noting the play as it happened and by the end of it had written 4–3–4–3–4–3–4, using all of the one square plus two more next to it. Coach laughed.

"Sometimes the structure of the game fails when things get out of hand," he told him.

Mikey shrugged.

At the end of the half inning, the public address announcer came crackling on with a message: "Christoper Miller, please report to the box office to meet a member of your party."

Coach looked at me. "I wonder if that's you?"

"My last name isn't Miller."

"Yeah but does anyone here know your last name?"

I shook my head. "No. But yours is common enough."

"Should go and check at least. Go on."

"What if it's your Christian name they have wrong, instead of my last name? Maybe it's for you."

Coach didn't argue except to push me with the sole of his shoe. I stood up slowly, keeping my hands in front just in case there was a stain. I looked at Coach and he didn't seem to notice anything. "Alright," I said and wandered slowly over to the box office.

The ticket window had no one in line. I presented myself to the attendant. He was maybe two years older than me, with a wispy thin moustache like a line drawn in chalk. It did not make him look older.

"The PA said for me to come here," I told him.

"You're Christopher Miller?"

"I guess."

He nodded behind me and, from the other side of the popcorn concession, Reg Law emerged wearing the same street clothes we had seen him in on the bus. He was laughing at nothing and holding out his arms. When he got close enough, he grabbed me by the shoulders and yanked me in for a hug. I had my hands still clasped over my lap and just got them free in time to avoid sandwiching them between my nether parts and his.

"Kiddo," he said, clapping my back. "How are you?"

I cleared my throat and then found when I tried to speak I needed to do it again before managing. "I'm good, Reg. You?"

He showed his palms to the air. "Moving from adventure to adventure."

"Where's the team?"

"Buffalo I'd guess. We had an argument and I asked to sit out a game or two."

"You want to talk to Coach?"

"No," Reg said, so chipper it sounded like a song. "I can talk to you can't I? You're the brains."

I didn't know how to cover my crotch and make it look natural anymore so I leaned one hand on the ticket wicket and kept the other by my side. Reg, like Coach, didn't seem to notice or care. I pretended to look at the dirt and still didn't see a stain.

"Thanks for saying that, Reg. What can I do for you?"

"I'm looking for a place to toss my stuff until tomorrow. I've a lady friend in town who I can stay with, no need to put me up or anything, but I was hoping you could hang on to some equipment for me." He pointed to an overfilled sports bag by the booth. It was the kind of thing that could have held a half-dozen bats, or a closet's worth of laundry, or a whole human body laid out head to foot.

"I'd have to ask Coach."

"Why?"

"He's boss. Hang out here. I'll be back in two minutes."

I went back to the grandstand and asked for Coach's keys. I didn't say why or what the message was or even whether or not I was Christopher Miller. He was incurious about all of it. The road team had tied the game up at two apiece on what Mikey's scorecard said was an infield single and all attentions were firmly on the field.

"How'd you know where we were staying?" I asked Reg as we walked out of the stadium to the car.

"I know a few motel guys around. Called three of them before dialing Burdick at your spot, asking for a trio under the name Miller. Came by and you weren't there so I left a message."

"Is Burdick the clerk?"

"No, he's the cleaner. The clerk's name is Broderick. We're not close."

I thought about how little time Reg had spent in the Northern League and how a person comes to have this many casual acquaintances this quickly. "You're a real extrovert, Reg," I said.

He put his big hand on the top of my head, long fingers reaching to my eyelids, and said thank you. I let him but was glad when he stopped.

"You smell like piss, kid?"

"No?"

"Something does."

"It's the factories," I explained. "That one over there with the smokestack produces ammonia. Ammonia smells like urine."

"Huh," Reg said and made like he believed me. We walked two blocks more until we were in the expansive parking lot of some furniture store. The Buick was parked in the backmost corner.

"Reg, can I ask you something?"

"Sure thing, slick. You got girl problems?"

"No. I mean, yes. But it's not that. Those rumours you heard about Topps refusing to sign guys who had contracts with other companies—"

"Sure."

"You just heard that from one guy, or a few?"

"You doubt me, kid?"

"It's not that—"

"Look." Reg put his head down and leaned forward, like the world was heavy, and the whole conflagration was pressing down on his shoulders, and the job of explaining business to a child was more than he'd signed up for. "Do you think that licensing, that idea of licensing, was something Topps ever thought about before other people came looking to get in on the card racket?"

I didn't answer but I must have made a face like I didn't know.

"Licensing doesn't exist as a concept in a monopoly. You just pay what you want, if you want, and charge what you want on the other end. That idea of licensing, that's an in. It's a way for duct-taped outfits like yours to generate cost, to make life harder for the comfortable guys. If Topps has to pay players for their beautiful faces, they're not just printing money anymore."

"So you do think it's real?"

"I think making the licensing noise go away by putting everyone else out of business is the only way to keep the money machines running off in Brooklyn. Same as the owners of the teams. If they keep the players away from understanding their value, then they cut out a big hunk out of their costs. Players can't even get organized because they don't have the money to hire the lawyers.

You think of another job in America where you're not allowed to quit and go work for someone else?"

"The Army?" I guessed, after a few paces to think it over.

Reg kept walking in silence. "Okay, I accept that. Can you think of a second?"

I immediately thought of the Navy and Air Force and the Marines but held back on saying so. When we got to the Buick I opened the back and Reg folded the giant bag into the trunk. He thanked me and asked if I wanted a soda, so we crossed to a soda bar halfway back to the stadium. I checked my watch. The game might be over.

"What was the argument, Reg?" I asked.

"Argument?"

"With the team."

"No, no." He sucked back a swing of cola, which came in an oversized glass bottle and was called Spur. We didn't have it in Minnesota. The suction made a popping sound when he finished. "Wasn't an argument with the boys, just Simmonette."

"Oh."

He grinned. "I know what you're thinking but no. Do you remember when we shared those Popsicles, us and your girl, at the Akron game?"

"Yes."

"Well, seems it was deemed unprofessional and he wanted to fine me over it. You didn't tell him did you?"

"Nosir."

"Well. Someone did."

"There were, like, a few hundred people there, Reg."

He leaned forward and blew over the top of his bottle; it gave a low moan that, as he manipulated his lips around it, rose into a whistle. I tried to do the same with mine. "It may have been to do with the other thing too, a little."

I made my bottle squeal. "He knows?"

"Knows?" Reg snorted. "Knows. Men like that only know what they feel they have to. No more."

"Are you and Dora in love?"

Now he doubled over laughing, loud enough that the owner of the soda bar looked up from washing glasses, concerned it was someone making trouble. I gave Reg the time he needed to compose himself.

"Man, kiddo, I don't know about you. Did we look in love?"

I didn't know but Reg sure thought I should. I sat back in the chair, confused by how quickly talking to Reg put me at ease, and how the fear of him never left despite this. I was still scared of him, but I wanted to stay where he was. He finished his drink, then grabbed mine and necked the last third of it. "Come on," he said.

The Hamilton fans were leaving the stadium as we walked back towards it. Their faces and gaits were neutral, unreadable. I took this as a sign the home team had lost. Wins were rare enough here that they'd be a cause for celebration. Losses were presumed.

"What are you going to do now, Reg?" I asked him.

"Tonight? I told you. You can tag along if you want."

"No, I mean with the team."

"Oh, Simmonette will come around. Once the owners figure out I'm not playing, they'll roll on him and I'll be back. I have a friend who goes to Buffalo from Toronto twice a week. He can pick me up tomorrow and take me stateside. Always good to have connections in the world. Lets you act rashly."

"Do you have family around?"

"Nope. My mom's people are mostly down south, and my dad's—he's gone now, the war—they're in Ohio, but they don't talk to me. He was a white man and his parents didn't approve."

"He died in the war?"

"Indeed. One living Black mother and a dead white daddy."
Reg scratched the stubble on his chin and eyed the passing shops
and boutiques like he might check them out on his next visit.
"Folks never know what to do with me. You?"

"One white mother and the same. Folks sometimes don't know
what to do with me either."

Reg made a noise with his tongue against his teeth like cold
water in a hot pan. "Look at us, kid. A couple of orphan adjacents."

I wanted to ask Reg what kind of music he listened to. What
movies he liked and what clothes he preferred to wear when he
had his full choice, but we were already back at the stadium. Coach
and Mikey were at the tail end of the crowd leaving through the
main gate, a sign one or both of them had fallen asleep. We met
them by the field fence as players from both teams were packing
up to leave. The scoreboard confirmed what I suspected, that the
Zaps had come back to win it. The hometown pitcher's good
start went to waste.

I kept expecting Reg to wander off with the crowd, but he
stayed by my side, touching the brim of his cap at everyone, though
no one seemed to care that he was there or even recognize him.
The cap was his Clippers cap, the one he wore in games. They
only gave him one, I guessed.

Mikey saw us before Coach and stiffened. I put on my calmest
face as they approached.

"Where were you?" Coach asked.

"It was Reg here at the box office. He wanted me to help him
store his bags for the night."

Coach reached forward and shook Reg's hand. I could tell he
shook it tighter than normal because the skin on his knuckles
blanched. He jerked Reg's arm as he shook. "Law." He nodded.

"Miller." Reg nodded back, not bothered by the extra squeeze.
Reg began to explain himself to Coach. It was a simpler version

of events than he had given me, but I learned that he was asked to leave the team; he didn't leave them on his own. And then he went so far as to ask Coach for a place to grab a shower, which he had never asked me. Coach equivocated a little before Reg said he'd just try the YMCA and Coach agreed to let him in, like he had been waiting for evidence of Reg's desperation before consenting. I grabbed Mickey and led him off to where the staff and players were packing up equipment.

"How'd the game end, Mick?"

"Why'd you bring him here?"

"I didn't. He followed me. How'd the game end?"

Mikey looked at this scoresheet. "Top of the tenth. Single-8, single-7, runner to third. Strikeout looking. Ground ball, E4. Fly out 7. Bottom of the tenth. Strikeout. Put-out 1–3. Put-out 6–3."

"Losing on an error, that's rough."

"It was the Hamilton second basemen who did the error, and the same guy was the last out."

I looked back. Reg was going off about something or other while Coach stood with his arms crossed in front of him.

"I'm sorry I brought him back with me, Mikey. I tried to keep you two apart."

"It's okay," Mikey said. "I'm sorry you peed yourself."

"Shut up, Mikey."

The last Zaps came out of the dugout and then Spitter Sheridan himself, slapping a player on the back and stooping to tie his own shoe. I called out to him. He gave a friendly wave and then, seeming to recognize that we'd met before and we weren't just random Hamilton baseball fans, he jogged over to the fence.

"Aren't you two supposed to be in London?" he said, his red face shiny with sweat and both armpits stained a dull yellow.

"Car trouble," said Mikey.

"Hey coach," I added, "where's Clara today?"

"Oh, around for a bit, but she wasn't feeling great so she went back to the motel. We got your message. I'm sure she wanted to say hi, but you know how the road is."

Coach came up and greeted Spitter. "Captain Sheridan," he said. "Good win today."

"Thank you, Miller." He smiled. "I hear you three got thrown off course."

Coach nodded. "We're making the best of it though. Got a meeting with the Wings tomorrow and then back to London after that."

Spitter nodded, already distracted by the incongruous site of Reg Law behind us. The men didn't greet each other but, unlike the crowd of Hamilton fans, Spitter recognized him straight away.

"Well, I understand you're deep in your business," he said, "so I'll leave you to it. Kids, I'll tell Clara you said hellos."

We congratulated Spitter and he waddled off, his left leg struggling to keep up with the right.

Coach watched him leave and then turned around, looking first to Reg and then to Mikey and me and said it might be time to head home.

After the game was simple enough. I was desperate to shower but let Reg go first to get him off to his date. He brought in his bag and stripped whole-ass naked in the motel room, even before he picked out underwear or socks, and then he rooted around all skinned knees and foreskin before pulling out a crisp new shirt. Mikey kept his eyes so tight to his Bible stories his nose brushed the gutter of the book. Reg started to talk about his girlfriend, who was some sort of waitress, until Coach got tired of looking at the ceiling and threw a towel at him and he got the hint.

I called home to Mamma and she told me that the grocery was out of my favourite cereal, but that was okay we could go together next week and they'd have it then. I told her I missed her and she appreciated that. When Mikey got on he told her all about the Bible stories, which included some he already knew but also a bunch of new ones from the Mormons, including some about men who lived not far from where we were staying. Coach was on the phone when I went in to get cleaned up, and just hanging up when I was done.

Hamilton,
Sunday, July 13th, 1952

	W	L
Buffalo Bisons	41	24
London Maple Leafs	37	27
Akron Zaps	36	27
Erie Sailors	29	36
Windsor Clippers	28	36
Hamilton Red Wings	22	43

Last Night's Games
Wings 2, Zaps 3; Bisons 7, Clippers 0; Leafs 4, Sailors 2

WOKE UP TO A PITCH-BLACK ROOM AND WHISPERS. THEN regular talking. And soon a high-pitched cackle and a loud long monologue in a voice I recognized. I scrambled up and looked out the window. It was dark, but the streetlight just reached the lot and I could see a red coupe parked next to the rental, its engine still running. There were two people inside, one of whom I knew was Reg Law and the second was a woman. Neither of them was in the driver's seat. Their heads were close enough together in the backlight, they could have been sharing the passenger side.

I closed the curtain and looked back into the room. Coach and Mikey were asleep in the far bed and Mikey, always on a hair trigger when he slept and prone to start flopping about the bed at first light, was still for now. I looked at my watch. Four in the godforsaken morning.

I swapped my pajama bottoms for regular pants, dragged Reg's bag from the corner, and stepped out into the night. It was cold, colder than it had been at the game. The hair on the back of my neck stood up.

"Hello?" I called out to the car, holding the bag up as best I could. The heads had been moving about but stopped when they heard me.

Reg Law poked out. "Kiddo!" I knew he was drunk right away. The lilt in his voice. Like -do was an answer and Kid- the question.

"What's going on, Reg?"

He got out of the car and walked over. His shirt was untucked and riding up so that I could see the muscles in his stomach as he crossed into the light.

"Hey, kid." He put a hand on my shoulder. "My girl's roommate's family is in town so we are hanging out in the wild tonight. I thought it'd be alright if we parked here awhile."

"Where were you planning to spend the night, Reg?"

"Night? Shit, it's morning already. I'll be fine."

The driver's side door opened and a woman a couple inches taller than Reg, and a whole head more than me, stepped out. She wore a peach swing dress that hung down to her shins with a thin leather belt in the middle. Her hair was done up, and she looked like she belonged in an advertisement.

"Who's this, Reg?" she asked. I couldn't place her accent.

"This is my boy Chris," Reg said, not looking back to her but staring at me, following my eyes as I took her in.

"He live with you?"

"Not usually no."

I whispered. "Does she think this is your room, Reg?"

He shook his head and finally turned to the woman. "Essie, this is Chris. Get my boy a drink please, he's a businessman."

She looked at him like he had told her a bad joke, then reached into the car and pulled out an opened beer that looked like it had about two-thirds left. It was new enough that it still had bubbles. She popped open the back seat of the coupe and held the bottle out towards me. "This is a child, Reg. You're going to hell."

Reg nodded at me to get in the car. I asked him where we were going and he said nowhere, this was the end of their night.

"What about this?" I said, nudging the heavy bag with my toe. He said it could go in the car too.

I looked back just a second towards the motel room and then I found myself walking on light feet towards the vehicle. I said thank you to Essie, tossed the bag onto the back, and cupped the beer in both hands like it was a mug of hot soup. Reg and Essie got in and she turned towards me, smiled again, and rolled her eyes.

"How old are you?" she asked.

"Sixteen," I said.

She laughed at that and then she looked me up and down.

I took a sip of the beer and wiggled my toes. It was warm and tasted like it hadn't fully come together from its ingredients, like it hadn't been mixed up right. The four or five times I had taken a sip of a beer they always tasted that way. Like a platter of wet vegetables. Like salad.

Essie leaned forward and turned up the radio. "Sorry, Mr. Chris. They don't have good stations here."

I didn't recognize the song, but I could tell the singer was not a young man. It might have been recorded live, or the radio crackle just might have sounded like scuffing chairs and coughing.

"What are we doing?" I asked.

Reg didn't take the question seriously enough to look at me, just hung his hand out the window with his beer bottle loose between his fingers. Like Coach when driving. "Toasting the night."

"It was a good night," Essie said, drawing out the word *was* with a long exhalation. Reg nodded and grinned at her. I could count his white teeth in the light from the street.

After the song ended and a speaker came on talking about what a beautiful part of the country it was and how lucky they were to be there, a second song started, with that shuffling instrument in the background people played in bluegrass songs. Like an old washboard.

"Can we move the car to the other end of the lot, Miss Essie?" I asked her.

"Your brother asleep in there?" Reg tilted his head side to side like he was trying to see through the curtains. I didn't answer, but Essie still said sure, sweetheart, and put the car in gear, reversing out and moving to a spot at the far end of the C, facing a dark room with no vehicle outside to mark it as occupied.

Reg sat up and leaned over to her. He kissed her neck and ears and took her hand by the wrist, placing it in his lap. He was whispering something and she giggled and said no, not here. I took a big swig from my bottle and held it there until it was all gone except that last stubborn drop rolling slowly down the side like sweat. I looked out either side window while they rolled around up front. He stood up a little to pull his pants down but she slapped him in the chest with the back of her hand until he quit.

"Take the top off at least," he growled, grabbing her by the hair and pulling back so he could kiss her collarbone. She obliged, reaching behind herself to unclasp something and then he pulled her dress straps off both shoulders. She wasn't wearing a brassiere and both breasts popped into view. I wasn't prepared for them. Nothing held them up—they had their own gravity—and were dotted by perfectly round brown nipples just a shade darker than her skin. I wanted her, or him, or anyone, to let me reach out and touch them. Reg locked eyes with me as they kissed, his hands on her astonishing breasts, holding them like he was showing them off to me. I thought I should want to get closer, but I found myself pushing away as hard as I could, bracing my feet against the backs of their seats. I looked out the window again. There were no cars driving by. I imagined that last lone drop of beer still crawling down my throat, tracing its slow way towards my stomach. The music was ticking along at a walking pace, the singer scratching, "I asked my captain for the time of day. He said he threw his watch away." The blood in my ears chugged louder. I checked my watch but couldn't make sense of the time. I looked back at Reg. He broke the kiss a little, then stuck his tongue out his mouth, just an inch or two, and Essie sat up and took his tongue between her lips and I saw her cheeks dimple in like she was sucking on it.

I popped the door and squeezed out. Reg spotted me doing it and almost got to the door handle first, reaching over the front seat with his free hand. I shouted goodnight over my shoulder and ran for the motel room but Reg caught up to me. He pushed me in the back and I stumbled and flayed out in the dirt. I heard Essie yell as I climbed to my feet. Reg was pulling up his pants and saying something I couldn't make out but that sounded like a cuss. My chin was wet, but not with blood. Spit.

"What's your problem?" he shouted.

"I'm sorry Reg. I should just go home," I mumbled, holding my hands out. I looked down at the beer bottle still clutched in my fist and saw its bottom half was missing, a sharp shard left from where it broke. I dropped it and the rest shattered between us.

"You don't even know how to have a good fucking time?" he asked, though it sounded like a statement. Essie was still in the car, both doors on the passenger side open. I heard a voice behind me and then a whoosh of white cotton. Coach. Reg put a finger up and told him to stay out of it. He pushed past me and shoved Reg, then reared back to swing at him, but Reg was far too fast. He moved his head to the side and punched Coach right in the stomach, then when he lurched forward, another to the side of the head. Coach fell to one knee.

This got Essie out of the car. She called Reg's name and he followed it halfway, then stopped short and ran back to Coach like he was about to hit him again. Coach cowered, his hands over his head. Reg spat and yelled, "That's for snitching on me!" and then retreated to the car. Essie got in the driver's side and they pulled out, tires squealing once they hit the pavement, speeding around the corner, and were gone.

I looked at Coach. He was rubbing the side of his head, which was red but not bleeding. I turned towards the motel, where Mikey stood in the open doorway. None of us spoke. Coach got to his feet and looked at the glass on the ground.

"Were you drinking with that fucking animal?" he asked, catching some of the words in his throat.

I couldn't find an answer, so Coach just walked past me and told my brother to get inside. He was holding his ribs as he walked. I followed. Coach looked at himself in the mirror, then picked up his travel bag and threw it across the room. It hit the far wall and slouched to the floor.

"What were you doing out there?" he yelled.

"Just hanging out," I said, following two steps behind him.

He turned and slapped me. It jerked my head to the side but didn't knock me over.

"Hanging out?" Something from inside him, sweat or snot, leapt out and landed on my chest. "What the Lord of fuck is wrong with you, boy? I'm going to tell your mother and she'll have you sent to prison."

"Coach, no," I said, holding my jaw in my hand. "It's not like that, I was just worried—"

He made like he was going to slap me again and I flinched and overcorrected, losing my balance and falling into the corner of the room. I reached out to save myself with something stable and brought the curtain down with me instead.

Mikey made a noise that sounded like a squeal of complaint, or of pity, but it never rose to the level of words. I pulled myself up and reached for the first thing I could find, ready to hit Coach with it, heck even hit Mikey with it, whoever dared to interrupt me explaining myself. My face was burning and my head hurt from where I hit the wall as I fell.

The first thing I got a hold of turned out to be the doorknob. I pulled on it and the door opened and I discovered myself outside.

"Chris, I'm sorry," I heard Coach behind me. "Come back in."

But by then I didn't know anything except that he wanted me to stay, which meant all I wanted on the Earth was to leave. So I ran, with just enough bearings to aim for the direction opposite of Essie's exit. I heard Coach give chase so I turned down a side street and then into an alley and he was gone. I climbed a fence and then another until I knew that I was nowhere, nowhere a car could find me and nowhere Coach could get close enough to try and do something like apologize.

I spent the rest of the night sat next to someone's doghouse, crying and thinking about Minnesota. After a couple hours, the sun started to dye the far edge of the city and I stood up, wiped my face on the white undershirt I had been using as a pajama top, and started to climb over obstacles until I got to a road. It was abandoned in all directions. It took me two blocks before I saw someone: the driver for a local newspaper unloading a cube of papers by the door of a general store. I watched the man work but he never noticed me.

There were thirty cents in dimes and nickels in my pants pocket, plus the motel's map of Hamilton. I took it out. My first option was to go back to where I started and hope that Coach's guilty feelings held out and he wouldn't just give me another slap and send me on my way. It would be the brotherly option, but I found myself just as mad at Mikey as I was at Coach. I had gone with Reg and Essie halfway to get them away from him. Halfway anyway. The other half I couldn't explain properly, even in the dark. I wanted to know what they would do. I wanted to see it, and then I didn't. I was fleeing Reg's car before I even told myself I needed to. I was stepping into the back seat before deciding whether I should. Want and panic are both single-sighted things.

If I didn't go back to the motel I could try to find Darlene Young's mission house. The Elders would be out soon, if they got up early on Sundays. But the area of the city represented in the map didn't seem to stretch that far up the hill, and in either case this wasn't a long-term solution. There was no path from the mission house back to Minnesota, outside of going from there to the police station and declaring myself a missing child. A lost American, trafficked across the border by a dangerous fantasist in the guise of lowly commerce.

I knew I would have to go back to Coach eventually. So where did I want to be until then? I walked to the nearest corner to orient myself. Barton and Birch. The stadium was eight blocks east; Coach's motel was six blocks south. I walked east, and then north a touch when I could see the tall grandstand of the football field. The sun was mostly up. I stopped at the bit of pavement where Coach and Mikey had practised fielding to tie my shoes and take an audit of my breath. It wasn't great.

There was nobody at the desk at the inn. A notepad was open under the reading lamp. I looked it over and pulled myself up so I could see the tall postal cabinet. Most of the boxes had a little tented-up scrap of paper with a name and number written on it. Jacobson, 1; Moody, 2; Howard, 1. I read through until I found it: Sheridan, 2. Room 203.

I grabbed a mint and ducked through the doorway to the stairs as I heard footsteps return from the kitchen or bathroom or wherever. The inn had wood panelling throughout its halls that looked old and ornate but was warping a little in places, it was just a veneer with water damage beyond it. A man in a good suit and briefcase exited room 211 at the hall's end and walked towards me, checking his wristwatch and redoubling his pace. By the time I got to 203, the whole floor had gone quiet. I put my ear to the door and waited, eventually hearing someone close a drawer or maybe just a heavy book.

I knocked. There was no noise from the other side. I knocked again. The door opened a crack and from behind the chain lock I saw Clara's eyes and a single red ringlet of her hair.

"Hello?" she asked.

I had given exactly no thought to what I would say or how I would explain my presence at their door first thing in the morning on their day of rest.

"Who is it?" I heard Spitter call from somewhere in the room. Clara looked behind me. "Are you alone?"

"Yes."

"Why?" But by then her father had gotten up and noticed me. He closed the door, unlocked the bolt, and opened it wide. They were both still dressed for sleep. He in an undershirt like mine and shorts. She in a faded pink T-shirt that hung very loose around her neck and grey wide-legged pants that looked soft. I didn't stand out, except that I was wearing my good pants. I wished my undershirt covered more of my arms and chest than it did.

"Christopher?" Spitter said. He looked like he was about to ask me what I was doing there but decided not to, and instead invited me in.

Their room was nice but messy. Clara ran around tidying up, throwing what might have been panties in a travel bag and more or less making the beds. Spitter pointed at an upholstered chair and I collapsed into it. The tired soaked into my shoulders all at once.

He asked if I wanted coffee and I opted for water instead. He brought it to me in a ceramic cup with the name of the inn on its side. As I drank it down in small sips they sat on the bed opposite and waited for me to speak.

"Thank you," I said once the ability to do so had risen in my throat.

Clara was first to ask the question of the moment. "What are you doing here, Chris?"

I breathed in, held it for a second while I thought about the answer, and then very slowly exhaled. "I had a bad argument with Coach and ran away."

Spitter nodded his head. Clara looked at him with concern, but like the concern a mother animal would have for its young, and then back at me. I wanted to get up and wipe the expression off her face.

"I see," he said. "Well, you're free to stay here for a bit, but we should eventually tell him where you are. Don't you think he'll be worried?"

"Probably," I said. "But can we let him stay worried, for at least a little bit?"

They made me tea and shared the sandwiches Clara had put together. They were liver on toast, the liver a kind of smooth clay-like thing unlike the pan-fried liver Mamma made at home. Like in their Windsor motel room, there was a TV, though they kept it off, opting instead for the tabletop radio that played religious music before they tuned to the Canadian news program when it came on at nine o'clock. I wondered if it was the same music show Essie had listened to in her car, but surely the men who played those songs were now asleep.

They both had showers and then asked me if I wanted to get cleaned up as well. Spitter told Clara to see if there was a shirt of his small enough I could wear. I went to the bathroom and she followed me, going through his clothes while I watched until she pulled out a button-up the colour of shredded wheat.

"This doesn't really fit him, I don't know why he packs it," she said. "Here." She held it up against me, pulling at the fabric where it hung down past my stomach.

"Are you feeling better from last night?" I asked her. She shook her head.

"It wasn't any kind of illness. Some nights I just want to be alone with my thoughts." She leaned in and examined my face for a minute. I held my breath. Clara raised a slow hand and pressed the back of it against my cheek. "Did you get hit?" she asked.

"Why'd you think that?"

"I know what getting hit looks like."

I took a half step backwards. "Do you get hit?"

"Of course not. But I hang around ballplayers so I know how a punch shows up on the cheek. It looks like that."

I touched my fingertips to my jaw. "It wasn't a punch. A slap."

She pressed her lips together like she was going to argue with me, like she was an expert and it really was a punch, but instead she just lifted a sprig of hair out of my eyes. "I'm sorry, Chris. Here, wear this. You'll look silly but you'll feel good."

I took the button-up and set it on the counter and turned on the shower. The water took ages to warm up and I felt self-conscious standing naked in their bathroom where I could hear Clara clear dishes on the other side of the door. When I got out Spitter told me it was time to call Coach, and asked whether he should do it or me. I asked him to do it.

Spitter finished his coffee and wandered out the room to track down a phonebook and use the payphone. Clara was sitting up in her bed reading a book she told me was for school. She patted the mattress next to her.

"My hair's wet," I said. She shrugged and pointed to the big upholstered chair by the desk. I sat there and watched her read another page or so before she dog-eared the book and put it down.

"My dad's pills aren't for his heart exactly. That's more a metaphor. He gets sad easily, and the doctor gave them to him to cheer him up. He's not about to have a heart attack."

"Okay," I said. My hands were folded in my lap over a loose clump of Spitter's shirt where it hung off me like a tablecloth. "Why'd you need to tell me that?"

"When I stayed home last night, I wasn't being irresponsible or dangerous. He wasn't about to die because I didn't watch."

I nodded. I wondered what kind of pills they were.

"Is it from the war?"

She made a gesture with her hands like she was stirring. "And everything else, I guess. Life."

"My dad went nuts after the war," I told her. "The city said he had a car accident but we're all pretty sure he did it on purpose. Drove into a building."

"Anybody in the building?"

"No."

"That's good at least."

"Suppose so."

"My dad's not nuts though."

"No."

"I just said he gets sad."

I listened to the radio announcer. He was talking about armistice attempts in Korea, but also about a battle that was going on there at the same time. Imaging dying in a war while the countries talked about ending it. Every war must have had someone who died in it last.

Clara was smoothing down a wrinkle on the hastily made bed. She turned her head back to me. "I want you to know that I don't date boys yet. My father says I'm not old enough. I think you're fine and everything, but I agree with him about that."

I blinked at her and cleared my throat. "Okay," I offered, stalling to gather my thoughts. "I understand. But I think you're better than fine. You're great. And I don't think there's any harm in you knowing it."

Her cheeks flushed and I thought her eyes got a little shiny. She opened them wide and pursed and unpursed her lips. I knew I didn't want her to get off the bed and come over to me. I wanted to sit in the chair next to her forever. And not just to wait her out until she decided she was ready. I wanted to sit in the chair and have her sit on the bed and for nobody to grow any older.

The radio newsreader announced the time and then a song began the next program.

I had forgotten how close we were. At night, every new block had felt like another country, but it was basically just the stadium, a school, and a park and then we were in sight of our motel. Clara stayed behind again, not because she asked to but because her father had required it, and he and I walked there alone. Sometimes, directing us through intersections, he put his hands on my shoulders and they felt warm and soft, like the paws of a giant dog. I kept my head down while he talked about arguments he'd had with his old man, with his high school football coach, with a minister. He once fought a pitcher who ended up going on to the majors, where he gave up three consecutive home runs to the meat of the Yankees' Depression-era order.

"One day you just stop fighting people. You either start speaking civilly, or you let them stand in the opposite corner of every room and be wrong. Can't fist-fight them all."

I hadn't fought Coach, or Reg for that matter, or anybody. I once put a kid in my class in a headlock because he called my mother a name, but even then I hadn't closed my fist at him. I held his skull against my ribs and squeezed until his ear got so hot it felt like it would brand my arm. I hadn't done anything wrong.

"What about if it's family?" I asked him. He seemed surprised; it was the first thing I'd said beyond simple answers to his questions since we'd put our shoes on.

"Well, I understand Coach feels like family, and that's a good thing, good you have that in your life. But even people you're close to, you can hold them at the distance you need. Except your mamma and your brother probably. Her you're attached to until she passes, and him, you're likely stuck with him until you do."

I liked that Sheridan spoke like this. He was trying to cheer me up but he still wanted to talk about death and dying, about letting go of people. Nobody spoke to me like this.

"Did he hit you?" he asked me. I said no. He looked at me like he wasn't convinced but didn't ask again. I didn't know if Clara had told.

"Can I stay in Hamilton and then go back to the U.S.A. with you, instead of heading to London with them?"

Spitter put his hand on my back briefly even though we were well clear of any intersection.

"No. But if you want me to hang around while you talk to your coach, I can. If it doesn't work out, just walk back to our place with me and we'll try again later."

I looked at him and he gave me a big goofy wink so I forced myself to laugh and said thank you. He put the paw back on the small of my back and I leaned into it until I was balanced on the heels of my feet.

Spitter didn't say much to Coach except to shake his hand and accept a thank you. He left us with an invitation to join Clara and him at church.

"That's kind of you, Coach. We actually had an invite from the Mormons to attend their sacrament meeting today, but I'm afraid we're too late for it now."

"Well, the family and I are Episcopalians, and we sleep in. Usually." He shot me a friendly smirk. "One p.m., there's a little church across from the gas bar there. You can get lunch first."

Coach thanked him again and then I thanked him again and Mikey—solemnly from the washroom doorway and half under his breath—thanked him as well.

We watched him leave the room and turn the corner. I knew he was going to hang out a few minutes just in case, somewhere out of sight, and I was calmed and buoyed by that. It made it easier to turn back towards the room and look Coach in the eye.

"Mikey," Coach said when I got there, "take the keys from out of my grey pants and go and sit in the car until I come get you. Chris and I need to talk a bit in private."

Mikey did what he was told. As he walked past me he leaned over a little and pressed his shoulder into my side, which I took to be a gesture of support. He closed the door behind himself.

It was dark in the room. The light switch was just a foot away, but I didn't want to move first. Coach did. He walked over to his bed and sat down on the edge, his feet flat on the floor and his head hanging loose like he had fallen asleep. After a few ticks from the clock on the wall he looked back up at me. His face was red, but he wasn't angry. He looked like he'd been holding his breath.

"So obviously," he said, slowly, glancing from object to object in the room, "the first thing that has to happen is I have to apologize to you. I'm not someone who hits people smaller than me. I was upset, very upset, at you and at that low-life Law and at myself. It's never happened before, and it won't happen again."

I watched him until I was confident he was done speaking, then turned away and reached for the light and flipped it on. The beds were both made and our bags were packed and the desk chair at the other side of the room was pushed in. I leaned against the door. Coach or someone from the motel had even put the curtain back.

"Okay," I said. "That's okay."

"Do you want to go home?"

I frowned. "Do we have to?"

"No."

"We have work to do."

"I know." He rubbed his hands together. His feet were still flat on the ground and the posture was one I'd never seen in him before, knees far apart and his weight forward. It was like talking to someone in a full-body cast.

"I would understand if you wanted to go home, is all I was saying."

I only realized then that we were whispering. I cleared my throat and spoke up. "No. It's important to me and to Mikey, and you want to do a professional job."

"I do." He nodded, raising his own voice to meet mine.

"Are you really Mikey's dad?"

He stopped rubbing his hands and put them together like he was praying, the tips of his index fingers just under his bottom lip. "Why do you ask?"

"I want to know."

"Yes."

"You promise?"

"Yes."

"Are you going to ask Mamma to marry you?"

"I already have. Twice."

I breathed out through my mouth, trying to control the air so it didn't sound like I was nervous. Still, it came out in bursts, like I was shivering or sobbing. I wasn't.

"Did she say yes?"

"You don't keep asking once you get a yes."

"But both times?"

"She said no and then later she said probably not." He looked up at me and smiled a weak smile. "Which means I'm making progress."

I didn't smile back, which didn't seem to bother or surprise him. I wanted to ask him what would happen if she said yes. Would we move? Where? But it seemed like I was asking what would happen if one of us was hit by lightning or struck gold. What would happen in the case of an impossible event. I had watched Coach negotiate, in practice and real life, enough to know when he was losing. He was losing on the Mamma file, and he knew it.

"Why'd she say no?"

He held his hands up to say he didn't know, and then looked at the ground a little more when it became obvious I wanted a real answer. "She said that she's happy with her life right now."

"Why wouldn't she be?"

"I can't say. But life is hard for unattached women. You don't know. Especially alone with kids? I told her I could make it less hard if she'd let me."

"We're doing okay. She got a raise last year from the college."

"I know, I know. She's an incredible woman—"

"She knows that it's hard. Maybe she doesn't think it would be easier with you."

I noticed I was gripping the side of my pants in my fist. I so badly didn't want to seem angry, or upset, or anything, that I was taking it out on my pants. I put my hands behind me but pressed both shoulders against the door so I could be sure I didn't slouch.

"Maybe not," Coach said, looking out the window beside me. "But it sure would be nice to try."

Spitter's shirt was made for a grown man, and a big one. I had tried to tuck it in on the walk over but it had bunched up and looked funny so I pulled it out. Now with it hanging down halfway to my knees, I wish I hadn't.

"Are you going to tell your mamma about this?" he asked.

"About what?"

"Christ, boy," he said, not shouting but certainly underlining his words. "You are plenty difficult."

"About what?"

"About me hitting you? Alright?" He stood up but didn't come towards me. He walked towards the bathroom and put his head in the sink, running the water. When he came out, his hair was stringy and stuck to his face in awkward curls. His shirt front was wet and he had undone his belt, which hung in front of him like he was being led around by a leash.

Years ago, when Mamma had just started at the college, she came home with a strange woman. This woman was older, a few years from retirement, and she worked in the recruitment office. She wore bright floral clothes, and her hair was dyed and treated to the point that it made a crunching sound like dead leaves when she touched it. Mamma introduced her to me and said that the flower lady, whose name I've long forgotten, was learning a new job where she helped people become, "happier and more successful in their lives."

The flower lady was unmemorable except for the exercise she made me do before she left after dinner. She was practising how to do it with strangers. The exercise was very simple and something I did all the time back then: drawing yourself. Mamma got me some paper and pencils, and I drew a quick stick man holding a gun and pretending to be a cowboy. The lady said to try again and to really think about how I looked when I pictured myself in my mind's eye. She suggested I focus on just one part of myself, maybe my face, so it would be easier to draw in detail.

I spent a good twenty minutes drawing my eyes and nose. I didn't even get to my mouth. I'm not a great artist, but the flower lady encouraged me to really think about how I looked. When I touched my cheekbone, she gently moved my hand away and told me to only use my memory, my mind's eye, and not my hand or a mirror or anything that would tell a plain truth.

When I was done the eyes didn't look right but I told her I was happy with it to make her feel good. And then she said to me the part of the exercise that stuck, she said, "People draw the versions of themselves they feel is the truth; what they draw is *their opinion of themselves.*"

It occurred to me that with the breath-holding and the weird posture and now this messy sink bath that Coach was drawing me his opinion of himself. His imagined self was this version that had fallen apart all over.

I decided he had had enough.

"Okay," I said. "It's all in the past. What's the agenda for today? When's Hamilton's pitch?"

He wiped his hands and the front of his shirt on a towel. "Are you going to tell your mother, Chris?"

"I said it was in the past."

He stood in the doorway of the bathroom, the very spot Mikey held when I first came home. Father like son. He looked like he might cry from gratitude, but only for a moment. He gathered the end of his belt and fixed it in his pants loop. A hand swept the wet hair across his head. He rallied.

"Okay then. The Red Wings are practising this afternoon. I thought about four p.m. We can go to church with Spitter and your friend first."

"Thanks. I'd want to."

"And then you said Erie plays in London tomorrow. We can leave after the meeting and make it there, or stay the night here."

"Here," I said. "I need to sleep and so should you. We'll leave in the morning, get the Hornet back then."

He nodded. "Are you hungry?"

"Yes," I told him, opening the door to the motel room. "Go find Mikey and take us where he wants."

He walked past me out the door to do as I had said.

Mikey couldn't decide what he wanted to eat so we ended up just going to the first cheap-looking spot we saw, where Coach and I both had fried bologna and Mikey ate a grilled cheese and left the soup that came with it to get cold. I ordered a coffee when Coach did, but I didn't drink all of mine. Even when I opened four sugars, it still tasted like it was angry with me. All the same, I felt properly awake when we parked and crossed the street to the church.

The building had a cozy, textured look as if it was made out of clay and twigs, though once you got close enough it was obviously just masonry. The name "All Saints" hung over the door and once we walked in it was dark, full of wooden beams and low on windows. It was about as full as the baseball stadium, proportionally, and Clara was wearing a smart white shirt and black skirt topped, I was thrilled to see, with the fashionable circle hat I had swindled for her in Windsor.

Spitter was making do with the same clothes he wore earlier. We slid in next to him and I handed him his shirt. Everyone greeted one another and we prayed.

After, we wandered on foot back to their room in the townhouse inn. Spitter had invited us for tea before the Zaps gathered for a team meeting and optional bullpen for the pitchers.

"Why the Zaps?" Mikey asked as we crossed the street. "Why are they called that?"

"It's a good question, Michael," said Spitter. "There's a college in the city where we play, and the college team is called the Zips. So, the owner thought if we had the Zips, why not have the Zaps too. I guess it was a little joke."

Mikey followed along behind us for a half block, deep in thought before responding. "But why is the college team called the Zips?"

Spitter laughed. "You may have stumped me there, Mike. I do know they used to be the Zippers, so maybe that's where they come from. Maybe zippers were invented in Akron?"

"Zippers are Canadian," I interrupted. "I read it on a poster."

Eventually we stopped bothering Spitter about zipper trivia and landed at their front door. It was a lot of people for a small room so we kids shared Clara's bed while Coach took the upholstered chair and Spitter made tea and put out the cookies they had bought at the corner bakery. Coach had given Mikey a warning against another run on the Sheridans' TV.

"It was a good service, Sheridans. Thanks for inviting us." said Coach.

"Well sure," Spitter said, pouring tea. "I'm not the most religious man by nature, but we do like to take a breather on the road. It keeps our minds anchored when we're away from the rest of the family, doesn't it, Clara?"

Clara flattened her skirt out over her legs and agreed. There was an old copy of the Baseball Encyclopedia by the bed, a big thick book it would have been hard to carry around, so maybe it lived at the inn, and she had it out and was showing Mikey through its sections.

"Do you get home to Jersey at all during the season?" Coach asked.

"Once or twice during breaks. Louisa's used enough to me being gone all spring and summer that she doesn't really expect or need me around. But she misses Clara something terrible."

"She knows you're chasing the dream."

"Oh maybe." He handed Coach a mug of tea. "But it's also a job. I'm not sure I would do it for free anymore."

"Of course. I wouldn't do mine for free either."

"Right, and you've just reminded me." He dug around until he found a pair of reading glasses. Clara raised an eye from the big baseball book. "On that subject, I thought you should see this. Arrived at the team offices last week. Our doctor brought it with him when he came to look at the shortstop's eye bones."

He handed Coach an opened envelope. Coach frowned and accepted it. In it was a letter on a single piece of paper, which he read silently to himself, his lips moving and an angry flush on his face. I looked at the envelope. It was addressed to the Zaps and the return said Topps Chewing Gum Company of Brooklyn, New York.

Coach finished reading and pressed the palm of his hand hard against his forehead. "Well," he said. "That's certainly aggressive, though I don't necessarily feel like it changes our position."

"Your position is your business," said Spitter. "And I won't tell my boys to act any differently. I just thought you might want to know what the head of the dragon you've caught by the tail looks like."

Coach passed me the letter when he saw me leaning over to try and read it. It was on Topps letterhead and was from their legal department. I scanned it quickly, one ear out for the adults' conversation. Essentially, Topps wanted the Zaps to know that if they signed a licensing agreement with another provider, they would forfeit the ability to sign with Topps when they made the major leagues. The letter said that those licences were bought for two hundred dollars apiece. I couldn't imagine all that money for a face. It was the threat Reg Law had told me about. It was real.

"They're gonna run us out of business," Coach said.

"Well, they were always gonna try, Mr. Miller. That letter was always coming, ever since you and your colleagues started to come out to leagues like the Northern. You know the pattern: they did the majors, so you did the minors. Then they did the minors, too, so you did the low minors, then C-ball, then D-ball. Heck some even tried the colleges, until kids started losing their scholarships. Now this, all the way to nothing ball, so low the dogs can't sniff you out. But eventually they do. They've got a cracker pack of dogs, folks like Topps and Bowman."

"Reg Law was right." Coach shook his head. "We should have gone to the market with exclusive contracts only. That way we'd own what we got instead of just borrowing it until the big boys came to take it all away."

Coach closed his eyes and sat very still while the rest of us drank our tea and I tried the cookies. They were oatmeal. Even Mikey didn't like oatmeal as a cookie.

"Thanks for telling me," Coach said, smiling with one half of his mouth. "Always somebody trying to starve you, isn't there?"

"It's rough treatment, certainly. But don't despair." Spitter gestured around the room with his mug. "You got to show these boys another country and eat all the baseball they could take. And they're good boys, good company. You found some wins in the end."

Coach looked out the window like he was trying to find a way to believe that. At three thirty, we all walked to the stadium, Clara and Sheridan to see if any Zaps wanted to practise curveballs and the rest of us to check whether the Red Wings had received the same letter.

Coach's contact for the Hamilton team was a young man who said he was the assistant general manager. He also seemed to handle the concessions as when we found him he was fixing a popcorn maker, turning it on its side and digging around under the trolley bed with a fork. He informed us that often the kernels got stuck.

We introduced ourselves and he said his name was Brian. Brian would be our guide as his boss, Mr. Cassels, and most of the rest of the non-playing staff, were off for the Lord's Day. The stadium was empty except for fifteen Red Wings running sprints from foul line to foul line and, in the distance, two or three Zaps throwing bullpen while Spitter watched and Clara wandered the outfield stands with her camera.

"You guys are from the merchandisers?"

"Baseball cards. We work with the Four Corners Card Company."

Mikey pulled out an example card while Coach spoke. Brian leaned in and squinted at it. "Have you ever heard of us?" Coach asked.

"Baseball cards? A little. I'm not a collector or anything. They come with gum, right?"

"Yes, sure. Gum or candy, or sometimes just by themselves. Have you heard of Four Corners?"

Brian shook his head. "You mean like a rectangle?"

"Sure."

He confessed that he wasn't really into baseball and that this was more of a job for him. His uncle owned the paper company that sponsored the team. His interests were in payroll and managing the concourse.

"I see. Well, did the GM tell you why we are here?"

"He did not."

"Okay." Coach cleared his throat and fiddled with his hands. "Well, we are agents. We're touring the Northern this week looking to meet with players and have them sign licensing contracts so that our company can use their images should they ever make the major leagues. Are contracts an interest of yours?"

Brian said yes so I pulled an agreement from the pile and handed it to him. He stood in the sunshine and read it to himself, pausing to nod approvingly every now and then. The contract was a hit where the card wasn't. I took a moment to imagine the life path of a man who liked contracts and payrolls but not baseball.

"Excellent," he said. "Are you affiliated with the Topps Chewing Gum people at all?"

Coach swallowed and said no. Brian asked us to sit tight and went over to his bag and pulled out the letter. He handed it to Coach.

"We received this on Thursday I think. Or maybe Friday. So the players have to pick which one they go with?"

"Well, no," Coach said, waving Brian away like he would a mosquito. "Topps isn't offering them anything right now. They're saying that should they get to the majors, they'd be interested in signing them then."

"And if they got there and had previously been signed by you, they wouldn't be interested anymore?" Brian had his thick freckled pointer finger out, scanning for the offending line.

Coach looked over the letter and made a face. "Is that what it says? Sorry, this is the first I'm seeing it. In either case, our agreements are non-exclusive, meaning that you can sign with another company as well as Four Corners."

"No, Coach." Mikey pulled on Coach's shirt from the side and it came untucked at the hip. I opened my mouth to stop him but he didn't see me. "Brian's saying that Topps's contracts are exclusive. You can't sign one if you already have the other."

Brian nodded, and I closed my eyes for a moment. Coach blew a gust of air out. Nobody spoke until Brian broke the tension with a clap of his hands.

"Well, we're in last place. How many of these guys are making the major leagues anyway? Let's call them over and give them the lay of the deal and see what happens. I'll get the coach."

Their field manager looked young for the role, maybe younger than Coach, and wore the same uniform and gear as his team. I suspected he was still playing or, if he wasn't, had just recently given it up. We watched him and Brian confer on the foul line and after a minute Brian waved us over and everyone shook hands.

The Red Wings clumped around us in a loose circle. Their uniforms were white with red trim that didn't look clean. There were memories of sliding stains on the shins and stomachs. Among the players, I saw more different kinds of faces than in the other clubs. More Black and Spanish-looking men. They chewed gum or tobacco and looked at us without appraisal or opinion, waiting for us to speak.

Coach walked forward holding out his arms but Brian stepped in front of him.

"Okay. These men are baseball card agents," the assistant general manager told his players, shuffling about in front of us and speaking quickly, his breath running out before his words did. "You can sign with them for five dollars and they'll use your faces for their baseball cards or you can wait until you're in more advanced leagues and sign for Topps Gum for two hundred. It's up to you. Basically sign now if you don't think you'll get that far. Anyway, their names are Leonard and, I'm not sure what these two children's names are. Kids, you got names?"

Mikey said his name but I was too busy pinching the bridge of my nose. I looked at Coach, who seemed about ready to tackle poor Brian to the dirt. He sniffed and shook his head and, when he took over talking, it was at about half the volume I was used to.

"Thanks, Brian. My name is Lawrence Miller and the company I represent is called Four Corners. Have any of you heard of Four Corners cards?"

None of the Red Wings answered him.

"It's no problem if you haven't. We're a newer outfit run by some good people from Utah, and we are touring the Northern this month looking for players to sign what's known as a non-exclusive licensing contract. What that means is, basically, we'd like to pay you cash today for the rights to put your faces on our cards should you one day make it to the big leagues. My assistant Christopher here has the contracts in hand. Chris?"

I stepped forward with agreements. The first Red Wing didn't move. I held it out for a second or two before giving up and leaving it on the grass by his cleats. I went around the group; some took their contract, others didn't. One man accepted his, scanned it over a moment, and handed it back.

"Now I understand that you are ballplayers, not lawyers. But don't worry because I'm not a lawyer either." Coach laughed in a way so dry and barren it might have been heard as sarcasm. "That contract is a half page long and clear as day. Take the five dollars, and if you get a better offer, mail it back to us at the address at the bottom."

"What's this about Topps?" a tall thin Red Wing asked from the back of the crowd.

"Well I don't work for Topps, friend," Coach explained. "So I can't say much for how they run their business. If they don't believe in non-exclusive contracts, that's fine by me. As I said, mail our five dollars back if you need to."

"But when Topps comes looking and we're listed with you, we're out two hundred bucks."

The Red Wings grunted as a team.

"Well." Coach started to squint as he smiled. "There are legal cases in front of the courts about all that right now, but I won't bother you with their details. In either case, this will only come up if you make it to the big leagues."

"You don't think we're going to the big leagues, Miller?" said a new voice. A stout young player in catching gear.

"I can't be sure," said Coach, trying on a crooked smile I know he thought was friendly. "But if I look around the country at how many jobs there are for major-leaguers, I'd find maybe one for every hundred talented young men playing in places like Hamilton."

Some of the Red Wings puffed out their chests and some of them rolled their shoulders and looked up into the sky. Imagine standing in this field in Canada in dirty pants on a Sunday if you didn't believe you might make it to the major leagues.

"I think you can keep your fiver and I'll take my chances," said the tall one. His neighbours nodded.

"Well, no one's forcing you to sign," Coach said, his voice thinning a little as he spoke. "Especially not today. Take it home if you like. And about our contracts: they live in our vault in Utah and aren't shared with others. Topps has no way of knowing who did or didn't sign one."

"Won't they know when your cards come out?"

"Ah! The cards." Coach grabbed Mikey by the elbow and hurried him into the centre of the crowd. "My young associate—isn't he cute?—should show you our cards. They're all full-sized and capture dynamic moments on the major league field."

Mikey held out a card and the catcher took it and looked it over. "Who the fuck is Jim Waugh?" he asked.

Coach explained that Jim Waugh played for Pittsburgh and was a promising young starting pitcher. The catcher said he had never heard of him before or seen a card of his.

"That's right!" Coach came back breathlessly. "Jim is among the big-leaguers who can only be found on Four Corners cards! We're very proud to have him."

I saw where this was going before Coach did, but I didn't know how to stop it. Above us and several hundred feet away in the left field grandstand, Clara turned her camera on the meeting. Had she snapped the picture, and had I asked her to print the negative, I wondered if the image would tell the story of the meeting. Could you see it, from that distance, the wall up ahead?

"He doesn't have a Topps card?" the catcher asked.

"Nosir. But again, his contract is non-exclusive, so we'll allow him to if he wishes."

"But does Topps wish? I've never heard of a major-leaguer not having a Topps card. Did your boy get blacklisted like Brian said?"

Coach opened his mouth to keep pitching, held it there for two endless seconds while a few of the Red Wings started to laugh, and then closed it. The catcher gave Mikey back our Waugh and patted him playfully on the head. In the distance, Clara had moved on to shoot the city.

"Alright, men," said the field manager, stepping between us and the team, "I feel these gentlemen have said their piece. They'll be available for the next little while for questions and to receive signed papers. Take five and we'll set up defensively first."

The Red Wings dispersed. Two of them who had taken contracts came back to politely return them. I picked several more off the turf.

For a while no one approached us until the field manager wandered over and asked for a contract.

"Sure," I said. "For who?"

He chuckled. "For myself, junior."

I looked over at Coach and his mouth tightened. "Are you still playing, Coach?" he asked.

"Sure am. I'm a relief pitcher and I back up the outfielders."

"I see. And how old are you?"

"Thirty-six. How old are you?"

"Thirty-six."

"Well, aren't we a pair?" The Red Wings manager had moved past me and was now faced off with Coach, looking up into his face with a mouth full of grey teeth. "Where'd you'd serve?" he asked.

"First Marines, Seventh Regiment. You?"

"Canadian Grenadiers. Fourth Armoured Brigade."

"Well." Coach cleared his throat. "I'm afraid I don't know that outfit."

"It was a big war, Marine. Are you gonna give a fellow soldier five dollars or what?"

Coach scratched his forehead while he thought this over and eventually signalled to me to hand him a contract. I did and Coach wandered over to the dugout to sit down while I watched the soldier sign.

Ten minutes later, while the starters were drilling defence, another backup slinked shyly by to submit his paper. And that was it. Two measly contracts: one for a thirty-something lifer and one for a bench piece. Pathetic.

We went and found the car and drove back in silence. When we got to the motel Coach left to call Utah and Mikey and I read his Bible stories to each other. Coach was gone a long time, and when he came back his tie was loose and his top button undone and his face was red like he had been yelling. Mikey watched him with interest as he crossed the room and sat down on his bed.

"Can we go eat?" he asked him. "I'm starved."

Coach gave a short hot sound that might have been a laugh. He tossed his hat at the bed. "You two are really looking for a night out after a performance like that? You were awful. We all were."

Neither of us said anything. I could see Mikey's hand crumple the page we were reading as he stared back at Coach.

"I had the rare luck of getting through to Anna Forbush on the Lord's day. She said that letter is in every league on the continent. Lawyers are on it but who knows how long that'll take. We're to try our best, but if we can't get at least sixty signatures league-wide they'll close up shop on the Northern and the like and wait until the matter is settled. Which means of course that I'm out of a job."

He leaned forward and held his chin in his hands.

"But sixty's only twenty more," I said. "Ten from each club. We're still on track."

Coach shook his head. "You don't understand, Chris. That letter is arsenic. Once Erie and London see it, it's done. It'll be like here or worse. We'd be lucky to scratch out another half-dozen broke veterans. We need to go and get the car anyway, but this is it. We're on our way home for good tomorrow."

Mikey looked from Coach to me, his nostrils flared. I put my hand on his shoulder. We listened to each other's breathing as Coach stared at the wall for what felt like an hour, though the wall clock disagreed.

"I'm not hungry, fellas," he said after the moment passed, rubbing at the skin under his eyes with both hands. "Go grab a sandwich at the restaurant and then call your mother. We need to get a good night's sleep. Last night wasn't adequate for anybody."

Mikey and I got sandwiches and ate at a two-seater. He asked me if I thought we'd see the London game tomorrow and I said probably but not for sure. He asked what Coach might do for a job if the baseball cards dried up.

"He's still got the sports store, and the schools pay him to coach. He doesn't need the money."

"He told me he did," Mikey said, mouth full of egg sandwich. "Said he's got tons of expenses."

"I heard. But what expenses?"

Mikey shrugged and swallowed his sandwich with a swig of milk. I wondered about bringing Coach back something for dinner, but I didn't want to be scolded for spending money if he really wasn't hungry.

Later in the meal, just to break the boredom of the adult faces and my chicken club, which didn't even have mayonnaise, I asked Mikey more questions about Coach.

"Why were you so sure he wasn't your dad when he told you?"

"I dunno," he said. "I just knew it."

"But how?"

He put his sandwich down and looked thoughtfully at the table. "If you forgot what Mamma looked like and then she showed up in a crowd of people, do you think you'd know it was her when she introduced herself to you?"

"Suppose?"

"Well"—he scooped up some egg salad with his finger—"it was the opposite of that."

I asked him if he was mad at me for bringing Reg Law back into our lives, and he said no. I had to ask Mikey about our important things all at once because he ate so quickly and it was our only time alone. It felt like I was giving him a quiz.

We paid for the sandwiches and I ran back to leave a nickel tip. Walking through the restaurant, we swung our arms like we lived there. A pretty girl who looked like she might've been old enough for college was using the phone so we waited for her to finish talking to her boyfriend. She looked back at me once or twice and I tried a cool smile, which I thought she noticed and appreciated. When she was done I asked Mikey whether he wanted first or second. He said first, so he could go shower right after. They talked for five minutes about Hamilton and the church service, and Mikey didn't let slip about Coach and me or about my night out of the motel. I was grateful, although knowing Mikey there was half a chance he'd just forgotten. When they said goodnight, Mikey told her that he missed her much more than he thought he would, and that it was hard for him to sleep at night.

She was coughing when I picked up the phone.

"You alright, Mamma?" I asked. Mikey was already out the door and zigzagging between parked cars on his way back to the room by the time she caught her breath and got a sip of water. I wondered if Coach had it in him to scold me again for not staying by his side.

"Yes, dear. Just some tea down the wrong trench. One of the ladies in recruitment brought it by Friday, some fancy Indian brand. Not Native, like India-Indian. It tastes like charcoal but it's apparently good for digestion."

"I had a chicken club for dinner just now."

"The proper choice!" Mamma chirped. She always ordered the chicken club sandwich if she saw it on the menu at a new restaurant. This was because so many places made them that it created a standard test of quality, she said, a way for a restaurant to prove itself against the competition on a fair field where everyone had the same task. Then, if you liked the sandwich, the chicken was cooked properly and there wasn't too much condiment, you'd go back and order their speciality.

I wasn't likely to ever come back to the motel restaurant, or Hamilton, or who knows probably even Canada, so the trial was all for naught, but I still did it so I'd be able to report home.

"It wasn't very good. I don't think they use mayo. Dry."

She clucked. "Well, now you know what not to do, don't you?"

I asked what she got up to today. She went to church by herself and Father inquired where we were. He was very impressed to learn we were travelling abroad. Nobody at church knew much about baseball except, secretly, the music leader, who was trained in Europe and spoke with a thick Dutch accent but who rooted for the Yankees, having made his way to Minnesota via New York after the war.

"How are you three holding up?"

"Good I guess. I told you we got off-course, so we're doubling back tomorrow to do London."

"Say hi to the new queen for me."

I smiled, which I knew she couldn't hear, but suspected she detected it in my voice when I told her that it was not the same London, though it apparently sat on a river called the Thames.

"How's Coach holding up?"

I said he was fine too, but then went on to tell a version of the Topps letter story, and how poorly we had done with the Red Wings, and how Coach felt that this might be the end of his job with Four Corners, so in the end not very fine at all.

"That poor man. He tries so hard and puts himself out there. You be grateful, okay? Say your biggest thank yous and don't let him spend too much money."

There was quiet on the phone line for a moment while I thought about these demands.

"How are you sleeping, Chris? Miss your bed?"

"Last night was a rough one," I told her. "Nightmares."

"Nightmares? That sounds like your brother, not you. What about?"

I turned away from the phone booth and looked out into the hallway. It was painted a soft yellow that was likely meant to soothe but looked too much like pee to do so. There were no footsteps because the guests made it to their rooms via the outdoors. Just a little alcove and, somewhere to my right, the clerk scratching in his notebook. I wetted my lips and thought about my nightmare.

"Fire," I told her. "I remember sitting in the back of a car—not our car or the Hornet, it was a different car. A red car. There was a man and a woman in the front, and the man had some sort of fire-holder. I couldn't tell what it was made of, like bone maybe? Like those bowls made of bone we saw at the museum. Remember? Those.

"Anyway, the man was just pouring the fire from the bowl onto the dashboard, the foot rest, and onto the lap of the woman. She was in the driver's seat. And nobody was screaming or upset, and I don't think she was in any pain or anything. I was the only one who told him to stop. He didn't listen so the car just filled up with this fire, which started like a liquid, like the lava from a volcano. But eventually it turned into flames. Like campfire.

"And I tried to get out of the car but I couldn't. The handles were covered in the fire. And I remember calling for you, and for Mikey, but I was all alone and I couldn't stop it."

Mamma was breathing into the phone receiver. "And then what happened?"

"I don't know. I woke up, I guess."

She told me that the men in the psychology department would say that fire meant anger, and getting burned alive in a dream meant you were overwhelmed by your anger. She asked if I felt anger.

"Everyone feels anger, Mamma."

"Do you feel more lately?"

I thought about it. "Yes?"

"Well." She paused to drink a bit more of her charcoal. I could pick up the sound of her swallowing. "In a lot of ways, that's part of growing up. Both because growing up is confusing—it comes with all those changes inside your body we talked about, and those can make you angrier. But also, the older you get, the more you notice people, and some of those people make bad choices or are unkind, or they don't act with God in their hearts. And that'll make you angry because you were raised right. And you know what? Good. It's correct to be angry sometimes."

The clerk next door closed his ledger book with a bang that wasn't all that loud, but it still made me jump a little. "Mamma," I asked her, "how long have you known Coach?"

"Coach Miller?" There was a ripple of worry in her voice. "Why'd you ask?"

"I don't know, just curious."

"Well." She sighed a bit and paused, or thought it over, or in any case took a second before speaking. "Just after the war, I guess. He was a friend of your daddy's like you know. That's a good man, Christopher, and I mean it. He came back to help his friend who needed help, and then he stuck around to help me and help you and Mikey. There are nuns and priests out in Africa who haven't given that much of themselves to the service of others. It's important that you be grateful, especially when he's down. Understand?"

"I will, Mamma." The payphone cord didn't have that corkscrew style—it was just a long stiff rope—but I still tried to wind my finger around it. It didn't bend enough. "Did he come right after the war?"

"Pretty close to, I think."

"You should bake him a cake. Every year on the day he moved to town, like it's his birthday, to commemorate."

Mamma laughed. "That's a good idea. Maybe you should bake it though. I've told you ten times we should make sure you know how."

"Do you remember what day he moved in? I'll practise."

She was still laughing a little. "Let me think. So they got discharged early that summer. Daddy was in the hospital first. Late summer, early fall maybe? And then Lawrence the year after?"

"1946?"

"Don't recall. To be honest, that whole time is a blur. I can barely remember that stretch after your father came home to us. It was difficult. Days felt like months, but weeks felt like days"

I could tell she had stopped laughing.

"I'm sorry I made you remember this, Mamma."

She sighed. It wasn't a sigh of exasperation, or even sadness. She was thinking back on her life and wondering how long ago it was and not being able to remember. Which is a way of being lost, like you're walking through a strange town at night, except the town is the life you used to live, and it only looks strange because it's been so long since you've lived there.

"It's alright, Chris. It's still a fun idea. Maybe I'll ask Lawrence to go through his papers and see if he can figure it out."

"I love you, Mamma," I whispered.

I don't know when it started, or how it happened. And frankly I was surprised, given how closely I had been paying attention to the sensations of my own body, but I was crying. Not just wet around the eyes, but fully crying. I first noticed it when a tear trailed down my cheeks to tickle my chin. I sucked in air.

If she noticed, she didn't seem fazed by it. "I love you too. Please tell your coach to keep his head up, from me, alright?"

"Okay," I said and hung up. There were no human sounds in the hall. Somewhere far away a car squealed its tires. I wrapped my arms around my shoulders and squeezed as hard as I could, then felt myself sinking, back to the wall of the phone booth, until I was sitting on the ground with my knees tucked in and my head at rest between them. I stayed like that and nobody came for me or came to use the phone. Every few minutes, I looked up to make sure the booth door hadn't closed, that I wasn't locked in, that I could stand up and walk away when I needed.

London,
Monday, July 14th, 1952

	W	L
Buffalo Bisons	42	24
London Maple Leafs	37	27
Akron Zaps	36	27
Erie Sailors	29	36
Windsor Clippers	28	37
Hamilton Red Wings	22	43

Last Night's Game
Bisons 6, Clippers 1

ON THE DAY OF MY MISTAKE, WE LEFT HAMILTON BEFORE breakfast and were well on the road as folks were just starting their weeks. Coach had a schedule. First we'd get the Hornet and return the Buick, then he had a meeting lined up with Mr. Leahy, the gentleman who had messaged the motel. We wouldn't have time to tie our shoes until after lunch, and then Coach hoped to get both teams done before tonight's game and back on the road to America tomorrow. For better or worse, the end of the trip was oncoming.

We stopped for coffee and gas and Coach had me get a paper to check the game time. It listed Sailors versus Maple Leafs for seven p.m. Given the Sunday blackouts in Ontario, there had been only one game last night, a win for the Bisons at home over the Clippers. I was surprised to see Reg Law got back in time to play and that they let him on the field, at least for most of the game, before the box score said he was subbed out in the sixth. There was no write-up to explain why but I pictured Simmonette finding out mid-game and storming the dugout.

"Who's this Leahy guy, Coach?" Mikey asked, as the city started to assemble around us. It was wealthier and older-looking than either stop so far. Even the factories looked fancier and more robust. I noticed fewer hotels but guessed Coach had found something reasonable somewhere. We saw buildings making beer and buildings making maple syrup and then an endless run of big smoke-stacked buildings making something or other without the explanation of a sign. Downtown, we saw a long brick wall that looked like the side of a prison or even a castle. And sure enough, a River Thames, which forked in the city's middle.

Coach had his hand out the Buick window like he did when driving his own car, though we were sitting far higher up now so the feeling this imparted of a man floating downriver with his fingers in the current was gone.

"He's just a businessman. Said he had an opportunity for me, and now that I'm in the practice of seeking opportunities after this one ends, I said I'd visit him at his shop."

"What's his business?"

"Cardboard," Coach said. "More cardboard."

Mikey asked him what London was like and Coach said it was a fine place. Not as friendly as the border towns, but cleaner and more comfortable. He knew a place that served hamburgers we might like, if we had time before the game for proper food. He seemed at ease, if glumly so, resigned to his new reality and willing to make the most of it. He also still seemed like he was trying to make up for himself, to me and to Mikey, by being kind and presupposing kindness in others, as a way of restitution. When I recognized this, I felt a rush of something akin to victory.

The factory where Mr. Leahy worked was one of the more anonymous ones. It had a single white brick wall and three others that were flat and red like rusty old iron, even though they couldn't be iron; it would be too heavy. It was three floors big. There was a loading door on one end and a small entryway on the other, over which a sign read "O-Pee-Chee" in script like handwriting, which might've been a word in a language I had never seen. So if not exactly anonymous like certain of its neighbours, at least reticent about declaring itself in English.

Coach led us through the small door. There was a wooden receptionist's desk with no receptionist, a lobby area with loungers and magazines, and a man standing in the middle. He had been waiting for us, his feet shoulder-width apart and his hands on his hips like a comic book hero whose power was being perfectly average-looking. The man had nothing to remember him by: medium build and height, no moustache or beard; not fat or skinny. The only thing I noticed were his eyes, which were always squinting like he had been looking, with a great intensity of purpose, into the sun.

"Mr. Miller," said Leahy, "welcome to London. I hope you found us easily enough." He shook hands and asked us to follow him through two sets of doors into a big open factory full of presses and mixers. The smell in the air was sweet like bubble gum. Low-hanging lights swung above us and about twenty men were fussing about, carrying everything from bags of popcorn kernels to wheelbarrows full of sugar to flats of cardboard. I guessed the factory floor was two storeys, which meant there was a third somewhere overhead.

It was loud but Leahy, who asked us to call him Frank, was used to speaking over it. He pointed out all the machines. There were men making what he called Krackley Nut, which I understood to be a kind of caramel corn and was immediately interested in trying. When a woman came by holding a clipboard, Frank asked her to fetch samples. Most of the floor was given over to gum. Frank said they had the most modern gum production in the world here, that they could fill their factory to the rafters every week. I didn't see anything that a person couldn't eat, and the smells were entirely confection. Coach kept nodding in a way that I guessed meant he was impressed but didn't understand why we were getting this lesson in candy production. Eventually, Frank ended his spiel and had us follow him upstairs.

The top floor was quieter, though you still picked up the whirring and banging from the factory floor below. There were drafting tables where artists were putting together ads and packaging, and offices on the side with telephones and desks. It served as welcome notice that not all adult jobs were dull and abstract. Some kids grew up to sell candy.

The floor had two boardrooms, a large one with leather chairs and drink service and a smaller one with a square white table around which we sat in plain wooden seats like the ones they had at school. The clipboard woman came in with a tray full of samples and what I assumed was coffee for Coach and Frank. She served it out of a round kettle painted red to look like a giant gumball.

"It's an impressive outfit, Frank," Coach told him, pulling his chair in. "You've built quite the place here."

Frank waved him away with his hand. "Oh, I'm just an employee. Vice president. All the owners have been McDermids. First John and his brother Duncan and now John Jr. They're the builders here."

"What does O-Pee-Chee mean, Mr. Leahy?" Mikey squeaked out around handfuls of Krackley Nut.

Frank winked and reached for the far wall, taking down a framed broadside decorated with a watercolour robin that had been resting on top of a bookshelf alongside a certificate of thanks from the local little league team. On it was a snippet of a poem, which read:

> He it was who sent the wood-birds,
> Sent the robin, the Opechee,
> Sent the Shawshaw, sent the swallow,
> Sent the wild-goose, Wawa, northward,
> Sent the melons and tobacco,
> And the grapes in purple clusters.

"It's spelled differently," Mikey observed, and Frank made a happy little grunt of recognition.

"Good eye, son. I believe the McDermids thought it might be confusing to say out loud without the hyphens or the extra *E*. They were smart about that stuff."

"How's your card business?" Coach asked him, and Frank rapped his fingers on the table.

"Thanks, Lawrence. Obviously that's why I called you. Your people are in quite the battle down there with Topps and Bowman. I'd ask how it's going, but I don't want to put you on the spot."

Coach pulled his shirt front down and straightened his tie. Frank got a few cards out of a drawer, all of them mounted on wooden backboards, and slid them across the table. We each grabbed one. Mine was Buddy Myer, a second baseman with a big wide nose. I had never heard of him before, though I could tell he played for Washington from the *W* on his hat.

Mikey's was Charlie Gehringer, and I couldn't see Coach's though he was impressed enough he let out a small low whistle.

"When are these from?" I asked.

"Why, son, these are our very latest set!" Frank said. "From nineteen hundred and thirty seven."

Coach had a dreamy look like he was deep in pleasant, important thoughts. He turned his card around. It was a Joe DiMaggio.

Or, as O-Pee-Chee had printed it, Joe De Maggio. They should have called him Joe-Dee-Maggio.

"So not exactly a going concern anymore." Coach laughed.

Frank shared a lopsided smile, which I understood to be a self-effacing one. "Not currently, no. But as you can imagine from my inviting you here, I'm eager to get back in the business."

"Haven't you done any research, Frank?" Coach leaned back in his chair and rested his hands on the table. "Baseball cards are a two-horse race, and all the other horses get shot."

"In America they seem to, but we have reason to believe things are different on this side of the lake."

Coach didn't quite sit up straight but did pause, like he had been gearing up to give a lecture but now wanted to hear the other side first. He arched his eyebrows to urge Frank on.

"We've done sets since these old die cuts. Hockey and football mostly, then some military stuff right before the war. Heck, we'll do whatever a paying customer asks. We once took a contract to make wax candles in the old candy machines. During the war, when sugar shipments dried up, do you know what we made? Dried eggs. That powder you mix with water to make scrambled eggs at the front."

"You bastards," Coach said, and both men lost themselves to laughter for a moment.

"Every year I take the train down to Brooklyn and I sign up for the tour at the Topps facility and I scan the machines for signs they're doing something different. They got into bubble gum, then we got into bubble gum. We train for quick reflexes when it comes to following the leader. Do you know what I see now when I go there?"

"What's that?"

"Nothing. The same machines, the same designs. Heck, go look at last year's set: half of them are the same photographs. There are rumours they're going to fill the card backs with statistics next because they think what kids really love is math, but I haven't seen the proofs. And they aren't protected by divine right to sell baseball cards. Not in Canada they're not."

"That sounds swell for you, Frank, but how many kids in Canada collect ball cards?"

Frank shrugged. "Quite a few, though I understand your point that it's a smaller market. But unlike everyone else who started from scratch since the war, it means that we can build a battle chest out here first while we wait for American courts to put the world right with the card market. Once the feds call antitrust on Topps in two or three years, who would you rather be? The guy with a small clutch of gold, a world-class factory, and distribution to wherever you want to go? Or the guy digging out after his third bankruptcy and passing the hat at church to raise cardboard money?"

Coach seemed to think this over. I hoped he would ask the question I wanted to hear, and eventually he got around to doing so.

"Breaking the monopoly is fine, but what about licensing fees? I don't think Topps is any less likely to outbid you because you're only selling in Canada."

"That's just it, Lawrence. As far as our lawyers understand, we don't need player licences at all to sell cards up here. It's an invented market, and we can just ignore it."

That idea hung thick enough in the room that it got Mikey's attention too. It was like he was telling us that water wasn't wet once you crossed into Canada. I looked at Coach and for the quickest second, he slid his eyes over to meet mine.

"If you don't need licences, Frank, then why'd you call on a licences man?"

"I didn't," Frank said. "I called a salesman."

"Well, what am I selling?"

"Real estate."

"Where?"

"Grocery stores. Sometimes drug marts."

Frank explained that he wanted his relaunched line of baseball cards to show up in the snack aisles of supermarkets. He wanted them for sale next to candy bars at the checkout. He wanted them at the eyeball height of the average twelve-year-old boy; he even made me stand up to illustrate, though I told him I was tall for my age.

"You want me to relocate to come be your employee?"

"I thought you might want to be a partner in the new division. I sent a man down to your store in Minnesota: you're doing well there, you could get a meaningful cheque for it. Then sure, London's a nice place." Frank gestured to Mikey and me. "Bring the family and move here. I'd give you equity."

I felt the hairs on my arms stand up, and my face flushed hot. I didn't look at Mikey. Coach shifted into a more comfortable position. He had his chin in his hand and was studying the DiMaggio.

"You're not really in a position to take on partners as VP, are you, Frank?"

"No," Frank admitted. "You're right. But John Jr. isn't well and the board told me I'm next up. So we can hold the door open for that part. Then who knows. Either we'll be big enough to fight Topps or we'll be big enough to join them, and either way, you'll be a rich man, I'll be a richer man. This is a good town for rich men. I've a spot at the club here, just full of men like you who made one good decision and the rest was wind at their backs. So think it over, at least. Call on me when you've had the chance."

Frank loaded us up with gum and popcorn and more baseball cards from before I was born, though no more DiMaggios. Mikey and I said effusive thanks and Coach, silent while the presents were being given out, shook Frank's hand and bid him the best of luck. He had a lot to think on.

We switched the Buick for the Hornet, which no longer smelled of gas and instead smelled of the cologne the mechanic wore. I don't know what it cost, but it was enough to redden Coach's face when he found out. He shoved the receipt in the glovebox without telling us any details and we backed out of the garage at a keen pace. On the road, we drove past three interesting hotels, one of which had four floors and a spotlit sign, before landing at our old reliable by the highway, another flat C. This one, like in Windsor, with a central hallway and no parking lot access to the rooms.

Coach's hamburger place made for lunch. It was a round room with pictures of local heroes on the wall and a stink like a damp dog. The regulars all worked at the Labatt Brewery, which was the largest in Canada and hung its names on public buildings throughout the city like a malted Carnegie. The baseball park was Labatt, and according to an ad for it posted near the men's room, it still claimed to be the oldest ballpark in the world, just as Coach had told us. I looked at the picture. The grandstands were low-rising, and it wasn't particularly big, but the front was dour and imposing, with a religious seriousness. They had recently painted everything blue.

"What time are our meetings?" I asked Coach.

"I booked the Sailors first for three p.m.; we'll get them before they're fully set up, I guess. And then the Leafs said to meet at four but at the visitors' clubhouse, so I suspect that's an error. Hopefully it doesn't mean the time is wrong too. We'll know more when we get there. Contact for Erie is a Mr. Malcolm, who

I think is the GM. London doesn't have a name, but we can ask for leadership when we get there."

"The owner is the commissioner."

"I've been told as much, but suspect we'll end up with another assistant or a field hand. Commissioners are hard to push yourself in front of."

"Mamma said to keep your chin up," I told him.

He salted his French fries and looked at me. "Yeah? What'd you tell her?"

"Just that Hamilton went poorly."

"That it?"

"I told her about the Topps letter too." I took an oversized bite of my hamburger and Coach stopped asking me questions while I chewed. Mikey wasn't hungry. He'd eaten a lifetime's worth of caramel corn on the drive over and complained that his stomach hurt.

"What did you think of Mr. Leahy's factory, Coach?" he asked him while I worked on swallowing.

Coach opened his eyes a little wider and used his French fry to point at the space in front of him. "Who knows, boys. The world's full of ambitious men waiting for the sky to open up above them. Maybe it'll rain or maybe not."

"Are you interested in his job?" Mikey's voice went a little soft as he asked, and I didn't believe it was from the stomach ache.

"No," Coach assured him. "I don't think so. I'm flattered he'd want to look into me, but I can't move to Canada. I don't know anybody, and to be honest it's too far away from you."

Mikey grinned at him, and I may have made a noise.

"And Chris, and everything else," Coach added, pointing at me with a second fry.

The park was charming up close. It stood exactly in the fork where the Canadian Thames broke into its northern and southern selves. All along the river on either side were walking paths and trees. The core of downtown was across the river, and looking out from the grandstand you'd see factories, office buildings, and people going about their days as unaware of you as you might be of folks in another country.

We saw all this on our approach over the bridge from downtown. The lighting rigs stood high like eagles' perches on top of thin white poles, and as we came off the bridge and around to the front of the building, there were advertisements for the team bearing players' faces everywhere. We parked across the street and walked up to the ticketing window.

There was nobody there, so we stalked along the front of the building to the central entrance, and that was closed too. There was some fencing at the far end and a sign that read "Caution" like there had been a car accident or a break-in and the police were still investigating. The stadium was open at the edges like Windsor so Mikey had the idea to run ahead and see if he could get the attention of someone on the field, only to report back that there was no one there either. The field looked empty. I checked my watch. We were a little early at two thirty, but not so much that the place should be deserted. We sat on the curb and waited for a sign of life.

After exactly sixteen minutes, Coach asked me to run back to the car and get the newspaper. I found it folded up on the front seat. The picture on the front page, which I hadn't looked at when I bought it, was of the new queen, whose face was absolutely everywhere in Canada. It had been taken from overhead, looking down at her as she greeted guests at a garden party. Dressed all in white including gloves and purse, she had a similar hat to Clara's, pressed tight over her head like a second scalp. Not red though.

When people said she was pretty, they said it as if they were implying she was pretty for a monarch, but I thought she was beautiful for anybody. I rubbed my thumb over her face and thought about her skin for long enough that the Canadians would've probably found it disrespectful had they caught me, then hurried back across the street with the paper.

Coach put Elizabeth on the sidewalk and leafed through the sports section. He read a little, blinked, and then flipped to another page. He put the paper down, dropped his shoulders to a deep slouch, and covered his face in his hands.

"What's wrong, Coach?" Mikey asked. I felt my heart rise in my throat as Coach shook his head real slow and mumbled something sour under his breath.

He passed his hand down his face and gave an expression like when he ate the mouldy bread back in Windsor. "Okay," he said after a minute. "Chris, I understand this hasn't been a fully pleasant trip for you, and that I gave you a lot of responsibility, and we haven't been paying attention to the news since we left so it's easy to miss things. I want you to know; I promise I'm not mad."

"What?" I mouthed, not quite getting the sound out.

"This stadium had a fire last month. Not a bad one, but they're closed for repairs. The game's in Erie. That's why the team said to meet them at the visitors' clubhouse. They're on the other side of the lake."

I didn't say anything. He had his eyes closed, like he was giving all his energy to maintaining calm, performing calm. Mikey asked if Erie was far from London. It was.

"But the guidebook from the league said the game was here," I said, quietly, trying to form an argument that would change the facts of the situation.

"Chris, look," Coach said, a little snappier. He was pointing to the part of the building with the tape. "See that down there? That's cordoned off by the fire department. Do you see people getting ready to play baseball here? I don't. Mikey, do you see any baseball players?"

Mikey got up and looked around and said no. Coach stood, gathered the paper in his hands, walked five paces away, and screamed. First just noise and then a stream of sacrilege and swearing that made Mikey cover his ears. The skin on my head began to itch. I braced against the stadium wall as Coach bent over and whacked at the ground with the rolled-up newspaper. It made a sound like a ball hitting a glove. Then, he reared back and threw the paper into the street. The wind caught it and fluttered it open, pages spreading loosely in the middle of the road. Elizabeth and her party somewhere in its wings.

We stayed there long enough that a teenaged boy and a small black dog passed us, did whatever business they had in the park, and returned the way they came. I was saying "I'm sorry" but not loud enough for Coach to notice. Mikey said it was okay, it was just a mistake. I was thinking back to the side of the highway and wondering if it wasn't Coach, not me, who suggested today for London. But saying so felt like a provocation.

Eventually, Coach walked back to us, looked me right in the eye, pointed, and shouted "Fuck!" and then "You!" as two sharp staccato notes, precise, fully felt and from maybe two feet away, then crossed the street to the Hornet where I briefly imagined him driving home without us, but he didn't. He sat in the car with his head against the wheel and cried.

Mikey wanted to follow him to help but I convinced him to wait. At three o'clock, the side door to the stadium opened, proving itself not fully abandoned after all. A woman appeared. She was tall, as tall as Coach in her heels, and might have been in her sixties. She was well-dressed in a puffy red blouse and black pants, and her hair was primped and curled ten different ways. She had diamond earrings and more stones on her neck and fingers. She wasn't looking for us but noticed Mikey and me sitting on the street, and as this was a nice part of a nice town, kids on the street must have been unusual enough to get her attention. She called out and asked if we were alright. I looked to Coach, who didn't seem to have noticed her.

"We're fine, ma'am, thank you," I said.

She took two more steps towards us. "Where's that accent from?"

"Minnesota, ma'am."

That got her all the way interested. She smiled and walked towards us, the swaying walk of a woman who had looked good for her age at every age. She had white gloves on, like Queen Elizabeth, and took them off as she approached us.

"Whereabouts?"

It was unusual to tell a stranger your address, but my sense of the unusual had been fogged by recent events so I told her. She said she was from St. Paul originally, had moved to Canada when she met her husband. She could pull out the altered Os and Us that separated an American Great Lakes accent from its Canadian cousins like a sommelier sniffing cork. I didn't know what a sommelier was.

She asked us our names and said hers was Marthanne. Coach still hadn't stirred from the car so I asked her how long she'd been in Canada and she said since she was twenty. Everything Mikey or I said seemed to make her giggle.

"What are you two doing this far away?"

We told her we were baseball card agents, what Four Corners was, and how the trip worked. She giggled again and said it seemed like a big job for men our age, so I pointed across the street and said our boss was having a nap. She lingered a little over the sight of Coach in the car then asked if we knew the team was out of town and I said yes, thank you, we'd actually just discovered that. She laughed again.

"The office is closing early for the day, but I don't live far away. If you want to rouse your boss, we can chat at the house. As long as you don't mind entertaining some grandkids while you're there."

"How do you mean, ma'am?"

And then Marthanne told us that her last name was Eccles, and not only did she own the London team, she was the commissioner of the whole league, and we could talk about baseball cards over tea.

The first challenge was convincing Coach that Marthanne Eccles was a real person, and not a fairy godmother we had invented to fix our problems, assembled as if by magic from our fear and guilt and panic. If she hadn't given us a business card, with her address penned elegantly on the back, we might not have brought him around.

After that, there was still the matter of his mood, and our moods, and the downward slope of the day. I apologized for missing the venue change, even though being made the trip's planner was a ceremonial kindness, the kind of thing that adults winked to each other about that made me feel like an infant, not at all like a budding young man. Now that it had gone off the rails it was suddenly a serious duty, and I had been delinquent in performing it.

Coach told us that he had just needed a moment to plan in the car, like it didn't have windows and Mikey and I, and probably Marthanne Eccles, hadn't seen him shaking his big fists about and shouting. I let this lie pass as a needed step towards the Hornet's engine being activated and us pulling out to follow Marthanne home.

"The team is in Erie," Coach complained once we hit the main street again. "What's chatting with the owner's wife over tea gonna fix?"

"She didn't mention a husband," I said. "She said she's the owner. Herself. And commissioner."

Coach said that rich women always did that, take their husbands' titles, even though Mikey piped up to agree that he thought she ran the team.

"But she can't forge their signatures," Coach argued. "Those boys are free men."

I agreed she probably couldn't but told him, without the backing of any specific legal idea, that she struck me as someone in control of her surroundings, and that speaking to her still felt like a strong use of time. At minimum, she'd make a good business contact and carried the benefit of being in town, unlike the Maple Leafs or Sailors. Erie was too far away to drive to, and after that catch-up game, the two clubs would go their separate ways. The trip was extending out in front of us whether we stopped to speak at Marthanne's house or we didn't.

I was briefly unsure after we started driving and the landscape grew grittier and more industrial, but all at once it lifted into gardens on the far western edge of the city. Marthanne had told us to go down Horton Street on the park side of the river and keep the water to our right, eventually. We found her street, which was hard to follow because the civic numbers were set so far back from the road behind copses of thick old trees or iron gates. We eventually found hers. It was a gorgeous Victorian mansion with a few extra additions stuck on like stacked blocks. The front yard had apple trees and a giant stately maple, plus a natural pool of water that must have been fed by the river, as the main trunk of the Thames, half a mile before the forks, ran along behind the house.

The house wasn't the only building. There was a converted barn, now with two rows of dormered windows and a snake of green ivy along the front, painted bright blue with a London Maple Leafs pennant hung over the entrance door. The grounds in between the two structures were full of sheds, the ruins of an old batting cage, and other loose bits of recreation: a picnic table, a child's bike.

"Okay," Coach said. "So this all feels very real. I'm sorry I thought it wasn't."

A man who identified himself as the household manager, which from his behaviour and politeness made me think meant a butler, had heard us drive up and was already out the main door of the house, waiting on an expansive patio covered by wood slats cut into a trestle pattern.

He called to me by name and asked if this was the rest of my party. I nodded and he invited us inside.

I had been in old houses before, and I had been in fancy houses, but the Eccles mansion was a new experience. Mamma's boss invited us over once a year for holidays in the new subdivision on the edge of town, and his place was fancy but not old. You could tell from how they used wood over brick and how the design prioritized big open spaces. Plus there would always be another house just like it going up somewhere further down the same street. I had likewise been in a lot of old houses that weren't fancy anymore; they had been given up to apartments and were rented by families of kids from school that Mamma wanted me to know were less fortunate than us in our bungalow, even though their Mammas worked secretarial jobs just like my Mamma did, their fathers were dead from the war like mine.

The Eccles mansion was what happened when fancy held on, and was updated every few years to changes in style or the string of personalities that made up a line of ownership. It was the product of family wealth that rooted and expanded. The Eccles family business was beer, which outside of a dry period during Prohibition when they switched to temperance ale and soda, was sound. Catholic Irish immigrants in a sea of continentals, just like us. They weren't as successful as the Labatts, a few neighbourhoods away and Anglican, but they were friendly with them and lived well just under their shadow. Even the baseball team, a family property since its founding, lived under a big bright Labatt's sign at the park for which they paid rent as a tenant. The Labatt cousins who could stomach baseball showed up for the odd Leafs game, sitting in reserved seats. But there was a scattering of Eccleses every day. Marthanne was a hands-on owner to the point of hosting unmarried players free of charge in the boarding house built out of the old barn. Aside from her, an average game might see her son or daughter-in-law sitting in the cheap seats with bottlers and delivery men, the grandkids running the bases during warm-ups. One of the Labatts got kidnapped and held for ransom back in the '30s, but the Eccles were common enough to run free.

We learned all this from the household manager, whose name was Mr. Pass, and whom both Mikey and I immediately called Passepartout in our heads, as he was quiet and neat and reminded us of the character in the books Mamma had read to us last winter.

Marthanne Eccles reappeared once we had settled in her drawing room on couches with ornate wooden legs. Mikey swung his feet and hit the legs with his heels until I put my hand on his knee to make him stop. When she came in, she was finishing off a conversation with someone, Passepartout maybe, from the adjoining room. They were talking about children, not us, and what they might want for dinner.

"Hiya!' She waved, tossing her curls around like a younger woman. She cracked her knuckles and reached out to shake our hands, going in the order we had sat on the couch: me, Mikey,

Coach, instead of starting with the adult and working down like I was used to.

Coach thanked her for the invitation and promised we wouldn't be long, going so far as to apologize in case we boys made her feel like she needed to bring us over. Marthanne looked benignly confused by all this until she stopped him.

"I understood you had business for me," she said, holding a palm up. "I'd like to go through it, but first let's wrangle up the kids and have tea."

Passepartout showed us the way to a dark dining room. There must have been seating for twenty, with two serving stations along one wall and a bookcase stacked to the ceiling with leather volumes on the opposite. Marthanne swung in after us and switched on a radio, turning the volume down until it registered as background noise. It was the play-by-play of a baseball game.

"Sorry," she called back to us, lowering her head to the speaker, "I've got this device to gather signals from the coast, and the Red Sox are staging a comeback."

"Are you a Red Sox fan?" Coach asked her.

She shrugged. It was another gesture that seemed strange on a woman of her age and good clothing, like she had changed bodies with a teenage shopgirl. Or maybe I was just more likely to tie a woman's gestures to her clothing than I was a man's. Mamma would have corrected me on this if she had known. "I'm a baseball fan, Mr. Miller. I collect unusual turns of luck. And the Sox were down seven-nothing halfway through the ninth. They've a shot at coming back on the Browns now."

Mikey asked her the score, and she said 7–3. This didn't quite seem like an unusual turn of luck was imminent. Marthanne Eccles didn't care; she said she had the Northern axe their mercy rule this season because that fingernail chance at the unusual made the blowouts worth enduring. When Mikey asked who was hitting she gave a conspiratorial, almost flirtatious, wink and said it was Dom DiMaggio. Joe's brother.

Passepartout brought in a plate of cookies which we lunged towards before remembering our manners and sitting on our hands. The tea came in the form of three big pots in proper English cozies. Marthanne was cuddling the radio when, all at once, excitement came from several directions. The Boston announcer sparked alive, declaring that DiMaggio's swing had found a fastball and was carrying it over the Green Monster to make it 7–5. At the other end of the room, the French doors flung open and three children rumbled in screaming and shoving. Marthanne reached towards us, cuffing Coach on the arm and asking if he saw that one coming. He shook his head to said he hadn't. The kids put six hands in the cookie pile and started to chomp away, crumbs and handprints corrupting the good wood table. I joined in.

Once the play-by-play quieted down, Marthanne took a seat at the head of the room and introduced us to everyone. Matty, five, and Elisabeth, seven, were her grandkids and the eldest, John, was her nephew's son. John was nine.

This was the first time Mikey had seen kids more or less his age since we'd left home, and he was struck shy by their arrival. He gave a small wave and then said no thank you when asked if he wanted a cookie. I took one and gave him half, while Coach took his tea with a drop of fresh milk.

"So," Marthanne said, smoothing her dress front and leaning a little to the side so she could still take in the radio narration. "Your boys said you got your days mixed up."

Coach smiled sadly and explained the situation without assigning me the blame. He asked about the fire, which Marthanne said was the fault of a contractor—someone sneaking a smoke break where he shouldn't. It should be cleaned up by the week's end.

"One benefit of tenancy is we don't need to foot the bill, though refunding those tickets did hurt," she explained.

Coach asked her how long she'd had the team, and she said since the new league was formed in '46. Before the war she and her late husband had an Intercounty club and before that a stake in the old London Tecumsehs. Her husband had passed that first season, a heart attack, and the team and league had been her primary concern ever since.

"They let whoever invests the most money chair the league, so it seemed wise to throw in a little extra for the gavel. Most of the rest of the gang is good enough to work with. Akron's a riot. Hamilton are fine people. We make do with Windsor."

We all said nice things about the league, Coach dipping into details from past tours in previous seasons. He complimented the parks and the experience of the game. Marthanne lost interest in this flattery as the play-by-play announcer told us that the Red Sox had grounded to second for their last out of the game. The unusual had not come to pass. She looked briefly devastated, before bringing hot tea to her lips for comfort.

Mikey had been slowly wooed by the brood of Eccleses, and the four young kids were taking turns telling jokes. Mikey's contribution was one I'd heard before: How do trains hear? They hear with their engine-ears. It went over mildly but the youngest child applauded and Mikey took another cookie to celebrate. Mamma would say that was too many, especially after the morning haul of candied corn.

Passepartout came in holding an envelope, which evidently Marthanne expected as she thanked him for finding it. It was, to no surprise, the dreaded Topps letter.

"I take it you've seen this?" she asked.

Coach frowned and nodded.

"What do you make of it?"

He sipped his tea while Passepartout crossed behind us to change the radio over to classical music. "Well, it's not a tactic we haven't seen before. Baseball cards are a duopoly, and the incumbents have always put pressure on upstarts like us. They want to use their position to bully new competitors away. We think they've overplayed their hand this time though. The letter has been sent to our litigators and will be evidence for the antitrust hearings kicking off this fall."

This was a pitch. Obviously Coach had called in to Utah and taken it down as dictation. It had the tone of something memorized, but Marthanne seemed impressed either way.

"You're right. I sure hate shit like this." She glanced at me when she swore but didn't apologize. "It runs so far against the spirit of independent baseball, and worse it uses our boys' own dreams against them."

She got up and whispered something to Passepartout, then stood behind Elisabeth, balancing a cup in the little girl's hair while she dipped a soggy cookie in her tea. "You know how many league titles we've had here since '46? Three. That's not bad. Last season we finished second and we'll likely do it again this year. You know how many ballplayers we've sent on to the major leagues, where they're likely to show up in baseball cards?"

Coach said he didn't know.

"A giant fucking zero." Elisabeth Eccles's eyes bugged out in shock or protest. There must've been someone in her life who told her that her grandmother swore too much and that she wasn't to encourage it. "None. I got one guy in Montreal, giant beautiful lug of a man, can hit it five hundred feet so long as it's a fastball at the belt. I'd say he's twenty percent to make it at this point, but that'd be a first. Your company's going to throw away, what, four hundred bucks this summer, hoping for just one lottery ticket? When these little card outfits started out, they went looking for major-leaguers and got chased to the minor leagues. Now they've been chased down here. And that's still not low enough? Spit! Those scaredy cats in Brooklyn think you're not going bankrupt fast enough talking to indie-leaguers in the Northern, they need to put their foot on your neck. It's not fucking American business, I tell you. It's a scandal. DOJ's going to eat their lunch and serve them their own shit for dinner."

Coach gazed at Marthanne Eccles with a devotion I've never seen him show before as he leaned back in the chair, hands folded in front, taking in the splendour of her argument.

"I really appreciate you saying that, Mrs. Eccles. It's about where we've been coming from this whole time."

Passepartout returned with a stack of papers, all gathered together by string in a loose package. They looked like they had been folded and unfolded many times, so when Marthanne untied them, they puffed up like a pile of leaves.

"I hold proxy for all the boys on the team," she said, and I didn't know what that meant but felt Coach did from how fast he sat up at attention. "Here."

She handed him the topmost sheet and I tried to read it myself until she noticed this and passed me the next one on the pile. It didn't help much, but I saw it was signed by Marthanne and initialed by someone named Dominguez who I guessed was a Maple Leaf.

"Marthanne, are you saying you can sign the licensing agreements yourself?" Coach asked.

She huffed out a noise that sounded like a yes. "They're just baseball players, Miller. Half the people who come knocking on our door are there to sell them magic beans or trick them into marrying their sister. One of the services I offer, as a more familiar owner than most, a habit from running a family firm, is business advisory, and that comes with decision-making over matters like this. If one of these boys shocks the world and figures out International League pitching or how to drop the hook in for a strike, great. Let your lawyers and Topps fight over what that means. In the interim, I'm slipping a shiny new five dollar bill in each of their tuck bags when they get home from the road next week."

Then she looked me directly in the eyes and told me to get out the contracts.

Not ten minutes later, with a stack of contracts signed "Marthanne Marilou Eccles (obo)" in our bag, we were let loose in the backyard while Marthanne and Coach talked about shared experiences: Minnesota, baseball, life on the road. I had been angling to stay with the adults until Marthanne took me by the shoulders and said she needed me to make sure that her grandnephew John didn't slug any of the little ones.

"He's a big bully. We're working on training it out of him, but it's hard because he's the oldest on his branch of the tree," she whispered.

"Yes, ma'am."

"If he gets out of line, just come tell me or Mr. Pass, alright?"

"Yes, ma'am."

She stepped back and surveyed me. "And if we're not around, you look reasonably intimidating for your age, so I'm going to need you to scare him."

"Yes, ma'am, I will."

"Good kid." She punched me very lightly in the chest and spun me towards the door. Likely she was letting me down easy by making me think I was needed in the land of children, but I didn't mind. I had earned my keep by finding her, or at least by being found by her.

The gardens behind the house were a mix of formal design and chaotic flourishes. A tricycle was parked in a rose bush. John Eccles had organized the kids into a line and was handing out baseball equipment, which they had in every size and colour, though more blue than anything else. Mikey pulled out a thick forty-inch bat that would have been too much for most of the Maple Leafs but managed to get it more or less swung around himself without toppling over. He switched to a little league standard and John settled in on a makeshift mound the kids had made out of sand harvested from the sandbox at the far end of the property.

I was volunteered to catch while the other two Eccles children took positions on either side of second base. John wound up and missed high, which Mikey took as an opportunity for a couple of warm-up swings. This trip was, ironically, the longest he had gone without swinging a bat all summer, and I saw his body relax with the practice. The second pitch was also high but Mikey chased and swung through it. John Eccles let out a little whoop and told Mikey not to worry; he was the captain of his ten-and-under team and the kids he pitched to there got private lessons from professionals. Mikey didn't seem worried.

The third pitch was outside, and the fourth, Mikey got a hold of like I imagined Dom DiMaggio got a hold of his, and it shot out over Elisabeth's head and, had there been an age-appropriate fence in right field, maybe a hundred feet away, it would have cleared that too, but instead it took a bounce and landed among the bushes separating the game from the Canadian Thames.

John didn't react, no compliment and no protest. Neither he nor his cousins thought to retrieve the ball; he just fished another one from the bucket by his feet and wound up again. This time

Mikey cleared it over the invisible wall past Matty in what would have been centre field.

"Alright, give someone else a turn already," John shouted, and Elisabeth trotted in. She adopted a restful stance with the bat sitting on her back shoulder and let four or five strikes go by. John teased that she wasn't going to impress the new boys that way so she leaned into the next ball, a soft curve, and poked it just over her cousin's head. Her younger brother got an athletic jump on it and, as she took off for first, Mikey fell back to receive the throw. Matty's throw was offline and Mikey had to catch it off the bag and try to swipe a tag, which he did, hard, on the back of Elisabeth's head.

"Ouch!" she complained, holding the spot where the glove had clapped her, more angry than hurt. She pushed Mikey with her free hand as he tried to apologize.

"Lovers' quarrel!" John chirped as she walked back to home plate to take a second at bat.

This time she was less patient and swung on the first pitch, which was a good six inches outside. It clunked off the end of the bat and bounced down the first baseline. I was worried it was going to be my responsibility before Mikey came charging in calling me off and fielding the ball comfortably in front of Elisabeth. This time he had plenty of room to plant a professional tag so it was all the more shocking when he let her squeak by him just enough to spin and slap her on the backside so loud it moved birds from their branches overhead.

Elisabeth let out a high yelp and grabbed her butt, slowing to a walk and then slumping onto both knees. She bit her lip and tears began to fall.

I didn't help things by letting free a disappointed "Mikey," but by then John Eccles had thrown his mitt on the ground and ran over to confront my brother.

"The hell are you doing to my cousin, hayseed?" he shouted, which I thought was questionable as Ontario wasn't really any less "hayseed" than Minnesota. He stuck a finger under Mikey's chin.

"Fair play," Mikey excused, and pushed him away at which point John grabbed his arm and tried to throw him to the ground. But Mikey, always quick to understand where his body was in space, shifted his weight to stop him, then pushed him in the chest, sending the older boy tumbling onto the seat of his pants.

"Mikey!" I yelled.

"What?" he yelled back, and I couldn't come up with an immediate answer.

John Eccles shouted at him to apologize so Mikey turned around and approached Elisabeth, who was holding herself around the shoulders and sniffling, her fair hair out of its pigtails and the knees of her sundress stained with grass. He held his arms out for a hug and she didn't do the same, but still he grabbed her, roughly, and pulled her in, then leaned in and kissed her on the forehead as she tried to squirm away.

"Hey!" I heard John shout. He was up again and charging headfirst at Mikey. He caught him in the stomach but Mikey kept his wind once they landed in the dirt and let the momentum spin them both around until he was on top. Thankfully he didn't try to hit the commissioner's grandnephew, but he did pin his arms to the ground and leered forward at the older boy with a wide goofy grin.

I got there and pushed him off. John, Elisabeth, and little Matty booked it around the house towards the front door and the Maple Leafs' dorm.

I turned and Mikey was brushing dirt off his good pants. "Mikey what the heck is wrong with you?" I asked.

He tossed his head back and whistled at me. "I didn't like those kids. They were saying bad things about America."

"No they weren't!"

"They were thinking it."

"Mikey." I softened my voice and gripped him by the shoulders. "I know it's been a hard week but you can't treat girls like that, and you can't be a terror of a guest."

He took a big breath in and then spat on the ground next to us. "You're right, Chrissy," he said. "But it's all over now so let's go on like I didn't."

Back in the house Marthanne and Coach were laughing over their drinks and the Eccles kids were nowhere to be seen. She saw me and called me closer.

"The contracts man! Can I bother you for our copies, please?"

I went over to my bag and fished out the signed agreements while Coach kept on laughing, sometimes bringing a hand to his mouth to hide a bad tooth buried far enough back he'd need to be laughing really big to risk someone seeing it.

Marthanne took a sip of whatever new drink they were sharing. It wasn't an Eccles beer, but it was definitely alcoholic. "I need your full name, Lawrence, in the top section."

"You've got it there," he pointed. "Lawrence Miller."

"I'll need your middle name too. Lawyer will complain he can't track you among the other Larry Millers."

Coach made a clucking noise. "Lady, you can't have my middle name."

She grinned. "Why not?"

"Private."

She grinned harder. "Oh come on, spill. How bad could it be?"

He didn't say anything, just crossed his arms and looked out the window to the yard.

"If it helps, mine's Marilou. It's awful. It sounds like what the farmer calls to get the cows."

"Alright, compromise," he said, reaching into his pockets. "Chris, grab this and go into the other room and write in the full name on my driver's licence, and Marilou here can look at it, but only after we're on the road back to the motel. Fair?"

She giggled and rolled her eyes. Coach tossed me his wallet and I took it and the fifteen contracts next door to the sitting room.

Coach's middle name was Rudolph, which is something I knew once and forgot. It didn't strike me as particularly embarrassing and maybe even a touch better than Lawrence. Who cared what your middle name was anyway if you never used it?

I wrote Rudolph on every page and stuck the licence back in his wallet. I had the papers stacked and ready to hand over when the open wallet looked back at me from the corner of my eye.

Glancing at the door to the dining room, I spread the billfold open and counted the money. Twenty-four dollars Canadian and ten U.S. In the other pockets were a library card and about a dozen business cards, some of which I recognized. Buried under the flap was a birth certificate for Lawrence Rudolph Miller. February 4th, 1916, in Buffalo. Had we ever celebrated Coach's birthday?

An American Legion card. A membership for the savings co-op and an expired one for our chamber of commerce. And then the student card, which wriggled out the back like a loose tooth. I picked it up and turned it over in my hand. It said Genesee County Schools, Adult Division, New York State, and it was for the 1945–46 school year.

I stared at the student ID and tried to calmly understand what it did or didn't mean. A door swung open somewhere and I jumped, but it was just the Eccles children returning to the dining room. I could hear Marthanne ask how it went and Elisabeth say we played too rough, which her grandmother treated with the airy nonchalance of adults. I looked back at the card.

Daddy came home late 1944. Mikey was born in 1945. Maybe Coach had come home with him and stayed there for a bit. Maybe Mamma had gotten pregnant, and he got scared and ran back to New York, finished high school and sorted himself out, and then came back. But I didn't remember that and nobody'd ever said it.

I put the ID in my pocket. Then took it out to look at it again. Coach's hair was longer over his ears, like he hadn't yet gone back to cutting it after the Army stopped demanding he did. He was maybe ten pounds lighter. I stood up and found myself dizzy, so I put out a hand to catch the fancy Eccles couch and spun myself down to sit. I stayed there until the others came to get me.

Coach said we had eaten our dinner in free cookies even though I only had one and a half, so we skipped the restaurant plans and just grabbed sandwiches from a German deli on the way home. It was fine by me. I wanted to show him the student card in private. I kept reaching into my pocket and touching it, flipping it around against my thigh.

"How was playing with those other kids?" Coach asked, filling the air in the car with a bit of loose conversation after several minutes of silence.

I looked at Mikey and waited for him to comment or confess. He was staring at the back of the passenger seat. Listening, but just staring ahead.

"Did you guys play some ball? I hope you kept your elbow up like we talked about."

"He did good," I said. "Put two nearly into the river."

"Attaboy," Coach hollered, punching the roof in celebration.

Mikey still hadn't said anything, and the way he loosened at the shoulders when I spoke made me suspect he thought he was getting away with it.

"Mikey has a crush on the middle girl, Elisabeth," I told the closed window on my side of the car. This immediately prompted brays of laughter from Coach and a flailing eruption of complaint from Mikey. He leaned over and clubbed me in the shoulder, which hurt but not enough to stop me grinning.

"Interesting! A younger woman, but okay, to each their own," Coach commented.

"I don't!" Mikey screamed. "I hate her, she's ugly and she's bad at baseball."

"Then why does your brother say otherwise, Mike?"

Mikey was bright with anger. Nostrils flared and fists still clutched. "I don't know! He just likes to make people mad like you said!"

We all quieted down on the "like you said." Coach made out like he had to fiddle with the radio even though he never listened to the radio, got his news from overheard conversation and thought Perry Como was a lake.

I cleared my throat and looked at the buildings going by beside us. I didn't know why, but the idea of Coach and Mikey complaining about me in private didn't bother me much. It presented as a quick painless shock, like when you see a splinter go in but before the pain, only the pain never hits; it wasn't that bad. It wasn't as deep as I feared.

Mikey and Coach lived in worlds of their own making. Mikey because he was seven and kind of a dummy, so until he reached out from his small land of make-believe heroes and struck an actual second-grader on the ass, he was harmless and a source of joy and whimsy.

But Coach was a man. A whole adult who lived right next to the meaningful world, ducking in to visit it daily but otherwise keeping warm in his private fantasies of who he was, what he was good at, and what the people of the real world meant to him. When he reached out, it wasn't to grab or hit anybody: it was to pull you in with him. He had reached out and grabbed Mikey. Maybe Mamma too. Sometimes maybe me.

"Coach," I said as we parked the car, "you finished high school, right?"

"Now, Chris, I get I'm not the most polished man you ever met," he said, carrying our bags through the front doors of the motel, past the empty clerk desk. "But yes, I managed to graduate high school."

"When?"

He hesitated for just a minute. "Normal time I guess, round about eighteen or so."

Mikey spoke up. "But you said you went to those adult education classes Mamma found you at the college."

"That's right, Romeo, I remember. But those weren't for high school. It was to learn enough bookkeeping so I could do the store's myself and didn't spend all my money keeping Merle Sanderson in rum."

"Is that all you did—no other courses after high school?" I asked.

"Wish it wasn't true, especially given all the interesting young people your mother gets to meet, but those few weeks were my only college."

"You had classes in the war though," Mikey added, throwing his bag on the bed.

"True. Though that's different. Why do you ask, Chris? Wondering how I got so stupid?"

I let it go by saying yes, and we all crashed around each other laughing and unwrapping sandwiches.

Putting fifteen contracts from London in our bag changed the math on our quota. If Utah wanted sixty signatures, that meant that Erie would only need to produce five. Coach scoffed at all this: sixty would be the fewest he'd ever returned with, but given the Topps letter it still seemed like a victory, and at least we would have done what the bosses said we had to.

Coach said, despite this, that Marthanne's math was right and the Forbushes were tearing through their money. The big boys had chased them out of the majors, chased them out of the minors, and now had them pinned against the bottom of the barrel. The numbers didn't make sense. There might be, in a good year, one eventual major-leaguer in the whole Northern, and to be certain we'd sign him, we'd need to spend $75 a club, $450 for the league. Plus expenses and administration and whatever few dollars they threw Coach. When Topps could just take a long vacation until this star of the hypothetical future appeared in a major league clubhouse, offer him less than half that amount, and have him for life. We'd do better to bid for DiMaggio ourselves, walk right up to him and offer him the $450, hundreds over what Topps paid.

That's the solution that would make Reg Law happy, and all the other Reg Laws out there, hopeful that the lucky lottery winner hiding out in the Northern League was them. They had invested their whole lives in the possibility of that ticket; why shouldn't they want us to invest there as well? The dream of the major leagues was worth more than our five bucks. Otherwise Four Corners was just waiting to be killed. Coach was waiting patiently, like a stupid dog, to be killed. There was nowhere to go after this, unless you were Frank Leahy and decided the rules didn't apply to you, and maybe they didn't, or maybe that was just the only logical choice a person could make when faced with the option to die or cheat. Cheating was what there was.

I dug into my bag and pulled out the O-Pee-Chee cuts and looked into Buddy Myers's ambitious face. I'm not sure where Coach had put the DiMaggio misprint, probably had it squirrelled away somewhere on the guess it'd be worth money one day. Not the stupidest dog.

We called home but Mamma didn't have much time to talk and was worried about blowing Coach's budget of nickels. She had twisted her ankle taking the step down from the streetcar, but it wasn't a big deal. An excuse to put her feet up. Mikey did most of the talking about the Eccles house, and because once in an earlier life, a suitor had brought Mamma's father back a case of Eccles beer from a trip north to Toronto, she was duly impressed to know we had met a true-life Eccles. She said Grandpa claimed the beer was the highest quality, though the suitor wasn't. Mikey barely mentioned playing baseball and I kept his name out of the papers when Mamma asked me how that had gone.

Back at the motel, local radio had the game we had missed reporting in from Erie. Not a play-by-play, but regular enough updates between gospel songs to tell the crux of the story. The Leafs beat the pants off them, won by ten.

Mikey said he still had a stomach ache but retracted the complaint when Coach suggested we should limit his sweets. We needed to decide where we'd go to get the Erie club. They were playing tomorrow night at home, a second make-up game against the Leafs, which Mikey was interested in because of how much Marthanne had talked up her team. But Erie was maybe a twelve-hour drive, and here we all lay in a motel room, not on the road trying to pull an all-nighter against Mamma's strict demands that Coach not drive at night with us in the car.

"I fought a war at night. I know my way around in the dark," Coach had argued, without effect. She had not made many demands after he volunteered to take us, but she had made that one.

If we left first thing in the morning we would pull in, if all went well, sometime in the early innings and then either see the Sailors just after they got whipped again at home or see them the next morning as they boarded the bus and went up the south side of the lake to Buffalo.

The other choice was to just wait for them to get to Western New York: take a travel day tomorrow, maybe eight hours or so, and pull into town before they did. Mikey was interested in this option because it meant we could stop by Niagara Falls and watch water go over a hill. So Mikey was interested in both options; he was a swing vote.

I wanted Buffalo because we had only landed nine signatures when we visited them on their bus, but they were a strong team and we could try our luck adding a few more if we caught them in a good mood after a win. That might make the difference between sixty and fewer than sixty. Marthanne Eccles said she'd call the Erie team to make the argument for signing up on our behalf; maybe we could stretch her kindness to her rivals at the top of the standings too. Then we'd either go home through Pennsylvania or cross back into Queen Elizabeth's Canada and make our way to Detroit.

Coach was cold on Buffalo, though, and he wouldn't say why. He said Erie was a better place to bring children, that Buffalo was run by gangsters and pimps. I trawled my memory for any reference to Buffalo, positive or negative, in movies or comic books, and came up with nothing. But he said you couldn't move around at night and were better off staying put in the daytime too. I asked how people got to grocery stores and he just looked at me like I had asked him to tell a long, gory story he was opting to save me from hearing. He had fought a war at night but wouldn't brave Buffalo.

His story was bullshit, but he had the expense account and the driver's licence. And a student card from New York State dated the month Mikey learned to walk. I spent time in the motel trying to remember when I met Coach, but he had always seemed to be there. He was Coach before he ever coached us in baseball. He was in photos dating back to Mamma first getting a loan of a friend's camera. Me with no front teeth outside his store. Coach lifting Mikey on his shoulders.

If there was an event made of his arrival, maybe I'd remember it. But Coach wasn't like that. He snuck in, appearing casually and always for a reason until one day after the fact I realized that something had shifted. He had made himself our family. He came by as a matter of habit.

I was antsy. Mikey was falling asleep and Coach had slowed already and the student card was stuffed in my pocket like a pistol. I considered just reaching over to him with it in my hand, dropping it on the bedside table, and looking at him until he said something. If I came in making accusations he'd frustrate them with some reasonable story. He applied but never attended. He left and came back when he found out she had his baby, whatever. But if I just dropped the card in his lap, I'd know. I'd know from how he looked at it and how he looked at me.

Mikey had conked out but was still on my bed. I looked at Coach and he shrugged and said to leave him. But I didn't want to leave him. I pushed my toe between his ribs and he jumped a little.

"Hey." I clapped my hand at him. "I know you're tuckered out from trying to bag the Eccles girl, but you need to switch beds."

He grunted and closed his eyes. I kicked him harder and Coach shouted at me to stop.

"Mikey!" I yelled. "Get up. I don't want to wake up in piss again."

Mikey stumbled to his knees. "You're the one who pisses himself," he grumbled. "And you're the one chasing after girls all week."

"Yeah? There's a wet mattress in Windsor would say differently, Michael."

Coach gave me a dirty look and told me to calm down. I looked away and stuck my hand in my pocket to feel the card. It was a little cracked down the middle, and maybe that was new, like it was slowly disintegrating in my pants from lack of use. Like my window of confrontation was closing.

I sat up. Michael had settled down and Coach's eyes had wandered away from me, were now looking at his bare right foot and some sort of toenail problem it was giving him. Mikey's book of Bible parables was open on my bed. I took it, weighed it in my hands a moment, and then lobbed it across the room in a long arc, gently enough that I could make it out to be a mistake if I needed to. But it wasn't a mistake. It fanned out like Coach's newspaper on the street that morning but because of proper Mormon binding it didn't come apart, it just dropped from the sky like some miracle of heavy metaphor, hitting Mikey on the mouth and bouncing to the edge of the bed.

He yelped and cried, thrashing his arms and feet around like a sped-up version of his normal nighttime snow angel routine. Coach yelled and jumped up, laying a hand on his chest long enough to know he wasn't badly hurt and then turning on me. I was ready for him to let me down again with violence and had stood up to receive it. But instead he grabbed me by the arm and dragged me first towards the bathroom before deciding to change paths and hauling me towards the room door. I thought he might put me through it before it opened at the last second and we were beneath the bright lights of the motel corridor. There was a couple at the end, keys halfway in the lock and faces like they were embarrassed to have been found staring. Coach put a hand up to wave them away and, still holding my arm with the other, marched me down the hall to the main doors, out into the parking lot in his bare feet and undershirt, and to the Hornet, where he tossed me in the passenger seat and came around to sit in the driver's side.

He slammed the door and we sat there, breathing heavily, for long enough to make the windows start to fog.

"Do you want to listen to the radio?" I asked.

"Christopher, you have to stop daring me to hit you," he hissed through closed teeth. "I promised God I wouldn't."

I snorted and looked away. It occurred to me I was checking the rear-view mirror to see if Mikey had followed us out. I was grateful he hadn't.

"What the hell got into you?" he asked. And as an answer, I shifted my weight and dug the Genesee County student card out of my pocket and placed it square on the dashboard between us. I stared directly out the window in front of me, paying attention to the twitchy little movements he was making, until they stopped, and he was just as still as I was.

I turned to look at him. His face was notepaper white and something, sweat or a tear, had started down his cheek.

"Where'd you get that?" he whispered. I didn't tell him. He knew anyway. I wanted to wait until he told me what the card meant. I didn't want to ask. Though I knew I would know right away, and I did. I knew that he was a liar.

Eventually, he leaned back in the driver's seat and pressed his head against the headrest. He closed his eyes. "Are you scared of me, or ashamed?" he asked.

I thought about this. The answer was both, which felt impossible as I had been taught that fear was an overriding emotion. Fear took up the whole room. But I was both scared of Coach and ashamed of him. Grateful and confused and intimidated and embarrassed. Just as I was scared of Reg Law and in awe of him. Fear shared the room.

Coach had taken my silence for a rejection of the question. "Fine," he said. "I'm not Mikey's dad. I didn't meet your Mamma until she was plenty pregnant. It was whatever year it was and you were however old you were then. My leg hurt the whole war, but Uncle Sam still squeezed use out the rest of me until just before it ended."

I found myself slowly shaking my head. "Five," I croaked out. "I'd have been five."

"Your daddy wanted me to come visit. I don't think he meant forever, but that's how it is when you die unexpectedly sometimes. All your loans go permanent. I liked your mamma, and I wanted a fresh start so I stuck around."

"Why?" I whispered, still looking away from him.

He sniffed and cleared his throat. His voice was syrupy and thick. "Sometimes I say things I want to be true like they are. There are suppliers at the store who think your mamma and I are married. That you and Mikey are our sons. We all live together. Usually there's no harm to it; I understand that this is different."

"Mikey's had no father his whole life, Coach. Do you know what it would be like? To roll away that sadness and then put it back?" I wiped my eyes and angled my head so I could stare right up into his face. "You're a fucking monster."

He looked back at me. His eyes were red and small. He took two short breaths, then measured his courage and spoke again. "I do have a son. He and his mother are in Buffalo. I left them for good when I moved to Minnesota."

I opened my mouth and closed it. My tongue felt hot. I looked into the back seat of the Hornet, for something, I don't know what. Evidence or an explanation. Fire. Paperwork.

"What?" I asked him, my voice still low and raspy like I was dying for a drink.

"I don't know much about them; she doesn't tell me. But I sent the extra money for tuition and she said he got a job this summer at the college. Bits and pieces. He was your age when I left, twelve. We were kids when we had him. He's eighteen now. You remind me of him, when you're angry."

I looked down at my hands and tried to chew on the part of this I couldn't understand.

"If he was twelve then and eighteen now, then that was '46. Not 1945."

Coach didn't say anything but he dropped his head to his chest.

"Dad was dead by then. You didn't come to stay with him. You spent that whole year at school. He was gone already when you got to town. I wasn't five; I was six. Mikey was alive." It felt like I should remember him entering the house for the first time, that six was old enough I should remember a time before. Even with Coach's skill at sneaking in. I tried, but I couldn't.

It took him long enough to speak again that a car behind us parked, its driver got out, gathered two bags from the trunk, and got almost all the way to the front door of the motel.

"When we were in Guadalcanal and he was struggling, he asked me to come back to Minnesota and help him, and I didn't. Men who were struggling—I mean really struggling, a notch above everyone else—they carried a kind of fog around. You felt bad and you worried for them, but you knew if you got too close, you might get lost in that fog along with them. Often when they asked for things, it was best to just say sure and leave it be. Keep your distance. But when I found out he had died and I knew I was finally running away from Ann and Larry anyway, I ran there. It was the only place I could think of where I thought I might be needed."

I cleared my throat. "So that was another lie? Just now?"

He nodded and looked at his bare toes. "Yes. That was another lie."

"And the kid in Buffalo? Larry? That's a lie?"

"No." Coach used the flat of his hand to slice the air between us. "That's real. He's real, I swear it."

We sat there in our thoughts. I was beginning to wonder about Mikey alone in the motel room with a fat lip. I pictured us wrapped in fog: the three of us, the Hornet, the Northern. Cold green fog like where trolls hide in fairy tales.

"What do you want to do next, Chris?" Coach asked.

I blinked my vision clear. I hadn't realized it was up to me. "You have to tell Mikey. Not now, but back when we get home."

"And your mother?"

I thought this over. "That's up to you. I don't care."

"But what if Mikey tells her?"

"He won't."

"Why?"

I picked the student card up off the dash and handed it to him. "He knows you're full of shit. He always has."

We got out of the car and as far as the motel door before Coach put a hand out to stop me. For a second I was worried he would hug me, but he asked another question.

"What about the trip, Chris?"

I leaned on the door frame and thought about it. Buffalo or Erie.

"Is Buffalo really run by gangsters?" I asked.

"No more than anywhere."

I nodded. "Okay," I told him. "Then we'll go there. I want you to find your son. I want to see him, and I want you to see him. I want to know he's real."

"Chris, I'm not exactly wanted there—"

"That's okay," I interrupted. "He doesn't have to notice you, but I still want us both to see him. From whatever distance you like."

He looked at me like the instinct to assert himself and say no, don't be silly, we'll get the signatures and leave, rose up inside him and then faded again, and he just nodded. This was the first time he had looked at me like I was an adult. As I've come to understand it, the first time anyone had.

Niagara Falls,
Tuesday, July 15th, 1952

	W	L
Buffalo Bisons	42	25
London Maple Leafs	38	27
Akron Zaps	36	28
Erie Sailors	29	37
Windsor Clippers	29	37
Hamilton Red Wings	23	43

Last Night's Games
Sailors 4, Leafs 14; Wings 4, Zaps 3; Bisons 3, Clippers 4

THE FALLS WERE BETTER THAN I IMAGINED. I HAD IT IN MY head that anywhere people went on their honeymoon was going to be a bore, and moreover anywhere that consisted of just one famous sight, like the Grand Canyon or Mount Rushmore, would start to disappoint once you began to turn your head. I had never been to either of those places, but I found myself wanting to give them a chance as I leaned over the protective railing and felt the cool mist of the falls rise up in my face.

The American side was supposed to be better, but Coach agreed that we could stop after the border and look once more with eyes clear of petty patriotism and decide for ourselves if this was true.

Mikey was in a great mood all morning despite the long drive across Ontario to the falls. When we stopped for breakfast, he joked with the waiter and later impressed a couple of grey-haired ladies by recounting one of his Bible stories.

As for the flying book, it hadn't hurt him much. The worst of it was being left alone in the dark and even that wore off to the point that he was asleep once Coach and I got back. Everyone was at their best and this culminated at the falls. Coach was relaxed, like he had been lifted somehow by the episode in the Hornet. I was at ease with who the people around me were and were not. Even the Erie team and the looming question of our last five signatures didn't bother any of us. Coach had this year's tuition cheque covered, and if he had to go look for a new job for his son's sophomore year next summer, there was time for that.

The only clouds were coming north from Buffalo. Coach pulled me aside as we were walking to the lookout to let me know that if he spoke to Larry it would be a problem with his ex-wife. I said not to worry about it. He told me at breakfast that he hadn't seen him since he left, could only guess at what he looked like. He didn't know where his job was and while it was a small enough campus, what if he wasn't even working that day? What if he was out of town? I told him not to worry; all a person could do was try.

Mikey ran back and forth along the lookout, weaving through crowds of families and newlyweds and appearing in some unknown number of photographs set for the continent's slide projectors and sitting rooms. There were men selling ice cream and popcorn and men who would paint your picture if you sat beside the water for them. We did neither, preferring to look out upon the inexorable reign of gravity, sometimes pointing out a bird or a boat as one approached the mist.

We had been there for half an hour when I felt a tap on my shoulder. I turned around and froze a moment looking at the man who had done it, a tall slender gentleman in his twenties who gave the sense, almost imperceptible except as a lightness of posture, of being a ballplayer. I had seen too many in too short a time and now every man of that age, boyish but no longer a boy, read to me as an athlete, when most of them were still soldiers or students or apprentices in shops.

"Excuse me," the man said in a long, drawling accent that could have been from anywhere but sounded Southern in a non-specific way. "I was wondering if you might help us take a picture."

I looked at the camera around the man's neck, which was silver and black and so big it bounced against his breastbone like a medieval shield. It was large on him but had been even larger on Clara.

"Is that a II B?" I asked, pointing at the lens.

He gripped the camera and nodded, surprised but pleased to find an aficionado. "Why it is, actually. Do you know them?"

"I've used one once or twice." It was once.

At this point Coach and Mikey had been lifted from the spectacle and were watching us, the fronts of their shirts specked with river water. The man, with more than a little concern, had taken the camera off from around his neck and looped it carefully around mine. It's possible I had looked older, more reliable, from behind when standing on the ledge by the lookout, but now he understood he was entrusting this expensive toy, and the memory he had bought it to capture, to a child.

He showed me the necessary switches and dials, all familiar enough from Clara's explanations. Then I ducked my head, and he and his wife gathered in the square of the optical viewfinder, a top-of-the-line feature according to Clara's recitation of the II B's catalogue copy. It was then that I saw them both for the first time, not as examples set against my experience of young adults, but as people captured as-were against the empty expectations of the camera. He was short and she was his height, maybe an inch taller. He had a checked shirt and khaki pants. Her shirt was billowing in the vortex stirred up by the falls. They were both handsome but neither was beautiful. There was a practicality to them, a sense of the body as utility, and clothes and posture as necessities for presenting that tool, and nothing else. Not athletes. This was how regular people looked to regular people. I asked them to smile, then fiddled with the magnification until they were chief in the image but the falls surrounded them on all sides. They smiled and I snapped them, and then again for good measure.

The man walked up to me and gathered the camera up safely. "Thanks, kid," he said. "We're on our honeymoon and were worried no one up here would know how to work this thing."

"Children and technology, huh?" Coach said, getting their attention. They smiled.

"Your son's good with a camera, sir," said the woman, her voice high and sweet and a little hard to hear in the din.

Coach didn't correct her, and Mikey coming around to stand by his side made us look all the more like a family. The new husband told us to have a good day, and we said the same to them.

We left for the border just after noon, having grabbed some more sandwiches at a shop on the hill that rose dramatically from the lookoff. Coach told us to say goodbye to Canada and quizzed us on what we had learned. The capital was Ottawa, which was in this province but far to the east. Neither of us knew the name of the prime minister, but luckily Coach didn't either. The leader was the queen, who kept popping up in shiny new framed photographs on walls and the sides of government buildings, serene and long-necked in her clothes that looked like candy. We hadn't got to see a game in London but still both ranked it as the best stadium. Windsor was my favourite city; Mikey declined to say his.

The bridge to America lacked drama, perhaps for the best with the falls still visible along its south side and sure to upstage any scrap of iron. It was a flat two-laned highway cut straight across the Niagara River, on the safe side of the waterfall. We drove right through the Canadian checkpoint with its familiar cabins and its men in grey. Mikey waved and a border man waved back.

Once across to U.S. soil, Coach steered us into the shortest-looking line and we waited, like shoppers in giant painted grocery carts, filing forward towards the checkout.

"Shall we sing the national anthem?" Coach leaned back and asked us. I laughed and Mikey actually started it, picking up Coach for a few lines before they both trailed off when next it was time to edge ahead.

The officer at the front of our line wore sunglasses that made his eyes invisible to us and what might have either been a helmet or a very thick baseball cap. He spoke to Coach and ignored Mikey and me.

"Nationality and identification please."

I didn't know what exactly Mamma had left him with beside her letter, but there was a whole parcel of documents in the glove compartment. Coach pushed aside the garage bill and handed a selection to the man, and told him that we were American. I could tell Coach wanted to get out and stand next to the officer, but he was standing too close to the door to open it safely without asking him first to move. The man leafed through the papers, looking up from time to time to match a face to the image on a document.

"What's your relationship to these two minors?"

"I'm their baseball coach."

"Is this trip in relation to that?"

"Coaching baseball? Not in direct relation, no." Coach seemed unworried by the conversation, which made me just a little worried.

The officer kept cycling through the documents, looking up between pages at Mikey and me. In the lane next to us, there was a long line of white cars, so many that I wondered if the cars were sorted by colour and if we were in the red lane. Or maybe the red cars were meant for a different lane, and that was the source of our delay.

"Sir, can you please pull over to additional processing? I'll meet you there," said the man in the mirrored glasses.

Coach didn't question this but, whistling "The Star-Spangled Banner" under his breath, just pulled the Hornet around, through a gap in the white lane, and up next to a little shed hugging the wall of the exit ramp. We waited there while the border man waded through traffic to join us, Coach casting his eyes up into the rear-view and smiling a small smile while we sat.

When he got to us, the officer had Coach open all the doors and step out of the car. Mikey and I did the same and were shuttled to the other side of the vehicle. Looking behind us, there was a long expanse of pedestrian sidewalk on the passenger side going all the way back to Canada, about a hundred feet from end to end. We couldn't see the falls though its rumble filled the background.

The officer walked around the car and stopped at the trunk where he started to pull out pieces of luggage and the remaining example set.

"Sir," he said, apparently to Coach though he never looked in his direction, "can you tell me why there's a slice through the trunk upholstery and why this money is hidden inside?" The envelope was clearly depleted but still had enough unclaimed fives to warrant an elastic band.

Coach's posture stiffened all at once. I tried to remember whether he had done anything to better hide the envelope after it was discovered by the border man in Windsor. He wet his lips and took a big breath before speaking. "It's for safety."

"Safety?"

"Yessir."

"There's only like a hundred dollars here, but it's all uncirculated bills. Can you tell me why?"

I could tell Coach wanted to take a moment to think through his excuse first, but also that he felt compelled to answer quickly enough that the border man didn't get suspicious. These desires were incompatible.

"I've been on a mission. A business trip, with my boys here. We've been giving money away as part of the business. It's legitimate." He was sweating. The front of his shirt stuck to his chest and I could see the shine on his forehead.

The officer looked back at us. "And these boys aren't related to you?"

"Not legally no."

"How do you mean not legally?"

"They're not related to me. I'm not their father."

I didn't look back at Mikey, though I wanted to. I wanted to reach backwards and grab his hand in mine, but the officer had a weapon and I knew he didn't like Coach's answers already. He would like us jostling around behind him even less.

"So you're travelling internationally with a car full of uncirculated bills and two minors who aren't your children?"

"Yessir," Coach said, and then rallied to add, "There's a letter confirming they're safe in my possession from their mother among those documents."

"I saw it. It's a handwritten note on blank stationery." He took a step towards Coach and Coach blinked, his hands locked at his side like he was a new recruit at basic training, stare fixed slightly above the officer's helmet as he took in the nothing just above him. "Do you have anything else, Mr. Miller?"

Coach was too scared to hear what the officer really wanted, too focused on his answers to understand the question. I know because I felt the same way at first, that the officer was asking for something else, a little something extra, to help us glide through the checkpoint to Buffalo. Coach broke his pose and looked over into the trunk of the car.

"What sort of something else, officer?"

"Something better."

"Sure, sure." Coach rubbed his hands together and stepped towards the car. The officer flinched and put his hand to his hip but no further. Coach leaned into the back of the car and dug around, then bent down and opened one of the bags.

"Do you like baseball cards?" he asked.

The officer made like he hadn't heard him correctly.

"No?" Coach said. "Okay, well, that was enough for your colleague on the Canadian side of the last bridge. Here."

Coach walked forward holding five, maybe six, of the crisp new bills from the trunk. The officer took a step back and stared at him. I may have gotten most of the words "you Jesus idiot" out under my breath before the border man raised his voice.

"Sir, are you offering me this money as a way to gain passage into the United States?" I could tell from the way he said this that he was trained to say it that way.

Coach didn't fall all the way into the trap, but he fell far enough. "Well, I'm offering it, if it helps," he stammered.

The officer asked him to turn around, and he put a hand under his armpit and told him he was under arrest. At that point, at least three things happened at once. First, another officer, identical in every way to the first, came jogging out of the shed by the wall, his face radiant with a big open smile, tongue sticking out a bit from his mouth like a dog chasing a stick. Then I heard Coach break. He screamed at the officer that he misunderstood, he thought money was what he meant, and the officer put his palm on his own forehead and said he meant, like, Mamma's phone number or something, and that Coach was a big dummy and that now he was in real trouble. And lastly, and somewhat as an afterthought until its meaning fell fully upon me, I turned to my left and noticed Mikey was gone. He wasn't over my shoulder, and he wasn't behind the car.

When the second officer got there, he put his hands on Coach's back and pushed him to the pavement. Coach was flailing his legs and yelling his apologies. I shouted to him to just explain, but I didn't know how he could do so and I didn't think he'd be able to follow instructions if I had any. And then I remembered my brother and turned around again.

"Mikey?" I shouted, and this got the first officer's attention. I ran around the far side of the shed. Nothing. The officer appeared next to me and I ducked away thinking I was next for border prison. He asked me where my brother went and I said I didn't know. First he and then I cast a cautious eye over the side of the bridge but saw no ripples in the water below. I swallowed and the other officer called out to ask what we were doing. Then we saw him, a small retreating speck far down the long corridor of the bridge's pedestrian span. The fastest kid in our whole little league, faster than any of the coaches or dads. He didn't know where Canada started exactly. In the middle of the bridge? If it did, he was already there, and if it wasn't Canada until the opposite bank, then he was catching up to it fast.

"Shit," I heard the officer say, and I believe I said it too.

I yelled for Coach as the officer ran back to the scene of the crime. He said something to his partner and they pulled Coach to his feet. The twin officers released his wrists and pushed him into the Hornet and I opened the passenger side door and got in the front.

"What's happening?" I asked, but Coach wiped his eyes and said nothing. Outside, the officers were directing traffic and a path opened up across the front of the line and into the Canada-bound lane.

"Are they sending us back to get him?" I asked.

The initial officer appeared with a start, putting his hand in the driver's side window like he was trying to force it open. Coach rolled it the rest of the way down. The officer tossed the loose documents at us. I looked behind and saw his partner packing up our trunk. The first one reached through and grabbed Coach by the collar.

"Listen to me," he said. His words had a seething, whispered quality, and he strung them together so tight it was hard to follow, but I thought he said that if we came back via their bridge, Coach would be arrested on sight. They had his name and the Hornet's licence plate. They never wanted to see his stupid face again.

They stepped away from the vehicle and Coach looked at me, open-mouthed, like he was waiting for permission. An international border crossing's worth of vehicles waited behind us. All at once, I nodded my assent, and one of the officers stepped forward and kicked the Hornet in the side with their work boots. It made a clanging squawk.

"Get out of here!" he shouted and Coach accelerated, pulling the Hornet into a great screeching turn like the stock car runs it was built for, and we were off, doing twenty miles over the limit across the bridge and back to Canada to look for my brother.

We both knew where to go but we got lost on the way. Coach was wet with sweat. I saw it flick off his eyebrows when he moved his head, and soak into the material under his pits. I kept looking back to check for the border police, like there was one more turn in the maze and we weren't really driving away, we weren't home free. Like I'd look back and Coach would still be in handcuffs on the first few feet of American asphalt and the car would disappear around me and I'd be right there standing next to him.

Coach told me to relax, to keep my head, and then immediately missed the off-ramp back to the falls, sending us along some sort of freeway that split the tourist district from the town full of tour guides beside it. Coach swore and took the next exit, then doubled back through a residential grid until we were on the road leading along the riverbank again. I looked from side to side, hopeful for an early sighting but also knowing how fast Mikey could run when he needed to, and how long we were taking to get there, and not expecting him until after we parked the car and got out where Coach and I knew to go, though neither of us had said so.

There were too many tourists at the sweet spot of the lookoff so Mikey was sitting on a bench nearby, drawing attention but no good Samaritans as his chest heaved in and out, catching his breath and sobbing. He saw us and made to run again, but either he didn't really want to or he couldn't. He plopped back down and Coach and I sat on either side of him.

"Thanks for bailing me out," Coach said after Mikey's little body stopped panicking for air. He smiled and I smiled, and Mikey looked a little confused and didn't smile back.

"You're not under arrest anymore?" he asked.

"No," Coach told him. "Not right now anyway."

I put my hand on the back of Mikey's neck. There was a pool of sweat in the nape and when I pressed on it, I felt it squish out under my palm and down his back. "Is that why you ran, Mike?"

He pushed his lips together tight and shook his head no. I removed my hand and put it in my lap. Coach was looking at me with arched eyebrows like he was awaiting my approval for something.

It clicked into place. I nodded.

"Mikey," Coach said, "were you upset when I told the man we weren't related?"

He didn't say anything but his breathing finally calmed down to where we couldn't hear it.

Coach rubbed at his mouth with his hand. "Okay. Well, I had to tell the truth, is the thing. I love you, and your brother, and hell I love your mom too. I want us to be a big family. I want it so bad that I told you it was the case when it wasn't. Chris said he thought you knew I was telling a fib before. Did you?"

They both looked down at the ground in front of them, perhaps contemplating the weight and dimensions of that word *fib*, or perhaps only I did that. We all listened, or didn't listen, to the tinkle of happy visitors around us, and the long broad groan of the falls. I listened to these things. I don't know what they heard. When I thought about the word *fib*, I thought only of replaceable things.

"I knew," Mikey sniffled. "But I didn't want you to tell it to a stranger."

Coach's eyes were round and sad as he leaned back on the bench. He put his arm around Mikey and Mikey let him, and then Mikey did the most unexpected thing, tilted right over into Coach's soggy mess of a chest like he was going there for shelter. We stayed there, me watching the crowds go by and soaking in the voices, until one voice, thin and sweetened with a French accent, came more clearly from the fray.

French Wind saw us first, completely ignored the scene with Mikey and Coach, and started shouting for my attention. I sat up straight and cocked my head, but didn't stand. If the last hour hadn't been a fever dream, I might have been keener to recognize him as unexpected in that space; maybe I would have even asked him how he got there. As it was, he made it all the way to our bench and even slapped my shoulder before I said his name, or what I understood to be his name.

"French," I said, my eyes lidded like I was just waking up.

French told me something I couldn't hear, and then Coach was next to him, shaking his hand. Mikey stood up, tucking the shaggy ends of his hair behind his ears.

"You made it to the falls," French said.

Coach said it was a last-second decision on our way to Buffalo, and then he asked them what he was doing there, whether it was his day off from the Clippers.

"Non, non," French told us. He gestured with his chin to the parking lot behind us and there again, as it always seemed to when there was no other way forward, was the Ford Transit Bus the Clippers called home, sitting low on its tires even with the team spread out around the falls. The team.

"Where's Reg?" I asked him, surprised to find I was shouting though we were too far away from the falls for me to need to.

French cleared his throat and told us he was on the bus, that he had been injured and they were going to take him to a special doctor in Akron when they got there. He thought word had gotten around.

"You're going to Akron via Canada?" Coach asked him.

"We won last night," French said. "Somehow or another, we took a road win from the bastard Bisons. Manager said today was as good a day as any to go and see the falls. We'd been asking since April. We're off to Akron right after."

Coach looked at me and I tried to think of something to say. Two of the Clippers showed up and swallowed French in a teasing embrace. One rubbed his head until his hair stuck out at odd angles while the other asked him to come translate for the benefit of a Québécoise girl he liked. I fell back with Coach.

"Did you hear that?" Coach said. "A sign from the gods."

"How so?"

"They're headed to Akron. That's out via the bridge, south past Buffalo, and then west along the lake."

"You're not—"

"You got another option, Chris? I know you're worried about me and Law, but for an unbothered ride across that river, I'll split a seat with Satan himself."

"Let's just chance the bridge again."

"The great tower of fuck we will."

"How would we get back?"

"There's another bridge in Buffalo that will take you to Fort Erie. We walk that, jump on one of the dozen tourist buses they run back and forth to the falls, grab the Hornet right here and go home via Detroit."

"We're just leaving the Hornet?"

"Why not?" Coach gestured to the crowd. "This place is full of people every minute day and night. No one's going to think it out of place. Go grab the contracts and the rest of it out the trunk."

It occurred to me that I was tired of this. Tired of the pattern, Coach going bust on some confidence mission, getting in over his head, messing up, only to shake it off like stardust and reemerge having learned no humility, carrying an oracle's self-belief towards the next disaster. I was tired in the sense of being annoyed, worn thin by him, but also I was tired. Tired in my bones and body. I wanted to sleep in a warm room without him there to let me down and then insult me by suggesting that he was what I needed.

But there was nothing else to do. "You need to sit with Mikey if we go with them again," I told him. "Stay close to Mikey."

Coach didn't know why I said this but he liked that I did. He stood up straight and fixed his shirt.

The three of us followed French around and asked him questions about the team and how they managed to beat Buffalo on the road. It was a close game, he said; their starter ran out of gas in the eighth and walked four straight men. We asked whether Simmonette was travelling with them and he said no, so we asked who was in charge and he said he was, of course.

"Then, French, it might be to you we need to ask this favour," Coach said. French looked up at him with uncertainty. "The Hornet's on the fritz again. We got it here but it won't make it to Buffalo for us to catch the Sailors. Do you think you could give us one more ride?"

French filled his cheeks with air and blew it out. "Well, from me it's a yes but I need to clear it with Coach Dunn."

"He didn't have a problem with us last time, did he?" Coach asked.

"Non," French mumbled, scratching at his neck. "I suppose he did not."

"He slept through the whole time," I pitched in.

French chuckled. "He sure did."

"Where's he now?" Coach asked.

French pointed at the bus with his chin again. "Asleep," he said. "He's not much of a traveller. In there with Law."

"Why's Law in there?" I asked.

French reminded me that he had been injured. I asked just how injured and he told me I could go in and see for myself.

"I must corral these animals before they find the cafés," French said. "If you want to check with Coach Dunn you can wait for us there. Try to fit in among the laundry."

We crossed the lot and approached the Transit Bus from the back. Coach had French's keys and skipped happily in front of us. I ran up beside Mikey and put my hand on his shoulder.

"Mikey," I whispered, "do you understand who's on that bus?"

"I do," he said. His voice was calm. Not courageous, but calm. Steady. I told him to stay close to Coach.

They popped the door and climbed the stairs. Coach ducked into the first available seat and Mikey followed, leaving me standing at the front. There were two men sprawled out on separate benches, three and six rows away. The hard thin Clippers coach was in the back, as asleep as French had promised, while Reg Law sat with one leg angled straight out in front of him, staring into the seat ahead like it was ten miles away.

I turned and looked at Coach and Mikey. Coach had an arm around him and they were leaning into one another, just like on the bench, smiling as they watched the falls in the distance. Unburdened by fibs. I looked back at Reg and walked down the aisle until I was in his row and sat down right next to him. There were plenty of seats anywhere I wanted. I had no excuse.

I shucked off my bag and sat with my hands in my lap. Reg allowed his eyes to crawl over and take me in. He was dressed in an oversized shirt and a pair of short pants. His left leg was wrapped in blankets and what looked like two big splints held it steady.

"Are you the angel of mercy?" Reg asked. His voice was wet and drowsy. So low I had to lean in to hear it.

"Excuse me?"

"Have you come to escort me to the next life?"

"No, Reg," I told him. "I'm only going as far as Buffalo."

The door opened again and the Clippers drifted in. One looked down at Coach and Reg and shouted about stowaways, but then grabbed a ball cap and plunked it onto Mikey's head. It was a Buffalo Bisons hat, taken as a bounty in last night's celebrations.

"Look, and Law's got himself a nurse!" one yelled out. They filed by, reaching over me to clap him hard on the shoulder. His body shook with each slap, and he closed his eyes and gritted his teeth.

"Suppose they couldn't convince any woman nurse to take the risk," said another, and four or five of them stomped about laughing.

French showed up and asked if the manager had okayed our being there. Coach told him yes. The engine of the Transit Bus gurgled to life.

I looked over at Reg a few times before coming up with anything to say. "You manage to see the falls in the end, Reg?" I offered.

He tilted his head a few inches to my side. "I got the gist of them."

We went over a curb and Reg winced. He whistled ahead to the player in the next row.

"Davis," he grunted. "Grab me two more of those pills."

Davis seemed unsure. "Alright, just let me check with French first—"

"He's not a fucking doctor, rook, grab me two more pills and the vodka to wash them."

Davis went up to Coach and Mikey's seat and had them move around until he got his hand to a medical bag. When he came back, Reg pawed two white tablets into his mouth and spilled a half-empty bottle of booze on his lips. He kept the bottle by his side.

Slowly, Reg loosened up and even shifted his weight for the first time, moving his bandaged left leg ever so slightly along the way. The Clippers around us were talking about women and debating whether anyone had ever survived going over the falls.

On the bridge, we merged into a separate lane just for trucks and buses. When we pulled into the checkpoint I scooted down a bit in my seat. An officer spoke to French for maybe thirty seconds, and then smiled and waved us by. I turned and watched Canada slip past without anyone noting it or breaking into song.

As we hit the highway south, Reg rolled his head over to me

and smiled a dopey little smile. The hairs on my neck and arms stood up.

"D'you want to know what happened?" he asked.

I exhaled. "We read in the paper you got subbed out on Sunday. Did you hurt it then?"

"Oh, not substantially, you ask the Buffalo doctor he'll tell you. Just a pulled muscle. Possible even I was philandering, he told Coach."

"But then?"

"Yesterday I barrelled some goofy curveball in the first, rounded into second, and slid. I was safe, too, was the worst of it, didn't even need to slide. They carried me off the field over their heads, like I was the flag dragged out for Memorial Day. Shit. They had to give me a shot of something just to put me to sleep."

"Christ, Reg, I'm sorry."

He started to giggle. The laughter had a drowning quality, like his throat was full of drain water. "No you aren't, junior, don't lie. This is just what was deserved, far as you're concerned."

I frowned and looked at my knees. I didn't feel that way, though admitting so sounded like a failure of clarity, like I was being sentimental. I asked him how bad it was.

"Feels like my knee doesn't exist," he told me, holding all the *S*s in his words too long. "Feels like there's a hot rod shoved up the soles of my feet all the way to my hip, screwed in real tight, and burning."

"How long till it's better?"

Reg got quiet and looked out the window for long enough that a new town was announced along the highway and we watched it shoot by in its entirety outside the bus's left side.

"They called my mamma, while I was asleep," he whispered to the window. "Said they'll send me out on a bus after the Akron doctor gets a look at me."

"For the season?"

"Forever as I understand it," he told the window. "Quack Buffalo doctor said I'll walk in a month or so, but limping. If I'm lucky, I might still be a heck of a beer-leaguer."

He took a long slow drink from the bottle. I sighed. I thought about asking for some too. I knew that he would share.

Reg looked over at me like he had just remembered something. He chewed on his lower lip and then spoke. "Kid, I need to tell you a thing quick, okay, and if it upsets you to hear it, I'll need you to keep that shit to yourself. I won't have you getting panicky on me again, you get me?"

"Sure," I said, starting to get a little panicky.

"It's incumbent upon me," Reg licked his lips and swallowed. "That I need to apologize to you. And to your brother. One man's fun is not everyone else's. Sometimes I get carried away a little with the Watch Me stuff, I know, guys on the team expect it, but I shouldn't have involved you. Surely not yet."

I nodded.

"Give it ten years and a miracle of medicine, we can go hit the town together properly, right?" He grinned at me with the old grin, and I tried my best to follow him there, but I knew my eyes were giving me away and that he saw it, and so the grin dropped between us.

"Christ," he said, breathing in as he swore. He brought a hand up and rubbed the slick away from his forehead, then took another hard swig of the bottle. It was mostly gone.

"Kid," he added, swallowing air, like the word *kid* was a hiccup. "I want you to know that there's something wrong with me. I know it just as clear as you do. It's not good, not right, and I want you to know I understand all about it."

"Reg—"

"I wanted you to know that I know, and I'm sorry. That's the whole deal."

He let out a big gasp and grimaced something that might have been "Okay," and then went quiet. Eventually I heard him snoring. Then as we peeled off the highway towards Buffalo, his head fell onto my shoulder. I sat stone-still, heart beating like chattering teeth and skin so itchy I could scream, but I didn't make a sound. I pressed my sweaty head against his until the Transit Bus stopped, then propped Reg back up in his seat, grabbed my bags, and followed Coach and Mikey outside.

Buffalo,
Wednesday, July 16th, 1952

	W	L
Buffalo Bisons	43	25
London Maple Leafs	38	28
Akron Zaps	36	28
Erie Sailors	30	37
Windsor Clippers	29	37
Hamilton Red Wings	23	44

Last Night's Games
Sailors 6, Leafs 2; Wings 1, Bisons 5

I WAS THE FIRST TO WAKE UP. AFTER LYING THERE ALONE IN the bed for ten minutes I stood and went to the bathroom and brushed my teeth. Then I watched Mikey's and Coach's chests rise and fall in the other bed and waited for them to stir, but they didn't. After sitting quite patiently for several more minutes, I slipped on my shoes and left a note behind so they would know I hadn't run off again.

The Buffalo motel was not shaped like a C. It was shaped like an I, which is to say it was just a single line of rooms parallel to the highway, south of the city centre and close enough to the river—or the lake, or the widening point where the river became the lake—that you could see Fort Erie over gaps in the neighbouring buildings. I watched the cars go by and then wandered south to what signage called the Entertainment Lounge. I knew if I committed to coming in early I'd have a chance, and sure enough there was nobody in the Entertainment Lounge when I got there. The trio of teamsters' kids staying off-site for a union meeting were gone.

The television was a floor model. A Zenith. The speaker was in the bottom third of the cabinet and then all the rest was dials and screen. I dropped to my knees and began the prayerful work of tuning the machine.

The first view was just a white screen. I turned the dial again and it became a man reading the news. I twisted again and the first white screen had grown the word *Today*. The *O* in Today was a clock and the clock was set to, if I read the hands right, six forty-five a.m. I looked at my watch, which had a clearer difference between hour and minute hands. It was eight.

We didn't go to bed so late as to make sleeping in a need. If Coach and Mikey were tired, it was cumulative. All we did last night was get a bite to eat and then walk uptown to the university campus and poke around for a few minutes. Everyone who could look up a name or direct us to the student employment office was home for the evening. Coach told us that he had come here once when he was my age to listen to a man talk about the planets and show a bunch of slides.

The Civic Stadium, which locals called the Rockpile because it looked like an ancient ruin, wasn't far from the motel, but we missed it because Mikey said he was too beat to keep going in the strange city, and Coach was of a mind to let him have his way. The two of them barely left each other's physical contact the whole night, like somehow all of these lies and discoveries had brought them closer. Maybe the world just seemed a little less reliable, more dangerous, and Mikey sought out the first tall body to crouch beneath, unaware or not caring that Coach himself was the source of all that chaos. That he was both the rainstorm and the canopy of leaves that kept him dry.

The *Today* program consisted of a man in a striped bowtie and glasses smoking a cigarette and wearing what looked like a table leg attached to his chest that was, I figured, the microphone recording his speech. He told us about the news in New York City and then there was a weather report. The bowtie man picked up a telephone and spoke to someone whose job was to know the weather. There was a big chalkboard map of America and the weather predictor told the bowtie man the forecast, and the bowtie man sketched the weather on the map. I pressed my hand to the screen, light enough to not leave fingerprints, and thought long and hard about how in some wire-fed room in distant New York City, that man was talking to me right now, and here he was also right in front of me, even though he had never left.

Last night we had called Mamma and told her we'd be a day late coming home, and if I had the patience to let someone else cry in front of me, she might've. She said she'd make plans to take us for dinner and I said no thank you, we'd had enough restaurant food for the whole summer and maybe we could just have homemade hamburger steak and she could read us the book we had started before we left, which was a great big book about ancient Egypt, a novel, written by someone from Sweden of all places. She got very quiet and told me she was looking forward to that. I was too.

Mikey padded into the Entertainment Lounge as the bowtie man was playing us a record. He sat next to me and, like I had, put his hand on the screen to feel its electricity. We stared into the square box for ages and eventually, as much to my surprise as his, I told him that I loved him and I wanted him to be happy. He said the same, and then lifted a thin finger to his lips to make me quiet.

We had to push Coach out of the motel like a stubborn donkey. First he slept the longest, and then he spent extra minutes plucking hairs in the bathroom, and then we had to talk him down from his plans for a full breakfast. If I was eager to spin the morning forward to get us out the door and on the scent of Larry Miller, Coach was forever turning it back. I was worried we wouldn't have time to do the college first before meeting the Sailors. Coach said we'd need to be at the stadium by noon, which was ridiculous, and we settled on a three o'clock appointment in the visitors' locker room, which meant we'd leave the campus at two. No matter what. Two o'clock and we'd be gone. Sight or no sight of Larry Miller.

The administrative building was the one with the biggest American flag. The three of us gathered under it and Mikey looked up in what I thought at first might have been spontaneous patriotism but upon investigation was just novelty. He hadn't seen a large stars and stripes in public since we crossed the bridge for the first time. He had nearly forgotten it.

"It's like how I couldn't remember yesterday what colour the house was," he told me. "It's weird how things go away."

I put my arm around his shoulders. "The house is white. Let's head in and look around."

We had brainstormed the sort of people we could be when someone asked. A contractor and his sons. Two brothers doing research for a boy scout project. A lost child looking for his cousin Larry. Coach told us what he thought he might look like, the product of old memories and a single photograph from a school field trip, taped in secret to the roof of the Hornet's glovebox. He had brown hair, maybe not as dark as Coach's. Tall for his age at one point. Like me. In the picture, he stood before the gates of a museum, gesturing at a poster whose specifics had been smudged out or otherwise lost to wear. I asked to hold the photograph in my hand and found myself rubbing it between my fingers the way a suspicious bank teller would do a personal cheque.

At a university, during the school year, it's hard to search out someone in charge. There are too many bodies, and to me they all looked reasonably adult or at least about the same age. Professors and administrators were younger than I imagined, and students always looked older. However in the summer, with the students spread out at their various homes, it became easier. Almost anyone you walked past worked there.

We marched up to a reception office and found someone who staffed a desk between semesters. They directed us to the student jobs bureau three floors up. The young woman working there was also a student, handling the job of jobs until September. We asked for help, and she kept her gate closed at first, explaining that student worker information was private. She had straight blonde hair that looked almost liquid, like if I reached out I could gather it in my hand like lemonade poured from a pitcher.

"We're his cousins from Minnesota," I told her. "He doesn't know we're here. It's a surprise." I gave a sidelong look at Coach, who was hiding behind the door.

"I see. Do you know where he might be assigned?"

"Assigned?"

"What's his department? What job does he have?"

"Oh." I patted my lips with the tip of my index finger. "Something with books I think." This seemed broad enough at a centre of learning not to shut any doors.

"Alright, let me check the roll. Maybe the bookstore." She got up and opened a big binder on the table behind her. Three desk phones lined up beside it. "What's his name again?"

"Miller. Larry Miller."

"What's Larry short for?"

"Um." I turned and Coach pointed to himself. "Lawrence," I told her. I knew that.

She turned the pages back and forth, stopping at one point to answer the middle of the three phones and tell someone on the other end when they closed. I looked at the clock. It was already past noon. Hopefully he didn't take a lunch.

"You were close," she said, closing the binder. "Library clerkship."

"Is he working today?"

She shook her head. "I wouldn't be able to tell you that. It's up to the librarians on staff to set hours."

We got directions to the library and said thank you. Mikey and I skipped halfway out the building before we noticed Coach wasn't behind us. We turned back and found him on a bench under a framed painting of Millard Fillmore. The former president, who had helped found the university according to a plaque beneath his painting, was shown sitting in a captain's chair facing away, to our left. Coach did the same.

"What's wrong?" Mikey asked him, getting there three steps before I did.

Coach glanced up at us and then resumed a presidential slouch. He shook his head. "I'm not up for this, boys."

"Sure you are," Mikey said. I said nothing. I wasn't certain.

"No. It's more complicated than you two can appreciate. It's of no value to me, and it's unfair to him."

"You said you weren't going to let him know you saw him," I said. "That's fine by me."

Coach held out his palms, either a gesture of recognition or a stop sign.

"Wait?" Mikey turned. "Why wouldn't he let him know?"

"He's not allowed to."

Mikey made a noise I recognized from our mother. A quick chirping tongue against the back of his teeth. "Then what are we doing here?"

I waited a beat, my legs fidgeting back and forth like I was pantomiming running.

"I wanted him to show me."

"Show you?" Mikey squinted. "What do you care?"

"Chris doesn't think that he exists," Coach explained. Mikey looked at me like I had poisoned his food.

"It's not that—"

"Then what is it?" Mikey asked, his voice loud enough that a passing janitor took notice. This was not a challenge I had expected or was ready for.

"I just thought it'd be good for him."

Mikey shook his head. "Of course he exists. C'mon, Coach." He pulled on Coach's shirt and then turned and lunged ahead a step.

Coach didn't move. "It's not good for me, Mikey."

"But we're right here!"

"No," I said and dropped my chin to my chest a moment. "No, he's right. I don't know why I said he should do this."

"I can't believe you don't want to go say hello. It's your son." Mikey's voice was thinning in the way it did when he got upset. The skin on his cheeks was red.

"But I still want to go," I whispered.

"Who cares that *you* want to go?" Mikey turned and pushed his fist into my chest. More of a shove than a punch. I took a step back.

Coach scolded us and told us to sit down. I did but Mikey didn't.

"You're so weird, Chris," Mikey said, leaning over Coach to lecture me right to my face. "Why's it important to you if he doesn't even care?"

I shrugged. "I just think it would be good."

Coach put his hand on my knee. "Chris, you don't need to do this. Let's go to the game."

"I want to; it's not for you. It's for me."

Mikey threw his hands up in the air and turned away. Another gift from our mother. "Fine," he said. "I'll wait here with Coach."

I looked at them both to make sure they knew they were welcome to come, and both of them avoided my eyes. Mikey with frustrated disbelief, flaring his nostrils and clenching his fists, and Coach politely, demurely, that small social smile on his lips. I stood and walked away from them both.

The library was in the centre of campus, a beautiful old stone building, stately like a minor palace. I took the stairs and found a lobby that faced a giant study room with two rows of dark wooden tables overlooked by several floors of books. The circulation desk was to the left. I sought out a woman just in case Larry himself was manning the desk. The one I found was piling returns onto a creaky old cart that looked like a Victorian baby stroller.

I asked if she knew Larry Miller and she said no, sorry, but if he was a student clerk he'd be somewhere in the stacks doing shelve and sort.

"What's that?"

"It's where you go through all the shelves and check if the books are in the right order, alphabetically or by decimal system."

"Is that boring?"

She laughed. "Does it seem boring?"

"Yes."

"Well"—she dropped a pile of returns on the stroller and slapped the topmost one—"there's your answer."

I was worried about missing him so I planned a specific path through each level, starting by the windows and zigzagging through the stacks, then moving up a floor. There was a potential Larry in the periodicals, a short kid with hunched shoulders and hair buzzed tight like a soldier, but when I asked he just said huh and told me his name was Desmond.

All the clerks on the second floor were girls. It wasn't until floor three that I spotted two more targets. They both had dark brown hair that swept across their head in waves that reminded me of Coach. They both seemed young for a college student, giving more the impression of high schoolers. They wore black trousers, both of them, with white shirts and could have passed for a pair of companions from the mission house in Hamilton. One had glasses and was tall, taller than Coach, while the other, shorter and wearing a necktie, had no glasses.

They were on either side of the same shelf and each had their own stroller full of books, which they weren't using for returns but as short-term storage, a place to arrange and reorder rows of titles as you fixed them. The tall one was mouthing names and numbers under his breath as he worked. I looked at the books on the shelf by my knees. Science. Physics and astronomy and that sort of thing.

The tall one noticed me first.

"Can I help you?" he asked while he worked.

I looked up. I couldn't make out his eye colour but then again I couldn't remember Coach's either. Green? Or was it mine that were green?

"Yes please," I told him. "I'm doing a school project on the solar system. Is this the right area?"

The tall clerk looked around and pointed to a part of shelf at his belt. "About there should start you. What sort of information do you need?"

"Basically anything," I told him.

The shorter clerk spoke up from the other side of the shelf. "There are encyclopedias downstairs too. If you're just getting started that might be the best place."

"Thanks," I told him. He caught my eye through the stacks and smiled a little. It was a small smile.

"Do you go to school here?" the tall one asked.

"Oh no," I said, only realizing after I answered that he meant it as a joke. "But my brother does, and I can borrow his card. He's a junior. Are you juniors?"

"We're both freshmen," the short one said.

I picked up a book. It had some sort of moon or maybe a big satellite on the cover, looping around a planet. "It's nice to meet you," I said, holding out my hand. "My name is Lawrence."

The tall one shook my hand. "How about that. I'm Jason. And that's another Lawrence over there."

Lawrence put his handful of books down and reached through a gap to shake my hand. His hand was soft, his fingers thinner than I expected. He was crouched down to work a lower shelf, and I could see where his white shirt hung loose, a little big for him. One button on the collar was cracked.

He didn't notice me staring because he went back to work. Something tripped him up and he looked back a foot, mumbling a little and then twisting up his mouth while he thought. Jason excused himself around me as he skipped along. I wandered over to the end of the shelf to watch Lawrence struggle with his task. His pants had suspenders but he had loosened them and one had fallen comfortably down to his bicep. His shoes were brown like his hair. As a boy, he had been tall for his age, but now he was average height or worse. I wondered what he had eaten for lunch; I hoped it had been sufficient.

Lawrence caught me staring and smiled again. "How's the search going?"

"Huh?"

He pointed to my space book.

"Oh, I don't know, fine enough." I asked him if this was a good school and he said he hadn't started with classes yet but it seemed nice so far. I asked if he was from Buffalo and he said nearby. I told him I lived near the highway. All the time he worked to fix his mistake before hurrying along to catch up to his colleague.

"What do you think you want to study?"

"Business, probably? Maybe law. Why, what's your brother study?"

"Business," I told him.

"Oh yeah? Does he like it?"

"Yes," I said. "He says you learn a lot about people."

"Does he want to make a bunch of money?"

"I think so. Do you?"

Lawrence nodded and was about to say more when Jason appeared at the end of the shelves, pointing at his watch. Lawrence held a palm up to apologize. It was a form of apology I recognized. He turned to me. "I should concentrate. Good luck with your project though."

I said thank you and moved away a few rows but kept watching them both. The nearest books were now about banking and trade. I picked up a history of the New York Stock Exchange. A young woman came by and Jason gave her directions while Lawrence watched. Eventually they took the empty strollers into a labelled room and closed the door behind them.

I wandered out of the building the long way, walking through the stacks and tracking my fingers over the book spines. I left by the door I came in. Outside on the stone steps I saw Mikey and Coach on a fancy bench maybe thirty feet away. They weren't coming inside; they were just there to meet me. Mikey waved and pointed to his watch like Jason had. I looked at mine: it was time to go.

Coach rested his chin in his hands and looked back towards the administration building and the centre of campus. He shifted towards me when Mikey said something but didn't wave or join in the call to hurry. His sad eyes just waited. To my left, I saw Jason, the taller clerk, emerge from the library. He was done for the day or maybe off for lunch. Lawrence didn't seem to be with him. Jason saw me standing there and tossed me a quick nod. I waved back and noticed Coach had seen this, and that suddenly his eyes were wide and aflame. He sat back against the bench, jostling Mikey where he had leaned on him. All at once, he was the most scared I had ever seen him.

I don't know why I did it, but I know it wasn't a decision I thought through with my whole mind. As Jason walked down the steps, in Coach's direction and away from me, I lifted my arm and pointed to him. I didn't think to do it, and I say this not to deflect blame but to relate the novel sensation of my body acting without an expressible thought to guide it. Maybe I wanted to hurt Coach, or maybe I just wanted to force his hand. Single-sighted, either way. I did not plan nor direct my finger. It pointed at Jason's back and Coach froze in a clean perfect terror, his teeth locked tight together and his face like a sculpture of a knight felled in sword fight. Sickly, in pain. Jason passed them by without knowing they were there, and only Mikey looked his way, following the line of my arm to the lanky boy treading on past them towards the bus stop. I descended the steps and thanked them for waiting. Coach needed a hand to stand up.

Coach asked to stop for lunch along the way but it wasn't really lunchtime anymore so I had us take a cab to the Rockpile. I sat in the front passenger seat and Coach didn't speak out against this;

he just settled in the back next to Mikey. Mikey was confused by it all. He kicked my seat to the rhythm of the gospel song the cabbie had playing on the radio.

Coach kept shifting his big body to get comfortable and never seemed to get there until we arrived and he stood up to stretch.

In my memory, the younger Lawrence Miller looked like Coach but spoke and acted like me. I wondered if I should switch from Chris to Christopher. I wondered what he told people about his father. Did he say he died in the war to keep it simple, like me? What was Lawrence's mamma like?

Downtown Buffalo was a parade of brick factory buildings and the main street was wide like a highway. We found the Rockpile's back entry and spoke to someone who worked for the team. She brought us glasses of ice water without our asking, which I worried predicted a long wait but turned out to be no more than manners. We were called in before any of us took a second sip.

Our walk to the clubhouse was done with a guide, a young man named Gomez whose accent was new to me and who said he was born in Mexico. I thought of the novelty of moving to a new country and then settling in the farthest-away part of it, right up against the northern border of America. Coach told Gomez that he had visited Mexico before and asked him where he was born. Gomez said something I didn't recognize and Coach made like he understood it. I didn't know if he did or not, and I didn't know whether Coach had ever been to Mexico. It had never come up and Coach had a penchant for travel stories.

Gomez dropped us off beside a closed door marked "Visitors." Coach said goodbye in Spanish, but maybe not correctly because Gomez gave us a look of good-natured confusion on his way back to the office. Coach opened his arms and brought Mikey and me into a loose huddle.

"Look, boys, I think it's appropriate to say a quick prayer to mark the end of our tasks," he said. Neither Mikey nor I volunteered so he started. "Lord, we sinners walk the world with the desire to please you in our hearts. Please look upon our actions with charity. Amen."

"Amen," we agreed.

"Okay." He clapped his hands and rubbed them together. "Strategy. Let's find out early if they've seen the Topps letter and whether Marthanne Eccles has been in touch. The GM should be in there; let's speak to him first. Good Idaho boy named Derkins. Chris, last time I came through this club they had more outfielders than men who knew how to read, so be sharp with the explainers, okay? Mikey, you've got the samples?" Mikey did.

Coach sounded confident and calm, but I knew this pep talk was for him and not us. All he needed us to do was stand there, hand out pens, and be cute.

The door opened and a man came out with a toothpick in his mouth. Derkins. He and Coach spoke, then Coach thanked him for the opportunity and asked if now was a good time. Derkins said indeed, and with that we spilled into the Sailors dressing room.

The Sailors wore grey and navy blue, which was reasonable if boring on the eyes. Their room had little dividers between the stools on the far side where men could change with a shade of privacy. In the middle, a spread was laid out with bread and cheese, and two Sailors were making sandwiches on a cutting board. No one looked up when the door opened. Mikey made his way to the only unused surface, a repurposed school desk, and put the sample set down..

I waited for Derkins to get their attention, but he didn't seem like he was about to. He crossed to the sandwich station and jumped the line, grabbing two slices of bread someone had left behind after cutting their own. I looked at Coach, who was watching this, and

I saw that the initial calm and confidence of our chat had been rinsed out of him. Coach's rule was that if you took a meeting and the other party sat to hear your pitch, you sat too. But there was nowhere left to sit. His knees buckled, and he almost took a seat right there on the dirty floor with the bread crumbs the Sailors had left for the Rockpile's mice. He didn't look right.

Coach licked his lips and rubbed them together and I saw him reach into his coat pocket and pull the lining inside out like how characters in the funnies show their readers they're broke. Meanwhile, some of the Sailors had noticed us and began to take their sandwiches back to their stools, where they sat down to eat and wait for whatever we had to say.

But we had nothing to say. Coach left his pockets alone and let his head roll over at me in a way that reminded me of Reg Law, the queerest smile splintering out between his lips. I made a sharp gesture with my chin, trying to supply him his cue to start, but we had no signal for this. Coach always started.

I looked at Mikey. He looked as worried as he ever got, which is to say he seemed curious. Coach opened his mouth, which made a couple more Sailors quiet down, but then didn't say anything behind it. In a minute the room was very clearly waiting on us, but Coach still didn't start. I could hear his breath whistle in his nose.

Some of the Sailors looked at each other, or at Derkins. Derkins was the only one left ignoring us now, eating a sandwich with the aggression of someone who was late arriving but still planned on having a second. His toothpick stuck out above his ear like a carpenter's pencil.

I looked to Coach one last time—his eyes were a little crossed as he gripped and released his pocket liner—then back to the team, and I found myself beginning to speak.

"Excuse me," I said, and several sets of eyes moved from Coach to me. "Good afternoon. My name is Christopher Johnson, and my associates and I have travelled in from Utah this afternoon to speak to you."

Somewhere one of the Sailors let out a quick laugh, but only one Sailor and only one laugh. I moved along.

"We understand your time is valuable, so we won't take much of it. We represent the Four Corners Baseball Card Company, a newer printer and marketer of baseball cards from Utah, and we'd like to pay you today to allow us the right to feature your faces in our product, should luck and talent take you someday to the major leagues."

I asked them if they had heard of us, and one player nodded yes. I thanked him and said for the others that we were a company founded and staffed by Christian baseball fans who wanted to help younger ballplayers early in their careers cash in on the popularity of baseball cards. One asked how much cash and I said five dollars and nobody balked at that number.

"No, wait," a voice kicked up. It took me a moment to recognize it was Derkins, on a break from his sandwich so able to focus on the meeting. "That other outfit was offering more though. Here." He stood up and rooted through his pockets until he found the Topps letter. I checked in with Coach, half expecting him to have rallied and be throwing me threatening looks for commandeering his pitch. He had not rallied. His pockets hung loose at his sides and he was tightening and untightening his necktie.

"Yes, right here. Let's see." Derkins scanned the paper. "Okay, it's the Topps company, which I believe is what my nephew collects. They want to give you two hundred dollars."

Someone whistled and there was a quick build to a cheer, which resolved into a room full of hard eyes fixed back on me. I looked to Coach for help. He was deep in thought, and not about the Topps offer. He had begun to lilt over to one side, away from me, like a sheaf of wheat in the wind.

"Derk, when do we get that money? They coming today too?" someone asked, and I took the space offered by Derkins's return to the paper in service of that question to answer it myself.

"That money's not coming," I told them. "Or if it does come, it's coming years from now, and when you get it, you'll be getting paid ten different ways by then anyhow. Topps won't sign you until you're standing in a major league clubhouse wearing a uniform."

I looked at the room. Maybe they were humbled by this knowledge or maybe they were annoyed by me. Derkins scanned the paper for a rebuttal and didn't find one, so he folded it up and put it back in his pocket.

"We are offering five dollars cash. Today. If you get to that clubhouse, gosh knows we'll all be proud of you, and you can pull a fiver off your great overburdened billfold and toss it in the mail back to us in Utah if you don't want to do both companies' cards. That's a promise spelled out in these agreements."

Normally Coach would point to me now, but I was the one in a position to point, so I pointed with the stack of contracts to the Sailors. I gave them to the nearest man and asked him to pass them along. The first few players took a contract, glanced down at it, and then looked to Coach or Derkins for confirmation. Neither provided any.

"Are we allowed to sign both contracts if we get to the bigs?" one player asked. He looked about ten years too old to need to worry about ever making the majors.

"From our perspective, yes," I jumped in to say. "Our agreements are non-exclusive. As for other printers, I can't really comment, but, again, if they demand exclusivity and you like their offer over ours, just send us our five dollars back. There's an address there that goes to a Mrs. Forbush. She's the wife of our founding president, and she'll take your money and donate it to our church charities, and everyone will be better off."

Out of the corner of my eyes, I watched for Derkins to make a move, to remember something from the Topps letter and dip back in his pocket to see what it said about exclusivity. I felt conflicted, just a little, like a distant voice somewhere—Mamma's voice? No, it couldn't be. My own?—was raising an objection, but then I thought about Marthanne and what she said about lawsuits, and I remembered that in her eyes and the eyes of all reasonable people, we were the angels here. Coach and Mikey and me.

Marthanne. I reviewed the Sailors and tried to judge if they needed one more push. "Mr. Derkins," I said, and Derkins looked up, addressing me with his eyes but not his head or posture. "We've just come from the London, Ontario, team where we spoke to Marthanne Eccles, their owner and the commissioner of the Northern. She said she'd try to get a message to you about our cause before we arrived. Did she make contact?"

Derkins had gone back to his sandwich. A bright yellow bit of cheese fell out the bottom. He leaned over and picked it off the floor and ate it. I stood my ground and waited for him to acknowledge the question. He seemed to think.

"Eccles? I don't recall. Here let me check." He stood up and went through his pockets again. He pulled out the Topps letter but didn't open it. A folded bit of card caught his interest, and he cleared his throat.

"Ah yes, here. So, boys, this is from Mrs. Eccles—she's the wife of our last commissioner and she's a reasonable enough woman. And I quote: 'Dear Erie, Three men, two under the age of majority, will be through to see you this week. I don't know them any more than you do, but have met with them at my home and found their offer fair and equitable. Please take caution when dealing with external businessmen, most are swindlers and cheats, but to my understanding both Lawrence R. Miller and the two young Mr. Johnsons are honest exceptions to that rule.'"

Derkins put the message in his pocket. "That lady always talks more than she needs to. Anyway, Miller is the tall one," he said, pointing to Coach and then moving on to the food table to fix his second sandwich.

I smiled at the Sailors. "We're hopeful you'll consider our offer. My brother, Michael, has some sample cards there, and any of us can be available to answer questions."

The Sailors got up and went back about their business. I didn't breathe until I saw the first one kneel beside his changing stool and sign his name. And then another. One tall player with muscles like corded rope came over and asked if the offer was valid for foreign players. He had an accent I couldn't place, similar to Gomez's but not the same. I said absolutely. He handed me a signed paper. I felt the blood rush to my face. Mikey came over and grabbed Coach by the arm and pulled him against the wall of the room. Three more contracts appeared in my hand. I picked one up off the floor, signed and then forgotten in the meal rush. I shouted out to the Sailors that we'd be watching them tonight and would pray for their success. Someone appeared to my right with a contract and shook my hand, absolutely collapsing it inside their thick grip. I waited some more. I saw a man fold his contract up and stick it in an equipment bag. The older player who asked about signing both contracts brought his back and one from a friend. Derkins appeared next to us. In five minutes the players were back to changing and making jokes. I tried to weigh the contracts with my hand without counting them. Coach tripped over with fivers and handed them out. Derkins tracked down the signer of the copy from the floor to make sure that he was paid, then Gomez slapped me on the shoulder and said it was time for us to go.

I got all the way out of the Rockpile before looking at the contracts in my hand. There were ten of them. No need to go scrounging at the Buffalo team: that made sixty-five in total. I cackled, then squeezed creases into the contracts and held them up for Coach to see.

"Look!" I shouted at him, crowding right up under his chin, against his chest, waving whole handfuls of contracts in his face. "Look!"

Coach allowed a thin smile and said it seemed like plenty. I took off running for the Hornet to put them safely in the trunk, then remembered it was in Canada and, laughing, drew Mikey into a bear hug and we both stumbled, spilling onto the parking lot pavement next to some stranger's car and hollering our victory. There were not enough people around for us to make a scene. Only Coach saw.

Mikey, for his part, lost any interest in the matter of Coach's performance at the Rockpile before we even cleared the property line. I suggested we go looking for a bite to eat, and he and Coach stuck close together, sharing one half of a diner booth while I used the other and piled our bags at my side. I ate something called a western sandwich, which was basically just a ham-and-egg sandwich with green onions. I had wanted to give up on food that didn't look like it could be prepared inside of five minutes by my mother and was disappointed when my plate arrived showing nothing more complex. The trip had started with new smells and tastes and had since become a grim procession of hand-held meat. Coach got a burger and Mikey ate the fries that came with it.

Coach wasn't sick, and while he was tired it wasn't like him to just turn off like that. It was new. Mikey asked him if he knew I was going to give the pitch and he gave a noncommittal shrug and said he knew I wanted to try. I kept trying to goad either of them into a conversation about my success but they never joined in until, while I was doing nothing more aggressive than picking green onions out of my ham, he finished chewing and asked if I felt my approach in the pitch room was Christian.

"Excuse me?"

"Do you think you rose to the level of Christian honesty Four Corners should expect?"

"Where wasn't I honest?"

"I don't know. You tell me."

I crumpled my napkin in my lap to get the ham grease off my fingers. My face was hot. "Well, I thought I was pretty honest."

"You didn't say that Topps would turn them away."

"We don't know for sure that they will. Derkins had the letter right there; if he was worried about it, he could have said."

"Derkins was useless."

"You were useless."

I saw his colour catch in the light. A flash of red on his cheeks and forehead. He put his burger down, then reached across the table and took my plate. "Give me that."

Mikey looked on. I asked Coach what he was doing.

"You can eat if you apologize."

I wasn't hungry enough to do it. But I knew that if I didn't back down this would go on. Maybe I'd find myself looking for my own motel room later, or my own ride back to Minnesota once we crossed the bridge to get the Hornet.

"I'm sorry," I mumbled.

"Say it again and look at me."

It took me two tries, but I got my head level and still and told Coach face to face that I was sorry. He took a bite of my sandwich and handed it back.

"Good," he said, and gave Mikey a French fry dipped in ketchup.

It wasn't certain that we would make it to the game. Our job was done and we could try to get back to Niagara Falls before nightfall. The Hornet awaited us from inside its crowd of newlyweds. Coach had a schedule for the tourist buses out of Fort Erie and they came every hour. We could walk the bridge right now.

But Mikey had begged for one more game, and Coach relented. I was keeping my distance at the back of the group, and when we filed in I took the row behind them. It was hot again, the run of cool wind earlier in the trip was gone and people baked until the sun started to dip in the early innings.

It was my first time watching the Sailors, who had spent much of the week getting whooped from one side of the border to the other by Marthanne Eccles's boys, and I wasn't impressed. The first four batters all struck out on middling pitching, trying to put anything that looked like a baseball into the sponsor signage behind left field. The home team got one in the second inning and two more in the fourth, and by the time the heat started to temper off it was four-nothing and the Sailors hadn't seen first base. Coach stood up in the middle of the fourth and asked me if I was responsible enough to get Mikey back safe to the motel. I said sure, but why? He just patted me on the shoulder and said he was sleepy and wandered off towards the exit. Mikey frowned and moved back a row to sit with me.

We watched the Sailors try and fail again in the fifth. I asked Mikey what was up with Coach.

"He said he had his fill of baseball for now. He's got to go again next month for the Pioneer League remember."

"His fill? Of baseball?"

"Dunno. He's mad at you too, you know that. You were cheeky."

"I wasn't cheeky." I sniffed. "I was the hero."

Mikey didn't say anything to that. Eventually he asked whether I had seen Coach's son and I said I did and I described him the way you'd describe a stranger. Height, weight, hair colour. He listened.

"Are you eager to get home, Mikey?" I asked him.

"Yeah."

"Me too." I pulled a bit of fluff, from the car or maybe the motel, out of his hair. "Do you wish we hadn't come?"

He thought about this a bit as we watched another Sailor strike out. "Yes. But there's no point to that."

I didn't say "me too" to this. I wasn't sure.

Midway through the seventh inning, the crowd started to come alive, and it took me some time to realize why. The PA had announced 1,600 people, a good number for a weekday, though the Rockpile was cavernous and could seat ten times that for football. Their collective buzz began to echo around the building after a promising line drive landed in the glove of the Buffalo centre fielder to end the top half of the inning. The score was 6–0, but more importantly the pitcher, who still didn't look like much to me, had now gotten the first twenty-one Sailors out. Six more for a perfect game. As if they knew where our attentions sat, the Bisons went quickly in the bottom half, and the pitcher, a tall young man all elbows and obtuse angles, came out to applause. The first batter grounded to first and then the second wasted a 2–0 count with a pop-up to the catcher. Some people stood for the third out, a slow fly-out to the middle depth of left field. Three down. Twenty-four.

The Bisons took their time in the eighth, as a string of bench players came up to prove their worth. Two home runs and an RBI single, and the game looked like a lot more of a blowout than it felt at 10–0. They eventually settled down and the Bisons utility infielder grounded out to first to end it. If it wasn't for Marthanne Eccles's offseason intercession, that would be the ball game. Mercy rule, everybody go home.

"Has Coach ever seen a perfect game?" I asked Mikey. He didn't know. We wondered if we could dash out of the park and back, maybe fifteen minutes round-trip, and catch the last out with him. Or maybe the game was on the radio and he had heard about the situation and would run back himself, letter of invitation fished from the garbage, to see the end.

The three Sailors due up were the fifth through seventh hitters. A barrel-chested first basemen who led the team in home runs but only hit .210, then a speedy second basemen and a player who normally sat the bench as a backup, playing right field today to give the usual guy a rest.

The first basemen did what everyone expected. Down ten and not even a walk all game, he got way out in front of two change-ups and fouled them off and then, dutifully choking up, missed the fastball entirely. Drinks and popcorn flew in the air when we all raised our hands to cheer.

Perfect games have just enough possibility to hang over base-ball games like an unopened letter. There had been three in the majors, and none since Coach was younger than me. I don't know if the Northern League had ever seen one but likelihood would predict not. Statistics would guess that none of us 1,599 left in the grandstands ever had.

The second basemen was more difficult. Elbows missed outside twice and then got lucky when a liner careened foul, apparently hitting someone in the third base stand and causing brief concern before the fan stood up to start a victory chant. One more foul and then a really beautiful curveball, just enough hook to drop into the top of the zone, struck out the 26th batter on the game's best pitch.

The Sailors manager stepped up to the top of the dugout and said something to the umpire. It was a pinch hitter. Specifically, the team's usual right fielder, and one of their best, most consistent batters, was stretching and lumbering over to the plate, his face fixed in a tight frown as if he hadn't necessarily asked to interrupt his off day, dust the peanut shells from his pants, and be pressed into service just to potentially show up in someone else's press clipping. When the crowd saw the replacement made, they launched into boos. The Sailors manager stood through it with a firm face; nobody told him he couldn't try to wriggle out of being a conquest. In the other dugout, old Coach Gibbs chewed tobacco and supplied his young pitcher with reassuring nods and claps. Elbows took a walk around the infield, cheered on by his teammates and the breathless crowd.

The first pitch was taken all the way for a strike, and this brought on the loudest applause yet as the hotshot replacement, brought in against an unwritten rule about messing with a perfect game, got one-third of the way to out. The second pitch missed high, and then a curveball had the movement but not the line and drifted outside. Elbows took his cap off and wiped away the sweat. The fourth pitch was called low, but not by much, and everyone put their hands to their heads in anguish. Mikey stood up and I followed him; we had been the only ones in our section still sitting.

"What do you think, Mike?" I asked.

"Three-one is tough," he told me.

Everyone in the park inhaled and waited. The pitcher delivered and it could have been ball four, if the batter hadn't swung. It didn't look like much at first until the wind got hold of it, or the ball's natural spin started it curving for the corner of the outfield. The Bisons right fielder gave chase, though he didn't have the best jump, and at the last second he gave up on it, stopping short to play it off the wall. He got it on one hop and threw the ball into second, narrowly missing the put-out as the Sailors pinch hitter slid safely.

Everyone groaned. All the players, the crowd, the coaches; I thought I even heard the PA crackle on to mumble regret. It was over—just another ten-run game now. A parade started for the parking lot.

The pitcher walked the next guy and there was conversation in the stands about a reliever, but the number nine hitter turned out to be the relief pitcher. The Sailors were out of bench, and he let two meatballs go by him before a game attempt at strike three ended the night.

"That was a good one," I told Mikey.

He was already up and running down the grandstand steps. He wanted to go and find Coach.

The trip east wasn't long, though we extended it by stopping to watch people in bars and restaurants or people engaging in conversation on the sidewalk or (in my case) to observe one beautiful girl chase a late streetcar down the street.

I wondered how Mikey would be when we got home. Coach would come by often, maybe more days than not, but Coach didn't often stay long and so he would need to spend most of his time with me or Mamma. He seemed to not mind being with me, but he was quickly distracted and sometimes went quiet or sad. Was this Coach's same quietness and sadness, the stuff that flooded the gaps between his times of wild function, rubbing off? It wasn't genetic, but that's not to say he didn't take it in as a lesson.

And I wondered what I would be like. Mamma talked about how boys my age were a product of their friends, but I had barely thought about my gang from school the whole trip. I had been travelling with a working adult and a kid five years my junior and, outside of Clara, hadn't spoken to someone within a year of my own age. I wanted to read books all the rest of the summer and write Clara letters. I would get her address from Coach after all.

And lastly, as the motel came into sight on our left, what would Coach be like? Was this trip a speed bump for his plans with us and Mamma, or a hard end in the road? Would he call the O-Pee-Chee man again? Did he think that I forgave him or that I've just given up on him, and which of those things had I done?

Mikey ran ahead and got to the door first. There were cars outside only four of the motel's units. All pre-war coupes or other older vehicles. I wondered if anyone else had had a breakdown on their way here.

The door was locked and Coach had the only key. We knocked and waited. It was late and I suspected he was asleep. Mikey knocked again, and we both hollered for him to wake.

Mikey ran over to the window. The light looked on.

He yelled for Coach. "We saw twenty-six twenty-sevenths of a perfect game!" he screamed through the window and cocked his head like a puppy when no reply came back.

I joined him. The room looked empty, Coach's pants and jacket still on the bed. A single shoe sat next to the bathroom.

"Maybe he went to the TV?" Mikey said. I told him we could go check but we couldn't watch anything until we found him.

We ran to the main entrance. Mikey got there ahead of me again and we ducked our heads in. An elderly couple was watching a program with the lights off, holding hands.

"Sorry," Mikey said. The man nodded. He had farmer's clothes, dirty enough I noticed them even in the limited light from the TV screen, and I imagined the cleaners would be angry in the morning.

We ran back to the motel door to knock and yell again. I surveyed the room more meticulously through the window. There was a second window, a high panel covered by a green curtain, on the opposite wall. A writing desk littered with our supplies. And a bottle. I looked close at the bottle, because I knew I had seen it before.

"Mikey—" I breathed. The bottle came back to me. This was the bottle Reg Law's pills came from. It was open and there were maybe ten left.

I turned to my brother. "Mikey," I said, grabbing him by the ears and bringing him in close, away from the scenes at the window, until our foreheads touched. "Go to the clerk as fast as you can and get him to come with keys. It's an emergency."

Mikey blinked once and then took off. I looked back to the room. The shoe had a foot in it. The foot was from someone lying on the floor. Once, and only for a flicker, I saw Coach's foot make the shoe twitch.

I looked around for something to break the window. The parking lot was a wasteland. Four cars and nothing else, not even stones.

"Coach!" I shouted and slammed my fist against the window. It didn't break or make much noise, but my hand sent back stabbing pain all the way to my shoulder. "Co-ach!"

I looked back to the entrance. No Mikey. I ran around to the rear of the motel. Behind our unit, there was a wooden fence for garbage bins. The bins were chained in place and too light to break glass anyway. I looked at the panel window up high, and after a couple of false starts I climbed the fence to where I could see into the window. I shouted again. Through the gap in the curtains, I saw Coach lying in the bathroom doorway. His hands and feet were moving, but not like he was directing them; he looked like an overturned car whose wheels were still running. The bottle was obscured by the ledge. I tried to remember how full it had been yesterday.

I saw something in the opposite window. The shape of a man. I shouted again and jumped off the fence, doubling back to the front of the building. It wasn't the clerk; it was the farmer from the TV room. Mikey stood next to him. I spat out that we needed to break into the room—did he have anything? He scanned the parking lot like I had and then back to the window, where he just pointed.

I followed his finger. Coach. Standing up on the other side of the window frame, watching us. A ghost.

No one spoke. After a moment, Coach reached over and unbolted the door. Mikey turned the knob and it swung open.

"I— Wait here please," I told the farmer, whose wife was now standing behind us by the main entrance. I followed Mikey into our room, not looking at the stranger as I passed.

The room smelled of sweat and chemicals. I glanced towards the bathroom. The door was ajar but it was otherwise neat and tidy. I looked up to the panel window where I had climbed in to see. Coach had closed the bottle of pills and was pushing it into his bag. Mikey stood next to me.

"Did you play a trick on me?" Mikey whispered.

"No," I said. "I promise."

Coach turned to face us, his expression unreadable. He asked how the game was and Mikey told him everything.

"What was the final score?"

"Ten-nothing."

"Wow." He whistled. "So many blowouts on this trip. Rough luck."

His eyes were clear and his speech crisp. He watched me watching him as he crossed the room to the bathroom doorway, grabbed its header and, as if as proof of life, pulled himself into a chin-up. Once he finished he turned and spat, or vomited, something or other into the bathroom sink and ran the water until it was gone.

"You boys should head down to the payphone and call your mamma," he said as he went back to swinging from the door frame.

Mikey moved to leave but I caught him. "We already did," I lied. "We're both in for the night now."

"Suit yourselves, soldiers," Coach said, sitting down on the bed.

Mikey found his Bible stories and joined him. The door to the room was still open but thankfully the farmer and his wife were long gone. I watched Mikey shuffle closer to Coach until their thighs touched.

Once I had my fill of them, I turned to close the door. A squeal came up from the din of the city, the sound of tires taking a turn too fast on a road somewhere. I jerked my head up to look but saw nothing. Either it was too far away or I had just imagined it.

A Bridge to Canada

ID I DREAM EVERYTHING? THE WHOLE TRIP? THE PITCHES, the bus, the factories? Reg and Clara and Spitter and Marthanne? Did I dream the encounter at the customs stop in Niagara? Lawrence Jr.? Did I fall asleep after dinner and dream Reg and Essie, or Reg and Dora, or Coach lying on the bathroom floor and then, just as strangely, not?

Everything I couldn't understand, or that was coloured by my misunderstanding, or that I felt others understood somehow better than I did—which is to say most of it—it all carried the tone of a dream.

The bridge to Canada, the third bridge, between Buffalo and Fort Erie, carried the tone of a dream. It looked, from afar, like waves. Like a line of waves cresting between countries. The bridge did not rise; it just reached—a simple road whose ground disappeared below it and the waves, five of them, were arched spans that kept it up across that sudden gap. It had three lanes for cars and trucks; one dedicated each way and a third that converted based on traffic, which was now pointing vehicles east towards us in America.

We had packed for the trip slowly and negotiated all morning about whether we would walk straight to Canada or get a taxicab to drop us off at the bridge first. As the bags grew heavy, the latter won out. Coach opened his wallet to check for American currency and made a cartoonish whistle like the sound of someone dropping a penny down an empty well.

Our shared tolerance for diner food had finally run dry that morning so nobody ate. Eventually hunger would overtake us, but we wanted to wait for its insistence. Maybe Fort Erie had better options. At arrival, Coach had the suitcases and the large travel bag. I had my school backpack, my clothes backpack, and the Four Corners equipment, and Mikey had his sack and, still in his left hand as it had been since Hamilton, his book of Bible stories. At least a half-dozen pages were dog-eared.

"I'm concerned it looks like we're planning on a long stay," Coach said of us. I couldn't argue, but there wasn't anything left we didn't need. The two full bags of shed memories, anchored by a pair of pants Mikey had outgrown, now left behind in the motel's fenced-in dumpster, attested to this. They had been joined by Reg Law's pain pills, the bottle of which I understood I hadn't dreamed when I found them among Coach's things and tossed them unspeaking into the throwaway pile.

"What'll we say if they ask us?"

Coach shifted a bag from one hand to the other. "I'm not sure, Chris. Let's maybe just think on our feet if we get there."

I didn't expect the bridge to be as long as it was. In a car, a bridge, especially an unremarkable bridge like this, is just a jump between two gathering points, like a door between rooms. You don't think of the span itself as a journey. But loaded down as we were and slowed by Mikey's desire to stop every ten paces and look at the river, it took us the better part of twenty minutes. The sun was near its peak and sweat ran uninterrupted down my face or soaked into my hair and made it itch. I saw Coach ahead of me grow a dark wet spot in the small of his back. Mikey didn't seem bothered, though he also had the lightest load. He looked me over approaching the midway point and asked if I needed help, but I couldn't accept any once he asked. So we treaded along, talking about plans for home and letting Coach lob back updates on how our progress met with the bus schedule on the other side. The only open question seemed to be where we'd sleep tonight. Would we make Detroit? Probably not. Somewhere in Ontario along the way.

We didn't see another pedestrian until just after the pair of flags at the middle of the bridge, which we guessed were meant to formalize the end of one country and the beginning of the next. A woman, maybe forty, with a big bob of brown hair, carrying a musical instrument of some kind. I knew it was a musical instrument, even though it was in a hard case, because there was a bloom at one end of it for the bell. Coach turned around and watched her, so I did the same and then Mikey, who had spent a minute straddling the midpoint flags, one foot in each country, before we herded him forward, joined us. She got right to the flags and stopped, then took out the instrument, which revealed itself to be a trumpet. Fiddling with the valves a minute, the woman put the mouthpiece to her lips and blew. We didn't hear the sound right away—she started quieter and built—and while I recognized the music, I didn't know the name of the song. The song sounded like talking, like she was playing sentences. It started and stopped, and each section was unpredictable both in its length and how it argued around its central melody. The pauses felt inflated, puffed up with air. When she was done playing to the river, she put the trumpet away and walked back the way she came.

She saw us standing there but didn't make eye contact or greet us at all, just shouldered through the narrow pedestrian span, separated for safety from the cars by iron fencing. As she passed Coach, I heard him say a soft thank you, but again she didn't stop, and if anything she sped up, pushing along back to the Canadian side of the river.

We watched her walk away and after she had passed the next light pole, Coach hitched his pack up like it was time to go. Mikey asked if he knew that woman and he said no, he didn't.

"What was the song?" I asked.

"'Last Post.'" Coach said. "You should know that. Song for dead soldiers they play at funerals."

We didn't say anything the rest of the way down the bridge. I tried to remember how the woman with the trumpet had dressed. I didn't think she was in uniform; I tried to imagine her again, but she came up as a collage, in my mother's clothes or with Marthanne Eccles's curly hair. I tried to push her from my mind completely, but this also wasn't possible.

The customs plaza looked like someone had taken all the little sheds and cabins from the other bridges and glued them together. It was a squat and misshapen building, and the pedestrian check-point was just the far end of the walkway where it pulled up to the side of the property, near the parking lot. A desk and a chair and a door for further processing. There was no one in line when we got there. Wherever the trumpet woman went, she was gone.

An officer approached us, smiling, and asked for identification. Coach gave him a handful of papers and he leafed through them. He was shorter than Coach, the officer, and if he had a weapon he kept it well concealed.

"Are these boys related to you?"

"No," Coach said, and I took a step closer to Mikey. "I'm taking them on a trip with their mother's permission."

"Where?"

"Niagara Falls. There's a letter confirming her consent at the bottom there." Coach pointed to a sheet of paper. The officer pulled it out and nodded.

"How are you getting there?"

"I'm told there's regular bus service from the tourist office in town."

"There is." The officer nodded, handing Coach back the papers. He walked back to the desk and stood next to it. None of us moved or looked at him until he clarified that we were done by extending his arm and telling us that the bus stop and tourist office were three blocks ahead and on the left.

We made a point not to celebrate until we were out of earshot but when we did, Coach kicked us off. He pulled Mikey into a hug and told us how he always knew it would be that easy. I grinned back at him and reached out to shake his hand, but their hug had grown into a wrestling match where Mikey was trying to bury his head in Coach's stomach. They collapsed on the grass and I gave up.

The tourist office was right next to a deli so we grabbed some more sandwiches and waited for the bus. Mikey was telling Coach about the TV room in the Buffalo motel, and I was not listening. The trumpet woman was across the street. Now that I saw her again I knew she wasn't in uniform. Her pants were black and she was wearing some sort of long blouse that draped over her front like a scarf. She was also eating a sandwich, maybe from the same place, maybe she was a regular, this being part of her daily routine. Birds gathered by her feet to catch crumbs. A man walked by and she raised her head to say hello. They were friendly but not family; he kept on towards his business. I watched her tear off a hunk of crust and throw it to the ground, and a panic of birds dove for it. I broke the heel off my own sandwich, which was beef, and did the same. There were fewer birds on my side of the street but attention was soon drawn and a crowd gathered by my shoes. Just like that.

Coach shouted a reminder to call Mamma wherever we wound up. She should know where we planned on sleeping. I said I'd remember, and as I had skipped calling last night, I felt there was a lot to say.

I wouldn't tell her about Mikey running for the farmer and his wife, but I would say I scaled a fence. I would tell her we crossed a bridge on foot to save money, and that in the end we signed the number of contracts Utah had requested, with more to spare. Coach was on the phone just this morning and said that they were pleased, though not enough to send over a contract for next year, at least not yet. She would ask if I was glad I came, and I decided I would tell her yes, both because I wanted to avoid any talk of why not and because it felt like the only honest short answer.

I was slouching as I ate my sandwich so I straightened up, pressed the full length of my back against the wall of the tourist office. There was heat in the bricks. I would tell Mamma I had learned a great deal.

Mamma, what I've found is that there's no learning that isn't in the body. That everything comes home to how it feels. How to swing without thinking, jump, how pain teaches and how the release at pain's end also teaches. The body teaches you when it breaks. How it loves. I don't know how to tell you all this without spilling people's secrets, even those who deserve to have their secrets told, Mamma, even me. Do you have secrets? Where do they live inside you? I'll come home and sit on our porch and have you tell me about the world, and those lessons you give, I'll keep them safe, I promise, in the only place I can. Held in any part of me that moves.

Historical Notes

THIS IS A WORK OF FICTION. IT CONTAINS MANY DOZEN FIC-
tional people and only one actual historical figure, namely
the eventual president of the O-Pee-Chee Company, Frank Leahy.
Care was taken to make Frank somewhat of a blank slate both
physically and as a person: outside of his interest in sports cards,
I don't pretend to know anything about the man, and so the
figure speaking his lines in *The Northern* is a bit of a cipher. The
poem in the O-Pee-Chee meeting room is Henry Wadsworth
Longfellow's "The Song of Hiawatha."

The Four Corners Baseball Card Company never existed,
though it has many inspirations. The work of breaking the baseball
card duopoly was ongoing between the 1950s and the eventual
1980 federal ruling in Fleer vs Topps, prior to which generations
of businesses attempted to break into the industry using tactics in
some ways similar to those described in *The Northern*. I moved our
timeline to the early '50s in the interest of telling a story about the
generation coming of age after World War II. This resettlement
has created some anachronisms, chief among them the fact that
Topps wasn't an entrenched incumbent in the summer of 1952,
having just released the first truly "modern" set of baseball cards
earlier that year.

If you are looking for better history than *The Northern* offers, I'd like to recommend Jon C. Stott's very thorough *Canadian Minor League Baseball: A History Since World War II* and Dave Jamieson's delightful *Mint Condition: How Baseball Cards Became an American Obsession.* I am grateful for these secondary sources.

Coach's factory-issued uncirculated Joe DiMaggio O-Pee-Chee rookie card with the typo in the surname is worth about $100,000 today. I hope he kept it.

Credits

*T*HE *NORTHERN* AND I ARE BOTH VERY LUCKY TO KNOW ALEXIS von Konigslow. I am hopeful some echo of her empathy, her talent, and her wit have made it to the final book. I am grateful that I get to share this life with her.

Thank you to Ben, Rebecca, and Zoe, for your readings and kind words.

Books, as commercial goods, do not historically do a great job of reflecting the breadth of labour that goes into their creation, and this might play a role in the struggle to communicate their value. Books are collaborations by diverse artists and professionals. In the spirit of Maris Kreizman's 2024 *Lithub* essay "It's Time We Added Full Credit Pages to Books," here are *The Northern's* creators, in rough chronological order from first appearance on the project. Asterisks indicate volunteer labour.

AUTHOR: Jacob McArthur Mooney
FIRST READER: Alexis von Konigslow*
EDITOR: Michael Holmes
PRODUCTION CO-ORDINATOR: Victoria Cozza

PRODUCTION EDITOR: Jen Albert
COPYEDITOR: Crissy Boylan
SALES AND RIGHTS: Emily Ferko
EARLY READERS (BLURBING): Ben Lindbergh*; Rebecca Rosenblum*; Zoe Whittall*
COVER DESIGN: Ian Sullivan Cant
BOOK DESIGN: Jessica Albert; Jennifer Gallinger; Christine Lum
MARKETING & COMMUNICATION: Caroline Suzuki
CO-PUBLISHERS: David Caron; Jack David
PUBLICITY: Claire Pokorchak; Elham Ali; Cassie Smyth
OPERATIONS: Michela Prefontaine; Aymen Saidane
PROOFREADER: Peter Norman

Entertainment. Writing. Culture. ————————

ECW is a proudly independent, Canadian-owned book publisher. We know great writing can improve people's lives, and we're passionate about sharing original, exciting, and insightful writing across genres.

———————————————— **Thanks for reading along!**

We want our books not just to sustain our imaginations, but to help construct a healthier, more just world, and so we've become a certified B Corporation, meaning we meet a high standard of social and environmental responsibility — and we're going to keep aiming higher. We believe books can drive change, but the way we make them can too.

Certified

Corporation

Being a B Corp means that the act of publishing this book should be a force for good — for the planet, for our communities, and for the people that worked to make this book. For example, everyone who worked on this book was paid at least a living wage. You can learn more at the Ontario Living Wage Network.

This book is also available as a Global Certified Accessible™ (GCA) ebook. ECW Press's ebooks are screen reader friendly and are built to meet the needs of those who are unable to read standard print due to blindness, low vision, dyslexia, or a physical disability.

This book is printed on FSC®-certified paper. It contains recycled materials, and other controlled sources, is processed chlorine free, and is manufactured using biogas energy.

FSC
www.fsc.org
MIX
Paper | Supporting
responsible forestry
FSC® C103567

ECW's office is situated on land that was the traditional territory of many nations including the Wendat, the Anishinaabeg, Haudenosaunee, Chippewa, Métis, and current treaty holders the Mississaugas of the Credit. In the 1880s, the land was developed as part of a growing community around St. Matthew's Anglican and other churches. Starting in the 1950s, our neighbourhood was transformed by immigrants fleeing the Vietnam War and Chinese Canadians dispossessed by the building of Nathan Phillips Square and the subsequent rise in real estate value in other Chinatowns. We are grateful to those who cared for the land before us and are proud to be working amidst this mix of cultures.

ecwpress.com